Although Ritchie never achieved the kind of name recognition that even lesser authors enjoyed, perhaps because he toiled in mostly one genre and in one format, he still garnered the respect of his peers and the admiration of regular readers of mystery digests.

Ritchie was nominated for three Edgar Awards, winning for his *Alfred Hitchcock's Mystery Magazine* story "The Absence of Emily." His stories were selected in *Best Detective Stories of Year* anthologies 21 times over a period of 21 years, beginning in 1961 with his story "Shatter Proof" for *Manhunt* until his death in 1983.

Ritchie's stories appeared in 117 issues of *Alfred Hitchcock's Mystery Magazine* and in 116 Alfred Hitchcock anthologies. Three television episodes of *Alfred Hitchcock Presents/Hour* were based on his stories and five episodes of *Tales of the Unexpected*, as well one episode of the Canadian television show *The Unforeseen*. His story "The Green Heart," which appeared in *AHMM*, was filmed as *A New Leaf*, an Elaine May film starring Walter Matthau.

—Jeff Vorzimmer from his Introduction

THE BEST OF MANHUNT 4
THE JACK RITCHIE STORIES

**EDITED BY
JEFF VORZIMMER**

Stark House Press • Eureka California
www.starkhousepress.com

THE BEST OF MANHUNT 4: THE JACK RITCHIE STORIES
Published by Stark House Press
1315 H Street
Eureka, CA 95501
griffinskye3@sbcglobal.net
www.starkhousepress.com

"War and Peace on a Postcard" ©2022 by Jeff Vorzimmer

"My Game, My Rules" and "Replacement," ©1954 Flying Eagle Publications; "Hold Out," "Interrogation," "Solitary," and "Try It My Way," ©1955 Flying Eagle Publications; "Devil Eyes," "The Canary," "Good-By, World," "The Wire Loop," "The Partners" and "Degree of Guilt," ©1956 Flying Eagle Publications, ©1984 The estate of John G. Reitci; "Divide and Conquer," "You Should Live So Long" and "Kill Joy" ©1957 Flying Eagle Publications, ©1985 The estate of John G. Reitci; "Don't Twist My Arm" and "Deadline Murder," ©1958 Flying Eagle Publications, ©1986 The estate of John G. Reitci; "Fair Play," ©1959 Flying Eagle Publications, ©1987 The estate of John G. Reitci; "Shatter Proof," ©1960 Flying Eagle Publications, ©1988 The estate of John G. Reitci; "The Queer Deal," ©1961 Flying Eagle Publications, ©1989 The estate of John G. Reitci; "The Deveraux Monster," ©1962 Flying Eagle Publications, ©1990 The estate of John G. Reitci; "Ripper Moon!," ©1963 Flying Eagle Publications, ©1991 The estate of John G. Reitci; "Going Down?" ©1965 Flying Eagle Publications, ©1993 The estate of John G. Reitci; "Anniversary of Death," ©1956 Columbia Publications, ©1984 The estate of John G. Reitci; "A Torch for Tess," ©1956 Flying Eagle Publications, ©1984 The estate of John G. Reitci; "Dead Cops Are Murder," ©1956 Flying Eagle Publications, ©1984 The estate of John G. Reitci; "Death Rail," ©1956 Flying Eagle Publications, ©1984 The estate of John G. Reitci; "Rainy Afternoon," ©1956 Flying Eagle Publications, ©1984 The estate of John G. Reitci; All stories reprinted with the permission of the estate of John G. Reitci.

ISBN: 979-8-88601-041-1

Book design by ¡caliente!Design, Austin, Texas

PUBLISHER'S NOTE:
This is a work of fiction. Names, characters, places and incidents are either the products of the author's imagination or used fictionally, and any resemblance to actual persons, living or dead, events or locales, is entirely coincidental. Without limiting the rights under copyright reserved above, no part of this publication may be reproduced, stored, or introduced into a retrieval system or transmitted in any form or by any means (electronic, mechanical, photocopying, recording or otherwise) without the prior written permission of both the copyright owner and the above publisher of the book.

Stark House Press Edition: December 2022

Table of Contents

Introduction: War and Peace on a Postcard 7
The Stories from *Manhunt*
    My Game, My Rules 12
    Replacement 18
    Hold Out 26
    Interrogation 30
    Solitary 37
    Try It My Way 44
    The Deveraux Monster 50
    Ripper Moon! 64
    Devil Eyes 77
    The Canary 82
    The Wire Loop 88
    Goodbye, World 94
    The Partners 99
    Degree of Guilt 107
    Divide and Conquer 112
    You Should Live So Long 119
    Kill Joy 125
    Don't Twist My Arm 130
    Deadline Murder 137
    Fair Play 149
    Shatter Proof 154
    The Queer Deal 158
    Going Down 167
The Stories from *Mantrap, Murder!* and *Smashing Detective Stories*
    Anniversary of Death 171
    A Torch for Tess 184
    Dead Cops are Murder 194
    Death Rail 202
    Rainy Afternoon 208
A Jack Ritchie Bibliography 211

War and Peace on the Back of a Postcard

John G. Reitci, better known by his pseudonym, Jack Ritchie, was born on February 22, 1922, one hundred and twenty years from the very day Victor Hugo was, but that is where the similarity of the two authors ends.

Whereas Victor Hugo wrote novels that numbered thousands of pages with hundreds of pages of descriptive prose, Ritchie wrote lean, concise prose in the form of short stories, nearly 350 in all, averaging fewer than 3,000 words in length.

Ritchie once said in an interview for *Ellery Queen's Mystery Magazine*:

> The short story seems to be my field, possibly by forfeit. I've always felt that there hasn't been a novel published that couldn't be reduced to a better short story. Often the very long novels are really collections of short stories and sometimes they even include what are basically articles. Victor Hugo was good at that. He put about 30,000 words into *Les Misérables* delineating the history, structure, and whatnot of the Paris sewers. Now if I'd been in his shoes I could have described the sewers in two paragraphs. Maybe one. *Les Misérables* itself would have become a novelet. Possibly even a pamphlet.

In his introduction to the Ritchie collection *A New Leaf and Other Stories*, Don Westlake closed with a very apt observation that Ritchie himself provided the best and most concise description of his own prose style in his short story, "Piggy Bank Killer," in which one of his characters says, "I had the feeling the boy could have written *War and Peace* on the back of a postcard."

Ritchie's stories seem to start in the middle of the action and we're left having to catch up with what's going on. The beauty of the Ritchie style, though, is how he quickly fills in the gaps in the setting and atmosphere though his brilliant dialogue. It's the very practice of Elmore Leonard's writing commandment: "Try to leave out the part that readers tend to skip."

A writer with whom Ritchie had much in common and whose career coincided almost exactly with his own and, with whom, in fact, he shared the same years and of birth and death was Gil Brewer. They both served in World War II and both decided on a career as a writer after the war. They shared the same venues with both of them appearing in issues of *Manhunt, Murder!, Alfred Hitchcock's Mystery Magazine, Mike Shayne Mystery Magazine, The Saint Mystery Magazine, Mystery Monthly, Zane Grey Western Magazine, Mr. Magazine, Men, Male, Swank, Topper, Adam Beside Reader* and *Escapade*.

Ritchie and Brewer shared the same stark, noir style of prose that grabs you from the first paragraph and maintains a constant tension until the brutal end. One way in which Ritchie excelled, even over Brewer in this regard, was the twist ending. In that he was more like another great practitioner of the short story form, O. Henry. Ritchie was the hard-boiled O. Henry. You get the feeling when reading a Ritchie story that he wrote his stories backwards from the surprise ending to the beginning, starting with just a button and sewing a whole jacket on to it.

Ritchie sold his first crime story to *Manhunt* in 1954, breaking into what had been an exclusive fraternity of writers represented by the Scott Meredith Literary Agency. Ritchie was at a disadvantage living in his home state of Wisconsin rather than in New York City where most of the publishing houses and crime magazines, such as *Manhunt*, were located. But once his Milwaukee-based agent, Larry Sternig, got his foot in the door at Archer St. John's Flying Eagle Publications, he placed five more stories in *Manhunt* by the end of August of 1955. By the end of 1956, Sternig had sold ten more stories to *Manhunt* and its sister publications *Mantrap, Murder!* and *Verdict*.

At the same time Ritchie was writing for the crime digests, he was writing sports stories for men's magazines, but had an even more lucrative, parallel career writing romance stories for newspaper syndicates, most notably The News Syndicate Co., Inc. Through these wire services, Ritchie's short stories, most fewer than 1500 words, appeared in newspapers such as *The New York Daily News, The Seattle Times, Buffalo Evening News* and *The Gazette* (Montreal). Between 1953 and 1964 he sold over 40 stories for syndication.

Although Ritchie never achieved the kind of name recognition that even lesser authors enjoyed, perhaps because he toiled in mostly one genre and in one format, he still garnered the respect of his peers and the admiration of regular readers of mystery digests.

Ritchie was nominated for three Edgar Awards, winning for his *Alfred Hitchcock's Mystery Magazine* story "The Absence of Emily." His stories were selected in *Best Detective Stories of Year* anthologies 21 times over a period of 21 years, beginning in 1961 with his story "Shatter Proof" for *Manhunt* until his death in 1983.

Ritchie's stories appeared in 117 issues of *Alfred Hitchcock's Mystery Magazine* and in 116 Alfred Hitchcock anthologies. Three television episodes of *Alfred Hitchcock Presents/Hour* were based on his stories and five episodes of *Tales of the Unexpected*, as well one episode of the Canadian television show *The Unforeseen*. His story "The Green Heart," which appeared in *AHMM*, was filmed as *A New Leaf*, an Elaine May film starring Walter Matthau.

In addition to the 23 stories Ritchie wrote for *Manhunt* between 1954 and 1965, we've also included, in this collection, four stories from *Manhunt's* sister publications, *Mantrap* and *Murder!* and one additional story from *Smashing Detective Stories*, all of which are from 1956. These follow the *Manhunt* stories, which are in chronological order.

Jeff Vorzimmer
Austin, Texas
September 30, 2022

THE STORIES FROM
MANHUNT

My Game, My Rules

July 1954

They thought they were through talking, but as far as I was concerned they'd just started.

"I'll have to know more," I said. "Especially the Why."

The man in the gray pin-stripe spoke. "I don't think that's necessary," he said.

"I haven't said I'll take the job," I reminded him.

The three of them shifted in their chairs and tried to come to an agreement with their eyes: the pinstripe, the small olive-skinned man, and the big man who'd been eating too well for fifteen years.

I pointed to the man in the pin-stripe. "You start it off," I said.

They exchanged glances again, and then he sighed and got up. He was the kind of man who made after-dinner speeches and he had to get up when he talked.

"My name is Frederick Harlow," he said.

I shook my head. "No," I said. "You're Marcus Whitney Adrian."

His mouth sagged slightly and he had to look at the other two again.

"I lived in this town once," I said. "Everybody knows Marcus Whitney Adrian."

They thought about it, and then the man who liked food too much said, "Go ahead, Adrian. He probably knows, anyway. I thought his face was familiar."

This one was Sergeant Matt Hogan of the Sixth Precinct. A few years ago he had been Chief of Police Hogan.

Adrian shrugged his shoulders. "Very well, then. As you say, everyone knows me." He frowned at how to begin. "This has always been a clean city. . . ."

Hogan opened heavy lids. "Never mind the crap. Get to the point."

"All right," Adrian said irritably. "The point. The point is Bull Moberg."

The olive-skinned man, smiling quietly to himself, was Gino Cosmo. "Good old Bull Moberg," he said.

Adrian ignored him. "Moberg is an ignorant lout from what is commonly referred to as the other side of the tracks."

"Adrian's Row," Cosmo said, amiably. "Shacks, tenements, no culture, and high rents."

Adrian turned angrily. "The rents are in line with costs, and the houses are perfectly sound. Certainly better than those Bohunks and Da—those immigrants had where they came from."

Hogan stirred. "Lay off, Cosmo. You're making Adrian nervous, and you know he can't concentrate on two things at the same time." He lit a big cigar.

"What Adrian's getting to is that he owns half the ground anybody walks on in this burg. Moberg's making him kick in a couple of hundred grand a year for protection."

Adrian was trembling with indignation now. "Moberg," he said, "threatened to have my houses condemned and torn down unless I agreed to pay him what he calls a 'percentage'."

He brought out a handkerchief and wiped his palms. "At first I refused to pay. I still have certain friends in the Judiciary. But then a lot of my houses began to catch fire, and the fire trucks always developed flat tires or got there too late. I've been paying ever since."

I looked over at Gino Cosmo, still smiling to himself. "What's *your* problem, Cosmo?" I asked.

"I see you know me, too," he said. He brought out a silver cigarette case and extracted a king-size. "Then you probably know I run a few places around town. Gambling houses, joints—places like that."

He lit the cigarette. "I liked Bull Moberg, and I was the one who gave him his first job. I stuffed him into an over-size tux and used him to scare the complainers."

He paused for a minute. "Yes," he said, thoughtfully. "Moberg is an impressive boy. Big and tough."

That touched something in Hogan. "If I was twenty years younger he wouldn't look so tough. I've cut his kind down to kindling before."

Cosmo eyed Hogan's stomach. "Just fall on him now. That's all you'd have to do."

They stared at each other for a moment, and then Cosmo cleared the smoke from his nostrils and went on. "Bull was a good boy. He was useful and he came up fast. In five years he was my right hand. A brother. Even a friend."

Cosmo ground out the cigarette. "And then one pretty night I came to work and Bull was sitting in my chair with his feet on the mahogany."

He reflected on it sadly and then resumed the smile. "You notice I smile a lot," he said. "That's because I've got good teeth. Also there are times when I can't do anything else."

"And so I smiled and he smiled and he kept his feet where they were. We had a new administration."

Cosmo showed his good teeth. "We're still friends," he said softly. "I get invited to his headquarters regularly for a drink, a look at his swanky furniture, and a peek or two at his dame.

"Her name is Helen," Cosmo said. His eyes hazed and his smile was envious. "If those blue eyes were for me, I wouldn't mind the seventy-five grand Bull costs me each year."

Not blue, I thought with sudden bitterness. *Violet.*

It was Hogan's turn now. He put a match to the dead end of his cigar and got it going. "If you know the others, you know me."

"Bull Moberg is just a small-time punk who got lucky. I knew he was growing and I figured to slap him down when he got too big. But I'm not the worrying type and I let it go until it was too late."

He chewed his cigar, remembering. "When I saw how things were—when I woke up and saw that he had the administration in his pocket—I was plenty willing to cooperate. But Moberg had other ideas and other men. Since then he's had me sitting in the Sixth sorting traffic tickets all day."

He took the cigar from his mouth. "Now you know everything."

The three of them sat expectantly and watched for me to talk.

"Moberg's got an organization," I said.

"Sure," Hogan said. "But he picked his own boys, and not for brains. Without Moberg, the organization won't last twenty-four hours." His eyes lit up. "The old days will come back. Adrian handles the property, Cosmo helps the citizens get rid of their dough, and I see that everybody stays in line. Everything under control. Just like a three-decker sandwich."

Cosmo leaned forward in his chair. "There isn't anyone we can really depend on in this city. That's why we've had to send for you."

The three pairs of eyes focused on me and waited.

I let them stew while I tasted my drink. "All right," I said. "You're all nice people, and you've convinced me. I'll take the job."

The first part of my job is always to find out a man's routine, if he has one. You've got to be able to depend on it that a man will be at the same place at least once during every day. If you're lucky, it'll be at the same time.

At one o'clock the next afternoon, I parked about a hundred yards from the entrance of the Lake Crest where Bull had a penthouse apartment.

I lazed until four o'clock until Bull came striding out of the place. He was trailed by two muscle men who kept a couple of steps behind him.

A dark-blue chauffeur-driven Cadillac pulled up to the curb and Bull and his friends got in. I put my car into gear and kept a careful block behind.

Moberg made almost a dozen stops in the next four hours. It looked like he was checking his operations to make sure everybody was happy and paying.

At eight-thirty, he picked up Helen. I'd known about that, of course, for a couple of years now. There are always some smiling friends who let you know when something like that happens.

They dined leisurely at the Merrill House and then at ten they moved on to the Green Cockade, where everything costs the best.

Because I was hired for it, I paid some attention to Bull. He was big, plenty big, over two-fifty and carrying enough of that in the shoulders not to be bothered by it. His heavy face liked to roar with laughter and it liked to eat and drink.

And because I'd never gotten her out of my mind, I watched Helen too. Her eyes were the remembered violet, glistening violet. Her honey-blonde hair shimmered with each movement.

I was at the bar at the far end of the main room when she saw me. Our eyes held for seconds, and then she looked away. She kept her eyes on her hands for a long time before Bull said something sufficiently funny so that she could smile.

She came to the bar after a while.

"Hello, Johnny," she said quietly. "I made excuses, but I can only stay a minute."

"That's plenty," I said. It wasn't easy to say. She had been twenty when I left, and now she was four years lovelier.

Her face was expressionless. "Did you come back for anything?" she asked. "Perhaps you forgot something?"

"Just passing through," I said. "Having fun?"

Her eyes met mine. "Lots," she said.

"It's a living, anyway," I said.

She bit her lower lip. "I'm untouchable now. Is that it?"

I signaled the bartender for a refill. "I wouldn't say that," I told her. "Try to keep awake after Bull leaves your place tonight. Maybe I'll come up and—say hello."

"I'll be too tired," she said, her face white. She walked quickly away.

Bull took her back to her apartment at one-thirty. His two gorillas waited in the car, and Bull was back out at four.

I slept late the next day, but, by the time Bull was ready to make his rounds, I was waiting for him in my car. The routine was the same as the previous day, and Bull and Helen were at the Green Cockade at nine.

I was at the bar again when she came to me.

"I know you're not following we," she said. "What do you want here?"

"I'm here for a drink," I said.

She put her hand on my arm, but then pulled it back. "If it's Bull, be careful."

"Worried about me?" I asked.

"Why shouldn't I be?"

I looked over at the ringside table. "I figured you stopped worrying when you took up with Moberg . . ."

Her face was white again. "I waited two years," she said. "You never even wrote."

The bitterness was gone from inside me, suddenly, because I knew she was right—or, anyway, as right as I was. "I was waiting to raise a stake," I said. "The trouble is, I'm still waiting. You'd better go back to your table."

They left for her apartment at two, and I settled down outside for the hours to pass. But Bull was out again in twenty minutes, and from the way he slammed the door, he wasn't happy. It looked as though Helen wasn't in a cooperative mood.

I let his car disappear while I smoked another cigarette. Then I got out of the car and went up to her apartment.

She wore a black nylon robe, small-netted and transparent. It was held together at her breasts with the sparkle of a diamond pin.

She stood in the doorway with one hand on the doorknob. "If it's just this once, I don't want you here."

"My plans aren't definite yet," I said. "You want me to go?"

"You don't back up an inch, do you, Johnny? It has to be your way or not at all."

"I make the rules," I said. "Always."

She was silent, watching my face. Then she turned and walked back into the room, leaving the door open. "No," she said quietly. "I don't want you to go."

She waited for me and I put my arms around her. Her lips were warm with hunger, and she held me very tight. My hands went over her, and when I let her go, she unfastened the diamond clip and the cloth slithered off her shoulders and was a black mist on the floor.

She was mine for now, and I knew that she had never wanted it any other way.

The next morning, I drove to Bull Moberg's hotel and walked to the entrance. I stood there looking up and down the street until I found what I wanted.

It was at the end of the block and across the street: a red brick five-story hotel called the Cary House.

I checked out of my own hotel and got a third floor room with a view of Bull's hotel at the Cary House. I had my suitcase taken up to the room while I had dinner in the Grill downstairs. Then I killed time at the bar until about twenty to four.

Upstairs in my room, I put the suitcase on the bed and opened it.

I began getting ready to do the thing the three of them had hired me for.

I assembled the pieces of the carbine and fitted the silencer. I opened the window, lit a cigarette, and waited for Bull Moberg.

At five after four, Bull and his two shadows came out of the wide doors of the Shore Crest. I ground out my cigarette and rested my elbow on the window sill.

The Cadillac pulled up to the curb. Bull began walking toward it.

I squeezed the trigger. The gun made no more noise than a rubber band snapped against a wall.

Bull Moberg took one more step and then he fell.

I closed the window and wiped away my fingerprints. The carbine was broken down and went back into the suitcase.

I put on my hat, picked up the suitcase, stopped to use a handkerchief on the doorknob, and then went out into the corridor.

I was in my car behind the Cary House three minutes after Bull died. In another twenty minutes I was outside the city limits and relaxed for the two-hour drive back to Chicago.

I wondered what kind of a scramble my clients would get into back there. I wondered whether they would return to the three-decker sandwich or whether one of them was big enough to step into Bull's shoes.

Not Adrian. He didn't have the guts for it and his line was more respectable, like rent gouging and slum profiteering.

It wouldn't be Matt Hogan either. That fat wasn't all belly. And he was getting old. His limit was being a crooked cop.

Cosmo was the best bet, but not a good one. He had it up there, but that smile got in the way. It made him too ready to be a good loser.

No. None of them had it. It took the three of them just to get up nerve enough to hire me.

I thought about the payment in my suitcase and I smiled until I thought higher.

I thought about the seventy-five grand Bull took from Cosmo, and the two hundred G's Adrian cried about each year.

I thought about those things and I thought about violet eyes and honey-blonde hair.

Bull was gone now and his machine would collapse because there was no one strong enough to take over.

Power, money, and soft blonde hair.

I slowed the car to a crawl and waited for an open spot in the traffic lane.

I made a U-turn and drove back.

Replacement

November 1954

If he hadn't been Ed Kubak, he could have disappeared almost anywhere and I never would have found him, even with the connections I have. He could have lost himself in any city in the country and been safe from me.

But he was Ed Kubak and that made it impossible. He had been my boss once and every hood across the country knew Ed. They knew his face and they knew that I would give fifteen grand just to know where he was.

I didn't have to chase after Ed. I stayed where I was and let other eyes do the finding for me. I waited and thought about Helen and about the organization that was mine now. I thought about the city that was mine now.

Ed had been alone on top when I was still a collector making the rounds from bookie joint to bookie joint. He'd been a king while my feet were still walking the dirt. But my eyes were looking up, ready for the break when it came and even ready to make the break myself.

And the break came when Stacey Hanlon made the mistake of getting drunk and running out of money the same night. Stacey was one of Kubak's top muscle boys and not too bright even when he was sober. And with nearly a quart under his belt, Stacey went back to the old days and walked into a grocery store to pick up a little change.

He picked a little store run by an old man who should have been silly scared and begged Stacey to take every cent in the cash register. But the brittle old man wasn't scared and he kept a .38 under the counter.

When Stacey finished trying to cough the slugs out of his lungs and coughed out his life instead, there was a job vacant close to Ed Kubak, and I decided it was going to be mine.

It was easy to get to Ed's door. I simply took the elevator as high as it would go and then walked up a flight of iron stairs and I was right there. But from then on it got hard.

Two big men with cautious eyes opened it slow and not too far. Neither one of them was quite as big as I was, but still there were two of them and so I smiled politely.

"Yeah?" one of them said, squinting against the smoke from his cigarette.

"I'm here with the week's take," I said, holding up the briefcase.

He frowned at me.

"I'm a collector," I said. "Horse parlors."

"Sonny," he said, taking the butt from his lips. "You must be shiny new or you'd know better than to bring it up here. Take it to Sullivan, he has charge of the collections."

"I know," I said. "But Sullivan's in there, isn't he?"

"So?" the one who didn't smoke and had red hair said. "Sullivan's got an office with maybe twenty clerks. Why the personal delivery?"

"It's a secret between him and me," I said. "He'll get peeved if I don't see him."

Their hard eyes kept sizing me up while they tried to make up their minds. I raised my arms above my head. "I'm clean," I said. "And I don't bite very hard."

The man who probably everybody called Red went over me with his hands and through the briefcase. He eyed the other one and shrugged. "We can ask."

They let me inside and I was in a small carpeted hall with a very solid door at the other end. Red went to that door and pressed a buzzer.

A wide man with no hair let us see his face. Red spoke. "Ask Sullivan if he wants to see . . ." he thumbed at me.

"Warren," I said. "Max Warren."

Baldy closed the door and there were just the three of us to stare at each other.

I smiled gently and let the briefcase slip out of my fingers. Their eyes instinctively followed it as it thudded to the floor and I took that second to drive a shoulder-powered right to Red's lean jaw. He had just time to look surprised before he dropped and that left me and the cigarette smoker. His hand went for his side pocket and he almost got out the automatic before I got to him.

I made sure they were sleeping, stepped on the cigarette smoldering on the rug and went to the second door and waited.

In a few minutes, Baldy opened it. "Sullivan says to throw the . . ."

My hand on his face stopped the conversation and I shoved hard. He teetered on his heels and then sat down hard. I stepped over him and into the room.

About a dozen people's eyes were on me and whatever they had been talking about died in quiet. Hands went for shoulder holsters and I was facing five steady guns.

Sullivan got the brunette off his lap and rose, his face flushed. "Damn it, Max," he said. "When I say I don't want to see you, then you don't get seen."

I turned toward Kubak. He was a heavy paunched man with dark brown eyes. His face was sallow and jowled and he breathed in a deep tired wheeze.

"I came to see you, Mr. Kubak," I said. "Not Sullivan."

A small flicker of interest came into his eyes. "Then why ask for Sullivan?"

"Would you have seen me?"

"No," he said.

"So I asked for Sullivan. That got me half way in and I took it from there." I met his eyes. "You'll need somebody to replace Stacey Hanlon."

His eyes traveled over me and the sound of his heavy breathing was the only noise in the room. Finally he said, "Stacey was tough."

I gave him time to hear Red groaning his way to consciousness behind me. "Do I look like I carry daisies?"

Kubak smiled slightly and looked at the others. He took the cigar out of his mouth. "Sullivan," he said. "Fix the man a drink."

Stacey's job didn't have much work connected with it and the pay was good. Mostly I'd just stick close to Kubak, mix his drinks, light his cigars, and give him a feeling of security. But once in a while I'd get a word from Kubak and leave for a couple of hours. Occasionally I'd have to clean my gun before reporting back to Kubak, but not as often as I'd expected. All some people need is a friendly word or maybe just a little rough stuff to make them realize it was bad to irritate Kubak.

I rode beside Kubak in the big limousine, always stepped out first, just in case, and got to all the drinking parties that Kubak did. That was why I was there when Sullivan brought Helen Wesley along.

I always thought that was stupid of Sullivan, but then I never thought much of his brain power in the first place. If I owned her, I'd make sure to keep her away from anybody who had more money than I did. But I suppose Sullivan thought that Kubak was too old and tired to be interested, and Sullivan couldn't have been more wrong.

We were celebrating our expansion over the county line when Helen came in on Sullivan's arm. And the second she walked in you saw that the rest of the women in the room were just dames who talked too loud and went heavy on the make-up.

Helen was a honey blonde with brown eyes and your first look was enough to tell you that money was the only thing that could make her melt. Not that she looked hard, but it was there just the same.

I was sitting next to Kubak when Sullivan brought her over and that was the first time I'd ever seen him struggle to his feet when he was introduced to a woman.

She looked at him with open calculation and then met my eyes. I grinned until she looked away.

Kubak hovered around her all evening and I noticed that she was more to him than a sparkle in the eye. It went a lot deeper than that.

And Sullivan knew it too, because he hit the bottle hard and by the time the party broke up, he had to be carried out. I had Red toss him over his shoulder and take him to his car. Red drove Sullivan to his place and I took Helen to her apartment in my car.

She didn't complain when I followed her upstairs and into her apartment. Silently she made drinks and handed one to me.

"Hello," I said.

She lit a cigarette and went to the other side of the room.

I smiled at her. "All you want from me is information. Isn't that right?"

She stared out of the window, frowning slightly in thought, and then turned. "Sullivan told me he was the boss," she said.

"Once in a while he thinks so." I put my feet on the hassock and relaxed. "And now you're dissatisfied."

Her eyes flickered over me. "Are you anybody important? I'd like to know if I have to be polite."

"No," I said. "You'll have to love me for my personality alone."

Helen drew slowly on her cigarette. "Kubak fell hard. Do you think there'll be any trouble if I say goodbye to Sullivan?"

"That depends," I said. "Whether he thinks you're worth trouble."

She smiled. "I'll keep out of the way until it's over."

I set my drink down, got up, and walked over to her.

She stood stiff and still. "It'll be cold. Ice cold."

I took her in my arms and it was cold, Her lips were firm, unyielding. And then as I held her tighter I could feel the beginnings of a thaw.

She pushed me away quickly.

"I understand," I said, grinning. "Raised on the wrong side of the tracks. Old man drunk all the time and beat you. Left home at fourteen. Had crummy jobs. Waiting on tables? Or was it burlesque? Finally decided that all work and no money was not for Helen. Tell me about it. I like those kind of stories. They make me want to cry."

She flushed slightly. "Don't forget your hat."

I picked it up and walked toward the door. "Kubak usually starts off with flowers, but don't be disappointed. The big stuff will come after a week or so."

The next day Kubak sent me out twice. Once in the morning and once in the afternoon. In the afternoon I brought the paper he wanted, opened it, and laid it on his lap.

He read the headlines and the lead story. "It says that Sullivan and a small-time bookie had a shooting disagreement somewhere way out in the country. No survivors."

"That's what it says."

He glanced back at the paper. "No witnesses either and nobody heard the shots. But the cops think it happened about ten. That right?"

"Closer to ten-thirty," I said.

He folded the newspaper and sat back. "See that he gets a pretty funeral. The bookie too."

I handed him a cigar from the humidor and lit it.

"And so?" he asked. "I think you got something on your mind."

"And so you'll have to replace Sullivan," I said. "I thought you ought to know that I can read, write, and add."

"That's nice," he said. He closed his eyes for almost a minute. "All right. You got his job. I don't care what you read or write, but don't make any mistakes when it comes to adding." His eyes opened. "And don't get too ambitious. I'll be watching you."

But he didn't watch me and that was what I was counting on. His eyes and his brain were busy with Helen.

I was grateful to her for what she was doing to Kubak. Sure, she was doing it for her own reasons, but it helped me too.

I had my shoulder in the door now and I eased in. Helen was good at making Kubak forget business, and it wasn't long before the boys came to me when a decision had to be made. Kubak couldn't be bothered.

I worked slow and careful at first, not taking too much on my shoulders, but the boys soon got the idea I was trying to put across. Kubak was slipping, he was getting old.

I even let drop a word or two that I thought Kubak's take was too big. I let it be known that the fact saddened me and that I thought there ought to be some adjustment.

It took about six months before I was sure enough of where I stood to call a meeting of the big boys and not let Kubak know about it. I brought the whole thing into the open and in fifteen minutes we all agreed that Kubak needed a vacation. It took a little longer for them to see that I was big enough to take his place. They tried to put up some argument, but I talked bigger than I had and they decided to go along with me.

At Kubak's next party we sat there smiling at him until finally he noticed that the smiles were a lot different from the ones he was used to getting.

I got up, rapped on a glass with my cigarette lighter for silence, and looked at him in a kindly fashion.

Kubak sat up straighter, a frown forming on his forehead.

"Kubak," I said. "We've noticed that you've seemed tired lately."

"The hell I am," he snapped.

I smiled at Helen and looked back at him. "In fact we've decided unanimously that you need a vacation."

His brown eyes were hard. "You're not shoving me out."

"You could argue about it," I said. "But I don't think you'll have much help."

His eyes went from face to face and he lost some of his color.

"But we don't like arguments," I said gently. "You know how tempers will flare and how messy things get for the loser." I paused. "And so if you take this real quiet, I think you'll have a nice happy old age to look forward to in some warm climate."

Kubak's head turned from face to face again and suddenly he became old. He sighed tiredly and I could feel some of the tension leave my body. We had won and the boys got up and headed for the door.

I lingered behind until they were gone. I picked up Helen's ermine and draped it over my arm. "Ready?" I asked.

Kubak turned sharply toward Helen. She was considering him dispassionately, weighing the pros and cons.

His eyes were bewildered. "Helen! Don't even think about leaving me!"

"I'm the boss now," I said softly. "The head man."

She glanced at Kubak once more and then came toward me.

Kubak rose from his chair, his voice desperate. "Helen! You know I love you."

I put the ermine around her shoulders.

Kubak tried once more. I could tell that now he realized what Helen was, but he wanted her anyway. "I have money, Helen," he said quietly. "A lot of money."

Helen hesitated and I smiled at her. "Well, baby?"

Our eyes met and I knew what she was deciding. *Kubak has money, but I think you'll have a lot more some day.*

I held open the door and she walked out.

"Max," Kubak said, tightness in his voice. "I love her and nobody is going to have her if I can't."

I stepped into the hall and shut the door behind me.

Kubak left town at the end of the week, but he stopped to do something before he did.

It was the afternoon I got the new Jaguar that I found out Kubak's last words to me weren't just hot air. I went up to Helen's apartment and when I used the key I walked into a room full of cops.

They showed me Helen where she was lying on the bedroom floor. There was no bleeding now from the brown-stained front of her dress and she was icy cold when I touched her.

There might have been trouble for me, except that I'd spent the time the cops pin-pointed for the killing at the auto show room and three salesmen could verify that fact.

They questioned me for a couple of hours, but I had nothing to tell them. I knew that eventually they would get the connection between Kubak and Helen and they would begin looking for him. But that would take time, and I wanted Kubak to get away. At least from the cops.

When they were through with me, I went to my apartment and began phoning. I let it get around that I wanted to find Kubak and that it was worth fifteen thousand to me. I just wanted to know where he was. I didn't want a hair of his head touched and I didn't want the police in on it.

It was two months before I got the telegram from Palm Beach. "A friend of yours is here," it said. "Be sure to bring the fifteen grand." It was signed Rieber.

It was near nightfall when the plane brought me in and I was met by a short wiry man wearing a yellow sport shirt. "The name's Rieber," he said.

We got in his car and drove out of the airport.

"You sure about this?" I asked.

He had a permanent tight smile on his face as his eyes watched the road. "You'll spend the dough tonight."

He switched on his headlights. "He's in a small motor court outside the city. It's pretty run down so there aren't many customers to bother you. I got a boy watching so he don't decide to move."

We drove half an hour and then Rieber braked the car and turned smoothly into a motor court. He stopped the car and pointed. "Over there," he said. "The one with the light in the window. No. 24."

I walked toward the cabin with my .45 in my hand. I took it carefully and on tiptoe and went around to a side window.

Kubak sat at a small table, a quart of bourbon in front of him and next to it a glass tumbler more than half filled with the stuff.

I went around to the front and turned the knob slowly. The door was unlocked and I pushed it open.

Kubak looked up at me without surprise. He seemed a lot older now. The skin on his face hung in tired flaps and his eyes were deep sunk and weary.

He fingered the glass of bourbon for a moment and then sighed. He put it on the window sill. "You found me because I stopped running, Max," he said.

"Drink the whiskey," I said. "It might make it easier."

His eyes went to the glass and then away. "I'm a dying man, Max," he said. "You could wait another month and you wouldn't have to bother." He looked up. "Liver, kidneys, everything inside worn out and gone bad. But mostly the heart."

"A month is too long, Kubak. Your troubles are over right now."

Kubak looked at me curiously. "You didn't love her, Max. Not enough so that you'd take care of this personally. What makes you mad is that somebody took away something you thought was yours."

"She *was* mine, Kubak. Sure I loved her."

Kubak rubbed his eyes tiredly. "I'm the one who really loved her. I loved her so much I was blind to what she was. But even when I knew, I still loved her."

I was getting impatient. "No prayers and no drink?" My finger tightened on the trigger.

It was a clean shot and he died easy. There was just that shock in the eyes of a man when he realizes that death is not quite what he expected and then he dropped.

I picked up the glass of bourbon from the window sill and downed it in a few gulps. "I loved her as much as you did," I said.

The drink burned in my stomach. I went to the water tap and swallowed a glass of water and waited for the burning to stop.

But it didn't stop. It got worse and worse until I doubled over, holding my stomach. I looked at Kubak lying there and suddenly I knew about the whiskey. I knew why Kubak had stopped running. That drink was supposed to be his last one on earth. But he had left it for me. For my victory drink. For my death drink.

I began cursing then. I cursed because of the white hot pain and because I was afraid to die and because I wished I had never seen Helen.

I hoped she was in hell.

Hold Out

May 1955

Fred drove the car and I sat in the back with Pete Harder. "Nice stretch of country here," I said to him. "Looks pretty in the moonlight."

"You two must be strangers here if you think you can get away with this," he said.

"Fred and me are doing fine so far."

"Why pick on me?" Harder asked.

"We stuck a pin in the phone book and there you were." I crossed my legs and idly tapped the heel of my shoe with the barrel of the automatic.

"I got five G's in the bank. That's all I got," Harder said.

I raised an eyebrow. "That all? You must be a spender. I figured you to have more than that, considering the size of your apartment."

"Not a cent more than five thousand," Harder said again.

"We picked on a poor man, Fred," I said. We passed a big nightclub at a highway intersection. "That's another one of Mike Corrigan's places, isn't it? How many has he got altogether?"

"Enough to make him a big man in this part of the country. He'll get hot about this." Harder was about medium-sized and he had black hair and a thin mustache.

"Think you're worth fifty G's to Corrigan?" I asked.

Harder glanced at me but didn't say anything.

"Anyway I hope so," I said. "That's what we're asking."

Fred cut the speed of the car and turned into a gravel side road.

"He's got until noon tomorrow to get it together. It's rushing things, I admit, but Fred and I like to operate fast."

Fred turned into the driveway to the small two room cabin and parked the car in front of it.

I turned on the flashlight and got out. "Be careful where you step, Harder. It's muddy right here."

We went into the cabin and I kept the flash on until Fred fit the kerosene lantern. I indicated a chair with the gun. "Take a seat, Harder."

"Suppose Corrigan doesn't raise the money by noon?" Harder asked.

"You wouldn't like to think about it," I said.

"If you two got any brains you'll let me go right now."

"Sure," I said. "We shake hands and forget this ever happened. That's right, isn't it?"

Fred rummaged through the cupboard. "Pork and beans okay?"

"Fine," I said. "You hungry, Harder?"

He shook his head. I went to the corner and picked up the rope.

"You don't have to tie me," Harder said.

"We don't have to, but we want to. Put your hands behind your back." I tied his hands and wrapped another coil around his legs. "Can't have you walking away," I said.

"How do you know I'm worth fifty grand to Corrigan?"

"It's a risk we'll take. You're his right hand man. We heard talk about how buddy-like you two are."

Fred heated the pork and beans and poured them on two plates.

"At first Fred and I figured on sending the note to Elsie Thomas working on the idea that you mean more to her than you do to Corrigan. But then we weren't sure she could raise the money. Probably have to go to Corrigan anyway. So we just cut out the middleman, so to speak."

"I don't care much for blondes myself," Fred said. "Pass the bread, will you, Ed?"

"Why not settle for the five thousand," Harder said. "If you get Mike mad he'll come for you."

I nodded. "That thought sends shivers down our backs. I understand Corrigan's a shiv man when he's irritated. Got a silver switch knife with a blade that gleams like all get out."

"Elsie could pawn her jewels," Harder said. "You'd get maybe five grand more."

"Take too long," Fred said. "We get fidgety."

Harder was quiet while we finished eating, but he was thinking. He didn't like to bring up what was on his mind, but still he wanted to be reassured.

He licked his lips. "When you get the fifty grand, you let me go?"

"Fred and I are thinking about it," I said. "Be happy you're alive now."

Harder didn't have much to say after that and around eleven Fred and I carried him into the bedroom and put him on the cot so that he could get some sleep if he wanted it.

Fred and I took turns sitting up with him during the night and at eight in the morning Fred made breakfast. Harder didn't want anything to eat, but I untied him so that he could have a cup of coffee.

I lit a cigarette after we were through and went to the window. "Looks like rain," I said.

"Hope not," Fred said. "The windshield wiper's giving me trouble."

"What time is it?" Harder asked.

"About eight-thirty," I said. I took Harder back into the bedroom and retied him.

He sat on the edge of the cot. "How are you going to get the money?"

"Fred and I find that the simple ways are the best. At twelve noon, Corrigan or somebody he knows tosses the satchel of dough out of his car right where that sign marks the county line. Fred will drive by and if everything looks okay, he'll pick it up."

Harder's forehead was damp. "What if nobody shows up?"

"Don't think about it," I said. "Try to relax."

Fred read comic books and I played solitaire until about eleven-thirty. "It's time to go now, Fred," I said.

He got into his coat. "It's beginning to drizzle."

While he was gone, I took my gun apart and went over it with a rag. I smiled to myself. "You know," I said. "I've just been thinking. If you and Corrigan aren't good friends like it looks, this would be a nice time for him to get rid of you."

"He wouldn't do that," Harder said.

"You know him better than I do."

"We've been together for ten years."

"That right? Partners?"

"No," Harder said. "He's the boss."

"Must be an interesting life." I began putting the automatic back together. "This Elsie is quite a looker. Caught her act a couple of nights back. Not much voice, but that's not what she's selling."

Every ten minutes or so, Harder asked for the time. About twelve-thirty we heard the car pulling up in front of the cabin and Harder turned his head toward the door to the kitchen and waited.

Fred came in and shook some of the mist from his hat. Harder's eyes searched his face.

"Did you get the satchel, Fred?" I asked.

"Nobody showed up."

"You must have missed it," Harder said. "It's probably in the ditch."

Fred sat down. "Nope. I checked."

I looked at Harder. "I guess Corrigan doesn't miss you like you thought."

"He needs more time to raise the money," Harder said.

"Fred and I think he just doesn't want to."

Sweat trickled down Harder's face as Fred and I stood looking down at him. His eyes went from my face to Fred's and back again and the terror shine was coming into them.

I picked my automatic off the table and pressed off the safety.

Harder almost screamed. "Wait! You'll get the money."

"No," I said. "If Corrigan wanted to pay, he would have."

Harder's voice was high. "I've got the dough. There's almost a hundred grand. You can have it all."

Fred and I looked at each other. "I don't know," Fred said. "I'd say he's stalling."

"I'm not stalling," he said desperately. "Elsie's got the money in the safe at her apartment. It's mine. I've been getting it together for the last couple of years."

Fred eyed me. "That's it," he said.

I put the automatic in my pocket and went into the kitchen. Corrigan was standing behind the open door.

"You heard?" I asked.

"Yes."

"I guess you were right at that. He's been getting away with two or three grand a week. Do you want Fred and me to finish it?"

"No," Corrigan said. "I'll take it from here." His hand came out of his coat pocket with the switch knife.

Corrigan went into the bedroom and he made it last ten minutes.

Interrogation

June 1955

When Pete and I reported in and signed the book, Sergeant Herrick filled us in.

"Her husband and his brother-in-law set up an ambush and had a lot of fun," he said. "They set the bait by hanging a lot of the pink stuff on the line and then took up a stand behind the ash-box. When this collector slid over the fence around midnight and began popping the clothes pins, they were waiting. The guy's unbroken, but he's hurting and lucky to be alive."

Herrick looked at the wall clock and yawned. "Like always, the creep says he can't remember a thing. His mind went blank and all that stuff."

Pete checked the bulletin board and came back to the desk. "We got any reading material on him?"

"A regular customer. Three times for indecent exposure and once he was caught under a window enjoying a free show. He got a working over for that one too. You'd think he'd learn."

I lit a cigarette and leafed through the charge papers.

"He's got a place near the river and we went over it," Herrick said. "It was loaded with silk, pictures, and symphony records."

"Where have you got the poor misunderstood soul?" Pete asked.

"Upstairs in 603 with Nelson." Herrick picked up two heavy folders from his desk and handed them to me. "Try him on the Dugan thing. We went over it with him the last time he was here, but maybe you're more persuasive. And the other one's the Harris collection. I know it's pretty dusty, but you never can tell. I'll give you a cigar if you can hang it on him."

Pete and I went down the corridor and took the elevator to the sixth floor.

"It's funny what some guys do for a hobby," Pete said. "Now me, I like to watch ice cubes melt."

We walked into 603. Nelson was sitting on the wooden table looking at the stack of snapshots. He got to his feet. "After the first fifty, it gets monotonous."

He thumbed toward the corner. "Every greasy inch of him is yours. I'm going outside to wonder about these things for a while."

The man was seated on a straight-back chair, his legs drawn up and he hugged his knees. His face was puffed and torn from the beating and the edges of the bandages around his head were dark with the oil of his hair. He kept his eyes on the floor and was hoping he wouldn't be touched.

I pulled up a chair and sat down, adjusting my trousers to protect the creases. "Talk to us," I said. "And start with your name."

He bit his lips and kept his eyes focused on the floor.

"He's shy," Pete said. "I think I'll roll up my sleeves."

"My name is Ralph Pittman," he said quickly. "I live at 826 South Travis."

"Tell us all about it," I said. "We're the kind who like to listen."

"I don't remember anything," Pittman said.

"You see, Pete," I said. "He doesn't remember anything. I think we ought to leave him go."

"I blacked out," Pittman said.

Pete went to the cardboard box on the table and fished among the lingerie. He held up a pair of briefs. "Hey," he said. "Monogrammed. I saw these advertised in the papers a while back." He tossed them toward Pittman and they landed on his knees.

Pittman's eyes watched them as they glided down his legs and flowed to the floor.

"Just between the three of us, Pittman, why the hell do you collect these things?" Pete asked.

"I don't know," Pittman said.

Pete pawed through more of the stuff.

I looked Pittman over before I opened the Dugan file. The collar of his shirt was soiled and there were moons of dirt under his fingernails.

Pittman's eyes went to the green folder. "You always ask me about those things," he said. "I never had anything to do with them."

"I believe you," I said. "But let's go around again. Marion Dugan. On October 21st of last year she was found in an empty lot. She was twelve years old."

"I didn't have anything to do with it," Pittman said. "You cops tried to pin it on me the last time too, but there was nothing to it."

"When was that?" I asked.

He looked at the floor. "In January."

"What were you here for then?" I asked.

He didn't want to talk about it, but I waited patiently.

"For that window stuff," he said finally. "I was just passing by, that's all. I didn't even look."

"Man! How this stuff slithers," Pete said, still bending over the box.

Pittman licked his lips and looked away.

I picked up the other folder and looked at it. "Edna Harris," I said. "She was eleven. Can you help us a little bit on that?"

Pete left the box and began going through the pictures. He looked up. "Take any of these yourself, Pittman?"

"No," Pittman said. "I bought them. I don't know who from. Just some guys I met on the street." He turned back to me. "I don't know a thing about the Harris girl either."

Pete came over with one of the snapshots. "Here's one I'd like to meet," he said.

I glanced at it. "Looks a little hippy to me."

"That's how you want them, Harry," Pete said. He showed the picture to Pittman. "She isn't too hippy, is she?"

Pittman turned his face away, but Pete shoved the picture under his nose. "Is this one of your favorites?" he asked. "Tell me what you think about when you look at her?"

"What's it like to talk to a psychiatrist, Pittman?" I asked. "I'm real curious about that."

"I'm as sane as you are," Pittman said. "A lot saner."

"He's not crazy, Harry," Pete said. "He's emotionally disturbed."

"How about that, Pittman?" I asked. "Are you emotionally disturbed?"

"I'm a lot better off than you are," Pittman said.

I moved my chair a couple of inches away from him. "Don't you ever take a bath, Pittman? I can smell you from here."

"He likes it that way," Pete said. "He likes to smell. It makes him feel comfortable and gives him a sense of security. Didn't you know that, Harry?"

"You're dirty, Pittman," I said. "Filthy dirty and you stink."

"Don't say that," Pittman's voice rose.

"You're greasy," Pete said. "Can't you feel the greasiness on your neck? Doesn't your skin stick when you move your head?"

"You're oily and you stink," I said.

"I don't stink," Pittman yelled, rising to his feet.

"Pete," I said quietly. "I think you're disturbing him."

"I didn't mean to do that, Harry," Pete said.

We waited until Pittman was seated again. He was breathing hard and his face was mottled with color.

"Say," Pete said. "Did you know that Pittman here has a collection of symphony records? Must be a couple of hundred."

"I like good music myself," I said.

"Tell us what you think about when you listen to music, Pittman?" Pete asked.

"Don't ask him, Pete," I said. "He'll spoil my appreciation of good music if he tells us."

"I wonder if they're all symphony records," Pete said. "You know some of those things have fake labels. I heard a couple the other day that were pretty hot stuff."

"I never thought of that," I said. "Let's bring them to headquarters and play them."

"Those are my records," Pittman said. "Leave them alone."

"We just want to borrow them, Pittman," I said. "I don't think we'll break any."

Pittman sat up straight in his chair. "Leave them alone. They're just music."

"Now don't be that way," Pete said. "You must have hundreds of them. You won't miss a few."

The muscles in Pittman's face began twitching.

"I'll bet there are some good ones in your collection," I said.

"Have you got the one about the two women and the doctor?"

Pittman leaped to his feet. "I'll kill you if you touch those records!"

I took out my pack of cigarettes and offered one to Pete.

"I really ought to cut down on smoking," he said, taking one.

"Me too," I said. "I wake up every morning with a cough."

"Why don't you sit down, Pittman," Pete said softly.

Pittman sat down.

Pete looked at the pair of briefs still at Pittman's feet. "You better pick those up before you step on them," he said.

Pittman picked them up and held them out for Pete.

"You can hold them for a while," Pete said. "I wouldn't know what to do with them."

"What kind of material is that, Pittman?" I asked. "Looks like silk to me."

"I don't know," Pittman said, not looking at the briefs.

"I don't think they make those things out of silk any more, Harry," Pete said. "Come over here and feel it."

I stood up and moved over to Pittman. His head shrank almost into his shoulders as I reached forward and took some of the material between my thumb and forefinger. "I can't tell, Pete," I said. "This could be nylon."

Pete fingered the briefs. "I don't know, Harry. I think nylon is used for stockings mostly. This could be rayon."

"You ought to know, Pittman," I said. "Run this stuff between your fingers."

Pittman let go of the briefs and hid his fingers in his fists.

"I think the lace does something for these things," I said. "If you know what I mean."

"I sure do," Pete said. "Come now, Pittman. You must know what kind of material this is when you take it off the lines."

"It's always dark, Pete," I said. "And he doesn't remember."

"Here," Pete said. "Let me put this in your hands and you can feel it, Pittman."

The chair tipped over as Pittman jumped to his feet. "All right," he shouted. His chest heaved as he breathed. "I stole those things off the line. What more do you want?"

"What things?" Pete asked with interest.

"Panties," I said. "Don't embarrass him, Pete."

"Stop it!" Pittman shrieked.

Pete went over to the ash tray and carefully tapped some ash into it. "Pick up the chair, Pittman," he said. "That's city property."

"Sure," I said. "Sit down and relax, Pittman. There's no point to getting excited."

Pittman righted the chair and sat down. Thin beads of sweat made claw marks from his temples to his shirt collar. He took out a handkerchief and smeared at his neck.

"Look at the handkerchief now, Pittman," I said. "You'll see that I was right. That's dirt. Filthy, greasy dirt."

His eyes went to the handkerchief for a second and then he stuffed it back into his pocket.

Pete paged through the Dugan folder. "I wonder what type of a man would do that to a twelve-year-old kid?"

"You couldn't call him a man, could you, Pete?"

"I'll bet he's something filthy," Pete said.

"How do you mean?" I asked.

"Inside and out," Pete said. "The kind of a guy who never takes a bath. Real dirty and sticky."

"Are you sure you're not sticky, Pittman?" I asked. "Doesn't the sweat trickling under your shirt and down your body bother you?"

"Leave me alone," Pittman said, his voice breaking.

"You never can tell about people, though, Pete," I said. "Maybe deep inside of him this degenerate bastard's got a sensitive soul and likes good music. The world just doesn't understand him."

"You may be right," Pete said. "The world's a cruel place for somebody who's sensitive."

"I think he's the kind of a man who's afraid of women," I said. "That's why he picks on kids."

"I never thought of it that way," Pete said. "How are you with women, Pittman?"

"Have you ever seen one with that look in her eye?" I asked. "You must know what I mean."

"Or have her come and whisper evil things in your ear?" Pete asked.

Pittman put his hands over his face and bent his head to his knees.

"On the other hand," Pete said. "I'll bet Pittman doesn't know a thing about women. If it's a man, Harry, would you still call him a virgin?"

"I think so," I said. "Or is it eunuch?"

"That's something else, Harry. But maybe he's got a complex. You know what that is, don't you?"

Pittman leaped to his feet again and his eyes were wild. He stood there with his body stiff and his face contorted. After about ten seconds he collapsed back into the chair and began sobbing softly.

I lit a new cigarette and tossed one to Pete. "Open a window, Pete," I said. "Let's get some clean air In here."

Pete went to the window and pulled it up as far as it Would go. He leaned out and looked down. After a while he pulled his head back in. "That's a long way to drop," he said.

"Six stories, Pete," I said. "Wonder what a man would look like if he fell that far."

"Depends on how he lands," Pete said. "But he sure would be messed all over." He walked away from the window. "I've been wondering whether you ever thought of a telescope, Pittman?"

"How do you mean, Pete?" I asked.

"You can see a lot of things with a telescope," Pete said. "Especially at night and if you look from a high place."

"That's right," I said. "A lot of people are careless about shades."

"It's a lot safer than window peeping too," Pete said. "What do you think, Pittman?"

Pittman still had his hands over his face and his breath made a noise through his fingers.

"I don't believe he knows exactly what you mean," I said.

"Leave me alone," Pittman moaned.

"I think he's a little confused now," Pete said. "If we showed him, he'd understand a lot better."

Pete took his left arm and I took his right. Pittman tried to shrink away and his mouth moved soundlessly as we half-carried him to the open window. His eyes looked down the six floors to the hard pavement below and they filled with horror.

"Look at all those windows across there," Pete said. "You ought to be able to see dozens of things every night."

"It makes me shiver to look down there," I said. "How long do you think it would take to fall, Pete?"

"Just a couple of seconds," he said. "But it would be a long time, hell, because you know what's waiting for you."

Pete flipped his cigarette butt out of the window and Pittman watched with terrible fear as it dropped.

"You know, Harry," Pete said. "I think the man is basically a coward."

"Who are you talking about, Pete? You mean Pittman?"

"I was thinking particularly of the killer of the Dugan girl, Harry."

Pittman's knuckles were white as his hands gripped the window sill.

"He would have to be a coward," I said. "A dirty, filthy little coward. Be careful, Pittman. We wouldn't want you to slip."

"I should say not," Pete said. "Remember the last time, Harry? Took us hours of paper work to explain it."

"It was an accident, Pete. You know that."

"Sure, Harry. That's the way I always think of it."

Pete and I both leaned forward until Pittman's body was out of the window from the waist up. His toes scratched frantically for the floor and he made small animal noises as he struggled.

Pete and I shoved him out a little further and held him there. After about a minute, Pete and I looked at each other and Pete shrugged his shoulders.

We hauled Pittman back into the room and let go of him. He sank to the floor and crawled to a corner. He crouched there, holding his knees tight to his face, his eyes wide but not seeing anything.

I picked up the two green folders from the table and Pete and I left.

Nelson was outside the door leaning against the wall. "A little noisy in there," he said.

"Don't know what you mean," Pete said. "Take good care of him. I think he needs a glass of water."

Pete and I took the elevator down and put the folders on Herrick's desk.

"Nothing doing," I said.

Pete and I walked down to the basement coffee shop. "You meet some queer ones," Pete said.

"I know what you mean," I said. "They always leave a bad taste in your mouth."

Solitary

July 1955

Jake shook my shoulder. "You want to spend these last couple of minutes saying goodbye? I'm the sentimental type."

I sat up and let my feet dangle over the edge of the bunk. "All right," I said. "Goodbye."

Jake's eyes studied me for a few seconds, his mouth edging toward a thin smile. "You strained yourself."

He peeled back the paper of his chocolate bar for another bite. "What does it take to make you happy?"

I rested my elbows on my thighs and stared at my shoes.

"Jeez," he said, after a while. "I hope I get a live one in here next."

"Sure," I said. "Put in for somebody who keeps his yap moving."

"It don't have to be much, but at least something. All you ever done since we been together is stare at the ceiling."

"That's what I done," I said. "And I'm broken-up it made you so sad."

Jake waited for a piece of chocolate to dissolve in his mouth. "According to some of the boys, you made a lot of noise when you first come here."

"Just like you still do. But I bit too."

"Them three months in solitary done something, though, didn't they?" He licked sweetness from his fingers. "I thought they ain't allowed to keep you in that long."

"It slipped somebody's mind."

The first bell sounded and I got off the top bunk.

Jake put on his cap. "Here's my hand," he said. "If you got the urge, you can shake it."

I shook hands with him and then we waited at the cell door for the second bell.

When it rang and the locks sprung, we stepped out on the steel walk. I marched to the main floor with the rest of the men and there one of the guards told me to fall out.

It was O'Leary who took me through the gates and out to the administration building.

"I like quiet guys like you," he said. "No fuss. No bother. You can come back any time."

"Thanks."

We went up the concrete steps. "Heard you were pretty tough once. But that was before my time." He glanced at me with guard laugh in his yellow-brown eyes. "We bend them or we break them. Nobody walks without a stoop for long."

I sat on a hard bench in the warden's anteroom with O'Leary beside me. There were no bars on these windows and the one o'clock sun made free patches of light on the floor. I stretched my legs into some of its warmness and let it seep through my trouser legs.

We lay on the bank beside the pool and watched the high clouds for awhile and then we looked at each other. Her legs were slim brown and she rested her cheek on her arm as she faced me.
Her hair was golden with sun and had the softness of smoke. It responded to the faint flow of wind and I looked into the gray eyes that were waiting for me.

O'Leary poked me with his club., "Wake up, Collier."
"My eyes are open."
"But you weren't seeing anything." He crossed his legs and shifted on the bench so that he could look at me. "Let me guess the first thing you're gonna do when you get out. Will you have to pay for it or have you got it waiting?"

When the warden was ready for me, I went in alone and sat down in front of his desk.

He picked up my file and scanned it briefly. Then he tamped the papers to a straight edge and began to talk with words that had lost their accent sharpness because they had been memorized.

I had paid my debt to society and I should not cherish bitterness. I could become a useful member of society if I worked hard. I must avoid bad company. I must not drink.

My eyes went to the calendar on the wall behind him. It was cheap and glossy, but it did show a green valley. A valley green and hidden in security.

Her hand was soft in mine as we walked and I could smell the crispness of the ferns beside the stream. We stopped beneath a large oak to look at all the quietness that belonged to us and my arm went around her waist.

The phone on the warden's desk was ringing and he picked it up. He listened with his head cocked and then spoke. "I'll take care of it in a couple of minutes. Just as soon as I finish here."

He put down the phone and his mind lingered on other thoughts. Then he returned his attention to me. "Did I cover the point about getting permission before you leave the county of your residence?"

"Yes, sir," I said.

His eyes dulled for a look into his memory. "No, I didn't," he said. He inspected me coldly and then resumed talking.

When he finished, his thumb carelessly riffled the records. "Well, that's that. Just be a good boy and we won't see you again." He consulted his watch.

"You could have got off more time," he said. "But those first wild years didn't help you any." He smiled slightly. "Ninety days in the hole made you a different man, didn't they, Collier?"

"Yes, sir," I said.

"It's the best way to handle the trouble makers. A few months alone with nothing but the dark. They can't stand that."

He enjoyed his reminiscent smile. "I'm hard, but I'm fair," he said. "Anybody who cooperates with me won't have a hard time. You learned that, didn't you, Collier?"

"Yes, sir," I said.

He laced his fingers in front of him. "Any questions?"

"No, sir," I said. And then I got up and went out to where O'Leary waited.

It was two more hours before they opened the last gate for me. I stood outside on the walk in my new black shoes and looked down the line of cars in the parking lot.

Amy sat in a small sedan that needed repainting and she blew the horn when she saw me. She got out of the car and hurried toward me and she was out of breath when she put her plump arms around my neck.

My eyes examined her face and went to her brown eyes. "You wear glasses," I said.

"Why, Eddie," she said. "I been wearing them for three years now. You seen me in them lots of times on visiting days."

"That's right," I said. "Lots of times." I began walking toward the car and she caught up with me after a few steps.

"They're tinted a little bit because my eyes are sensitive to light. That's what the eye doctor told me. I got some astigmatism too."

I got into the car and she went around to the driver's side. I glanced at the shabby upholstery. "What have you been doing to keep alive?" I asked.

"Honestly, Eddie," she said. "You're so forgetful. I been waiting on tables for six years now at Grady's. You ask me every time you see me."

"That's right," I said. "And you tell me I'm forgetful."

She turned the car onto the highway and leaned forward in driver concentration.

I opened the window on my side and listened to the hum of the tires on the road.

"Did they give you a job, Eddie?" she asked.

"Yes," I said.

She waited a while. "Well, what kind of a job is it?"

I thought about it and remembered. "In a warehouse. I'm supposed to put things in piles."

Amy drove at a conservative speed and several cars passed her. "I got a small cottage for us," she said. "Just three rooms. Nothing like we used to have. I made all the drapes myself. Chartreuse. I wasn't sure they'd go with the walls at first, but I took a chance and it turned out all right."

"Yes," I said.

"I bought a couple bottles of good whiskey," she said. "And some beer in cans. We'll just take off our shoes and wiggle our toes until the boys show up."

"All right," I said.

"I kept all your classical-type records," she said. "I don't have an automatic phonograph, though. You got to change the records yourself."

I closed my eyes against the light and listened to the whistle of air against the body of the car.

I knew she was there and I smiled as I listened for her and at last opened my eyes. She leaned over me and there was the fragrance of perfume in her hair. She spoke softly to me and her hand touched my face. Her lips came closer and rested lightly on mine.

The car came to a stop and I opened my eyes. I wondered at the darkness.

"Did you have a nice nap, Eddie?" Amy asked. She turned off the motor and put the ignition keys in her pocketbook. "There it is," she said, pointing. "That little place in the back."

I got out of the car and walked to the front door. I waited until Amy came with the key.

Inside she kicked off her shoes and began turning on lamps. I sat down in an easy chair and listened to the flat sounds her feet made when she walked on the part of the floor that was bare.

She came back from the kitchen with a tray of canned beer, a bottle of whiskey, and glasses.

"I don't mind if my man drinks," she said. "Remember how you used to just sit with a bottle and listen to those records. You could really put away the stuff without showing it. You always drank like a gentleman."

I poured some of the whiskey into a glass.

Amy punched open a can of beer and swallowed a few times. "I was true to you, Eddie," she said. "You can ask any of the girls where I work and they'll tell you the same thing. I even turned down dates with Mr. Grady. And he respected me for that. He said that if all women were as loyal to their men as I was this would be a better world."

I tasted the first liquor in ten years and it was nothing to me.

"Beer is healthier," Amy said. "But I miss the champagne. We'll fix that, though, won't we, Eddie?"

My eyes went to the stack of record albums on the table next to me and I picked up the Franck symphony.

The doorbell rang and Amy struggled to her feet. "Probably the boys," she said.

Benny Eckers and Mike Kurtz came into the room with their right hands searching for mine.

I remembered them again now, and that Benny was small with a flesh-starved face of lines and seams.

"Benny's a truck dispatcher for a gasoline company," Amy said. "Can you imagine?"

"It's a nervous job," Benny said. "All kinds of time limits and responsibilities. It's been ten months now and my parole officer is running out of gold stars."

Kurtz filled a water glass with whiskey and buried it in his big hand. "Life has been rough," he said. "A man my size sweats when he has to move around."

"We been looking places over," Benny said. "Mostly loan companies. Our idea is to hit about five or six in a week and then take off for someplace where we can spend it. We'll make up for all those years, Eddie."

I watched the smoke of the cigarette I was trying.

"I'd like to see Florida again," Amy said. "All that excitement and all them people. We wouldn't have to be alone for a minute."

"Florida is out," Kurtz said. "Every second guy at the tracks is a dick."

"Kurtz is right," Benny said. "We spend our dough in Cuba or Mexico or some of them places where they don't care how you got it."

I stared at the amber glow in my glass of whiskey.

Her voice was quiet music and it spoke only of things in which there was beauty. I listened to her words and marveled at the gentleness in them.

Kurtz bumped his glass against the neck of the bottle as he refilled it.

"I like them big parties," he said. "All that fancy grub and them babes from the shows."

I took a record to the phonograph and put it on. "You like that, Kurtz?" I asked.

"That's what I said." Kurtz drank and wiped his mouth with his sleeve. "Big parties. That's really living."

"What was it like in solitary, Eddie?" Benny asked. "I was a meek con and never got a taste of it."

"What's to tell," Kurtz said. "I was in a week myself for heaving a plate of stew across the dining hall. The last couple of days I would of give my right arm to hear somebody talk."

Benny's eyes went to the electric clock. "I'm getting on my horse," he said. "I gotta keep regular hours, being a working man and all. At least for another week or so."

"I got to shove off too," Kurtz said. "Think of it, Eddie. I'm a house painter."

When they were gone, Amy went to the bedroom. "I'll make myself more comfortable," she said.

She came back wearing a faded blue robe and sat down heavily in her chair. Her face was red and moist with the beer she had been drinking.

She scratched the calf of one leg. "Did you do much reading, Eddie?" she asked. "I remember you were all the time reading before you went to the pen."

"No," I said. "I don't have to read any more."

"That's good," she said. "Gee, sometimes you were a creep. Maybe now you'll learn how to enjoy life more."

I put another record on the phonograph.

Amy opened a fresh can of beer. "I guess one more won't hurt. But I don't want to overdo it tonight, if you know what I mean. You been gone a long time and I know what you want."

"Do you, Amy?"

"I know what boys want," she said. She laughed and her body shook with it. "No hurry though," she said. "We got plenty of time. I'm off tomorrow,"

When the record was finished, I put on the first movement of Smetana's Moldau.

"You're not going to listen to those damn records all night, are you?" Amy asked.

There would have to be music in our valley. Not the music that intrudes and must be listened to with attention, but the music that is always background.

Amy was standing up, her face splotched with anger. "I been talking to you for fifteen minutes and you just sit staring into space."

I looked at the record that had been played and was now revolving soundlessly.

Her eyes followed the direction of mine and then she moved. She grabbed the record off the machine and snapped it with her pudgy fingers.

She snatched one of the albums from the table and put it on the floor. The records cracked under her slippered heel.

She looked up as I rose and came to her. Her eyes showed fright before my hands went to her throat.

It wasn't at all difficult. My hands pressed mechanically until there was no more struggle in her.

I let her drop and looked down. Her face was ugly purple and her eyes were flecked with blood.

I dragged her into the kitchen where she would be out of my sight, then I washed my hands carefully and returned to the living room.

There was now the question of running away and I considered it with a tired vagueness.

Then I heard the new music that shimmered faintly. It was beckoning and I had to get closer.

I put the album back on the table.

It made no difference now about what Amy had tried to do.

I turned out the lights and made my way to an easy chair.

I was going back now to the world I'd found in the darkness of solitary, and I was going back to the girl I had found there in the valley. It wasn't a real world. It stayed quietly waiting in my mind and that was why I liked it.

They would find me sitting here staring the same way they had found me then. They would see that my body breathed, but my eyes would show that I was not one of them.

And this time they would not be able to bring me back. I knew that, as my eyes followed the moonlight and fixed on the night sky.

I came back to my valley in the music and the moonlight and she waited for me. She was pale and lovely and her eyes searched my face.

And then she smiled.

I had come to stay.

Try It My Way

August 1955

At four o'clock they thought of shutting off the water. I took the half-filled saucepan out of the sink and poured it into one of the big cookpots lined up on the floor.

Keegan stopped fooling with the automatic long enough to pour me a glass of vanilla extract from the quart bottle.

I took a couple of swallows and wiped my mouth on my sleeve. Then I pulled the bill of the guard cap lower and walked to the other end of the kitchen.

They were both in their underwear. Brock sat cross-legged, staring at the backs of his big hands without interest, and Stevens hugged his legs tight to his chest, his eyes trying not to look up at me.

I grinned. "Here we got two types," I said. "Notice the nice gray hair, the clear healthy skin, and them baby blue eyes on Stevens."

Turk was at the big window keeping an eye on the exercise yard. He turned his head. "A real nice grandpop. I remember the twinkle in his eye when he used his stick on my kidneys."

"Watch this, Turk," I said. I reached down and put my hand on Stevens' shoulder. He shrank away and began trembling.

Turk laughed. "That's good to see. I'm glad I lived so long."

"Stevens is remembering all the little things he used to do to make life interesting for us," I said. "And now he's scared silly that we got better imaginations."

I shifted my smile to Brock. "Now this here boy's got no imagination at all. He's got free hand but he can't think of the clever things like Stevens can."

Brock met my eyes. "I'm thinking of some now, Gomez."

I grinned at him a long time and then I went to the window.

The guards were in a straggling arc around the three sides of the messhall wing. Some of them were standing, but most were taking it easy, hunkered on their heels and waiting for the warden to think of something.

I went back to my chair. "Keegan," I said. "I'll tell you about Davis. You're too young in here to remember him."

I lit a cigarette and exhaled smoke. "Davis was afraid of cats. Crazy afraid about them and everybody knew it. And one day he made the mistake of using unrespectful words to Stevens and he got tossed into the hole."

I put my feet on the table. "Davis had one peaceful day and then he began screaming. Real interesting screaming and it was all about how there was a cat in the hole with him."

Keegan took the clip out of the automatic and examined it.

"After a couple of hours, Davis suddenly didn't make any more noise. When somebody bothered to wonder about that and take a look, he found Davis had beat his brains out against the wall."

I looked at Stevens. "In one of the corners was a black-as-spades cat licking his paws. Now I wonder how he could of got in there."

Turk turned away from the window. "The warden's waving a hanky and he's coming around to the main door."

Keegan got up and went into the dining hall and I could hear his footsteps as he made his way through the emptiness of it. He began moving some of the tables and benches away from the double doors.

There would be guards in the corridor, but they wouldn't try to force their way in as long as we had Brock and Stevens with us.

In five minutes, Keegan returned with Warden Cramer.

Cramer's eyes went to Brock and Stevens.

"They're doing just fine, warden," I said. "But they might be a little chilly."

His eyes moved to the uniform I was wearing and his mouth tightened. "This isn't going to get you anywhere, Gomez," he said.

"Tell us what we got to lose, warden," I said. "I'm the short-timer here, and I got ninety years to wait."

He shifted his attention to Keegan. "For one thing, you got your lives to lose if anything happens to Brock or Stevens."

Keegan sipped his glass of extract and smiled at him.

"All right," Cramer snapped. "Let's have what you expect from me."

"A nice fast car and an open gate," Keegan said.

The warden's eyes were hard. "It wouldn't do you much good. You couldn't get far."

"We'll have Brock and Stevens along to show us the way," Keegan said. "Something clever should come to us when it gets dark."

Cramer walked over to Stevens and Brock. "They haven't tried anything rough on you, have they?"

"Just words," Brock said.

Cramer came back to us. "You have one hour to give this up."

I smiled. "And if we don't, warden? Are you going to try what you haven't got nerve enough to do now?"

Cramer's face colored angrily.

"Remember," I said. "Keep it quiet and orderly out there. If you come for us, start thinking of words to use for Stevens' widow."

Keegan took the warden back out and while he was gone I searched through the kitchen drawers until I found a whetstone. I began sharpening the nine-inch meat knife I carried.

When Keegan came back, he refilled our glasses.

Brock uncrossed his legs and rubbed circulation back into them. "Before that stuff goes to your head, Keegan, do some thinking. If Cramer lets you three get away with this, there won't be a guard safe in the country. He's not going to let that happen."

"Start hoping you're wrong," Turk said. "Work on it real hard."

I got to my feet and went over to Stevens. "Maybe I should cut off a few ears and toss them out into the yard for Cramer to admire. It might impress him that we mean business."

I got down on one knee in front of him. "Whose ears should it be, Stevens? Yours or Brock's?"

Stevens licked his lips and tried to look away, but his eyes came back to the knife in my hand.

I grabbed a handful of his hair and jerked his head back. I put the tip of my knife under his jaw. "You got two seconds to make up your mind."

His voice was the strangled whisper of terror. "Brock. Make it Brock."

I let go of him and stood up. "See, Brock," I said. "He wants his ears real bad. He don't love you at all when it comes to that."

Keegan was watching me. "Did you get your thrill, Gomez?"

"Sure," I said. "I got a mean streak in me and it has to be fed."

Keegan lighted one of the cigars we'd found in Brock's uniform and took Turk's place at the window.

I went back to the table and sat down. "With Davis it was cats," I said. "With some people it's the dark or maybe high places."

I watched Turk pouring himself a drink. "I'm thinking of the time the drier in the laundry flared up," I said. "Just a short in the wiring and nothing to get excited about. Remember the size of Stevens' eyes when he thought he might get burned?"

I picked up a pack of bookmatches and lit one. I let it burn low and Turk watched it. When I blew it out, Turk took the pack and went over to Stevens.

Turk stood there grinning and then he tore one of the matches out of the pack and lit it.

Stevens' eyes got wide and he backed away as he watched it burn.

"Let him alone, Turk," Keegan said from the window.

"All I want is a little fun," Turk said. "I got it coming."

Keegan came away from the window. "I just told you something, Turk."

Turk met his eyes for a few moments and then he shrugged and walked away.

"Gomez, the idea man, and Turk, the pupil," Brock said. "You *got* nice company, Keegan."

"Stevens is with you," Keegan said. "Want to brag about him?"

Five o'clock passed and nothing happened. I relieved Keegan at the window and waved to the photographers who were behind the line of guards taking pictures.

The warden finished talking to a knot of reporters and then he started through the guards.

"Cramer's coming back," I said. "And he hasn't got a car under his arm."

Keegan left to let him in. When he came back with the warden, they took seats at the table.

"Well?" Keegan asked.

"You might as well quit this before somebody gets hurt," Cramer said. "You're not getting out of here and that's that."

"We're stubborn and we think different," Keegan said. He glanced at the wrist watch he'd taken from Brock. "We're not going to drag this out until there's snow in hell. It's ten after five right now. We'll give you until seven."

"It's out of my hands," Cramer said. "I talked to the governor and he says positively nothing doing."

"You got almost two hours to change his mind," I said.

"You know what will happen if you let anything happen to Brock or Stevens. You'll all be held equally responsible." Cramer's eyes went around the three of us and settled on Keegan. "You got sense enough to know that this won't work."

Keegan smiled thinly. "I'm the outdoor type, and I been in here six years. Don't count on me being able to think clear."

The warden got up. "Seven o'clock is going to come and go. It's not any special time on my clock."

He looked at the pots of water. "We can wait a long time out there. Longer than that will last."

When he was gone, Keegan sat at the table slowly smoking his cigar. It was quiet except for the sounds the guards made as they talked to each other in the yard.

At six Turk took my place at the window. I refilled my glass and lit a cigarette. "Cramer's got the notion that we don't have the guts to do like we say. I vote to build a fire under Stevens. He should get loud enough for even the governor to hear."

I let a whole book of matches flare up and tossed it at Stevens.

He shrieked as he skittered away from it. His face got pasty white and twitched with fright as he crouched in the corner watching me.

Keegan got up. "I thought I said words about doing things like that."

I glanced up. "Not to me."

"You're getting told now."

I looked at the bigness of his shoulders and the way his hands hung, ready to use.

I picked up the knife and smiled. "We'll leave it at your way for now. When it gets past seven we can argue about it."

At six-thirty the dusk began pushing into the room. Keegan went to the light switch and tried it. Nothing happened.

It was quarter to seven when the floodlights in the yard were turned on. Inside the kitchen pillars of light leaned against the windows.

Seven o'clock came and passed.

At ten after, I finished the last of the vanilla extract and threw the glass at the sink. "Now let's do it my way," I said. "Let them listen to Stevens die and they'll find us a car real fast."

Cellophane crackled as Keegan unwrapped another cigar. "Stop smacking your lips over Stevens and start thinking."

I sat on the edge of the table and began flipping the knife at the piece of light that lay over one corner of it and waited.

"Let's look at this thing with brains," Keegan said. "The party's over. We've had it."

I kept playing with the knife and neither Turk nor I said anything.

Keegan went on. "Like Brock said, if we get away with it here, the same thing will be tried in every pen in the country. That's why Cramer's not going to let it happen."

"He'll have to," I said. "If we do it my way. We give them one body. That makes them know we got nothing more to lose. We can burn only once and it'll be no cost to us to give them another corpse if they don't do like we say."

Keegan reached for his glass and then saw that it was empty. He pushed it away. "Use that beautiful imagination of yours now, Gomez. Suppose even that doesn't work. Start thinking about the hot seat."

Brock spoke from the darkness. "I watched a dozen of them take the walk. Ask me how scared they were."

I looked toward Brock and Stevens. They were in the shadows, but I knew they were watching and hoping.

Turk broke the silence. "It's not going to be a happy time for us when Brock and Stevens put on their uniforms again."

"I'm not looking forward to it either," Keegan said. "But it's better than frying."

There was another long quiet and then Turk sighed. "That part about being alive persuades me."

Keegan's face came into the light as he leaned forward. "Make it unanimous, Gomez."

Brock spoke again. "It's something to see when they turn on the juice. They jump against the straps like the devil was burning inside of them. They're supposed to be dead in a second, but it don't look like that to me, Gomez. Not when they fight it like that."

I stuck the knife into the table. "I'm finished," I said. "Just like you are."

Keegan relaxed back into his chair. "First I finish this cigar. It'll be a long time before I taste another one."

And then I saw it.

I whirled toward the window and it was there on the sill, a small silhouette against the light.

I whipped off my cap and smashed at it again and again until it was a broken stain on the stone.

"Jesus!" Turk said sharply. "You scared the hell out of me, jumping up like that. It wasn't nothing but a little cockroach."

Another floodlight flashed on outside and a slant of light cut across the room and fell on Stevens.

Iciness gripped at my insides. Stevens knew about them now and I knew what he was thinking about. He knew what I was afraid of. When we were back in our cells he'd know what to do to me.

I jerked the knife out of the table and went after him.

Keegan shouted and moved forward, but he was too late to stop me.

Keegan pulled at me, but I didn't let go of Stevens until I was through.

Keegan looked down at the body and then his eyes met mine.

"All right, Gomez," he said quietly. "Now we got no choice. We try it your way."

The Deveraux Monster

February 1962

"Have *you* ever seen the monster?" my fiancée, Diana Munson, asked.

"No," I said. But I had. A number of times. I smiled. "However, everyone seems to agree that the Deveraux monster rather resembles the Abominable Snowman, but with a coloring more suitable to a temperate climate. Dark brown or black, I believe."

"I wouldn't take this at all lightly, Gerald," Diana said. "After all, my father *did* see your family beast last night."

"Actually it was dusk," Colonel Munson said. "I'd just completed a stroll and was about to turn into the gate when I looked back. The fog was about, nevertheless I clearly saw the creature at a distance of approximately sixty feet. It glared at me and I immediately rushed toward the house for my shotgun."

Freddie Hawkins summoned the energy to look attentive. "You took a shot at it?"

Colonel Munson flushed. "No. I slipped and fell. Knocked myself unconscious." He glared at us. "I did not faint. I definitely did not faint."

"Of course not, sir," I said.

Colonel Munson, recently retired, and his daughter Diana came to our district some eight months ago and purchased a house at the edge of the village.

Fresh from Sandhurst and bursting for a good show, he joined his regiment on November 12, 1918, and that initiated a remarkably consistent career. In the Second World War he sat in England during Monty's North African campaign. When he finally wrangled a transfer to that continent, he arrived three days after Rommel's command disintegrated. He fretted under the African sun during the invasion of Europe and when at last he breathlessly reached France, the fighting had moved to Belgium. He still fumed at a training depot near Cannes when our forces joined the Russians in Germany. In the 1950s he set foot in Korea just as the cease-fire was announced and during the Suez incident he was firmly stationed at Gibraltar. It is rumored that his last regiment's junior officers—in secret assembly—formally nominated him for the Nobel Peace Prize.

Freddie sighed. "All I have at my place is a ghostly cavalier who scoots about shouting for his sword and cursing Cromwell. Rather common, don't you think? Haven't seen him myself yet, but I'm still hoping."

Diana frowned in thought. "Who else, besides Father, has seen the Deveraux monster recently?"

"Norm Wakins did a few nights ago," Freddie said.

I smiled. "Ah."

Freddie nodded. "I know. Norm hasn't gone to bed sober since he discovered alcohol. However, he has always managed to walk home under his own power. As a matter of fact on Friday evening he was quite capable of running. Norm left the village at his usual time—when his favorite pub closed—and his journey was routine until just north of the Worly Cairn when 'something made me look up.' And there he saw it—crouching and glaring down at him from one of those huge boulders strewn about. His description of the animal is a bit vague—he did not linger in the area long—but from what I was able to piece together, it was somewhat apelike, with dangling arms, a hideous face, and glowing yellow eyes. He claims that it was fanged and that it howled as it pursued him to his very cottage door."

"I shall have to carry a revolver loaded with silver bullets," I murmured.

"Only effective against werewolves." Freddie stretched lazily. "During the last ninety years the monster has been seen dozens of times."

Diana turned to me. "Gerald, just how did your family *acquire* this monster?"

"There are dark rumors. But I assure you, there is *no* Deveraux monster."

Freddie scratched an ear. "Gerald's grandfather had a brother. Leslie. Well, Leslie was always a bit wild and just before he disappeared . . ."

"He went to India," I said. "And eventually died there."

". . . just before he *disappeared,* Leslie seemed to grow a bit *hairy.*"

I remembered a few paragraphs of the letter my grandfather had left to his son—a letter which had been passed on to me by my father.

> I first became aware of what was happening when I accidentally came across Leslie at the Red Boar. It is not my usual pub—when I do go to pubs—but I was in the vicinity after seeing my tailor and thirsty for a pint.
>
> When I entered, I recognized my brother's back at the bar. I also noticed that the other patrons seemed to shy away from him and that the barmaid, in fact, appeared rather pale.
>
> When Leslie turned at my approach, I stopped in shock. His eyebrows had grown thick and shaggy, his hairline was almost down to his eyes, and his complexion had turned a dark brown. He leered when he saw me, revealing stained yellow teeth.
>
> I had seen him less than two hours before, but now I scarcely knew him!

"According to legend," Freddie continued, "Gerald's great-uncle never did go to Africa, or India, or some beastly place like that. His brother was finally forced to keep him confined. In the east room on the third floor, wasn't it, Gerald?"

"Someplace about the house," I said. "Though if you have a monster, I should think that a more logical place to keep him might be in one of the cellars."

"Too damp," Freddie said. "And you must remember that your grandfather was rather fond of his brother—monster or not."

Diana's eyes widened. "You don't mean that—?"

"Oh, yes," Freddie said. "Leslie is supposed to have turned into the Deveraux monster."

"How ghastly," Diana said dutifully. "But *why?*"

Freddie shrugged. "Heredity, possibly. The monster eventually escaped. Bit through his chains, I believe. The Deverauxs always had good teeth." He looked at me. "Either that or he was let out periodically for a constitutional?"

"My grandfather would never release a monster," I said firmly. "Matter of honor."

Freddie calculated. "If this monster is human, I mean solidly animal, then it would be about ninety years old—considering Leslie's age at the time of his metamorphosis. Rather decrepit by now, I should think. Did you happen to notice its condition, Colonel?"

Colonel Munson glowered at the floor. "Seemed spry enough to me."

"I know that people have *seen* the monster," Diana said. "But is it dangerous?"

Freddie smiled faintly. "Eighty-five years ago a Sam Garvis was found dead on the moors. He was frightfully mangled."

"Packs of wild dogs roamed this area in those days," I said. "Garvis was unfortunate enough to meet one of them."

"Possible. But fifteen years later your grandfather was found dead at the base of a cliff."

"He fell," I said. "Broke his neck."

"Probably he fell because he was being pursued by the monster," Freddie said. "It had been seen just before he died. And then there was your father. Died of fright practically at his front door."

"I did not *faint,*" Colonel Munson muttered.

"Father did not die of fright," I said. "Weak heart plus too much exercise." I glanced at my watch and rose. "I'll have to be running along, Diana."

Freddie got up too. "Mother's expecting me. Besides, Gerald needs an escort across the moors. Someone fearless."

The colonel saw us to the door. He was a short, broad-shouldered man with a military mustache in grey prime. "I'm going to hunt the beast."

"Best of luck," I said.

"I'll need it," he said morosely. "Hunted tigers in Malaya, leopard in Kenya, grizzly in Canada. Never got a blasted one."

Freddie and I said our goodbyes, adjusted our collars against the late afternoon's chilly mist, and began walking.

"I rather envy you," Freddie said.

"I'm perfectly willing to give you the monster."

"I mean Diana."

"Quite different."

Freddie brooded. "Of course I can't court her now. You do have some kind of a definite arrangement, don't you?"

"We're getting married in June."

He sighed. "My only hope is that the monster might slaughter you before then."

"No assists, please."

"Wouldn't think of it. After all, we've known each other since time began, so to speak. Served in the same regiment. I saved your life."

"Barely."

"I'm fumble-fingers with bandages and the like. Besides, I couldn't remember where the pressure points were supposed to be."

We walked silently for a while and then he said, "You don't really believe there is a monster, do you?"

"Of course not."

We parted at the branch in the path and I went on toward Stonecroft.

I made my way among the lichen-covered boulders and paused for a moment at the remains of the huts. They were low roofless circles of stones now, but once they had been the dwellings of a forgotten, unwritten race. Perhaps they were men erect, but I have always had a feeling that they might have been shaggy and that they crawled and scuttled by preference.

I wondered again what had happened to them. Were they all really dead and dust or did their blood linger in our veins?

The moor wind died and I glanced up at a faint rustle. A dark figure moved slowly toward me in the swirling wisps of fog.

When it was within twenty feet of me, I recognized Verdie Tibbs.

Verdie is simple. Actually quite simple and he likes to roam the moors.

I thought he seemed a little disappointed when he saw me, but he smiled as I said, "Hello, Verdie."

"I thought it was my friend," Verdie said.

"Your friend?"

Verdie frowned. "But he always runs away."

"Who does?"

Verdie smiled again. "He has fur."

"Who has fur?"

"My friend. But he always runs away." Verdie shook his head and wandered back into the dusk.

I reached Stonecroft ten minutes later. No one seems to know just how old my home is. It had begun existence as a modest stone building in a distant time, but generations of Deverauxs had added to it—the last substantial addition being in 1720. My contribution has been the installation of plumbing, electricity, and the telephone. At the present time I occupy only the central portion of the three-story structure and very little of that.

When I reached the studded front door, I heard the great key in the lock and the bolt being drawn. The massive door opened.

"Well, Jarman," I said. "Taken to locking the doors?"

He smiled faintly. "It's my wife who insists, sir. She feels that it would be wiser at the present time."

"I've never heard that the monster enters buildings."

"There's always a first time, sir."

Jarman, his wife, and their twenty-year-old son Albert are my only servants at present. I could perhaps do without Albert, but it is family history that the Deverauxs and the Jarmans stepped over the threshold of Stonecroft at approximately the same moment. Turning out a Jarman would be equivalent to removing one of the cornerstones or snatching away the foundation of Stonecroft.

At late breakfast the next morning, I noticed that Jarman seemed worried and preoccupied. When he brought the coffee, I said, "Is there something troubling you, Jarman?"

He nodded. "It's Albert, sir. Yesterday evening he went to the village. He wasn't back by ten-thirty, but my wife and I thought nothing of it and retired. This morning we found that he hadn't slept in his bed."

"Probably spent the night with one of his friends."

"Yes, sir. But he should at least have phoned."

Freddie Hawkins wandered in from the garden and took a seat at the table. "Thought I'd drop over and see if you're tired." He helped himself to bacon. "Sleep well last night?"

"Like a top."

"No sleepwalking?"

"Never in my life."

"You look a bit hairy, Gerald."

"I need a haircut and I haven't shaved yet. Bachelor's privilege."

"Do you mind if I examine the bottoms of your shoes?"

"Too personal. Besides, if I roamed the moors last night as the monster, I wouldn't have worn shoes."

"There is the possibility that you are a monster only from the ankles up, Gerald." He took some scrambled eggs. "I suppose you'll be dropping in at the Munsons?"

"Of course."

"Mind if I toddle along?"

"You're frightfully infatuated, aren't you?"

"Fatally. We male Hawkinses are invariably lanky, tired, and muddleheaded, but we are always attracted to the brisk practical woman. The moment I saw Diana and learned that she had once taken a course in accounting, I experienced an immense electrical reaction. You couldn't step out of the picture, could you, Gerald? For an old comrade-in-arms?"

"Not the thing to do."

"Of course," he said glumly. "Not gentlemanly. It's the woman's prerogative to break up things like this." He seemed to have something else on his mind and after a while he spoke again. "Gerald, last night Diana saw the monster."

I frowned. "How do *you* know?"

"She phoned my mother," Freddie said. "They get along rather well." He put down his coffee cup. "Just after she retired, Diana thought she heard a noise outside. She went to the window and there in the moonlit garden she saw the monster. By the time she roused the colonel and he found his shotgun, the creature had scampered away."

I lit a cigar and took several thoughtful puffs.

Freddie watched me. "I don't know what to make of it either."

After I shaved we walked to the Munson house.

Diana met us at the door. "Gerald, I'd like to talk to you alone for a few moments, please."

Freddie waved a languid goodbye. "I'll go on to the village. The Red Boar, if anyone needs me desperately."

When we were alone, Diana turned to me. "Really, Gerald, I cannot accept a monster."

"But Freddie is really very...."

"I mean the Deveraux monster."

"Diana, if the animal exists, I believe that it is actually benign."

"Benign, my foot! That thing is dangerous."

"Even if it is, Diana, it seems that only the male Deverauxs have anything to fear."

"Gerald, I am looking at this from the practical point of view. I simply cannot have you murdered after our marriage, especially if we have children. Do you realize that the death duties these days would force me to sell Stonecroft? I might even have to go to London to find some employment. And I do not believe in working mothers."

"But, Diana...."

"I'm sorry, Gerald, but I've been thinking this whole thing over. Especially since last night. I'm afraid I'll have to call off our engagement."

"Diana," I said—and winced. "Is there... is there someone else?"

She thought for a moment. "I'll be frank with you, Gerald. I've been examining Freddie. He does seem to need management. I've met his mother and we seem to have a lot in common."

"Freddie has his ghost too," I pointed out. "That cavalier who runs about looking for his horse."

"His sword. But he is entirely harmless. He's tramped about the grounds since 1643 and has never yet harmed anyone."

"Suppose he finds his sword?"

"We will cross that bridge when we come to it."

I went to the window. "That cursed monster."

"It's your own fault," Diana said. "You Deverauxs should have watched your genetics and things like that."

I left her for the village and stopped at the Red Boar. Freddie was rather pale. "I just heard," he said. "Jarman's son, Albert, was found dead on the moor a half an hour ago. Head bashed in. Quite a messy business."

"Good Lord! Who did it?"

"No one knows yet, Gerald. But I'm afraid that people are talking about the Deveraux monster." He smiled faintly. "Gerald, I'm afraid that I've given you a rather hard time about that. I just want to say that I really believe that you only need a haircut and that's all."

I returned immediately to Stonecroft, but the Jarmans had evidently gone on to the village.

I went upstairs to the east room and unlocked the chest. I removed the envelope and re-read my grandfather's letter.

. . . I believe the expression on my face gave Leslie considerable pleasure. I pulled myself together and was about to ask for some explanation, but Leslie took my arm and led me outside. "Later," he said.

We mounted our horses and rode out of the village. After half a mile, Leslie pulled up and dismounted. He removed his hat and then I watched a transformation. He pulled at his forehead and the coarse hair forming his low hairline came away in his fingers. His bushy eyebrows disappeared in the same manner. "And, my dear brother," he said, "my complexion can be washed away and a good tooth-brushing will remove the stain from my teeth."

"Leslie," I demanded sternly. "What is the meaning of this?"

He grinned. "I'm creating a monster. The Deveraux monster."

He put his hand on my shoulder. "Bradley, we Deverauxs have been here since the dawn of history. We were here before the Norman invasion. Deveraux is not French, it is simply a corruption of some prehistoric grunts applied to one of our ancestors. And yet, Bradley, do you realize that we are not *haunted* by anything or anyone?"

He waved an arm at the horizon. "The Hawkins family has its blasted cavalier. The Trentons have their weeping maid waiting for

Johnny to come home from the fair, or some such thing. And even the Burleys, *nouveau riche*, have their bally butler drifting through the house looking for the fish forks. But what do we have? I'll tell you. *Nothing.*"

"But, Leslie," I said. "These are *authentic* apparitions."

"Authentic, my Aunt Marcy! They were all *invented* by someone with imagination to add to the midnight charm of the homeplace. People are not really repelled by ghosts. They *want* them. And so when they do not tell outright lies about seeing them, they eventually *convince* themselves that they have.

"Bradley," Leslie continued. "I am *creating* a Deveraux monster. And what better way than this? The villagers actually *see* me gradually turning into an apelike creature. And in a week or so, I, the human Leslie Deveraux, will disappear."

I blinked. "Disappear?"

"Bradley, I'm the younger son. I cannot possibly remain at Stonecroft the rest of my life waiting for your demise. You seem remarkably healthy. I suppose I could poison you, but I'm really fond of you. Therefore the only course left is for me to go abroad to seek fame, fortune, and all that rot. But before I go—as a parting present, so to speak—I am leaving you the Deveraux monster. I will be seen wandering the moors—in full costume—and pursuing a passerby here and there. I have had a complete suit constructed, Bradley. It is locked in a chest in the east room and I will don it for my midnight forays."

I immediately and vigorously launched into argument condemning his scheme as absolutely ridiculous and insane, and, at the time, I thought that I succeeded in convincing him to give up the entire thing. But I should have known Leslie and that half-smile when he finally nodded in agreement.

He wandered the moors in his Deveraux monster suit the next week—though I did not learn about it until later. It seems that people were reluctant to bring the creature's existence to my attention, since there was a general feeling that Leslie was undergoing a transformation.

And then Leslie disappeared.

It was not until a year later that Leslie wrote me from India, but in the meantime I had no answer to those of our friends who cautiously inquired about his disappearance. In a fit of pique one day, I declared that actually I kept Leslie chained in the east room. It was an unfortunate remark and my words were eagerly taken at face value by a number of people who should have known better.

I might have exposed the Deveraux myth when Leslie's letter finally came, if, in the meantime, this district had not enacted the mantrap laws.

I have never scattered mantraps about my grounds. I feel that their jaws are quite capable of severing a poacher's leg. But I have nourished the *impression* in the countryside and at the village that I was quite liberal in strewing them about my property. That was quite sufficient to keep most of the poachers off my land.

But then, as I mentioned, the mantraps were outlawed, and if I have a reputation for anything, it is obeying the law and the poachers know that. They immediately descended upon me with their snares and traps, causing untold depredations to the American quail and partridge I had introduced on the moor.

I tried everything to stop them, of course. I appealed to the authorities, I hired a gamekeeper, and I even personally threatened to thrash any poacher I apprehended on my property.

But nothing availed.

It was in a moment of total desperation that a wild idea descended upon me. I gathered up the house keys and went up to the east room. I opened the chest Leslie had left behind and the Deveraux monster costume was inside.

It fit me perfectly.

I believe I have never since enjoyed myself as much as I did in the next few weeks. At night I would don the costume and wander about. I tell you, my son, it was with the most delicious pleasure that I pursued—with blood-chilling howls—the elder Garvis to the very door of his cottage.

The elder Garvis did not poach again—to my knowledge—but it is unfortunate that his experience, or his relation of that experience, did not make an impression upon his son. He persisted in poaching and eventually toppled off a cliff and broke his neck.

It is widely believed that his demise occurred while the monster pursued him. That is not true. I never met Sam, Jr., on the moors. But I have done nothing to discourage the legend. As a matter of fact, the monster has been "seen" a number of times when I did not leave the house.

And so, my son, when I depart, I leave you the Deveraux monster. Perhaps you too will find some use for him.

                Your loving father,

                            Bradley Deveraux

My own father had added a note:

> Gerald, it is remarkable how persistent the Garvis family is. Each Garvis, apparently, must learn about the monster from first-hand experience before he refrains from poaching.

I pulled the costume from the chest and slipped into it. At the mirror I gazed at the monster once again.

Yes, he was indeed frightening, and the good colonel had fainted.

Norm Wakins had seen the Deveraux monster, and simple Verdie Tibbs, and Diana.

But Albert Jarman? No.

After I let Diana catch a glimpse of me, I had returned directly home. I had met no one on the way and I had gone directly to bed. And slept soundly. Except for the dream.

I removed the head of my costume and stared at my reflection. Did I need a shave again?

At dusk I saw the Jarmans returning to Stonecroft and let them in the front door.

Mrs. Jarman was a spare woman with dark eyes and she stared at me as though she was thinking something she didn't want to believe.

"Mrs. Jarman," I said. "I'd like to extend my most sincere—"

She walked by me and disappeared into the back hall.

Jarman frowned. "Mrs. Jarman is very upset, sir. We all are."

"Of course."

Jarman was about to pass me, but I stopped him. "Jarman, do the authorities have any idea who might have killed your son?"

"No, sir."

"Is there any . . . any talk?"

"Yes, sir," Jarman said. "There is talk about the Deveraux monster." He sighed. "Excuse me, sir. I should go to my wife."

Before turning in for the night, I opened the bedroom windows for air. The rolling hills of the moor were bright with the moon and in the distance a dog howled. I felt the drift of the cool wind.

A movement in the shadows below caught my eye. I watched the spot until I made out a crouching figure. It moved again and stepped into the light.

It was Verdie Tibbs. He glanced back at the house for a moment and then disappeared into the darkness.

That night I dreamed again. I dreamed that I left the house and roamed across the moors until I found the circle of stones. I remained there waiting. For anyone.

Albert Jarman's funeral took place on Thursday and I, of course, attended. It was a dark day and at the graveside the mist turned to light rain. Most of the countryside seemed to be in attendance and I was conscious that a great many of the eyes found me with, a covert glance.

Freddie Hawkins came to Stonecroft the next morning while Jarman and I were going over the household accounts.

He sat down. "Frank Garvis was found dead in his garden this morning. Strangled. He had several tufts of hair . . . or . . . fur clutched in his fingers. Definitely not human, according to the inspector."

Jarman looked up, but said nothing.

I rubbed my neck. "Freddie, just what do *you* make of all this?"

"I don't know. Perhaps some ape has escaped from a circus or something of the sort?"

"The papers would have carried a notice."

He shrugged. "Could there actually *be* a Deveraux monster?" He looked at Jarman. "What do you think?"

"I have no opinion, sir."

Freddie grinned. "Perhaps Gerald rises in the middle of the night, gripped by some mysterious force, and goes loping about the moors searching for a victim." He shook his head. "But I guess that's out too. I hardly think that he would grow fur just for the occasion. Or does he slip into a monkey suit of some kind?"

Freddie looked at me for a few moments and then changed the subject. "My mother told me about your break with Diana. Dreadful sorry, Gerald."

"I think she rather fancies you," I said.

He flushed. "Really?"

"No doubt. She's impressed by your intelligence and drive."

He smiled. "No need to get nasty."

After he left, I went upstairs to the east room and unlocked the chest. I pulled out the Deveraux monster. Tufts of hair had been torn from both of the arms.

That evening I was in my study with a half-empty bottle of whiskey when Jarman entered.

"Will that be all for today, sir?" he asked.

"Yes."

He glanced at the bottle and then turned to go.

"Jarman."

"Yes, sir."

"How is Mrs. Jarman?"

"She is . . . adjusting, sir."

I wanted to pour another glass, but not while Jarman was watching. "Do the authorities still have no suspects for your son's murder?"

"No, sir. No suspects."

"Do *you* have any . . . ideas?"

His eyes flickered. "No, sir."

I decided to pour the glass. "Does your *wife* have any ideas? Does she think that the Deveraux—?" I found myself unable to go on.

I drank the whiskey and my next words came suddenly and were undoubtedly inspired by the drink. "Jarman, I want you to lock me in my bedroom tonight."

"Sir?"

"Lock me in my bedroom," I snapped.

He studied me and there was worry in his eyes.

I took a deep breath and came to a decision. "Jarman, follow me. I have something to show you."

I led him to the east room, unlocked the chest, and put the envelope in his hands. "Read this."

I waited impatiently until he finished and looked up.

"You see," I said. "There is *no* actual Deveraux monster."

"No, sir."

"Jarman, I wouldn't tell you what I am now going to if it weren't for the present circumstances. I must have your word of honor that you will not repeat my words to a soul. To no one at all, do you understand?"

"You have my word, sir."

I paced the room. "First of all, you know that the poachers have been plaguing us again?"

He nodded.

"Well, Jarman, I have been wearing the Deveraux monster. I am the one responsible for chasing Norm Wakins to his door. I am the one who met poor simple Verdie. Accidentally, I assure you. He is not a poacher. He actually tried to make friends with me and I was forced to flee." I stopped pacing. "My only intention was to frighten away poachers."

Jarman smiled faintly. "Is Colonel Munson a poacher?"

I felt myself flushing. "That was a spur of the moment thing. A lark."

He raised an eyebrow ever so slightly. "A lark, sir?"

I decided that I might as well be embarrassingly candid. "Jarman, you are aware that the colonel and Diana Munson came here about eight months ago? And that within two months I found myself engaged?"

"Yes, sir. Rather sudden."

I agreed and cleared my throat. "I was committed and I am a gentleman. A man of my word, but still . . ."

The corners of Jarman's mouth turned slightly. "You found yourself not quite as happy as you thought you should be?"

I flushed again. "I happened to see Colonel Munson while I was in the monster suit and suddenly it occurred to me that if the colonel, and perhaps

Diana herself, should see the monster, they might not be so eager for me to . . . ." I wished that I were downstairs with the bottle.

"I understand, sir," Jarman said. "And I am sure that Miss Munson will be quite satisfied with Mr. Hawkins."

"Jarman," I said. "I have frightened a number of people, but I have injured no one. I am . . . positive . . . that I did not kill your son." I stared down at the Deveraux monster in the chest and at, the bare spots on the arms.

Jarman's voice was quiet. "Do you still want to be locked up for the night, sir?"

There was silence in the room and when I looked up, I saw that he was watching me.

Finally Jarman said, "I *know* you didn't kill Albert."

"You *know?*"

"Yes, sir. Two nights ago Verdie Tibbs came to the back door and spoke to me. He saw Albert killed. He saw the murder from a distance, too far away to give aid to Albert . . . and the crime was over in an instant."

Jarman looked tired. "Albert was returning from the village and apparently he came across a set of poacher's snares or nets. According to Verdie, Albert was bending over them and he seemed to be tearing them apart, when suddenly someone leaped behind him and struck him with a rock."

"Who was it?" I demanded.

Jarman closed his eyes for a moment. "Frank Garvis, sir."

"But why didn't Verdie go to the authorities?"

"Verdie was afraid, sir. He's heard talk that he might be sent to an institution and he wants nothing to do with any public officials. But even if he had gone to the authorities, what good would that have done, sir? It would have been the word of simple Verdie against that of Frank Garvis."

"But then *who* killed Garvis last night?" I looked down at the chest again and wondered if I had only been dreaming when—

"Sir," Jarman said quietly. "The Jarmans and the Deverauxs have been together ever since the beginning. There are no secrets a Deveraux can keep from a Jarman—not for long." He smiled faintly. "My grandfather also left a letter to his son, and, in turn, to me."

He took a key out of his vest pocket. "This unlocks the chest top, sir, and the Deveraux monster fits me as it did my grandfather and my father whenever they wished to wear it."

Jarman sighed. "I would have preferred to remain silent on the whole matter and let it pass. But I could see that you were beginning to fear that you were responsible and so I had to speak. Now that you know, I will put my affairs in order and then go to the police with a full confession."

"What have you told your wife?"

"Nothing but that Garvis killed Albert. I did not want her to think what the villagers are thinking."

I rubbed my neck. "Jarman, I fail to see that any . . . good . . . can come of your going to the police."

"Sir?"

"The Deveraux monster murdered Garvis," I said. "I think that it is much, much better if we leave it that way."

After a while, Jarman spoke faintly. "Thank you, sir."

I pulled the Deveraux monster out of the chest. "However, I believe that we should destroy this, don't you, Jarman? After all, someone might manage to compare it with the tufts of hair Garvis had in his fingers."

Jarman put the monster over his arm. "Yes, sir. I'll burn it." At the door he looked back. "Is the Deveraux monster dead, sir?"

A sudden gust of moor wind whispered around the shutters.

"Yes," I said. "The Deveraux monster is dead."

When he was gone, I happened to glance at the mirror.

Strange. I rather needed a shave again.

Ripper Moon!

February 1963

"I am a lineal descendant of Jack the Ripper," Mr. Pomfret said.

"Really?"

He nodded. "Some families hand down secret recipes from generation to generation. In our case it is the knowledge that we have inherited the blood of that remarkable, and yet unknown, man."

Some of my patients choose to lie on the couch. Pomfret was one of them and now he lay with his hands folded happily over his small paunch.

He took a single sheet of paper out of the breast pocket of his coat. "Would you like to see my family tree?"

I had expected something as complex as the lineage of the Jukes or the Kallikaks, but his ancestry was a tree without branches. A succession of only sons led back to a nineteenth century bookkeeper.

I studied Pomfret again. He had mild blue, slightly vacuous eyes and he was evidently at home in his recumbent position.

"Mr. Pomfret," I said. "Have you ever been analyzed before?"

He hesitated. "Well . . . yes."

"How many times?"

"Four."

"And why did you leave your previous psychiatrists?"

"When I felt I no longer needed them."

It was my suspicion that he had done so when he had caught them yawning, however I said, "But now you've come to me?"

"Well . . . after a while I find myself slipping again."

"Slipping? How?"

"I get this mad compulsion to slash, slash, slash." He turned his head toward me and smiled amiably. "Doctor, you must help me. You must."

The phone at my elbow rang and I picked it up.

It was Henry Wilkerson and his hysterical voice carried well into the room. "Doctor, I'm on the twelfth floor of the Tarleton Building and I'm going to jump!"

"Is that right," I said. "And why did you phone me?"

Perhaps he blinked and there was a momentary silence on the line. "Doctor, aren't you going to *try* to talk, me out of it?"

"I never interfere with the free self-expression of any of my patients."

Another silence. "I said the *twelfth* floor. That's pretty high up."

"I understand your reluctance. Perhaps if you tried it from the eleventh?"

He seemed to be fighting tears. "Doctor, you're *no* help at all." He hung up.

Pomfret had risen to a sitting position, his eyes round. "Just what kind of a psychiatrist are you anyway?"

"Cold-blooded and competent. Also I happen to know that the Tarleton Building is only eight stories high. He probably called from a phone booth at ground level." And further, though I did not tell Pomfret, I did not particularly care whether Wilkerson jumped to his death or not. "Mr. Pomfret," I said. "You may lie down again."

He did so with a trace of reluctance.

"Mr. Pomfret, are you married?"

"No."

"Living with a maiden aunt?"

"With my elder sister. She's a spinster."

I considered that answer close enough to have been a vindication of my guess. "Do you have any other hobbies?"

"Other hobbies?"

Besides having yourself psychoanalyzed, I had meant, but I rephrased the question. "Do you have any hobbies?"

"No. I used to smoke, but I gave that up after reading some articles."

I put his name on the top of a blank sheet of paper and clicked my ball point pen into readiness. "Tell me what comes to your mind."

He closed his eyes and relaxed. "Where should I begin?"

"Where do you usually?"

"With my first impression. I was eighteen months old and got ear sick. It was a 1924 Essex."

There was a certain narcotic element to Pomfret's voice and I found myself drifting into thought. When I returned some thirty minutes later, Pomfret was in the midst of reciting one of his most traumatic childhood experiences when he had stolen a pencil-sharpener from a dimestore counter.

I interrupted. "When do you get this mad impulse to slash, slash, slash?"

"On foggy nights. When the moon is full."

"If it is foggy, how do you know the moon is full?"

He blushed at the obstacle of logic. "I just *feel* that it's full."

"And *have* your ever slashed, slashed, slashed?"

"Well . . . no." He rallied. "But it is *truly* a wild, mad impulse. *Very* hard to resist."

I doubted whether Pomfret was capable of a wild, mad impulse. Without great danger of error, I thought I could slip Pomfret into a category. Man desires some distinction, real or imaginary, to lift him above the humdrum. In the case of Pomfret, he chose to regard himself as a descendent of Jack the Ripper and capable of similar actions. "Mr. Pomfret," I said. "How do you *know* you are a descendent of the real Jack the Ripper?"

He smiled complacently. "The diary. It's been passed down from father to son for almost a hundred years."

I glanced at my watch. "Our time is up for today. I'd like to see you again on Wednesday morning at ten." At the door a thought came to me. "The next time you come here, would you bring the diary with you?"

After dinner that evening, I watched my wife, Laurette, at the dressing table mirror.

She glanced at my reflection. "I hope you haven't forgotten that we go to the Carsons tonight? Which earrings shall I wear? The white or the green?"

"The green."

She held the white pair up to her ears. "I'll wear the white."

"Why did you ask me? The green."

She turned and glared. "White."

"Green."

Laurette is one of two daughters whose father possessed the sum of two million dollars. Her will is of iron. Mine is of steel.

"You are being childish," Laurette said. "White."

"We are both being childish, but I remain adamant. The green,"

Though the youngest child, she had dominated her father and her sister, Melanie. Originally I thought that perhaps the arrangement suited them all—her father and her sister seemed to need direction—but subsequently I had reason to doubt it.

When her father died, he left his entire estate—with the exception of a paltry ten thousand a year—to Melanie.

It was a turn of events which shook me considerably.

Perhaps he did so because he thought I had courted Laurette for her money—which was true—or possibly it was a species of revenge upon Laurette for the domination he resented. Whatever the actual motive, the one he declared in his will was that he considered my income as a psychiatrist sufficient for me to support Laurette properly.

I had thought of resorting to the courts to break the will, but I soon discovered the hopelessness of such an action. Her father had slyly had himself certified sane and in full possession of all his faculties by three psychiatrists before making out the will.

Laurette picked up the green earrings and began fastening them. "How in the world did you ever get to become a psychiatrist?"

"My parents could afford it."

She surveyed her image for a final inspection. "If you had a lot of money—and I mean a *lot*—how would that change your life?"

"I would lock the door of my office and never return."

She slipped into her wrap. "We'll take a taxi."

"Our car."

"Taxi."

We took our automobile and arrived at the Carsons at approximately eight-thirty.

Eventually I found myself next to one of the other guests, Dr. Nevins.

He spoke enthusiastically. "Just wound up a conversion hysteric case. The man had absolutely no musical talent, but his mother hot-house forced him to practice the piano and even made a concert pianist out of him. On his twenty-first birthday he declared his independence by developing paralysis of the hands."

I yawned. "How's your golf game been lately?"

"I don't play golf. Anyway, his mother finally died and at the graveside his paralysis left him. Well-adjusted now. Got himself a job as a used-car salesman."

A young man-the kind who carries a cocktail glass from conversation to conversation—drifted toward us. "You're both doctors, aren't you?"

We acknowledged that and waited for his symptoms.

He tilted his head. "People become doctors for a number of reasons—for the prestige, for the money, because they like medicine, or . . ." He smiled cunningly. "Or because they have a burning desire to help humanity." He pointed a finger at Nevins. "Why did *you* become a doctor?"

Nevins made a confident choice. "Because I *like* medicine."

The young man shook his head sadly. "Don't you think there's something *wrong* with anybody who *likes* sick people? Who *likes* diseases?" He wandered away.

Nevins turned to me, mildly troubled. "Why did *you* become a doctor?"

"Because I have a burning desire to help humanity."

Laurette's sister, Melanie, arrived at the party at nine. We exchanged glances, but said nothing.

Once during the evening she touched my hand lightly.

I smiled and spoke softly. "Careful. Someone may see us."

At eleven-thirty, I approached Laurette. "Time to go home."

She frowned. "I do not *feel* like going now."

"I do."

We locked eyes. Then she turned to her hostess, shrugged apologetically, and slipped into the wrap I held.

On Wednesday, Pomfret arrived at my office promptly at ten.

He extended a large green volume. "Actually this is only one of a series of twelve, but the accounts of the murders are all in here."

I regarded the large diary dubiously.

"I have book marks in the pertinent places," Pomfret said quickly. "You don't have to read the whole thing."

I sat down with the book. When I finished the indicated passages, I thumbed through the rest of the diary.

Hiram Pomfret—for such was the Ripper's full name—had been single and living with his spinster sister. He had been a bookkeeper with the East India House. The over-whelming majority of the volume chronicled such events as the time he rose in the mornings, when he retired, what he ate, and the state of his liver.

I lit a cigarette. Each of his murders—if indeed the diary were genuine and he had not lied—had been immediately preceded by a violent quarrel with his sister. As a matter of fact he devoted more words to the quarrels than he did to the murders.

And when his sister died, presumably of natural causes—the compulsion to murder had suddenly left him.

I turned the book over in my hands several times. "Could you leave this here? I'd like to study it a little further."

After a moment's hesitation, he agreed. "But you won't show it to anybody else?"

"No." I stared at my cigarette smoke for a while. "When you get these impulses, what do you do?"

"Do?"

"Yes. Do you just lie down and wait until they go away? Or what?"

"I go for a walk."

"Just for a walk? That's all?"

"Well . . . I sort of think . . . dream, I guess . . . that I'm Jack the Ripper . . . looking . . . stalking. . . ."

"But you *do* nothing?"

He seemed almost ashamed. "No."

I heard the outer door of my waiting room open and shut. My next client had arrived. "Mr. Pomfert," I said. "I would like to see you again tomorrow."

At twelve o'clock, I locked up my office and met Melanie at Paretti's for lunch.

There is only a slight family resemblance between her and my wife, Laurette. Melanie is smaller, has sloping, rather than square, shoulders, and gray cat eyes.

We kissed and then she said, "Just one year more, dear, and then the divorce."

I sighed. "Plus that one year waiting period."

She patted my hand. "The waiting period is absolutely necessary. We'll need it so that it will appear that you fell in love with me *after* the divorce—not that you divorced Laurette because you fell in love with me."

"I know, but. . . ."

"We must avoid any talk that might injure your reputation. After all, dear, when we establish your clinic, magazine articles will be written about you and we don't want any raised eyebrows."

But still two years away from Melanie's millions was a frustratingly long time. Anything could happen. "Couldn't I get the divorce right now? That would save us a year."

"You must be married to one wife at least three years. This establishes the fact that you are mature, but eventually had to bow to incompatibility. People insist on mature psychiatrists." She smiled smugly. "*None* of my friends are married to psychiatrists."

"They are quite rare."

"I want a husband who *is* something," Melanie said firmly. "Not just a man."

Over coffee, she again returned to a point which seemed to plague her. "I just can't understand why you married Laurette rather than me."

I manufactured my usual smile. "I met Laurette first, and besides, I didn't think you were interested in me. After all, you said nothing."

She admitted that. "I thought there was plenty of time. But everything moved so fast. You were never even formally engaged to her. Suddenly you were married."

Yes, everything had moved swiftly. But that had been my doing. I had seen the million dollars behind Laurette's shoulder and that had impelled me to avoid a long perilous engagement. One had to act quickly before the prize wandered.

Melanie exhaled sadly. "Two years. It's going to be so long, but I can't think of any quicker and proper way to get rid of Laurette now."

I said nothing.

When Melanie and I parted, I went to the public library, selected the most comprehensive volume on Jack the Ripper and proceeded to read.

His crimes, and the accounting of them in Hiram Pomfert's diary matched perfectly. There was just one difficulty. The dates were not the same. Hiram chronicled the murders a week, sometimes two, after they actually occurred.

It was just as I had expected. Hiram had merely read about the murders in the newspapers of his time and had appropriated them for his dream world. It was even possible that eventually he actually believed that he *was* Jack the Ripper—such an assimilation is not too rare—but the fact remained that Hiram Pomfret and Jack the Ripper were two different persons.

I remained in the silence of the library for half an hour more and then made up my mind. One must make do with what one has.

I left the library, drove to a hardware store, and bought a long thin knife.

The next day I cancelled all my appointments—with the exception of Pomfert's. While I waited for him, I dissolved a dozen sleeping tablets in a partly full decanter of cold water and stirred thoroughly. Then I hung a calendar under my medical certificate.

When Pomfert arrived, I studied him more carefully. Was my patient as simple and placid as he appeared? Or did he suffer the hot frustrations of life? Was he capable of hatred? Violent rage? Was the seed of murder within him? I handed back the diary. "This seems to be authentic."

"Then you really *do* believe that I am the direct descendent of Jack the Ripper, don't you?"

"It is difficult not to." I allowed a thoughtful interval of silence and then said, "When you prowl about on these moonlit foggy nights—do you carry a knife?"

"No."

"And yet sometimes you wish that you did?"

"Well . . ."

I opened my desk drawer and took out the knife I had purchased the day before: I extended it, handle forward. "Take this."

He recoiled. "Why?"

"I merely want to study your reactions when you hold it."

He took the weapon gingerly. "Are you sure this is healthy?"

"You may trust me." I made a pretense of looking him over critically. "Now slash at someone imaginary in front of you."

He did so, clumsily and tentatively.

"Slash upward," I directed. "From nave to chaps. Imagine someone you hate stands leering before you. Your employer. A neighbor. A blood relative."

He slashed again, with more enthusiasm.

"Again," I said. "Again. With feeling." I had him repeat the action, some thirty times. "That will be enough for now," I said finally.

He stopped with a trace of reluctance. "Sort of gets you after a while. How were my reactions?"

I managed to look troubled. "Your eyes."

"My eyes?"

"Yes. At about the tenth slash, suddenly a steely determination seemed to leap into them."

"Steely determination?" He looked about, probably for a mirror.

"And the *way* you slashed," I said with awe. "It seemed as though . . . as though. . . ."

He leaned forward. "Yes? Yes?" I pulled myself together, took the knife out of his hand, and put it back in the desk drawer. I poured a glass of water. "Drink this. You look somewhat warm."

He took the glass and dutifully emptied it.

I picked up my pad and a pen. "We'll get on with the session. Lie down on the couch, Mr. Pomfert." I waited until he did so. "Now let me see, the last time you were in that position you were telling me about the pencil sharpener."

"Oh, that," he said deprecatingly. "I'd rather talk about Jack the Ripper."

I doodled idly on my pad. "Tell me what comes to your mind."

He rambled on and after a bit his speech slowed and he yawned. In another five minutes he was asleep and snoring softly.

I could not, of course, estimate to the minute how long he would sleep. I would have preferred that he do so for less than a half hour, however giving him too small a dose might have induced nothing more than drowsiness.

I got several magazines from my waiting room and sat down to wait. After an hour Pomfert was still asleep, but I thought the time had come to bring him out of it. I rapped a book sharply three times on my desk.

His eyes opened, closed, and then quickly opened again. He sat up and blushed. "I guess I must have fallen asleep,"

I dragged sharply on my cigarette. "No, Mr. Pomfret. It wasn't sleep. Not sleep."

He glanced at his watch. "But I've been on the couch for about an hour and I don't remember . . ."

"It wasn't sleep," I said again. "Not sleep. Something *happened!* Suddenly it wasn't *you* talking."

He blinked. "It wasn't?"

I rubbed my eyes as though they were tired. "Mr. Pomfret, were you born in England?"

"No. Peoria."

"Strange," I murmured. "And yet . . . and yet you spoke with an English accent. A definite English accent." I took a couple of obviously troubled breaths. "Mr. Pomfret, you were in a *trance.*"

"I was?"

I lit a cigarette from the stub of the previous one. "I've never . . . *never* believed in reincarnation until. . . ."

He leaned forward hopefully. "Until?"

I rose and began pacing. "I *still* don't believe it. It's impossible."

He rose to the defense of his reincarnation. "Why is it impossible?"

I turned on him. "But you couldn't possibly be Jack the. . . ." I rubbed my eyes again. "You are only a miserable bookkeeper."

He flushed. "*Jack* was just a miserable bookkeeper."

"But just look at you. Physically you are absolutely insignificant."

The flush deepened. "It just so happens that Jack was exactly the same weight and height that I am. He describes himself on page one, volume one, of the dairies."

"He was dominated by his sister."

"And *I* am dominated by my . . ." He stopped and cleared his throat. "I mean I just don't see why it's impossible that I could actually be a reincarnation of Jack the Ripper."

I resumed pacing and spoke aloud, but as to myself. "Fulfillment. That's who you . . . *he* said. Every man must seek fulfillment. He must prove, if only to himself, that he is not the insignificant creature that *everyone* thinks he is."

Pomfret nodded in agreement.

"And you . . . *Jack* said that at the next full. . . ." I stopped speaking abruptly and strode to the calendar on the wall. "We've got only a week until. . . ."

Pomfret joined me at the calendar. "Until the next full moon?"

I stared at him soberly. "Jack . . . I mean, Pomfret . . . I want to see you every day during the remainder of this week and the next. We've *got* to stop this from happening."

But, of course, quashing the reincarnation was the last thing I had in mind.

I cancelled all my other appointments and concentrated upon Pomfret—mornings, afternoons, and evenings.

The volunteer patient has a pathetically eager desire to win the approval of his psychiatrist. If his doctor frowns, he is shattered; if he smiles, he is delighted. During the next few days I ostensibly set upon a course of "curing" Pomfret of the obsession which he barely, if at all, had.

I kept emphasizing that he could not murder because he was mentally, emotionally, and physically incapable of such a positive action. In short, he lacked the courage. I also made it plain that basically, though I was fighting hard to conceal it, I absolutely detested people who lacked courage. Especially Pomfret.

That approach proved only partially successful, for while Pomfret had his narcissistic foible—his desire for continual psychoanalysis—it still remained that otherwise he was remarkably adjusted to his actual situation in life. That he was insignificant physically, that he was not particularly intelligent, that he dwelt under the thumb of his elder sister, these things he accepted with a minimum of resentment.

Even his belief that he was a direct descendent of Jack the Ripper was not a revolt from reality, not a relapse into a warm dream world. It was a "fact." His father had told him it was true and he had himself seen it in black and white.

Pomfret was therefore, a difficult problem for me, and now I concentrated on his relations with his sister and continually directed the analysis back to that point.

I revived the petty squabbles they'd had. I analyzed them viciously. I tore them apart and cemented them back together, but in distorted and giant proportion. I created trauma over a scolding for a broken dish, a mud track on the floor, tardiness for a meal.

And yet Pomfret loved his sister. This too was a fact that I could not destroy and did not wish to. I wanted him to hate and love. To love, to hate, to feel guilt for hating, and yet to feel *justified*. To feel rage, yet a helplessness to act.

But how does one purge one's self of consuming hatred and rage? How does one prove that one is really a man?

Now I channeled the hate I had created. It was not really his sister who was nagging, who stifled his manhood. It was *all* women.

And that was the light—the *relief*—for Pomfret. He couldn't possibly harm his sister—not someone he actually loved—but....

And I . . . his psychiatrist . . . *God* . . . subtly intimated that I might even approve.

Except for his "trances," I doubt that Pomfret slept much at all during the week. At the end of six days he had lost weight, was hollow-eyed, but frantically impatient for the advent of the full moon.

On the seventh day, he left my office perspiring and on the brink of action.

I had done as much as I could and nothing remained now but to wait. I spent the evening at home in my study listening to news broadcasts.

I had almost given up on Pomfret, for that night, at least, when the announcement came over the eleven-thirty news. A woman had been slashed to death on the west side. The murder appeared motiveless, but the method immediately led the commentator to make comparisons with Jack the Ripper.

I made myself a drink. Pomfret had come through.

The next morning I looked up Pomfret's address, drove to the neighborhood and cruised about. It was an old-fashioned section of the city with heavy shade trees and little known street names. The corner of Montmorency and Dill seemed an appropriately untraveled and potentially dark site. I made a note of the location and then drove to my office.

Pomfret arrived at ten. He seemed different now. More relaxed, the possessor of a certain new confidence. He smiled slightly. "Is it true that a psychiatrist is like a priest? When you tell him something he's not allowed to repeat it to anyone? Not even the police?"

"We do keep confidences," I said. "However not to that extent." I laughed lightly. "If someone told me that he had just committed a murder, for instance, I'd be obliged to turn the information over to the police immediately."

He seemed disappointed. He tried a side gambit. "Did you read the morning paper?"

"No." I poured a glass of water and pushed it toward him. "You look tired and thirsty."

He took the glass. "I seem to be drinking an awful lot of water here." He finished the glass and lay down on the couch. "Do you suppose I'll fall into a trance again? It's been pretty regular."

"We shall see."

He appeared suddenly worried. "Suppose I say something in my trance about murdering somebody. Recently. Would you *go* to the police?"

"Of course not," I reassured him. "Words spoken in a trance are not admissible as evidence in a court. Against the Fourth and Fifth Amendments."

When he woke an hour later, he quickly asked, "Did I say anything about a murder?"

"No."

He scratched his head. "I dreamed . . . I mean I *thought* I said something about last night."

"No." I looked puzzled. "But you did say a few other things. Really nothing much, except that you kept repeating, 'The moon is still full tonight.'"

His eyes went toward the calendar. "It is?"

"Yes. And you kept repeating two names. One of them was Montmorency. Does that mean anything to you? A town? A person? A tart red cherry?"

He gave it thought.

"The other name was Dill," I said. "Montmorency and Dill."

A light dawned in his eyes.

"And you kept saying, 'It is destiny. It is destiny.'"

He nodded sagely. "Destiny is a pretty important thing." He smiled to himself and repeated the message. *"The moon is still full tonight, Montmorency and Dill. It is destiny."* He frowned. "Did I mention anything else? Like a time?"

"I forgot," I said hastily. "You did mumble something about eleven in the evening."

When he left the office, he looked at me and spoke slyly. "Be sure to read tomorrow morning's paper. A fellow really ought to keep up with the news."

In the evening, Laurette and I got into our car for the drive to the party the Newmans were giving.

"Are you taking the 27th or the 35th Street viaduct?" she asked.

"The 27th."

"I prefer the 35th."

"All right. We'll take the 35th."

She looked at me. "Aren't you feeling well?"

"I simply do not feel inclined to argue tonight."

Sometime during that evening, at about ten-thirty, I would disappear for a moment, and when I returned I would draw Laurette aside. "I just had a phone call. Or rather it was actually for you, but the maid misunderstood and got me."

"What was it?"

"Betty Nelson. She phoned our apartment and Clara told her we'd be here."

"I thought Betty was in Europe."

"Evidently she returned. She seemed quite agitated."

"What was wrong?"

"She wouldn't tell me. But she said that she wanted to see you immediately. Alone. I wasn't to come with you. At the corner of Montmorency and Dill. She said it was terribly important."

Laurette would frown. "She didn't give any hint as to what it's all about?"

"No. But she said for you to hurry. She would be there at eleven."

And since Betty was her best friend, Laurette would take our car and go. What would I do about Pomfret after tonight?

I thought I could handle that. A few more of his trances and I would convince him that Jack the Ripper was satiated for this generation, at least.

Now I turned the car onto the 35th Street viaduct.

"Let me feel your forehead," Laurette asked.

"I am *perfectly* all right."

Laurette was silent until we left the viaduct. "Most people think I'm a strong personality, but actually I've never won an argument with you until now."

"Congratulations."

"I mean that most people think that I dominated my sister and my father. Actually that wasn't true. My manner was simply a sort of self-defense to prevent being subjugated. Melanie was the dominant member of the family."

I had suspected that ever since I've begun seeing Melanie. Naturally I had had to bend my own personality to some extent in order to create a favorable impression with her, but I had the uneasy suspicion that after our marriage I might have difficulty preserving my intellectual and emotional independence. Melanie was not obviously forceful, but she had the patience and wearing power of a leech. Laurette was much easier to deal with.

"Tell me," Laurette said. "If you had it to do all over again—and knew who was getting the money—whom would you marry, Melanie or me?"

"It seems to be getting foggy tonight."

Laurette smiled slightly. "Then let me put it this way. If both of us had the same amount of money, just whom would you choose?"

I spoke without hesitation. "You, of course."

Laurette was quietly thoughtful the rest of the trip and when I parked near the Newman residence, she touched my arm. "Money means an awful lot to you, doesn't it?"

"Of course."

"And frankly, it means a lot to me too. Much more than you might think. As a matter of fact, I've thought of killing Melanie."

I helped Laurette out of the car. "What good would that do?"

"Quite a bit. I happen to know that Melanie hasn't made out a will. If she died now, the entire estate would go to me."

At ten-thirty, I went upstairs to one of the Newman bedrooms and used the phone. "Melanie," I said. "I must see you right away. I can't explain why now, but it's dreadfully important. It means our entire future."

"All right, dear," she said. "Where shall I meet you?"

"Montmorency and Dill. I happen to be attending a party in the neighborhood and I can slip out for a moment."

At eleven o'clock I looked across the room at Laurette and silently toasted two million dollars and Pomfret the Ripper.

Devil Eyes

May 1956

Fred says that a hundred, a week is cheap enough and I guess that's one good way of looking at it.

Not that he could ever prove anything. There's nothing to show I hired him, and I didn't really.

Maybe I should stop paying, but I can't take any chances. You can never tell about those winos. And besides, it's Fay's money anyway.

I try not to let it bother me. Instead, I like to think about the two Jaguars, the forty suits I have at the Bermuda place alone, and about Fay's money.

And Fay, too, of course.

It was a real good deal, meeting her. I remember I was moody and depressed at the time. Mr. Bronson's detectives had me jumpy, following me that way, and I'd just phoned Mrs. Bronson and told her the whole thing was off.

I was kicking myself for not saving money for times like this when I saw Fay. She had shimmering black hair and devil dark eyes that were a flat invitation. I felt suddenly happier as I made my way through the cocktail crowd.

A real bitch, I thought, as our eyes came closer. But I wasn't complaining.

She arched an eyebrow as she smiled. "Mr. Philip Gillespie, isn't it? I've heard about you somewhere."

I returned the smile. "Some people are shocked. And others interested."

"I'm horrified," she said. "Absolutely shivering."

I touched her arm. "Tell me about it. No harm in that."

"Of course not," she said.

And that's the way it went, right from the start. We both knew what we wanted and we didn't waste time asking questions.

She let me know that her husband, Charley Whittier, was down someplace on the coast of Georgia looking over a new yacht, and that took care of that.

I took her to my apartment after the party and it was fine. It was fine that night and all the other nights. Even when Charley came back we didn't let that stop us.

Fay had a firm white body rounded so soft that you couldn't keep your hands off it. I used to wonder why Charley took so many trips until I made it my business to see what he looked like.

He was the type that always walked with his shoulders back and took in a lot of fresh air. But he'd been breathing the stuff for sixty-five years and now he got his kicks fishing for tarpon.

In two weeks I had a new car and I re-opened my bank account. The sun was shining for me and I could see that the setup could go on for a long time.

Just how long Fay had in mind I found out one evening as we lay there.

First she moved a lock of my hair away from my forehead. "I know you're no damn good," she said.

"Oh?" I said. "A fine time to start complaining."

"What I mean is that you're a complete rotten heel."

I reached for the cigarettes on the night stand. "What brought up the insults?"

Fay accepted the cigarette and a light. "I just thought you ought to know that you're not fooling me. And then, too, there's the terrible fact that I love you."

I tried to blow smoke rings. "I love you too. It's a maddening, soul-searing love."

"My dear Phil," she said. "You don't love anyone but yourself. There's your soul-searing love."

I looked back up at the ceiling and kept quiet.

"I suppose I could get a divorce," she said. "But you wouldn't like that. I probably couldn't get enough money out of Charley to satisfy you."

I was glad to see that she was being sensible. So many of them get the divorce idea without thinking about money. That's when I put on my hat and go for the door.

"And yet I'm stupid enough to love a rat like you," she said. "I like to have you around."

I met her eyes. I'll be damned, I thought. She really does.

I brushed my lips lightly over her eyelids. "Relax I'm around now."

"Sure," she said. "As long as Charley pays the freight and doesn't know what's going on."

She was quiet for a while and then she said, "I've been thinking about something else. I'd have money then."

I was interested. "And that?"

Fay watched me with thoughtful eyes. "Suppose we killed my husband."

I sat up and brushed the sparks from my chest. "Get that idea out of your head fast."

She smiled faintly. "It could look like an accident."

"I've heard that one before: Think about something else, baby. You're making me nervous."

Charley came back from another one of his healthy trips and I saw her only twice in the next week. Both times we nearly got into arguments because she kept harping on the accident subject.

I guess that's why I hit the bottle too hard that night when she had to go some place with Charley.

Ordinarily I go easy on the wet stuff because I know I can't handle it. But Fay had me worried with her talk and I could see a good thing coming to an end.

The drinks stacked up inside of me and by the time I was having trouble telling up from down, I was in the Third Ward.

I had a palm against a building to keep me from falling and was wondering where the hell all the taxis were.

That's when I met Fred.

He was a little sniffling man with frightened shoulders and he eyed me from the doorway of a closed grocery store.

"Keep moving, Bo," I snapped at him. "I'm not going to pass out."

He passed a grimy hand over his nose. "I wasn't gonna roll you, Mister."

He watched me, ready to move on if I came closer. "Mister," he said. "I ain't had a thing to eat in days."

"You make me cry," I said, after a hiccup. "Starve somewhere else." My hand slipped on the wall and I almost fell.

I closed my eyes for what I thought was a second, but it must have been longer. He was near enough to grab when I opened them.

I got him by the shirt front, but he was a wiry little bastard and he twisted away before I could throw a punch.

He scuttled twenty feet before he turned and snarled. "You rich slobs think you can push everybody around."

I considered going after him, but it seemed like work. He stood there hating me and then the liquor inside me began to talk.

"What'll you do for a couple of bucks?" I asked. "Anything?"

He stared at me, hope flicking in his eyes.

I fumbled for my wallet and took out two hundreds. "Pretty, aren't they, bending in the wind that way?"

His eyes fondled the money and automatically he cleaned the tips of his right hand on his pant's.

I found another hundred and fanned myself with the three bills. "Would you kill for three hundred? That's a lot of bottles."

His tongue wet his lips and I stood there grinning at the way he leaned for the money.

His eyes began thinking for his head and he looked at me. "What's his name?"

I should have stopped right there and put the money back in my wallet. But I was rolling and I pushed it further. "A real important man," I said. "Charley Whittier."

A taxi pulled around the corner then and I took my eyes away from him as I flagged it.

A second too late I felt the tug as he jerked the hundreds from my fingers. He slipped into an alley before I could even remember to curse.

That's how I met Fred.

Charley Whittier took off again, this time for Kentucky to look over some horses, and I took Fay to dinner after his plane left.

She started talking about it right away.

"I hired a man today," she said.

"Yes?" I said. I was enjoying the steak and wasn't paying much attention. "Somebody quit at your place?"

"Not a servant," she said sharply. "He's going to do what you're afraid to do."

I stopped eating. "What do you mean?"

Her words were clear and should have been whispered. "I hired a man to kill my husband."

She said it just like that. Real cold-blooded.

I put down my knife and fork and glanced around the room. I was pretty sure no one else had heard her, but I still didn't feel calm. "You're crazy," I said.

"Yes," she said. "You make me that way."

"You couldn't get away with it. Call it off."

She looked down at the tablecloth. "No."

I pushed my chair away from the table. Fay put her hand on my arm. "He'll make it look like an accident."

I shook my head. "Too many things can go wrong."

"It's the only way for us," Fay said. "I don't want you only part time."

I got up. "Part time is better than no time, baby."

She saw I meant it. "All right, Phil," she said slowly. "I'll call it off."

Charley came back from Kentucky with two yearlings. But he never did get a chance to see them race.

The day after he returned I picked up the paper to read about how he died.

It seems that Charley made a habit of taking walks in the evening. Usually he went to a lonely point where his estate faced the ocean.

It was here that he must have slipped, the papers said, and fallen down the steep palisades to the rocks below. There were no witnesses to the accident.

I kept away from Fay for two weeks and spent the time sweating over every item the papers carried about Charley's death.

The whole thing passed without making a smell. The death was ruled accidental.

I decided it would be all right to see Fay again.

She had her hand on her hip when I came. "Well," she said. "That was a nice long decent interval. How good to see you again."

"I'm glad you had sense enough not to phone me," I said. "You can never tell about wire tapping."

Her black eyes met mine. "What are you talking about?"

"As long as it's over, honey," I said, "we can forget about it." I watched the tightness of her dress and the way she moved. "I missed you a lot, baby."

She didn't quite believe me, but she came to me. Later I thought I might as well ask the question.

Devil Eyes

"Was it an accident?"

She ran a hand along my cheek. "Of course it was an accident."

"That's the way we'll think of it," I said. Then I smiled before I kissed her.

Fred came to see me a few days later.

He hadn't used any of the three hundred to help the outside of him and he smelled of dampness.

"You got a peculiar kind of guts," I said. "You steal from me and then you come up for a touch."

He trembled with hangover uneasiness. "You can't say I stole it," he said, his voice a whining flutter. "You remember, don't you?"

I felt coldness creep into my hands. "What the hell do you mean?"

He gained a faint confidence. "You read the papers, don't you? Like about the accident to Mr. Whittier."

"And you claim what?"

His face got wise. "I don't claim nothing. I just say I didn't steal the money. Get me?"

He tried a snaggle-tooth grin. "I had a hard time finding you. I sure could use another hundred."

He was a little man whose life was the warm sleep made by wine. It would be his word against mine, if he ever talked.

I could say it had all been a joke, or deny I had ever seen him before. But once the cops listened, they'd begin to dig and I didn't want that.

The main thing was not even to give them the idea.

Fred stood straighter now. "If I don't get the hundred I'll have to sleep on a park bench tonight. I might get picked up and cops make me so nervous I talk a lot."

And so I gave Fred his first hundred.

He gets it every week now. Sometimes by check, because since Fay and I got married we do a lot of traveling.

It's always a hundred. No more, no less. Maybe he's smart that way. For only a hundred a week I don't get any drastic ideas.

It just shows the way drinking can cost you. You get into a situation like that where you have to pay a faking runt like that.

Not that liquor doesn't help sometimes. It did the other time. I don't think I would have had the nerve otherwise or even considered the idea if I hadn't had too much to drink.

Maybe that's why I don't have nightmares about it.

Charley did an awful lot of clawing and screaming before I finally managed to throw him off that cliff.

The Canary

June 1956

I lay on the top bunk and listened to the canary in the second gallery and thought about the time when I had one in our cell.

Matt was listening too and he began to swear. He got off his bunk and spit into the toilet bowl.

I studied the damp prints my fingers made on the two thin sheets of paper I held in my hands.

Matt turned the faucets in the basin on and off a couple of times, just to have something to do, and then he looked up at me. I could feel him doing that.

"Too bad we ain't got a canary any more," he said.

I began to fold the papers slowly.

"I said it's too bad we ain't got a canary any more," Matt said. "Old man, when I'm talking, you look at me."

I looked at him.

He let himself get the smile that never went to his eyes. "Now why did you have to go and kill the poor little bastard?"

"Because I'm mean," I said.

He nodded. "That's right." And he waited.

"I'm a ratty weasel," I said.

He nodded again. Then his eyes went to the papers I was putting in my pocket. He came over and took them out.

I put my hands behind my head and looked at the ceiling. I thought about the canary and how I'd held it in my hand and then crushed it.

After a while, Matt said, "All right, runt. What are these?"

"Nothing," I said. I could feel my stomach tightening.

He reached up and pulled me off the bunk. I bumped my knee coming down and closed my eyes against the pain.

"Don't tell me it's nothing," Matt said.

I opened my eyes and blinked away the water. "They're tracings of some plans," I said.

He let go of my shirt and looked at the sheets again.

"They're tracings of some plans I found in the warden's files," I said. "One sheet shows a section of the old sewage system. The other one shows what part of it's being used today."

I took the sheets out of his hands and tracked with my forefinger. "This sewer pipe isn't being used today. It leads out of here down to the river."

Matt looked at me and then he smiled and sat down on his bunk.

"It goes under the carpenter shop," I said. "You got to get through four inches of concrete and five feet of dirt to get to it." I licked my lips. "It's two feet in diameter. And from where it ends, it's about two hundred yards to the river."

Matt kept his grin. "Anything more?"

"There's a grating at the end of it," I said. "You'd need a hacksaw."

He leaned back against the wall. "You been dreaming about this?"

"Just dreaming," I said. "I don't like tunnels."

Matt put his hands over one knee. "You got a job now. Get me into the carpenter shop."

I climbed back up on my bunk and lay down. I thought about crawling in a little tube with five feet of ground between you and the fresh air.

In the morning, after breakfast in the mess hall, I went to my job in the warden's office. I dusted his desk, the files, the window sills, and then I began sorting the mail.

The warden came into the office at nine and I stood up until he took his chair. Then I brought the mail to his desk and sat down with my pad of paper and a pencil.

He went through the stack and as he did he dictated answers to me. When he finished he lit a cigar.

"Morgan," he said. "I been hearing things. You want me to get you another cellmate?"

"No, sir," I said. "Not now." I closed my notebook. "Sir," I said. "Bronson would like to get a transfer to the carpenter shop."

He rolled the cigar in his mouth a couple of times and studied me. "Did he figure you got the influence to get him there? Nobody gets out of the laundry until he's put in a full year there."

"I was just asking, sir," I said.

He took the cigar out of his mouth. "How long have you been in here, Morgan?"

"Thirty-four years, sir," I said.

His grin showed the gold fillings in his teeth. "This is your home, boy. You wouldn't know what to do if I opened the gates for you."

I looked down at my notebook and didn't say anything.

"You got a nice warm and comfortable little cell," he said. "I hear you even put curtains on the windows."

"I took them down, sir," I said.

Out in the exercise yard during the free hour, I went to the sunny wall where Jim Wallace was sitting on the ground with the chess board already set up.

I sat down on the ground and rolled a cigarette.

"Nice day," Jim said. "Won't be many more like this."

"Right, Jim," I said. "Guess I'm getting old. I can't stand cold weather any more. I get twinges like rheumatism."

Jim started a Casablanca opening. "Drop in at the dispensary and have the doc look you over."

"I don't know, Jim," I said. "If you're not bleeding, the doc don't think you're sick."

"Try it anyway," Jim said. "If he don't give you nothing for the pain, I'll see if I can get you something." Jim studied the board. "'My canaries are three weeks old now. Would you care to have one?"

"I'll think about it, Jim."

"I know how you feel," he said. "I never thought I'd want another after Alfie died. But you get over it. They're good company."

We were down to the end game when Matt walked up to us and looked down. "What's going about getting me into the carpenter shop?"

"I talked to the warden this morning," I said. "But it's not that easy, Matt. Nobody gets out of his time in the laundry."

"I don't like the laundry," Matt said. "My hands get chapped."

"All I can do is talk to the warden," I said. "That's all I can do."

Matt studied us for a while and then he hooked a toe under the chessboard and flipped it over.

Jim kept his eyes on the ground. I looked up at Matt for a few seconds and then I looked at the ground too.

Matt stood there laughing softly to himself and when he got tired of that he walked away.

I turned the board back over and we picked up the pieces.

"That's the sixth time he's done that," Jim said. "I'm keeping track."

"I know, Jim," I said. "So am I."

"We never bother nobody," Jim said. "I don't like other people to bother me either." He looked up from the board. "Your move."

Matt had to finish his two months in the laundry, but at the end of that time the warden transferred him to the carpenter shop.

After the first day there, Matt sat on his bunk and pointed to his shoes. I got down on my knees and began unlacing them.

"It's a cinch," he said. "We'll break into the pipe where it goes under the tool room. We got some privacy there."

I put his shoes under the bunk.

"I had to let the tool-room boys in on it," Matt said. "But they're not taking the trip. They don't like tunnels either. Just you and me go." He stretched his legs. "It'll take at least a week. It's got to be done slow and easy."

It took almost two, but when it was done, Matt came back to our cell grinning. "Pack your valise," he said. "We leave at two tomorrow afternoon."

"Matt," I said. "I can't just leave the warden's office when I feel like it."

"The hell you can't. You been here so long you practically got the run of the place. You're trotting all over on errands for him the whole day."

"Matt," I said. "Why do you want me to come along? I'll just slow you."

His grin came back. "You're my insurance. I don't read plans so good and if everything's not right, I want you to share it with me."

Around one-thirty the next afternoon, I let the warden notice that I wasn't feeling so good and he let me go to the dispensary.

Jim was at the typewriter in the empty waiting room pecking away on some medical records. He stopped when I closed the door behind me.

"I leave in about fifteen minutes, Jim," I said.

He looked around to make sure that we were alone and then he opened a desk drawer and took out a small flat bottle.

"A half pint," he said. "About fifty percent alcohol and flavored with orange juice."

"Thanks, Jim," I said. I put it inside my shirt, under my belt, and we shook hands.

"Good luck," Jim said.

I went outside to the carpenter shop and nodded to the guard lounging against a work bench.

"The warden wants me to do a check on the tool records," I said. "I'll be messing around here all afternoon."

He was considering a yawn. "Go ahead," he said. "Help yourself."

I went to the far end of the long room and into the tool cage by the side door. Matt was inside with a con I knew as Eddie and they were trying to look busy.

Matt glanced out of the wire cage to make sure that the guard wasn't interested and then he squatted down under the counter. He shoved aside a big cardboard box, switched on a flashlight, and we looked down into the hole.

I felt the color leaving my face as I smelled the sick air coming from it. I looked at Matt and I could see that he was beginning to sweat.

"Once you're down, I'll slide over the box," Eddie said. "I don't think anybody's going to miss you until the five o'clock check."

"Who goes first, Matt?" I asked. But I knew.

"You do," he said.

I reached under my shirt and brought out the bottle and unscrewed the cap.

"What's that?" Matt asked.

"I'll need a little something, Matt," I said. "My nerves aren't so good."

Matt looked down into the hole again and then he took the bottle away from me.

He took a big swallow and while he stood there trying to keep the stuff down, I reached for the bottle.

He slapped my hand away. "I'm not through yet," he said. He took a couple more swallows, waited a half minute, and then finished the bottle.

"Don't brood about it," he said, looking into my eyes. He handed me the hacksaw and a flashlight. "Get down there and start crawling. You know how to do that."

I lowered myself into the hole cut into the pipe. I began inching myself forward on my stomach, holding the flashlight and hacksaw in front of me.

After ten yards I stopped and waited for Matt to follow me. It was a long minute before I heard him behind me.

The pipe was foul with dead air and the stench of the dirt that covered the bottom of it. I would have tried to back up, but Matt was behind me and there was only one direction for me to go.

I went forward about twenty-five yards and then I stopped to rest. But Matt slapped at my heels and I had to *go* on.

The small stones at the bottom of the pipe began digging into my knees and elbows. I crawled fifty yards more and then I had to stop.

Matt began slapping at my heels again and he even scratched my legs with his fingernails. "For God's sake," he said, his voice high. "Keep moving!"

"I got to rest," I said, over my shoulder. "You got to let me rest or I'll die here and you'll never get out."

At the end of five minutes I started forward again and the next time I stopped to rest Matt didn't bother me.

I lay there waiting for my heart to stop racing. When I began moving forward, I tried not to stop for rest again. But I had to stop twice more before I got to the grating.

I found that I had to remove the blade from the hacksaw in order to get at the ironwork and it took me about forty-five minutes to cut my way through.

I crawled out into the fresh air and looked back up the riverbank to where the prison walls were only fifteen yards away.

I thought about the canary I'd called Betty and I thought about how Matt had taken her out of the cage and put her in my hand.

I remembered how he'd put his big hands over mine and made me squeeze until she was dead.

I put up the collar of my jacket. It was cold out here. Too cold for a man who was in his sixties.

I started walking along the wall toward the front gate. I'd probably spend some time in solitary, but when they let me have my cell again, I could put up curtains. Matt wouldn't be there to laugh at them and make me take them down.

Nobody would bother to crawl through the pipe. I was pretty sure of that. They'd just seal it up and figure that Matt had got away.

Anyway, I'd tell them that he did.

It must have been about the halfway point when the barbiturates Jim had gotten for me caught up with Matt. There was enough in that bottle to kill him three times over.

The Canary

Maybe he was dead now, or maybe he was still breathing.
I wondered if the rats would wait.

The Wire Loop
As by Steve Harbor

August 1956

Karl Krader folded the newspaper and put it on the end table. "It's queer, all right. He kills the girls, but doesn't touch them otherwise. Either before or after. Evidently he gets his thrill just from the strangling."

His wife Laura turned her head to Norman Calmet. "Is that it, Norman? Is that how he gets his thrills?" Her gray eyes waited for him to speak.

Norman's small fingers drummed on the arm of the easy chair as he talked. "I'd hardly think so. He's killing something he hates and he'll do it over and over again until he's caught or finally decides he's even with the world."

Karl brushed a lock of blond hair from his forehead. "It's been ten days since the last one. Maybe he's finished killing now."

Norman Calmet was a small man of thirty-five with the neatness and primness of a man who hates germs and disorder. Usually he wore glasses, but it was a point of vanity with him not to when he spent an evening at Karl's house. He was beginning to get a headache, but he preferred that to looking owlish.

"I imagine he simply enjoys killing," Laura said.

"Perhaps he does," Norman said. "And perhaps he suffers terrible pangs of conscience."

Laura smiled at the thin stream of smoke from the cigarette she held. "That's remarkable. A conscience in a deviate."

Norman's moist fingers reached for his glass. "Well, I'd hardly call murder a deviation. Though technically I suppose you're right."

His eyes went to his carefully polished size six shoes and he felt the familiar waves of heat anger as Laura watched him. He brought the glass to his lips, wishing he were the kind of a man who could drink a lot without getting sick. He felt sure that liquor would help him to meet anyone's eyes.

"Perhaps he's been jilted by some girl," Laura said. "That could be possible, couldn't it, Normie? Or does he just hate women?"

"Evidently not all women," Karl said. "Just the small ones. Three high school girls, so far, and one office girl of nineteen. None of them weighed more than one ten."

Karl rose and began collecting the empty glasses, "He's been lucky so far. No one's even got a look at him."

"Someone terrifically strong, wouldn't you say so, Normie?" Laura asked.

Norman handed his glass to Karl. "Very little whiskey in mine."

"He didn't need any particular strength," Karl said. "He had a wire loop with some sort of a rod. All he had to do was to slip the noose over his victim's neck and twist the rod. It wouldn't take much muscle to do that."

He stopped in the doorway to the kitchen. "By the way, Laura, did you know that Norman's picked up a girl friend." He grinned. "About time too, Norman. You're not getting any younger." He disappeared into the kitchen and in a few moments they heard the clatter of glasses and the sound of the refrigerator door being opened.

Laura put her chin on the palm of her hand and studied Norman. "A girl? How nice. Is it an experiment?"

Norman turned on her, his voice soft, but angry. "Why do you talk to me like that?"

"Like what?" A smile flickered on her lips. "What's her name, Normie?"

Norman turned his eyes from her, "Vivian Kirk. A student in one of my classes."

She smiled as she watched him. "I've been wondering about something, Normie. You don't have to continue teaching at the University now, do you? Not after all the money your father left you?"

"No, I don't," Norman said firmly. "But I want to."

"I see," Laura said. "And of course you wouldn't want to leave the friends you've made here. Isn't that it?"

At a quarter to ten, Norman rose to leave. Karl and Laura saw him to the door.

"Now be careful, Normie," Laura said. "Take the lighted streets. And be careful how you walk. The strangler might have bad eyesight."

Norman cursed softly as he walked away, conscious that Laura still watched him from the doorway. He tried controlling his walk, making long manly strides, his body stiff against unnecessary motion. Turning the corner, he relaxed somewhat, falling back into the short mincing steps that were more natural to him.

At his morning ten o'clock class, Vivian Kirk, sitting at a desk in the front row, winked at him. She was a small girl with dark brown hair. Norman was quite aware that she was pretty, but he also regarded the temper lines near her eyes with some trepidation.

He fought down a flush of irritation. Damn the girl, he thought. Chemical Engineering is a man's subject. Why doesn't the girl leave me alone. But Norman knew why not and he wished almost sincerely that he had only his professor's salary to depend on.

All he really wanted from life was peace and the society of a few choice friends. And if it hadn't been for the whispers and smirks of the faculty members and the students, Norman thought that he still might have been able to keep her at arm's length. But he'd been unable to endure the talk, and finally had had to talk to Vivian, if for no other reason than to prove that he wasn't being frightened by a girl. Any girl.

He remembered the dates he'd had with her; the evenings spent in a movie theater, sitting rigid as Vivian put her hand on his and smiled, her teeth white and sharp in the semi-darkness of the theater.

Norman went through his lecture avoiding her eyes and when the bell rang, he gathered up his notes wearily and joined her in the hall. He wore his glasses.

"Hello, darling," she said, her eyes steady and her mouth smiling.

Norman glanced about self-consciously. "Hello, Vivian." He frowned ostentatiously at his watch. "I'm afraid I'll have to rush. I've an appointment in the cafeteria with Professor Krader."

Vivian lifted a knowing eyebrow. "How tragic. I thought I might have lunch with you."

"I'm really sorry, Vivian, but this is awfully important."

She ran a hand over his cheek. "Of course, darling. I wouldn't want to keep you from your work. But you will see me tonight, won't you? Call for me at about seven."

Krader was downstairs at their table. Norman noticed that as usual the tables around Karl were occupied by Coeds. It was always that way, Norman reflected. Karl, tall and with broad shoulders, always attracted women.

"How's it going with Vivian?" Karl asked.

Norman carefully conveyed a spoon of soup to his mouth and swallowed. "Fine. I'm taking her out again tonight."

Karl let his eyes go around the room and he smiled at some of the girls. "Nice red-head in the corner," he said.

Norman kept his eyes on his food and said what was expected of him. "You really shouldn't notice things like that."

Karl shrugged his shoulders. "There's no harm in being friendly." He stirred his coffee. "By the way, what's this between you and my wife this last week or so? What I mean is why does she have it in for you?"

"I don't know," Norman said.

"The other day I told her about how you saved my life on Okinawa. She laughed about it."

Yes, Norman thought bitterly, she would laugh. How ridiculous, Normie in the army? And a hero too? You must be joking.

"Somehow she got the idea that you were a 4-F, or something," Karl said.

Norman looked up to find Karl staring darkly at a petite blonde girl and a good-looking boy who took seats at a table nearby. "Damn bitch," Karl muttered.

Norman called for Vivian at precisely seven-thirty. She met him outside the Sorority House dressed in a fluffy sweater and with a light coat thrown over her shoulders.

"They have a new 3-D at the State," Norman said. "Should be quite absorbing and I understand educational."

She took his arm. "Who wants to see a stuffy movie on a night like this."

Norman had no choice but to fall in step with her. They passed couples strolling arm in arm and Norman was certain they turned to watch him.

Vivian led him to a bench and they sat down. She examined him with disconcerting objectivity and her eyes reflected the moonlight. "You love me, don't you, darling," she said.

Norman felt panic rising within him.

"You do, don't you?" her voice was silk with a hard glowing sheen.

The thought of the irritating smiling faculty members flashed through Norman's mind and he remembered the oblique taunts of Laura. "Of course, I do," he heard himself say defiantly. He was startled, but he repeated it experimentally. "Yes. I love you."

Vivian's smile was lazy and satisfied and Norman could feel a chill at the back of his neck. She moved closer to him. "Well?" she said. "Aren't you going to kiss me?"

Norman's arms went slowly and reluctantly around her. Their lips met for several seconds. Her lips were warm and in spite of himself he felt a strange excitement. He caressed her cheek, and his fingers slid down gradually just under her chin. Her throat was soft too, so soft, and he could feel the excitement growing.

He heard footsteps coming up the path and guiltily took away his hands. Vivian stood up and brushed her skirt. "I'm hungry," she said. "Let's go someplace where there are lights and people."

They began walking. "Lord how I hate that awful Chemistry," Vivian said. "I don't think I'm the type for college, do you Normie?"

By nine o'clock Vivian had developed her usual headache and Norman dropped her off at the Sorority house. He went away in a gloomy mood, following an aimless route until he found himself in the neighborhood of Karl Krader's house. He went slowly toward it and stood outside for a minute before going up the stairs and ringing the bell.

Laura answered the door. "Why, how nice to see you, Normie," she said. Her gray eyes glimmered with faint mockery.

Karl came out of the bathroom, lather on his face and holding a safety razor in one hand. Norman noticed the suppleness of Karl's arms, the smooth tan of his shoulders, and the perfectly tapered torso. He turned away and found that Laura was watching him with narrowed eyes.

"Sit down, Normie," Laura said. "I'll get you a drink." She spoke to Karl with an edge in her voice. "Go back into the bathroom and finish shaving."

Norman rested in an easy chair while Laura went into the kitchen to make the drink. He picked a magazine from the rack beside the chair and noticed that it was a physical culture publication. He leafed through the pages idly scanning the glossy photographs of nearly nude young men in poses emphasizing their shining oiled bodies.

Laura returned with the drink and Norman returned the magazine to the rack.

"Cigarette?" she asked. And then seemed to remember with a smile. "Oh, I forgot. You don't smoke, Normie."

Norman met her eyes tiredly.

"Sometimes Normie does smoke. And he shaves too, just in case you were wondering." Karl came out of the bathroom stuffing his shirt into his trousers. He picked up his jacket and put it on. "Sorry to leave you, Norman. But I've got a department meeting tonight. I can't get out of it and I'm late as it is."

"But you'll stay, won't you, Normie?" Laura said. "Unless you're afraid to be here alone with me."

"Sure," Karl said, grinning. "The strangler hasn't been doing anything for some time now, and who knows, this might be his night."

"We'll protect each other, dear," Laura said. "If he breaks in, I'll fight him off while Normie phones for the police."

Karl went to the door. "But seriously, Laura, I don't want you to leave the house alone."

After he was gone Laura turned on the phonograph for quiet music. "I've been wondering about you and Karl," she said. "You've been friends all your life, haven't you?"

"Yes," Norman said. "All our lives and we went into the army together. They accepted me without hesitation."

They watched each other silently and then Laura rose and went to the closet. She returned with her coat. "I'm going to the drugstore for cigarettes," she said. She picked up a large handbag and waited.

Norman got to his feet.

The moon glowed dully behind the scudding clouds and the streets were shadowed between the lonely street lamps. After they walked a block, Laura said, "I know that Karl is apparently more friendly with his Coeds than he should be."

"There's nothing to it," Norman said.

"I was quite disturbed by it at first. Considerably so. But not now. The truth gradually dawned on me that he really wasn't interested in girls at all. He was merely trying to show the world that he was something that he was not. He isn't interested in women, is he Normie?"

Norman's voice was low and controlled. "You really can't tell by the way a man looks, Laura. You can't tell it by the way they walk, or by their delicate manner. And quite a few of them do get married . . . for one reason or another. It must have been a surprise to you to find that out."

"In a way it's funny," Laura said. "I thought the real reason you came to the house was because you wanted to see me. I was flattered."

Norman shook his head sadly. "I may look like I'm one, Laura, but I'm not. And Karl is. And so we're friends, and only that."

Laura stopped. "I don't believe that. I still love him, Normie, and I don't believe what you're saying."

Norman looked deep into the darkness of the empty lot beside which they stood and then along the deserted street. This could be a place, he thought. A man could hide here and wait. Perhaps there would be a scream, but not if he were careful.

Norman heard the snap as Laura opened her purse, then dropped it. He bent down to pick it up.

"It's bad about those girls," Laura said, her voice above him. "But I didn't know then. I thought it was young women he wanted and I hated all of them."

Norman's head jerked back as the wire tightened around his neck. It cut deep into his flesh as Laura twisted the rod, and before the pain made him deaf to sound, he heard her low mad laughter.

Good-by, World

August 1956

Edwards sat on the bunk with his knees close together and sweat glossed the backs of his hands. His eyes were big with long-time fear as he watched me read.

I went through the papers slowly, turning each sheet face down after I finished it. I spent thirty seconds on the last one and then I turned it over too.

I shrugged my shoulders slightly and lit a cigarette. "I guess you've had it," I said. "There's nothing else left."

He leaned forward. "No, Mr. Hudson. You can try once more. You've got to."

I flipped the burnt match through the bars of the cell into the corridor. "Why not face it. I've done everything that can be done."

Edwards' voice trembled. "Try the governor again. He can stop it."

"He has," I said. "Four times so far."

His head moved in spasmodic jerks. "The Supreme Court again, Mr. Hudson. Please."

"It wouldn't do any good," I said. "Even if we had the time. I've had them refuse to review it twice."

Edwards' knuckles went to his lips. "Justice Barton," he said. "He's in this state now on vacation. He could stop it."

"Maybe," I said. "For a little while."

He got to his feet and he had to lean against the wall. "He's got a cabin near Harville. He's an important man. A big man. The people there would know where it is."

I dropped my cigarette and ground it with my foot. "What am I supposed to show him? I've run through every piddling little irregularity and they're not enough to get you a new trial."

His voice was sharp with panic. "I've got just five hours left, Mr. Hudson."

I glanced at my watch. "Four hours and forty-six minutes."

I put the papers back into my briefcase and then I stood there thinking and rocking slightly on my heels. "All right," I said, after a while. "I'll try to get to Justice Barton."

He tried to clasp my hand, but I shoved him aside and rapped on the bars.

The guard came and led the way back up the corridor. "The warden wants to see you for a minute," he said.

We went through the gates of the death house and into the sunshine outside.

The guard glanced at me, interest and coldness mingled in his eyes. "What do you do it for?" he asked. "If anybody deserves to die, Edwards sure as hell does."

"I'm a lawyer," I said. "I owe it to my client to try every means at my disposal."

"That sounds real nice, Mr. Hudson. Do you ever dream about the Jeffers kid he butchered?"

We went up the stairs of the administration building.

Warden Hall was waiting in his anteroom. He worked on his cigar with his lips when he saw me. "Did you say your last good-by to Edwards?"

"I don't know," I said. "I may see him again."

He took the cigar out of his mouth. "Do you expect to get a big reputation out of this?"

"I've got a reputation," I said.

"Then it's money."

"I'm not making a fortune from Edwards, if that's what you mean."

He moved to his office door. "Come into the office." He looked at the guard. "You better come along too, Jim."

We went inside and Mr. Jeffers was standing at the window looking out.

Jeffers turned and his mouth opened slightly when he saw me. He looked at the Warden and then at me again and there was silence.

"If anything happens to me, Warden," I said clearly. "I'll hold you responsible."

Jeffers met my eyes and he licked his lips. Then he nodded, as if to himself, and started walking toward me.

"I'll kill him," Jeffers said. "I'll kill the dirty shyster."

The guard and the Warden moved forward and forced Jeffers into a leather easy chair.

"Easy now, Mr. Jeffers," the Warden said. "I know just how you feel."

Jeffers struggled for a few moments and then became quiet. "All right, Warden," he said. "I promise I won't do anything."

I looked at Hall. "This is why you wanted to see me? You wanted a face to face meeting with the bereaved father and perhaps a few dramatics? Was I supposed to burst into tears of contrition?"

Hall reddened. "You know what I'd like to do, Hudson? I'd like to leave you alone in this room with him. Just for ten minutes."

I thought about it and smiled.

Hall came close to me. "You got a kid about the age of the Jeffers girl. Suppose it had happened to her?"

I didn't say anything.

"Edwards isn't innocent," Hall said. "There's not a chance of it. You know that and I know that."

"Yes," I said. "We know that."

Hall walked away from me and then turned. "Maybe you think he shouldn't die for it? Is that it?"

"No," I said. "He ought to die."

"You've got no use for him yourself and yet you've been trying every trick in the book to keep him from the gas chamber. You've dragged this out for three years."

I regarded him for a moment. "I think I'll be going," I said.

Hall looked at me curiously. "You got some place important to go?"

"Yes," I said. "One more try." Jeffers' eyes met mine.

"One more," I said. "I'm going to see Justice Barton." I turned to Hall. "You might get a phone call."

I drove back to the city and had a meal before I began the trip to Harville.

I got there at about six-thirty and dropped in at the office of the small weekly to ask about Justice Barton.

I had several cups of coffee and some sandwiches at a small restaurant and then I drove out of Harville. I followed the rutted mountain road for three miles until I came to the turn-off.

It was dusk when I parked my car in front of the cabin and went to the door.

Justice Barton was a small sere man in a plaid wool shirt and he looked at the briefcase under my arm.

"Richard Hudson," I said.

He nodded and smiled thinly. "I almost expected it. I almost made a bet with myself that you would think of this."

He stood in the doorway for half a minute, examining me, and then he turned and walked back into the cabin.

I followed him and we sat down at the table where a gasoline lantern hissed its bright light.

He looked at his watch. "It's almost seven-thirty. Edwards is supposed to die at eight, isn't he?"

"Yes," I said.

He rubbed the side of his seamed face slowly and stared at me. "You waited until the last minute."

"I didn't think of this," I said. "Edwards did."

His eyes moved to the briefcase.

"It will take at least an hour to go through it," I said.

He smiled tiredly. "New evidence? Prejudiced witnesses? Irregularities?"

I shook my head. "Nothing new, but this is his last chance. It's an hour of your time. Just one hour."

Our eyes met for awhile and then he got up. "I don't have a phone here," he said. "We'll have to go to Harville."

We stopped at a cafe in town and Barton went to the telephone.

I glanced up at the electric wall clock and it was seven-fifty. I ordered two cups of coffee and opened the briefcase.

When Barton came back, he sat down wearily. "I called," he said. "And now they're waiting."

He took a pair of glasses out of his shirt pocket and cleaned them with a handkerchief. He looked at the stack of papers and then began to read.

It was almost nine o'clock when he finished. He took off his glasses and rubbed the bridge of his nose. "There's nothing here," he said slowly. "Nothing at all to stop it."

I picked up the papers, tamped them into evenness, and slipped them back into the briefcase. I snapped the lock and ordered two more cups of coffee.

Barton stared at his coffee for a minute or two and then he got up. He went to the cashier for change and walked into the phone booth.

I got back to the city at about midnight and drove to the Raven Bar on the west side.

Jeffers was alone in a rear booth and I sat down in front of him.

He smiled at his bottle of beer. "They had to carry him," he said softly. He put his thumb and forefinger about an inch apart. "He was that close. That close and then they stopped and waited."

"It was the first phone call from Barton," I said.

He nodded and kept smiling. "It was just right. I liked it. I liked watching him wait to die."

Jeffers tilted the bottle to his lips and then wiped away foam. "And Lord how he screamed when they dragged him off the bench and went on with it an hour later."

The waitress brought my drink and we waited until she was gone.

Jeffers leaned forward and touched my arm. "He stopped screaming when they closed the door." He nodded his head and laughed. "Then he tried to hold his breath."

Jeffers was quiet for a while, thinking about it. "A thousand deaths," he said softly. "That's what I wanted for him."

"That's what you got," I said.

His hands gripped the bottle. "It makes up for what he did to my little girl, doesn't it, Mr. Hudson?"

"Yes," I said.

His eyes stared into mine. "I would have killed you if he got off, Mr. Hudson."

"There wasn't a chance of it," I said. "I told you that."

Jeffers put his hand in the pocket of his coat and brought out the brown paper wrapped package. "You did a good job, Mr. Hudson. You drew it out for three years and the last part was the best of all."

I tore open a corner of the package to make sure the money was there, and then I put it in my pocket.

Jeffers looked up as I got to my feet. "Mr. Hudson," he asked. "They always need witnesses for executions, don't they?"

"Yes," I said.

His eyes were bright. "Can anybody get to be a witness? Can I watch again?"

"I don't know," I said. "Why don't you ask."

I left him smiling to himself.

The Partners

September 1956

"Too bad," I said. "We all liked him."

"Let's hope you mean it," Lieutenant Palmer said. "Because it wasn't hit and run. It was murder."

I raised an eyebrow. "You can tell?"

"No skid marks. No paint chips. No broken glass. No nothing that goes with that kind of thing. He was beaten to death and dropped off on the road."

"And so?"

"And so I got to find who did it and why. This is one of the places I look." His eyes went over the three of us. "You three own this big, swanky nightclub?"

"That's right," I said. "Partners. Eddie Fletcher, Louie Nicolle and me. Danny Neil."

Lieutenant Palmer was a sandy-haired man with shrewd blue eyes, "What was Harold Romaine around here?"

"He was our bookkeeper," Louie Nicolle said. Louie's short heavy body was wedged between the arms of the gray leather chair. The rings on his fingers glistened as he brought the scotch and soda to his lips.

Lieutenant Palmer smiled thinly. "I always got my suspicions about bookkeepers. There could be something that smells in that direction."

Eddie Fletcher toyed nervously with his cigarette case. "Nothing at all there. He was as honest as they come."

Palmer still smiled. "You don't mind if I have your books checked? I might find that one or all three of you had a good motive for getting rid of him."

I returned his smile. "Not at all, Lieutenant. Any time."

"Maybe it was someone in his personal life," Louie said.

Palmer closed his notebook. "We're checking."

"Poor Harry," I said. "Any relatives?"

"None that we know of except his father. I already talked to the old boy, but he wasn't much help. He's not quite all in order between the ears."

Palmer put the notebook in his pocket. "About those books. I'll have somebody sent over later today. I like to be thorough." He opened the door and paused. "By the way, where were the three of you early this morning? Say between two and seven?"

"The three of us were playing poker," Eddie said. "Right here in this club until nearly eight."

"That's nice," Palmer said, nodding his head. "And probably not one of you even left to go to the can. Good bladders." He waggled a few fingers in goodbye. "I'll be back."

Eddie went to the corner bar and made himself another stiff drink. "You sure it won't show up in the books?" he asked.

"No," I said. "If Harry could do anything, he could keep books. It won't show."

Louie spoke around his cigar. "How much do you think he took us for before we caught on?"

"It's hard to say," I said. "Not less than twenty-five G's. Could be as much as fifty."

"The bastard," Louie growled.

Eddie turned to me. "You could of made it look better."

I shrugged my shoulders. "You guys were all hot and bothered for a rush job," I said. "Besides, it was getting daylight and I had to get rid of the body."

"I wonder if he really spent it," Louie said. "You think maybe it's stashed away somewhere?"

"You heard him keep squealing that it was the horses," I said. "We'll just have to believe that."

Maxie, the head waiter, knocked on the door and poked his head in. "Some old gent wants to see you. Any one of you. I think he's Harry's old man."

"Let's see what he looks like," I said.

Maxie had a surprised expression on his face when he came back with Harry's father. He slid the .45 across the desk to me.

I extracted the full chip from the automatic and then looked at Harry's father. Mr. Romaine was a small, frail man with silver hair and blue eyes that blinked often.

He looked about the room. "Fine," he said. "It would have been fine. All three of you here."

"All right, Pop," I said. "Tell us all about it."

His wild eyes met mine. "I don't know which one of you it was," he said in a high uncertain voice. "I don't know which one of you killed him, but I know you're all guilty."

I studied him. "Why should we be guilty of anything?"

"Because you knew what Harry was doing," he said. "He told me all about it when he thought you knew." He smiled slyly. "But I didn't tell the lieutenant. I want to take care of this myself."

He looked down at the gun on my desk. "I'll use something else," he said. "I'll use something else to kill all three of you."

I got to my feet. "You're going home now, Pop, and get some rest. You'll feel better tomorrow." I took hold of his arm at the elbow and steered him toward the door.

Behind me Louie spoke softly. "How much was it, Pop?"

The old man twisted his head as I shoved him through the door. "Thirty-one thousand," he said, and his laugh was almost a giggle. "Thirty-one thousand dollars."

"The bastard," Louie muttered under his breath. "The dirty crooked bastard."

Outside the office we stepped aside to let Jean Taylor pass. Jean has flowing gold hair and gray eyes that remain perpetually quiet and unsurprised. She is part of the floor show and she sings songs that are as simple and restrained as she is.

She stopped to look at the old man and then at me. "Be careful with him," she said. "Don't hurt him."

I smiled. "I won't disturb a feather in his head," I said. "I'm only showing him how to find the back door." I took Harry's father into the alley and pointed him toward the street. "Run along now and get some sleep. I know it's hit you pretty hard, but don't let it give you any bad ideas."

Jean was still standing where we'd met her in the corridor when I came back. "What did he want?" she asked.

"Harry's father," I said. "He didn't get what he wanted."

She tilted her serious face slightly. "I'm still curious."

"Something to do with Harry," I said.

"What about Harry?"

"I guess you haven't heard yet," I said. "Harry got himself killed last night."

She looked deep into my eyes.

"Yes," I said. "Murdered." I patted her lightly on the head. "Don't take it so hard. We can always get another bookkeeper."

After we closed the club, I went to my apartment and slept until two in the afternoon. I'd just finished shaving and was using the after-shaving lotion when the buzzer sounded. I grabbed a cigarette on the way to the door.

"Come on in, Lieutenant," I said. "Care for some coffee?"

"No," Palmer said and took a seat in the arm chair. He pursed his lips for a moment before he spoke. "I came to bring you the news. Louie Nicolle got his throat cut at about eleven this morning."

I thought about it and got to my feet. "Just a second," I said. I went into the kitchen, poured myself coffee and cream and brought it back into the living room.

He watched me. "Are you sure you're interested?"

"I could cry," I said. "But not until I've had my coffee."

Palmer seemed about to continue and then it looked like he thought of something else. He cocked his head. "What happens to Louie's share of the club now?"

"It goes to Eddie and me," I said. "The setup is now fifty-fifty." I sipped the coffee. "I was sleeping alone at eleven this morning," I said. "Should I phone a lawyer?"

Slowly he unwrapped a cigar. "No, you don't need a lawyer or an alibi. We know who did it and we got a witness."

"You could have said that right at the beginning," I said.

"For some reason I like to see you worried," Palmer said. "Not that you show it, but I know it's there." He sucked on his cigar until it was lit. "Around eleven this morning, a chamber maid was at one of the linen closets in the hall near Louie's door. She saw a little old man buzz Louie's door. When Louie opened the door, the little gent whipped out a sharp knife." Palmer drew his finger across his throat. "Just like that. No fuss, no bother, no talk."

"Are you sure you don't want coffee?" I asked.

Palmer rubbed the side of his face as he watched me. "And then the little man calmly wipes his knife on Louie's shirt and quietly walks away while Louie is still kicking."

Palmer sighed. "By the time the maid believes her eyes and makes a noise, he's disappeared down the stairs and out the front door. We're still looking for him."

"I hope you get him, Lieutenant," I said.

"Thanks," he said dryly. "A little old man, about five foot two. Gray hair and blue eyes. Does that strike a note?"

"Nothing at all," I said.

"It was a whole melody to me," Palmer said. "Seeing as how I'd had a conversation with a man of that description just recently."

I nodded.

Palmer went on. "I went to see Harry Romaine's father. Nobody home. The door happens to be unlocked and so naturally I check for burglars. When I leave, I have a couple of old man Romaine's photographs in my pocket. The maid does a positive identification."

He crossed his legs and leaned back in his chair. "There must be something you forgot to tell me the last time we met."

"Sorry, Lieutenant. I can't think of a thing."

Palmer stared at the ceiling. "Fifty-fifty now," he said thoughtfully. He got to his feet. "Anyway, I hope you think enough of Louie to give him a nice funeral."

When he was gone, I went to the phone and called Eddie Fletcher. "Palmer been there yet?" I asked.

"No," Eddie said nervously. "What for should he want to see me?"

"Louie got his throat cut this morning," I said. "Harry's father did the job and he's still loose."

I could almost see Eddie sweating and I smiled. "Relax," I said. "The cops will get him sooner or later. In the meantime make sure you know who it is when you answer the door."

I went back into the kitchen and had some more coffee and toast. It wasn't a bad deal at that, I thought. With Louie gone, that made me about fifteen grand a year richer. The coffee tasted good.

At seven in the evening I was getting ready to go to the club when the buzzer sounded again. I started for the door and then stopped as I thought of Louie. Better to be careful than to be suddenly dead, I said to myself. I wrapped a suitcoat around my left forearm and held it near my throat as I opened the door.

For an old man, he could still move fast. If my arm hadn't been up there he would have got me. But as it was, he just sliced through the coat and nicked my hand a little.

He was pulling back for another try when I got his wrist. I pulled him into the room and twisted his arm until he sank to his knees. The knife slipped out of his grip and thudded to the rug.

I jerked him to his feet and got ready to give him a good going over. He looked at me with those mild watery eyes and I saw that he was about as far off his rocker as you could get. He didn't have enough sense left to tie his shoe laces, and the only thing his mind was working on was the idea of killing me and Eddie.

To start off with, I let him have an easy right to the chin. He must have been weaker than I thought, because that took the light out of his eyes and he collapsed. I kicked him in the ribs as he lay on the floor, but it was unnecessary, for he was out cold.

I was reaching for the knife, when the idea flickered in my mind. I left the knife there and lit a cigarette. After a few slow puffs, I bent down again and picked the knife up, being careful not to touch the handle.

I put the knife in an empty half gallon milk bottle, wrapped that in a towel and put it in a shoe box.

Then I went into the bathroom and got a couple of sleeping tablets. I dissolved them in warm milk and waited until the old man came to. While he was still blinking, I put the glass to his lips and he drank automatically, like a child.

He got to his feet and I pushed him onto the davenport. He tried to get up, but I kept my hand on his chest until the pills took effect. When he was asleep, I left the apartment with the shoe box.

It was quiet beyond the door when I pushed the buzzer to Eddie's apartment. "It's all right," I said. "It's only me."

The door opened to the length of its chain while Eddie made absolutely sure. When he let me in, I saw a bottle on the table and Eddie had the smell of its contents on his breath. I put the shoe box beside the bottle.

Eddie licked his lips. "I'm not coming to the club tonight. I'm staying here until they find that crazy old coot."

"Good idea," I said. "You got to be careful."

"Maybe we ought to tell Palmer that Harry's old man is out to get all of us."

"Then he'd want to know why," I said.

Eddie fidgeted and then thought of pouring himself another drink.

I waited for him to finish and to put down the glass. When Eddie's eyes shifted away from me I slammed a hard right to his chin. I was ready to do more if that wasn't enough, but Eddie dropped and lay still.

I went into the kitchen for a knife. I turned Eddie on his back, and in a moment, being careful not to get any blood on me, it was done.

I washed the knife carefully and put it back in the kitchen. Then I opened the shoebox and got out the knife. Being careful not to get my prints on it, I put some blood on the blade and put it beside Eddie. On the way downstairs, I dropped the milk bottle and the wrappings into the incinerator.

After the first floor show, I spoke to Jean. She was wearing silver lame that clung to her like a hungry lover, tight and intimate.

"Honey," I said. "Sometimes I get the feeling that I've just got to have company after we close up."

When Jean looked at you, there were times when you wondered whether she was looking deep into your mind. "Sometimes I get that feeling too," she said. She regarded me soberly. "All right," she added, "you tell me what it's going to be."

"Your last show is at one," I said. "I'll knock off around midnight and go back to my apartment to change my shirt and then I'll be at your place at about two."

She looked into the distance and then back at me. "Two hours to change a shirt?"

I quit earlier than twelve because I was getting worried that Harry's father might wake up. I got back to my apartment at eleven thirty and used plenty of caution when I opened the door. I didn't want him waiting for me with another knife. But I had nothing to worry about. He was still stretched out on the davenport, breathing like one who's deep in sleep.

I looked down at him and thought for a moment that it might be better if I got rid of him permanently, but I changed my mind. He might babble to Palmer about the thirty-one thousand, but it would be the word of a loony against mine.

I went to the phone and got in touch with Homicide and Lieutenant Palmer.

"If you're still looking for old man Romaine," I told him, "you can stop. He's here in my apartment."

Over the phone I heard the sound of chair legs scraping and I guessed my words must have made him sit up.

"Be damn careful," he said. "The guy's nuts and dangerous."

"Not right now," I said. "He's asleep."

I went to the kitchen and got a knife. I put his fingerprints on it and added a few of mine. I put the knife on a table. I got a cold wet cloth from the bathroom and used it on his face until I got him back to consciousness.

He was still groggy when Palmer came with two plainclothes men.

"There he is," I said. "I opened the door and he took a swipe at me." I pointed to the knife. "I got nicked a little and had to put him to sleep."

Romaine was handcuffed then and the two detectives had to practically carry him.

Palmer's eyes followed the departing detectives. "I'd give a lot to know how much of what he'll say will be sane." He shrugged and went to the door. "This ought to make the other half of your fifty-fifty deal calm down. He was pretty jumpy when I saw him yesterday."

"I'm sure it will," I said. "Eddie likes security."

I got to Jean's apartment as fast as I could after they'd gone.

Her gray eyes went over me and she smiled ever so slightly. "You seem pleased with yourself," she said.

"I feel like I look," I said.

I sat down while she went into the kitchenette to mix drinks. When she handed me mine, I drank deeply with satisfaction.

She sat on the hassock, watching me. "Tell me about it," she said. "I'd like to know just what it is that can make you happy."

I rattled the ice cubes in my glass and drained about half of what was left. "Harry's old man tried to kill me this morning."

"I was wondering if he would," she said.

She watched my hand as I loosened my tie.

"I took away his sticker," I said. "And turned him over to the police." I yawned. "I had a hard day, baby." I stretched out my legs. "You know, now that I think of it, Harry was kind of a queer duck too. It must run in the family. I don't think he ever even went out with dames."

"The quiet type," she said. "Sometimes they give that impression."

"And yet that quiet bastard . . ."

I stopped and grinned sleepily. "How about sitting here next to me, honey?"

"And yet?" she asked, her eyes intent on my face. "What were you going to say?"

"Nothing," I said and closed my eyes. I felt relaxed—cozy.

"And yet that quiet bastard managed to steal thirty-one thousand dollars from you. Is that what you were going to say?"

I opened my eyes. "Who have you been talking to?"

Her face looked blurred to me. "We were going to make it fifty, Danny," she said. "An even fifty thousand dollars before we left."

It seemed to take me a while to understand what she was saying. "You and Harry?"

"Me and Harry," she said. "My husband and I."

I could feel myself sweating with the effort of trying to get to my feet. I didn't make it. "That drink . . ."

"And now I have thirty-one thousand dollars," she said. "But I don't have Harry."

I tried to shake the fog out of my head, but I was doing it slowly and it didn't work at all.

"I think Harry's father had the right idea about the way to do it," Jean said quietly. "Sleeping pills are too easy for you."

I heard her get to her feet. "It's going to be you now," she said. "And then I'm going to kill Eddie."

In the wild part of my mind, that seemed funny. She was going to kill Eddie. I let the laugh come to my lips.

It stayed there until I heard her in the kitchen opening a drawer, the rattle of cutlery.

Then I stopped laughing.

Degree of Guilt

December 1956

Jim Stauffer sat on the hardwood bench, and his right wrist was handcuffed to the radiator. He didn't look up at me.

"It's a mistake," he said tightly. "I swear I didn't do it."

Sergeant Morris had one foot on a straight-backed chair. He took the cigar out of his mouth and looked despicably at Jim. "You're going to have trouble persuading us."

I watched Jim for a few moments and then I turned to Morris. "I'd like to see my daughter now if it's all right," I said.

He took his foot off the chair, and I followed him into the next room.

Millie was sitting on a leather davenport with her hands folded on her lap. A lean man with quiet brown eyes was at the desk smoking a cigarette, observing her.

Millie looked up at me with dark eyes. "The doctor examined me," she said.

I put my hand on her head and smoothed her hair gently. "I know," I said.

The man at the desk got up, and Sergeant Morris said, "This is Dr. Kaplan."

Dr Kaplan glanced at the notes on his desk. "She says she's thirteen."

"That's right," I said. "Thirteen."

Millie's eyes moved to Sergeant Morris. "Mr. Stauffer and Daddy have been friends all their lives. They go fishing together, and I didn't think he would do anything like that."

Dr. Kaplan rubbed one of his eyebrows. "I haven't given her anything. I didn't think a sedative was necessary."

"I just went to get your tacklebox, Daddy," Millie said. "You said you left it at his house, and I thought you'd want it."

Her eyes went to the floor. "When Mr. Stauffer let me go, I ran next door to Mrs. Hendricks and she called the police."

I went to the window and looked out. Two hundred yards of green lawn separated the rear of the police station from the next building, a large brick warehouse.

"What are you going to do about it?" I asked.

"I don't know how it will end," Morris said. "The maximum is life, but some get as little as five years."

I turned around. "And eligible for parole in three?"

Morris shrugged his shoulders. "Maybe I agree with you that it isn't enough, but I don't make the laws."

Dr. Kaplan leaned against his desk and stared thoughtfully at a picture on the wall.

Morris unwrapped a fresh cigar. "He could have killed her," he said. "They do that when they know they can be identified."

"Sometimes," Dr. Kaplan said quietly. He smiled slightly to himself. "And then some of them aren't killers." His eyes came to me. "Is your wife here?"

"No," I said, "She died ten years ago."

Millie's eyes were watching me.

I walked over to her. "It's all right, honey. Everything will be all right."

I turned to Sergeant Morris. "I'd like to have one more look at Jim."

He exchanged glances with Dr. Kaplan, and then Kaplan came with us.

Jim had a cigarette in his left hand and he looked up momentarily as I entered the room.

I walked toward him, but one of the officers stepped in front of me.

"Easy now, Mr. Holman," he said quietly.

I stared past him for a few more seconds and then I moved back.

Dr. Kaplan spoke. "Mr. Stauffer," he said. "We have a polygraph, a lie detector. However, it's your right to refuse to take the test."

Stauffer licked his lips. "I refuse," he said. "I'm not going to take it."

My eyes went to the holster of one of the uniformed patrolmen. Dr. Kaplan was watching me and he shook his head slowly from side to side.

I met his eyes. "Do you know how I feel?"

He smiled slightly. "No," he said. "I really don't."

The door opened and a plainclothes' man came in. "Stauffer's lawyer is here," he said.

I walked out of the room and went back to Millie. "Come on, honey," I said. "We're going now."

She looked up. "Are we going home?"

"No," I said. "We're going to a hotel for awhile."

I registered at the Marshall Arms as Mr. James West and daughter, and we went upstairs to our room.

"Are you hungry, honey?" I asked.

She stood in the center of the room and looked at the vanity table. "Yes," she said.

I ordered a meal brought up, and when Millie was finished, I said, "Will you be all right for a little while, honey? I've got to go back home and get a few of our things."

She fingered the gleaming silver coffee urn. "I'll be fine, Daddy."

A dark blue sedan was parked in front of my house and I pulled up behind it.

Dr. Kaplan was on my porch swing smoking a cigarette. He stopped his dreaming and looked at me. "Your daughter isn't with you?"

"No," I said. "We're staying at a hotel."

He nodded. "There were reporters here when I came, and they'll be back."

I sat down next to him. "Well?" I asked.

He crossed his legs and looked out at the approaching dusk. "Stauffer talked to his lawyer after you left. They've decided to enter a guilty plea."

I watched his face for awhile. "You don't think he's guilty?" I asked.

He dropped the cigarette to the porch floor and ground it out with his toe. "I don't think he's innocent." He got to his feet and looked down at me. "Stauffer and his lawyer will probably try to get it changed to knowledge and abuse, you understand."

I waited. In the shadows his teeth were white in a thin humorless smile. He seemed to be listening to the quietness of the deserted street.

Then he said, "That's not rape."

I looked at my hand. "Why did you come here?" I asked.

He thought a moment. "A matter of duty," he said. "And perhaps curiosity. I wanted to know what your thoughts are."

I remained quiet.

His eyes went to his watch. "I'm having Stauffer brought to my office this evening. I'll know a little more when I'm through with him." He tapped a fresh cigarette out of his pack and lit it. He exhaled smoke. "Who does she take after? Her mother?"

I looked at him and was silent.

He went halfway down the steps and then turned. "I'll have to testify," he said, and there was a sadness in his smile. "I'm a doctor, you know." He hesitated another moment. "By the way, Mr. Holman. How did your wife die?"

I listened to the sound of a cricket on a neighbor's lawn. "A hunting accident," I said. "I shot her."

When he was gone, I unlocked the front door and went inside. I found a suitcase and went through Millie's things, packing what I thought she might need in the next few days.

I put her cotton pajamas into the suitcase and went to the closet. A patch of red between two folded blankets on a shelf caught my eye. I fingered the red dress for a moment, before I put it into the suitcase.

Then I sat down on her bed and smoked a slow cigarette. When I was through, I went to the dresser. I touched the brush and comb on top of it; then I opened one of the drawers. I took out a pair of antique pearl earrings and a lipstick and put them in my pocket.

I took the suitcase to the gun cabinet in my workshop. The 30/06, broken down, fitted diagonally in the suitcase. I put a handful of cartridges in my coat pocket.

I drove my car downtown and parked in the dark alley next to the furniture warehouse. By the illumination of the dashboard lights, I fitted the rifle together. Then I got out of the car and pulled down the fire escape on the side of the building and climbed to the second floor.

I slipped a cartridge into the chamber of the rifle and, using my 6X scope as a binocular, I searched the lighted windows of the big building across the lawn until I found Dr. Kaplan's office.

He was at his desk, a cigarette in an ashtray next to him drifting smoke, and Jim Stauffer was in a chair facing him. A uniformed officer sat on the davenport, one leg crossed over the other.

I steadied the forearm of my rifle on the fire escape railing. The cross-hairs of the scope lingered for a moment on Dr. Kaplan and then moved on to Jim.

Jim was leaning forward and talking, when I squeezed the trigger. I held the scope on the window just long enough to make sure I had done the job right. Then I went down the fire escape.

It took about ten seconds to break down the rifle and put it back in the suitcase. When I started my car and drove down the alley, the back doors of the police station were still closed.

At the Marshall Arms Hotel, I parked my car and took the suitcase with me up to our room.

Millie was in front of the vanity combing her hair.

She looked at me and smiled. "I phoned downstairs and had them send up a comb and brush. I thought you'd forget. I bought a nightgown, too, Daddy. It's lovely, A beautiful azure."

I put the suitcase on the floor.

She examined herself critically in the mirror. "Will my name be in the newspapers, Daddy?"

"No," I said. "They're not allowed to print it."

She ran the comb through her long hair slowly and smiled.

I sat down in a chair and closed my eyes.

"That's the worst crime in the world, isn't it, Daddy?" she asked.

"Some people think it is," I said.

She was silent for a few moments and then she said, "That's what I thought."

I opened my eyes, and she was still at the mirror. I reached into my coat pocket and took out the lipstick. I walked over and put it on the vanity.

She looked at it and then at me. "Lots of girls my age use lipstick." She smiled at me. "Of course it's all right, Daddy."

I went back to the chair and sat down.

"Mr. Stauffer is sorry now, I'll bet," she said. "And he'll stay in jail for life, or maybe they'll hang him." She turned and looked at me. "Even a lawyer won't get him off, will he, Daddy?"

"A lawyer won't help him," I said.

She smiled. "I'm glad. Because Mr. Stauffer has lots of money and maybe he could hire a real smart lawyer. He showed me his bank book once." Her eyes went back to her reflection and she studied it. "He's tight," she said. "A tight skinflint."

I sat quietly and waited.

After awhile, she said, "I don't look like I'm thirteen, do I, Daddy?"

"No," I said.

She turned again. "Do I look much like mother?"

"Yes," I said. "You're just like she was."

Millie was silent, thinking, and then she got up and came over to sit on the arm of my chair.

"Mr. Stauffer is desperate, isn't he, Daddy?"

I didn't say anything.

"What I mean is that he'll say all kinds of nasty things because he's desperate. But everybody will believe me, won't they, Daddy?"

"Most of them," I said.

She brushed my hair absently. Her eyes were gleaming as she stared into the distance, and there was a small smile on her face. Her lips moved and the words were soft and low. "The dirty, tight bastard. He'll be sorry now." And then she stretched, slowly and luxuriously. "I'm going to bed now, Daddy."

She went to the bathroom and when she came back she was wearing a filmy negligee. She pulled back the covers of one of the twin beds and got inside.

"Good night, Daddy," she said.

I looked down at her. Her face was freshly washed and her light hair was bound in a blue ribbon.

"Good night, honey," I said. "Good night, my little girl."

I leaned over and kissed her.

I went back to my chair and sat there, quietly smoking a cigarette until I heard her breathing deeply and evenly. Her face was relaxed, and she smiled as she slept.

I went to the suitcase and opened it. I pushed aside the red dress my money hadn't bought and picked up the rifle and put it together, methodically.

My hand went into my pocket and touched the pearl earrings that Jim had once shown me. They had been in his family for generations, and he always kept them in his wall safe.

I put two cartridges in the magazine of the rifle. Soon my daughter would be sleeping for good.

Divide and Conquer

February 1957

Charley phoned for me at around eleven and I walked the block and a half to the Green Dollar. The blackjack tables were going all right and the one-arms were taking heavy play, but I thought that something would have to be done for the faro games.

The Green Dollar is the one I started with, but now I've got two more places up the street. When I'm not around, I've got Charley running things.

He was sitting at the desk and looking worried when I opened the office door.

"We got trouble, Tommy," he said.

I lowered myself into a chair and lit up a king-size cigarette. "Don't we always have something on hand to annoy us?" I said.

"This is something different." Charley swiveled his chair to face me. "Maybe we got nothing to worry about and maybe it's big."

I bent the match and flipped it into an ash tray. "Somebody moving in?"

"Looks like it," Charley said. "A big gorilla was here sticking a finger in my chest. He let me know that he and his associates would appreciate a five hundred dollar weekly donation regular every week."

"You should have had him tossed out," I said.

Charley snorted at my suggestion. "I'm a cautious married man with two growing children. I didn't know how many friends he had and I wasn't anxious to find out."

"Anybody we know?"

"From the sound of him, I'd say mid-west. He couldn't be from around here. He thought I owned the joint."

"Think he might really be working alone?"

"Not completely, at any rate. I got the buzz that a runty little character is working the other side of the street. The big boy should get to the Four Deuces pretty soon."

I blew smoke into the air and rested my feet on a hassock. "Did he mention any names?"

"Said I could call him Mugger and that's as far as it went."

Charley took a cigar from the desk humidor and bit off the tip.

"Is anybody kicking in?" I asked.

"The way I get it, these boys just started." Charley lit the cigar. "Everybody's stalling and waiting to see what you're going to do about it."

Charley's eyes met mine. "I'm worried, Tommy," he said. "Gambling's legal in this state and pretty clean. I'd hate to see it spoiled."

The Four Deuces is the biggest and newest of my places. It's part nightclub and I run a floor show to keep the people entertained when they're not gambling.

The food costs me money and I break even on the liquor, but that's the way it always is in a place like mine. It's the big room with the machines, the dice, and the cards that makes it all worthwhile.

When I walked into my office, I found Juanita Reyes with her sandaled feet on my desk and making herself at home with a Manhattan.

She has a nightclub act with feathers and a lot of confidence and right now she was wearing her costume. It consisted of a little here and not so much there, and she had left her feathers in the dressing room.

She waggled a few fingers at me and smiled. "I knew you would come back," she said. "I'm irresistible."

Juanita took her feet off the polished desk and stretched herself lazily for my benefit. "How do you like my new costume? Just feel the material. It's the best."

"Why don't you take it off," I said. "It's a stifling hot night."

She fluffed her Mexican black hair. "It must be dreadfully warm for you, too." Juanita had long slender legs and softly curved thighs. She took a deep breath that put considerable strain on her black net brassiere and held the pose.

"Well," I said, grinning. "What I see seems all right."

She was reaching up behind her for the fasteners when the damn buzzer on my desk sounded.

I clicked on the switch and got the voice of Sid, the chief houseman.

"Something big out here is panting to see you. I smell trouble. You want to see him or do I form a posse and have him thrown out?"

"Send him in," I said. "But stick around in case I scream for help." I looked at Juanita. "You can toddle along. If you stay you'll just distract me."

"No," she said. "I want to watch. But impatiently."

The guy who came in was under six feet, but he carried the weight for somebody a good foot taller. You could blame heredity for his face, but you'd have a better case if you considered what a dozen barroom brawls could do.

He lifted a bushy eyebrow when he saw Juanita and she gave him a slow wink and a twitch of the hips. He stopped in his tracks and stared at her.

Standing at my desk, I snapped my fingers a couple of times. "I'm over here," I said.

He regarded me with acute distaste, but decided he might as well get down to business. "You the guy, Tommy Harrigan what owns dis joint?"

"Dat's me," I said. "And dat's me doll. Don't lay no finger on her."

He scowled at me. "Gettin' immediate to duh point, from now on you pay me five hunnert clams every week. Dis is for me bein' tender to you and not violunt. If you get what I mean."

"I bet he can scratch his knees without bending down," I said. "Juanita, will you see if the cook has any bananas."

"Personally," Juanita said. "I think he's kind of cute."

Mugger's cauliflower ears were reddening. "Dat wise lip makes it six hunnert a week."

"Is there anything else you might want, Bonzo," I asked. "I'll admit your case stumps me. I'm just used to feeding people."

He came toward me, his big ham fist beginning its swing. "Seven hunnert," he growled. "And dis is your receipt in advance."

I stepped away from the punch and picked up a piece of petrified wood I use for a paperweight. After I slipped under his second swing, I let him have the stone with a wallop to his jaw.

His eyes glazed and he dropped without argument to the rug.

Juanita watched his peaceful breathing. "Do you think that was quite fair?" she asked.

"Sure it was fair," I said indignantly as I hefted the paperweight. "This thing isn't heavier than two pounds. He still had a weight advantage of over forty."

Juanita lit a cigarette. "There's something wrong with your logic, but at the moment it escapes me."

I bent down beside Mugger and went through his pockets. Along with the usual things, he had a .45 automatic and a key to room 424 at the Holder Hotel. His wallet told me that his real name was Quincy Elwood Dowd.

"He's got seventeen dollars," I said, grinning up at Juanita. "He could really show you a good time."

"Ha!" she said, shrugging her shoulders. "Money isn't everything."

I unstrapped Mugger's holster and transferred it to my person.

"Why don't you call the police," Juanita said. "It would be so much simpler."

Sid stuck his head through the doorway just then and I had him get a couple of porters to carry Mugger out into the alley.

When I had on my hat and was ready to leave, Juanita put her hand on my shoulder. "Be careful," she said. "You don't know what you'll be missing if you should get killed now."

"Talk, talk," I said, brushing a strand of hair from her forehead. "I'll bet you're a virgin."

Some embarrassment touched her cheeks. "What a nasty thing to say about a modern girl."

At the Holder Hotel I went directly to Freddie, the desk clerk. "You got a big jerk registered here? Dowd is the name."

"Yeah," Freddie said, eyeing the bulge in my coat. "What for you packing a gun?"

"Was he alone?"

"He's got a single," Freddie said. "But he seemed to be traveling with a dame and a small guy." He spun the register around to show me. "They got three next to each other. 423, 424, and 425."

Dowd had number 424. Number 423 was registered in the name of a Miss Mavis Frawley and 425 to a Jim Beaker.

"The dame draws a whistle out of you," Freddie said. "Everything stacked right, but strictly out of stone. Doll face, but not a smile in a carload."

I drummed my fingers on the desk while I thought. "Freddie," I said. "Can you get me a clear empty medicine bottle? And fill it full of water, will you?"

"Okay," he said. "But I won't sleep tonight if you don't give me a glimmer of what's going on."

The smile I gave him was fond and affectionate. "It's too horrible for your young ears."

The man who opened the door to room 425 was a little squirt, but sharp. He had on a blue pin stripe shirt with button-down collar and a nifty blonde hair-line moustache.

I smiled gently as I put the heel of my hand on his nose and shoved hard.

"Hey!" he yelled as he went staggering back on his heels. "What's the big idea?"

I let the front of my sport coat dangle open so he got a look at the gun.

"You a cop, or something?" he asked suspiciously.

"Do I look like a cop, Shorty?"

I gave him a casual swipe with my open palm.

"Hey!" he yelled again. "Cut that out! Just who do you think you are, slappin' a innocent citizen around?"

"I'm practically nobody," I said, regarding him with a quiet smile. "But I represent the *Syndicate*"

"The Syndicate?" he squeaked. "What Syndicate?"

I shook my head sadly at his stupidity. "*The* Syndicate," I said. "And I'm from the Enforcement and Retaliation Division." I fixed him with a gimlet eye. "I've been briefed by the big boys that three of you Easterners are thinking of setting up business here."

He cringed when I lifted my hand to scratch my ear. "Just talk," he said nervously. "I kin listen without you getting free with the hands."

Beaker sweated while I studied him long and carefully. "Yes," I said finally. "You're the spitting image of Hoppy Nolan. Same type. Same build."

Beaker licked his lips. "Who's Hoppy Nolan?"

"Hoppy *was* a small time hood from Philly," I said. "He tried to buck the Syndicate about a year ago." I took off my Panama and held it over my heart for a few solemn seconds. "He got run over by an automobile."

Beaker's Adam's apple was traveling up and down.

"It was a tragedy and never should have happened," I said. "But the bottoms of Hoppy's feet were burned pretty bad and he wasn't so nimble."

I gave him a friendly shark grin and teetered a few inches toward him. "But how thoughtless of me," I said. "I forgot to introduce myself." I extended a hand. "The moniker is Matches O'Tool."

His head ducked between his shoulders and he stepped back. "You got me wrong, mister," he said quickly. "I was just passing through this burg. This minute I was packing to catch my train."

I got out a cigarette and after I lit it I allowed the match to burn almost to my fingertips before I blew it out. Beaker watched the small flame with horrified fascination.

"I'll be back in about an hour," I said. "You'll be on the train by then though, won't you?"

"Even," he said emphatically, "if there's no train."

The door of 423 was opened only part way by Mavis Frawley. Mavis had flaming red hair, green eyes, and the warmth of a bowl of ice cubes.

"Get that damn foot out of the door," she said, "or I'll scream for the cops."

"Go right ahead," I advised her, shoving my way in. "But you look to me like the type that doesn't do much screaming."

She watched me with smoldering eyes. "I charge a thousand bucks a minute," she said. "If you got less than that, see some of the girls down the hall."

"How unkind," I said. "Do I look like that kind of a man?"

Mavis walked over to a small table and put her hand on the phone. "Do I have to get someone to throw you out, or do you get what I'm hinting at?"

I smiled at her amiably. "Before you could get the operator I could toss you out of that window."

"You go to hell!"

"No need for animosity," I said. "I'm prepared to be friendly . . . this time."

Her eyes crackled with hate. "What do you want?"

"I wish it were you, baby," I said. "But this is business." I ground out my cigarette in the ash tray. "The name is Splasher O'Tool," I said. "The boss tells me that you've got a couple of monkeys trying to set up a stand in this town."

Mavis took her hand away from the phone. "The boss?"

"The boss," I said. "This town is sewed up tight and right. We can be downright unfriendly to competition."

"Why don't you try telling that to my 'boys', as you call them?"

"They've been informed," I said. I met and held her eyes. "Beaker got the idea right away, but Dowd is a little damaged."

For the first time, she seemed uncertain, but she said, "You're not scaring me!"

"Of course not," I said.

We studied each other for awhile and she was becoming uneasy.

"Did I ever tell you about Myra Lawson?" I asked.

Mavis said nothing.

Divide and Conquer

"Well," I said, cheerfully, "Myra used to deal blackjack at one of our places. Her take wasn't what it should have been and so we watched her until we found out why.

"She's still around, but she washes dishes for her meals now and doesn't go out in daylight," I said. "The acid, you know."

The little medicine bottle was now in my hand and I held it up. "Looks just like water, doesn't it?"

Her face got white and I gave her time to think.

Finally she asked, "How much time do I have to get out?"

"One hour," I said, as I rose and went leisurely to the door.

"I'll take it," she said bitterly. "But only because I can't operate without the boys."

Downstairs at the desk, Freddie beckoned to me. "Got a phone call from Sid. He says to call him right away."

In the phone booth I dialed the Four Deuces and asked for Sid.

"That baboon you laid out," Sid said, "left here fifteen minutes ago. On a hunch I had one of the porters tail him."

"And he's waiting for me?"

"Right. He ambled away but circled back. He's in the alley now with a piece of pipe. Should I call the cops?"

"No," I said. "I'm on a winning streak. I think I can handle it."

I walked back to the Four Deuces, but turned into the Bar & Grill that was on the other side of the alley. I went all the way through and into the back yard.

Peaking over the wood fence, I could make out Mugger in the shadows next to the rear exit. Evidently he was hoping that I'd step out for a breath of air.

Taking out the gun and reversing it, I tip-toed up behind him. Mugger had his attention glued to the door and so I had no trouble giving him a swipe behind the ear.

He sighed wearily and caved in, but before he could fall I got under him and slung him over my shoulder. He made a heavy load and I staggered as I carried him into the office and put him on the couch.

I put a glass and a bottle of whiskey next to him and waited. Mugger slept for ten minutes before painful consciousness returned. He groaned and grunted before opening his blood-shot eyes.

He directed a bleary glance at me. "Was dat you again?" he asked.

"Face it," I said. "I'm too damn tough for you."

Mugger kept his eyes closed. "Don't be so proud. You ain't touched me wid flesh and blood yet. What was it dis time? A gat?"

He forced open an eye to glare at me, but the whiskey bottle interrupted him. Aching every inch of the way, he managed to drag himself up to a sitting position and pour four fingers of the stuff.

Mugger drank deep and wiped his mouth with a sleeve. He stared moodily at the floor. "I feel ruint," he said.

"Don't take it so hard," I said. "Your friends didn't do any better and they're leaving town."

Mugger polished off the rest of the glass and tilted the bottle for a refill. "I knew it wouldn't work, but it's still discouragin'." He winced as he touched his head. "I'm gettin' too old for dis rough stuff."

He tasted the liquor again and examined the office and its furniture. "You get all dis splendor honest?"

"More or less," I said. "Brains had something to do with it."

"Don't rub it in," he said, brooding. "Well," he had a note of sadness in his voice, "I guess I better be leavin'. You ain't got a sawbuck or two for train fare? I'm near busted."

I considered his dejection for awhile. "The cops interested in you in any way?" I asked.

"Unless you're thinkin' of makin' a complaint, I'm pure as the driven snow right now," he said. "I just got out of the government boarding school and ain't had much time for bein' bad."

"You're getting gray hair, Mugger," I said. "Ever thought of trying legitimate? Like wearing a tux and a carnation and acting like a bouncer. Pays ninety-five a week."

"You serious?" Mugger's eyes rested on my face.

"But no pawing around Juanita," I said. "She's my claim."

"You're takin' the joy outta it," he said. "But I accept. The tear in my eye is hand-lickin' gratitude." He picked up his battered hat. "Only I need a day or two vacation. My head hurts."

When he left, I removed my coat and tie and stretched out on the couch. I thought, this divide and conquer business sometimes works. I closed my eyes.

I opened them when Juanita came in wearing a smile and an outfit that wasn't much more than the ribbons and bows holding it together.

She snapped the lock on the door and went around dimming the lights. "You look tired," she said.

"Had a hard day at the shop," I said.

She sat down beside me. "I've got a sparkle in my eyes," she said. "What are you thinking of?"

I reached for one of the bows.

She smiled and relaxed against me . . .

You Should Live So Long

April 1957

The phone call got me out of bed. I Had a couple of cups of coffee first and then got to Emma's place before eight.

Emma was there to open one of the big double doors herself. Her face was still flaky with last night's powder and her eyes were small in the bloat of her face.

She put a hand in front of her face and bit at her yawn. "Maylee Doyle," she said. "I got her locked up in room 23."

I draped my topcoat over a hanger and put it in the hall closet. "You're getting old, Emma, when you got to call the boss for help."

She shrugged. "Maybe tired. It just don't interest me to use the heavy hand myself any more. Besides, this isn't just the normal sassy tongue type of thing. I caught Maylee coming down the stairs with a suitcase in her hand this morning."

Emma fumbled in the pocket of her dressing gown and brought out a pack of cigarettes. "I been watching her for the last week, Freddy boy. When a girl has that look in her eyes, she wants to quit."

Emma took a drag on the cigarette. "Maybe she saved up her money. Maybe she wants to go back to Prairie Junction or wherever the hell she came from. Sometimes the girls start thinking about all-electric kitchens, a garden, and somebody to water the lawn on summer evenings."

In the big room downstairs one of the maids in uniform was cleaning up. She glanced at me disinterestedly and continued emptying and stacking the ash trays.

Emma pulled out a ring of keys and selected one. She scowled in the direction of the stairs leading to the second floor. "No blood, Freddy. We just got that room re-decorated. And don't make too much noise. Most of the girls are still sleeping."

The wide stairway was thick-carpeted and soft under my feet. The windows at the ends of the hall were opened for the morning ventilation, but there still lingered the scent of musky perfume.

I turned the key in the lock of room 23.

Maylee Doyle sat on the edge of the crimson bedspread with a small glass ash tray on her knees. She was in her early twenties and her gray eyes watched me almost impassively.

I closed the door behind me and locked it.

Maylee stubbed out her cigarette. Her hand moved into her purse and came out with a sharp nail file.

"Now, Maylee," I asked softly, "what seems to be the trouble?"

Her eyes narrowed with wariness. "There's no trouble if you unlock the door."

I moved closer. "You just want to leave, isn't that it?"

Her face was expressionless. "That's all I want."

I shook my head slowly. "It's not that easy. Maylee. You girls just don't quit when you work for me."

She had a half-smile on her lips. "Now tell me the story of the syndicate. Tell me I can't escape. Tell me that it reaches out into every nook and cranny of the nation and a couple of foreign countries besides."

I smiled at her. "That's the second step, Maylee. I use it when the first one doesn't work."

Her small hand held the nail file tightly. "There's not going to be a first step."

I grinned and drifted closer.

She tried for my eyes the way I thought she would, but I caught her wrist and twisted. She made no noise, but her face whitened at the pressure.

I picked up the nail file and tossed it into the waste basket.

Maylee sat still on the bed, her body stiff.

I slapped her hard across the face. Her head jerked with the blow, but she faced me again. There was only cold hate in her eyes.

I slapped her again and then stepped back to study her. Some of them cave in with just a little pressure. They whimper and they cry. And others you can beat to death and get nowhere.

I picked Maylee's purse off the bed and opened it. I examined the entries in the small green bank book. Maylee had less than two hundred dollars in the bank. According to the figures, she never had much more than that at any time.

I tossed the bank book on the dresser. "I'm curious, Maylee. I've seen the girls try to get out of the racket because they saved their money. What's your reason?"

She was silent.

My slap drew a little blood from her lower lip. I put my hands behind my back and looked down at her. "Somebody offer to set you up in an apartment, Maylee?"

She glared at me and said nothing.

I shook my head. "I guess that's not it then, Maylee. In the old days the boys with money weren't so particular. But now they like the amateur type. The innocent kind without mileage."

I smiled as I watched her. "I'll keep guessing, Maylee. I'll keep guessing and I'll hit it."

I walked around the room moving things absently. Then I glanced at Maylee. "But we got one thing straight, haven't we? You're thinking of leaving because of a man?"

There was just the slightest flicker in Maylee's eyes, but it was enough for me.

I grinned and folded my arms over my chest. "I think I can see it, Maylee. He's a clean-cut type you met while you were taking a walk in the park or something. You know what I mean, Maylee? And I'll bet he's sincere. A sort of boy-man. They always seem to appeal to you girls. I imagine he thinks of you as a goddess. Is that right, Maylee?"

Her cheekbones reddened. "You dirty bastard," she said tightly.

I rubbed my jaw. "I'm just wondering if you really deserve something like that. Think of how you've been earning your room, board, and perfume the last three years."

I teetered on my toes. "Suppose someone was to tell him, Maylee?"

There was something like a smile in her eyes and for a moment it stopped me. And then I got it.

I waited half a minute while I thought it out. "So he knows all about you and he loves you just the same? That must be it, Maylee."

She didn't have to say anything. It was there in her eyes.

I shook my head. "I just hate to lose, Maylee. I hate it like hell."

And after a few seconds I smiled again. "I'll bet you promised him that there would never be another man again."

I took a step forward. "But there's going to be one more, Maylee. At least one more."

Maylee tried to slip away, but my hand caught her and swung her to the bed. She fought and scratched, but my hand went to the neckline of her dress.

When I came downstairs, Emma was in an arm chair drinking a cup of coffee.

She looked up. "Well?"

I shrugged. "I don't think we can hold her."

Emma was moody. "Hell, she was one of the best we had."

I was slipping into my topcoat when the doorbell chimed. Emma groaned her way out of her chair and went past me to answer it.

A tall, thin man with shell-rimmed glasses stood in the doorway. He was extremely nervous, but at the same time there was determination in his chin. "I've come to get Maylee," he said defiantly. "She was supposed to meet me at seven-thirty at the railroad station, but she didn't show up."

Emma and I exchanged glances. She shrugged her shoulders. "I never seen him before."

"Come in," I said. "We've been expecting you."

He hesitated for a moment and then crossed the sill. He swallowed uneasily.

I lit a cigarette and looked him over. His clothes were obviously inexpensive and ready-made. "I suppose you were prepared to batter down the door or something like that?"

"If necessary," he said stiffly.

I grinned. "That would hardly have been necessary. All the girls are free to go whenever they want. I'm afraid you've been reading some of those old-fashioned novels."

I sighed. "We'll hate to lose Maylee. She's been with us for three years, you know."

I guess he didn't. That must have been a lot longer than Maylee had told him.

I shook my head. "I hope we don't lose any of our regular customers because of this. Maylee was quite a favorite. She had certain specialties."

He lost a little color, but his face remained stiff. "Maylee's told me everything I need to know."

"Ah, yes," I said thoughtfully. "These are all fine girls and happy. They like this type of work."

I turned to Emma. "Why don't you go up and see what's keeping Maylee?"

Emma looked at me questioningly for a moment and then moved on. She palmed the keys on the cocktail table as she passed it.

The thin man surveyed me with narrowed eyes. "I want to warn you that it will do you no good to blackmail us. In the first place we'll never have a lot of money. I'm just a bookkeeper."

I thought that was somewhat regrettable. Certainly from my point of view.

"And besides," he continued with a trace of smugness, "we're going a long way from here. And we'll make certain that we're not followed. I'll change my name, if necessary."

"It's really quite refreshing," I said. "To see a man of your caliber willing to marry a . . ." I held up my hand. "I'm sorry. I won't use the word. But still, it is refreshing. I imagine you must also have terrific confidence in yourself."

His eyes were puzzled and suspicious. "Confidence?"

"Why, yes," I said. "After all, in the three years Maylee's been here she's known . . . I believe that's the expression. Biblical, isn't it? . . . Well, she's known. . . ." I looked at the ceiling and my lips moved with silent mathematics.

I laughed self-consciously. "I'm not too good with figures, but you get the general idea of why I admire your confidence. After all, you'll be competing with probably a couple of thousand men." I thought it over. "Possibly the number of individuals is somewhat less. A lot of them were repeaters."

His face was dead white.

"I wonder," I said thoughtfully, "if she'll ever think of any of them." I smiled. "After you're asleep, of course."

From the way he threw his right, I'd say that he never had a fight in his life. I blocked the hook easily. My right to his jaw snapped the consciousness from his eyes and he dropped to the floor.

I bent over him and took the wallet from his pocket. His driver's license showed that his name was James Wells and I guess he was right about being just a bookkeeper. His last pay check was for less than sixty-eight dollars.

Emma came back alone. "Maylee will be down in a minute or two."

I put the wallet back in Wells' pocket. "I guess it must be true love, Emma," I said. "He's a nobody."

I propped Wells up and slapped him a couple of times to bring him to. After awhile he groaned and opened his eyes. He glared at me with hate and helplessness.

I lit a cigarette and took a puff. "I wonder if Maylee's going to miss this life. Once the girls get started on this type of thing, it's hard for them to quit."

Maylee appeared at the head of the stairs carrying her suitcase. The side of her face was swollen and she walked down slowly, her hand on the rail.

Wells stood up almost reluctantly. He seemed to look at her as though he had never seen her before.

I let Maylee get to the foot of the stairs. Then I took out my wallet and pulled out two tens. "Never let it be said that the boss doesn't pay when he samples the stock. I'm sorry about the face, Maylee, but you know that's the way I like to have mine. I guess you do too. At least you've never complained."

Maylee went past me without so much as a glance. There was a timid smile on her face as she looked at Wells.

He flinched slightly when she touched his arm.

It was an electric shock to Maylee and her eyes widened. "Jimmy, what's the matter?"

He couldn't meet her eyes. "Nothing," he said gruffly. "Let's go."

Maylee whirled on me and her voice was a hiss. "What have you done? What have you told him?"

I raised an eyebrow. "Why nothing, Maylee. I didn't have to lie."

I turned to Wells who was edging for the door. "I gather that you missed your train. Wouldn't it be more economical if you just left Maylee here until tomorrow morning? It would save you hotel bills for tonight."

Maylee's voice was high with panic. "No, Jimmy. I want you to take me away right now."

"Come now, Maylee," I said soothingly, "let's be sensible. What difference can twenty-four hours mean when you've been here three years already?"

Wells licked his lips.

Maylee met his eyes and knew by his indecision that I had killed something. Her face was white as she clutched his arm. "Take me with you now, Jimmy!"

He shook his head stubbornly and forced open her grip. I took a tight hold on Maylee's arm and kept her away from him.

Wells moved quickly to the door and opened it. There was the color of guilt in his face. "I'll call for you tomorrow morning, Maylee."

Like hell you will, I thought.

And Maylee knew it too. She screamed and tried to follow him, but I tightened my grip on her arm.

She struggled for half a minute more after Wells left and then burst into hysterical tears.

I let her cry until she was exhausted and then I gave her an order. "Get back upstairs, Maylee."

She picked up the suitcase and moved without spirit.

When I left Emma's place, I walked two blocks to where I'd parked my car.

A uniformed cop had one foot on the bumper of my sedan and he was writing out a ticket.

I came up behind him. "Hundreds of people get robbed every day, but you cops got nothing better to do than write out tickets for honest taxpayers."

He didn't look back. "You're parked practically on top of a fire plug, mister. As soon as I fill this out, I'll go chase a couple of rapists for you."

He tore out the ticket and turned around. Then he grinned and crumpled it up. "Hell, it's you."

He put his book back in his pocket and studied my car. "That's a pretty beat-up mess you got there, Fred. A detective sergeant ought to be able to show something a little better for his salary."

I opened the door and slid inside. "I'm saving my money, Al. One of these days I'm taking off for Cuba and buy myself a couple of estates. I'll have a dozen Jaguars."

He laughed. "You should live so long."

I grinned. "You're damn right I will."

Kill Joy

November 1957

I eased the car to the curb, and Frank got out. He went into the drugstore for cigarettes.

Fifty feet ahead of me, the exhaust of an idling sedan drifted toward the sidewalk. My eyes moved routinely to the license plate and the number rang a bell.

I checked with the clipboard on our dash, and then opened the right hand door to get out.

I stopped when I got one foot on the sidewalk.

The car was parked in front of a currency exchange office, and there was something going on up there. I could almost smell it; I knew that it had to be bigger than a stolen car.

The man behind the wheel reached across and opened the rear door of the sedan.

I slipped the shotgun out of its sling in the back of my car. While I waited, my fingers gently rubbed the cool metal of the barrel.

Two men came out of the building at a trot, and both of them had automatics in their right hands. The first carried a zipper bag and he tossed it into the sedan.

I leveled the barrel of the twelve gauge at his chest and pulled the trigger. The big No. 1 shot stopped him before he could get a foot inside the car.

I smiled slightly as I pumped another shell into the chamber.

The second man was short and heavy. His eyes widened at what he knew was coming, and his mouth opened to shout against it.

I fired again. His face twisted with shock as he dropped to his knees.

The driver of the car snapped his head back to look at me. He held a handkerchief over his mouth and nose, but I didn't need to see his face. The parallel scars cutting through his left eyebrow were as good as a signature.

I knew who he was and that made things different.

Our eyes met for a second as he pulled the door shut. He gunned the engine of the car and roared away from the curb.

I kept the barrel of my shotgun pointed at the back of his head all the way to the first corner. Then I raised my aim and fired high over the car.

Frank was out of the drugstore now, his .38 in his hand. He fired two quick shots at the sedan, but as far as I could see, he did no good.

My eyes went back to the sidewalk. The first man I'd shot lay sprawled on his face, but the other was still on his knees, staring stupidly at his own blood on the sidewalk. The automatic dangled loosely in his hand.

I glanced quickly at Frank. His attention was still on the sedan, and he was trying for another shot.

I pumped one more shell into the chamber and aimed at the kneeling man. I fired and finished him.

I slid back into the car and slammed the door. "Take care of them, Frank," I yelled. "I'll get the one in the car."

When I pulled away and kicked the siren, I glanced back. Frank was staring at the two bodies, and his face was gray.

The tires squealed as I took a corner. Ahead of me I caught a glimpse of the dark sedan. It took another corner.

When I got there, I kept going straight.

After a while I killed the siren and slowed down. I got in contact with headquarters and gave a general description of the car, but I mentioned nothing about the license number.

When I got back to the currency exchange office, three squad cars were already there and a couple of officers were trying to keep the souvenir hunters away from the bodies.

Frank was inside talking to a thin middle-aged man wearing rimless glasses.

I joined them. "I lost him, Frank."

Frank's face was stiff. "At least you got two for the morgue, Al. That ought to make you happy."

He studied me a moment more and then turned to the thin man. "This is Mr. Mader. He's the manager of this place."

I nodded and introduced myself. "Sergeant Williams."

Mader's face was pale and his hands trembled with nervousness. "They took about sixty thousand dollars. This is a Friday. We usually have that amount to cash pay checks."

An ambulance edged its way through the crowd on the street outside. The attendants got out and leaned on their folded stretchers while they waited for the picture crew to finish.

Frank lit a cigarette. "Mr. Mader, your desk is close to the window. You must have caught at least a glimpse of the driver of the car."

Mader's watery blue eyes became vague with thought. "Everything happened so fast. I really don't remember too much about him."

Frank turned to me.

I shrugged. "All I ever saw was the back of his head. But I'd guess he was an all-around average. Maybe five seven, brown hair, weight 145." All that was true enough.

Mader sipped water from a paper cup. "They came in shortly after we opened. The tall one came directly to my desk and the other stood near the door."

"How about your alarm button?" I asked.

Mader shook his head. "The tall one pointed the gun at me and threatened to shoot if I stepped on it. I'm positive he would have done that if I had been so rash."

The glass front doors swung open and Lieutenant Philips came striding through. He nodded to Frank and me.

"We just fell into this, Lieutenant," Frank said.

I started the story from the beginning. "Fifteen minutes ago I pulled up to the drugstore down the street so that Frank could get some smokes. While he was gone I noticed what was happening here."

I glanced at Frank. "When they came out, I called to them to stop and put up their hands. But they weren't having any of that. I had to use the shotgun."

Philips turned to Frank. "That the way it happened?"

Frank's face was blank. "I was in the drugstore and I didn't get to see much." His eyes flicked over me. "I didn't hear too much either."

Philips had a tight smile. "How many shots did they fire at you, Al?"

I shrugged. "I didn't wait for that."

He studied me. "That makes six you've killed since you joined the force."

Mader watched me with eyes that held a faint horror.

I grinned at him. "Be happy I'm on your side."

A half an hour later, Frank and I took Mader down to headquarters to look at the pictures. I leaned against the window frame and watched Mader going slowly through the big books.

When he started on the second volume, Frank left the room to see if any of the bodies had been identified.

Mader's forefinger flowed from picture to picture as though he were reading a ledger and he glanced at me uneasily from time to time.

At eleven o'clock I brought him the fourth book and I stayed near. When he got to the page with Charley O'Hara's picture on it, I was standing at his shoulder.

His finger touched Charley's picture for a moment, the thin face with the parallel scars through the right eyebrow, and then moved on.

I went back to the window and lit a cigarette.

Frank returned five minutes later. "We identified one of them. His prints were in our files. Edward Riley. He's the one you shot twice."

"He still had the gun in his hand, Frank."

"He wasn't going to use it," Frank snapped. "I could see that."

I shook my head and smiled. "You don't know that, Frank. I like to make my decisions fast."

Mader spent most of the day looking at the pictures but he came up with nothing. We let him go at three in the afternoon.

At five Frank and I checked out for the day.

He was silent until we got to our cars in the parking lot. "What keeps you on the force, Al? Is it the big pay and the retirement plan? Is it the hunting license that makes your kills legal?"

I smiled. "It gives me a good feeling to protect the weak and the innocent, Frank. That's what it is."

I watched his car pull away and then got into mine. I drove to the new housing development on the north side. I made my way slowly through the planned curves and pulled up in front of Charley O'Hara's ranch-style house.

Charley answered the door bell himself. He stood in the doorway, his thin face tense. "What do you want now?"

I grinned. "Just a routine check, Charley. Have a hard day at the shop?"

His face was sullen. "This is my day off."

I nodded. "But you look so tired, boy. Let's go inside and talk about it."

His stare was hostile, but he stepped aside.

I took a seat in the living room. "Having a hard time with the payments to this place, Charley? The shoe must pinch when you got a wife and two kids to support." I patted the chair I was sitting in. "This on time payments too?"

Anger flickered in his eyes.

I crossed my legs. "Where's the wife, Charley? And the kids?"

His lips were tight. "They're visiting her mother."

"I guess you were expecting me, weren't you, Charley?"

He didn't look at me.

I let half a minute pass. "One of the boys was Ed Riley. Who was the other?"

He lit a cigarette and took nervous puffs. "What the hell are you talking about?"

I smiled. "Aren't you grateful, Charley? I could have blown your head off."

I clicked my tongue. "Let's not play games, Charley. I saw you this morning and you saw me. We both know that."

He walked away from me and stood at the picture window watching the houses across the street. Finally he turned. "All right. Why didn't you blow my brains out?"

I smiled. "You've been wondering. Did you come up with any answers?"

His laugh was bitter. "I suppose you want half of the money?"

I shook my head. "No, Charley. All of it."

His temper flared. "Go to hell!"

"I want all of it. Every cent you took this morning. Either that or I take you in. Your wife and kids are going to miss you, Charley."

I let him have the time to think about it.

He ground his cigarette savagely into an ash tray. "I got it down in the basement."

I opened the button of my suitcoat and loosened my gun in its holster. "Fine, Charley. That's real fine. We'll take a look at it. But be careful, Charley. Real careful."

I followed him down the stairs. He went to the partially finished recreation room and reached up into the rafters.

I had the gun out, just to make sure he wasn't going to try anything, but he brought down the zipper bag and nothing more.

I took it from him and indicated a stool. "Sit there, Charley." I dumped the contents of the bag on a work bench and began counting.

Charley sat still, watching me, and moisture glistened on his forehead.

When I finished, I shook my head sadly. "That's only thirty thousand, Charley. That's only half."

He smiled thinly. "That's what I got. That's my share."

The thin voice came from behind me. "He means that the other half is mine."

I stiffened.

"Don't touch your gun, Sergeant. Turn around slowly."

Mader had an automatic in his hand. His eyes glittered behind the rimless glasses. He nodded at the expression on my face. "Yes, Sergeant, I was part of it, too."

I half rose. "Now wait a minute. We can work something out."

But he smiled.

The same way I do when I'm going to kill a man.

Don't Twist My Arm

April 1958

Pop told me to roll up the sleeve of my shirt.

"You can see for yourself," he said, "The kid's arm is all bent. He can't use it hardly at all now and it'll get worse year by year."

Mr. Ward leaned forward to look and the eyes in his heavy face showed nothing.

Pop waved a hand. "We'll hit them for all we can get. I don't care who pays. Either Peterson or his insurance company."

Mr. Ward rolled the cigar in his mouth a couple of times and then reached for his pen.

"Henry Peterson is the guy's name," Pop said. He watched Mr. Ward write. "Senator Henry Peterson."

Mr. Ward and Pop looked at each other for about ten seconds, and then Mr. Ward got a little smile on his face. "All right," he said. "Go on."

"My kid was crossing the street when he was run down by the senator's car," Pop said. "A big job in the five thousand dollar class."

I cleared my throat. "I was playing ball in the street."

Mr. Ward's eyes went over me without finding anything interesting. "Shut up, kid," he said.

"I was sitting on the stoop and I saw the whole thing," Pop said. "I picked up Freddie and took him to a doctor."

Mr. Ward played with his pen. "How come you didn't take the kid to a hospital? That's what usually happens in cases like that."

Pop shrugged. "The doc was nearer."

Mr. Ward smiled and rubbed his chin. "You were excited. That's natural. A father's first concern is for his kid and he's got the right to lose his head. What did Peterson do?"

Pop crossed his legs. "He came along."

I remembered the look on Senator Peterson's face when he saw how dirty Dr. Miller's office was.

Mr. Ward looked at my arm again. "When did all this happen?"

Pop shifted in his chair. "About two years ago."

Mr. Ward chuckled very softly.

Pop got a little red. "I figured the arm would turn out all right. But the kid kept yammering about it day and night. I finally took him to another doctor."

Mr. Ward puffed his cigar and waited.

Pop ran his tongue over his lips. "They'll have to break Freddie's arm and put it back together again. Even then it might never grow any longer than it is now."

Pop shook his head and looked down at his hands. "The kid's future is ruined. And look at him. He's lost maybe twenty pounds. He can't get no sleep nights because of the hurt."

Mr. Ward studied me. "How old is he?"

"Fifteen," Pop said. "He's always been a runt." Pop took a cigarette out of a crumpled pack and lit it. "I signed a paper with Peterson's insurance company and got five hundred dollars. I needed the money. But that don't mean a thing now. Not when the arm turned out this way."

Mr. Ward looked at the ceiling. "Why not sue the doctor?"

"You can't get blood out of a stone," Pop said.

Mr. Ward chuckled again and looked Pop over. "When we get together with Peterson, it might be a good idea if you shaved. Wear a necktie too."

We left Mr. Ward's office and walked down three flights of stairs to the street.

When we got near Danny's Bar, Pop slowed down and rattled the change in his pocket. He licked his lips, but I knew he wasn't going in there. Danny charges thirty-five cents for a drink. At O'Brien's you get the same stuff for twenty.

At Thirty-eighth, we crossed the street so that we wouldn't have to go past Ricco's. Pop doesn't go near there ever since he had that fight with Louie Milo who hangs out there.

Pop went into O'Brien's and I followed him.

Mr. O'Brien waited until Pop put money on the bar before he poured a drink. Then he looked at me. "Get the hell out of here, kid."

Pop yawned. "You heard him, Freddie."

"I'm not doing anything," I said.

Mr. O'Brien leaned over the bar. "Move before I put a boot in your rump."

Pop downed his drink and put some more change on the bar.

I looked at him for a few seconds and then I left and started walking home.

My arm hurt pretty bad. It gets that way when it's damp.

I went upstairs to the place where Pop and I live. There was half a bottle of olives in the refrigerator and some butter. There was a tomato too, but it was rotten. I found some bread and ate a little before I went outside again.

Turk and Pete and Gino were hanging around Harrigan's Grocery and they were wearing their Red Hawk jackets.

Once I nearly got one. I had eight dollars, but that was gone now.

They didn't pay no attention when I came up and leaned against the building next to them.

Pete got out his cigarettes and passed the pack to Turk and Gino. I put out my hand, but Gino gave the pack back to Pete.

Pete lit up for all three of them.

"I once read how that got started," I said. "You know, that business about three on a match being unlucky. It was in the First World War and if you kept a match lit long enough for three lights, a German sniper was liable to get a bead on you."

They didn't look at me and so I guess they didn't care about the story.

I waited a little while and then said. "I saw a couple of the Goldens today. I went through their territory."

Gino looked at me. "You beat their heads together? Is that it, Freddie?"

I changed my mind about what I was going to say. I shrugged. "I didn't want to start nothing there. I would of been mobbed."

"I'm surprised at you, Freddie," Turk said. "You're the brave type. It runs in the family."

Gino coughed on some cigarette smoke. "I thought I'd bust a gut when I seen little Louie chase Freddie's old man out of Ricco's. He's sure got speed when he's scared. Ain't that right, Freddie?"

I looked at the Poulos girls passing across the street and tried to quick think of something to say about the way they swung their hips. But I couldn't think of nothing.

Red Kelly's chromed-up Chevy pulled to the curb and Pete, Turk and Gino got inside. I thought there was room for one more, but Gino shut the door after him.

They took off and I watched them turn the corner.

Pop came home around ten o'clock with Willie Bragan. They had a pint with them and they began talking about the job they were going to do on Saturday night. I asked if I could be lookout, but Pop told me to shut up.

When they settled everything and finished the pint, Bragan went home.

Before Pop went to bed, he looked under the kitchen clock. He always does that ever since he found the eight dollars I set aside for the jacket.

I fixed myself some butter bread and went to the window and looked down. It was getting quiet outside and the traffic was thinning.

Pop woke at twelve. When he was through, I got the mop and cleaned up. Then I went to bed.

Senator Peterson was at the meeting and Mr. Jenkins, the lawyer from his insurance company, and Mr. Ward.

Pop looked mad. "You seen the X-rays. The kid's crippled for life."

Mr. Jenkins shuffled some of the papers on his lap. "This Dr. Miller who set the boy's arm. He lost his license several months ago for unethical practices."

"How the hell was I supposed to know what kind of a doctor he was?" Pop said. "The sign on the door said 'Doctor.' Am I supposed to drop the kid on the floor and check with the Medical Society first?"

Mr. Jenkins' voice was dry. "How did you happen to select him?"

Mr. Ward cleared his throat. "As my client explained, Dr. Miller was the nearest aid available."

Senator Peterson had grayish hair and he was about Pop's age. But his skin was clear.

He studied Pop. "It would seem that this Dr. Miller is the man to sue."

Mr. Ward smiled. "Dr. Miller disappeared shortly after losing his license. We've made an extensive search, but we've been unable to find a trace of him."

Pop pointed to Senator Peterson. "You're the one who's responsible. It was your car that hit the boy."

Mr. Jenkins sighed. "I fail to see that you have any case at all. At the time of the accident you absolutely refused to have the boy taken to a hospital. You refused to allow our doctors to examine him. In addition, you signed an agreement waiving all future claims, for which you received five hundred dollars. Under the circumstances, neither my company nor Senator Peterson can be held responsible for the mistakes of this Dr. Miller."

It was quiet for a while and then Mr. Ward took the cigar out of his mouth. "Perhaps we don't have an iron-bound case, from the legal point of view." He looked at Senator Peterson. "I believe you are running for the Senate again? Do you suppose the publicity might be harmful?"

Mr. Jenkins and Senator Peterson looked at each other.

"I see," Mr. Jenkins said. He put his papers back in his brief case and got to his feet. "Are you coming, Senator?"

Senator Peterson didn't look at him.

Mr. Jenkins smiled tightly. "At any rate, my company is not running for the Senate."

He went to the door and left.

But Senator Peterson stayed.

It was evening and I didn't feel like going to the movies. I got some candy bars instead and went back home. I went up the fire escape and sat down outside our window.

I heard voices inside the kitchen and shifted over a little so I could take a peek inside.

Dr. Miller and Pop were drinking from a bottle on the table. I could see the label and it was a real expensive brand.

Dr. Miller filled his glass. "The kid around?"

Pop lit a cigar. "No. I gave him a buck and told him to take in a movie." He slapped the table. "That bastard Ward took forty percent. He even said we were lucky he didn't take more."

Dr. Miller was bald and he wore glasses that made his eyes twice as big as anybody else's. He shrugged. "It's robbery, but there's nothing we can do about it. We still got twelve thousand out of the deal and we split that even."

I threw away the candy bar. I could feel sweat begin all over my body.

Pop's face was dark red. "I get a lousy six thousand. That's all I get for listening to that kid whimper for two years."

I shook my head. That was all wrong too. I didn't whimper.

Dr. Miller took a cigar out of the box on the table. "We had to wait at least a couple of years. I told you that in the beginning. We had to give that arm time to get real bad."

Pop pounded the table. "By rights, I'm entitled to more than a fifty-fifty split. I'm the one who got the idea for the whole thing the second I seen what a high price car hit Freddie."

Dr. Miller laughed. "Hell, all the kid got out of it was a trip to the movies. Be satisfied that he don't know what you did to him. He might get the notion to cut your throat one of these nights."

I gripped the cool railing of the fire escape hard with my good hand. There was a big knife in the drawer of the kitchen table. I'd wait until Dr. Miller was gone and Pop was asleep. Then I'd do it.

Dr. Miller stayed for another hour before he left. I settled down on the fire escape, waiting and watching Pop drink. I figured that he'd probably have enough by eleven o'clock.

Then I remembered that this was Saturday and he and Bragan were supposed to do a job.

I wondered if Pop could get out of it. He wouldn't want to take any chances with small stuff, now that he had the six thousand. But he couldn't tell Bragan that he had the money. You don't do something like that with Bragan if you want to keep it.

Willie Bragan came at ten and Pop looked surprised. I guess he forgot that it was Saturday.

Bragan looked at the bottle of whiskey and then at the cigars. "I thought you was broke."

Pop licked his lips. "A guy paid me back fifty he owed."

Bragan grunted. "Since when you been lending money?"

Pop laughed nervous. "An old friend."

Bragan wasn't buying that, but he shrugged. "We'll talk about it later. Let's get going. I got the truck downstairs in front."

Pop's voice had a whine in it. "Let's put it off, Willie. I'm not feeling so good tonight."

Bragan smiled a little and took a handful of cigars out of the box.

Pop didn't like that, but Bragan is a big man and you don't complain.

"Honest, Willie," Pop said. "I've been feeling rotten all day."

Bragan smelled one of the cigars. "Take a couple aspirins."

I watched them get in the truck down below and then I went down the fire escape.

It was cool in the streets and I began walking. Pop wouldn't be back for three or four hours and, I couldn't sit still that long. Not with what was going on in my head.

I don't know how long it was, but after a while I was in a long empty street and there were mostly warehouses on both sides. I was a little surprised to be there. But now that I was, I sat down in a doorway and watched the warehouse near the end of the block.

A cop turned the corner far down the street. He walked slow, shining his flashlight into the doorways.

And then he stopped in front of the warehouse I was watching. He seemed to be listening and then he took the gun out of his holster. He moved on his toes to the doors of the warehouse and he listened for another half a minute.

I wondered if I should do something, but then I remembered what I'd heard on the fire escape and I kept quiet.

The cop pulled open one of the sliding doors fast and jumped inside. The light poured out and I could see the cop's shadow stretching all the way across the road.

I waited a while and then I got up and walked toward the open door.

The cop had his back to me and he was standing just inside the door with his gun.

Pop and Bragan were facing him with their hands over their heads. Pop's face was white and Bragan was scowling. They were standing next to Bragan's big truck and it was about half loaded with automobile parts and new tires from the warehouse.

Bragan's eyes shifted in my direction and he saw me.

The cop noticed that and he jumped to one side like a scared cat. His gun swung back and forth between us. "Get over there with the rest of them."

I shook my head. "I don't have anything to do with this. I was just passing by."

The cop had a hard laugh. "At two o'clock in the morning, kid? Like hell." His gun jerked again. "Get your hands up."

I put up my right arm. "I can't lift the other one."

He looked at my short arm and his lips twisted. "So you got a cripple for the lookout work. Maybe that's all he's good for. He wouldn't be much help wrestling tires into your truck."

I looked at the cop and I saw that he had the kind of yellow brown eyes that Pop has.

Pop swallowed hard. "Look, we can fix this up." The cop grinned. "That's right. I'm just a poor cop. I don't earn too much."

I could tell from his voice that he was just playing, but Pop kept trying anyhow.

"Five hundred bucks," Pop said. "I can raise five hundred."

The cop kept grinning. "Keep going."

Pop was sweating. He had a record and it wasn't going to be easy for him if he got in front of a judge. "A thousand," he said. "I can get it to you in a day."

Bragan was looking at Pop now too and I guess he was wondering whether Pop was faking it or whether he really had the money. Maybe he was thinking about the whiskey and the cigars.

The cop's eyes flicked around the big room and he saw the wall phone.

Pop's voice got high. "Two thousand," he said. "Three."

For a second the cop looked interested. But then, I guess he took another look at Pop and figured that he couldn't have that kind of money.

The cop couldn't keep his eyes on everything. Not on Bragan, and Pop, and me, and the wall phone. I guess he decided I was the least important.

He took his eyes away from me for a few seconds when he started edging for the phone.

Pop looked at me now and he was asking for help.

There wasn't much time and I had to make up my mind. I hesitated for a second and then I stooped down and grabbed a tire iron leaning against the wall. I swung with all my might and the iron bit deep into the cop's skull.

Bragan came out of the shock first. He went to the door and pulled it shut. Then he knelt down beside the cop. After a while, he looked up. "He's dead."

I nodded and tossed the tire iron aside.

Pop was shaking. "The kid done it. We got no part of this."

Bragan got to his feet. "We're in it as deep as the kid is. We're in the big league now."

He picked up the tire iron and wiped my fingerprints off with his handkerchief. "All right," he said. "Let's go."

He went to the big doors and slid them open.

I stood to one side and watched them get into the truck. Pop put his head out of the cab. "Damn it," he yelled to me. "Get in."

I stood there for a few seconds, uncertain. I was sick with what he was. I didn't know if I wanted to stick with him any more—I didn't even know why I'd stuck with him this long . . .

"For God's sake, kid, get in," he said again. And I saw his frightened eyes dart over in the direction of Bragan.

Pop would have trouble with Bragan about the six thousand. *He might need me.* And as I thought it, I realized why I'd stuck with him, because no one else on earth had ever needed or wanted me for any reason, and, jeez, how I needed to be needed . . .

"All right," I said. "All right, Pop, I'm coming."

Deadline Murder

October 1958

Roy Tenney's day began at eleven in the morning.

I followed Cawber into the bedroom and sat down in an easy chair facing the bed, I crossed my legs, lit a cigar and blew a cloud of smoke at the ceiling.

Cawber pulled aside the long drapes and the bright sun slanted through the apartment windows.

It always took Tenney about ten minutes before he'd let go of sleep and take a look at another day. He was a thin, little man of forty-five with sick-looking reddish hair. He opened his eyes wide in a quick stare. I was there and that made the world safer.

Then he sat up in nervous alarm. "Where's your gun, Eddie?"

I brushed some cigar ash off my shirt sleeve. "In the kitchen, boss."

His voice was high and skittish. "Get it right away."

In the kitchen, Cawber was pouring coffee. "You scared the hell out of him. You had your fun for today."

I strapped on my shoulder holster and grinned. "Somehow I keep forgetting this damn thing."

Cawber followed me back into the bedroom with a tray. He put the tray on Tenney's lap and left the room.

Tenney picked up the coffee cup with the fingertips of both hands and sipped. "I've got a lot of enemies, Eddie. You never know when they'll try to get me."

"I wouldn't be worried," I said. "We're twenty-two stories up and there are two locked doors between us and the corridor. And then you got me."

Tenney shook his head. "You never know. They can strike when we expect it least. A man like me has to be careful. Anybody who prints the truth has to be."

Cawber came back into the room carrying the morning's mail.

Tenney slit open the first letter and began reading. After a while he giggled. "Jenny Williams is suing me. She wants a hundred thousand."

Jenny Williams is doing a Broadway show now, but she feels more at home before a Hollywood camera. Column talk has it that she's first in line for the big part in the film version of this year's bestseller.

I calculated for a moment. "That puts it over the two million mark."

His small jaw tried to be firm. "Nobody's collected a cent yet."

"That's right, boss," I said. "Your magazine prints nothing but the truth."

He nodded. "They all lead dirty lives. Every one of them. I can always dig up more about them and they know it. They're just after free publicity. Once they've got that, they drop their suits."

He took another sip of coffee and sighed. "It makes me ill. All this incredible filth in the world."

I glanced at the ceiling. "It's tough on a sensitive man. What you need is a vacation, boss. Why don't you try a little hunting trip?"

His face whitened. "No. You can never tell what might happen. I can't trust anyone."

He pushed the buzzer on his headboard three times and Miss Janicki came into the room with her pad and pencil.

Miss Janicki has a sallow skin, small features and she is a tense thirty-five.

Tenney began dictating answers to his letters. After a while he used his high giggle again and handed me a letter. "This is from Rick Balboa."

I read the letter and it compared favorably with one a President had written to a music critic. I handed it to Miss Janicki.

Her face became splotchy crimson as she read. Her eyes gleamed and she went over it again. "Horrible," she said. "Vile."

"I guess Balboa doesn't care for your kind of publicity, boss," I said. "He's got a wife and two kids now. Maybe he figures that being a prostitute's regular customer fifteen years ago is something that should be dead and forgotten."

"Time doesn't erase such things," Tenney snapped. "It's the public's right to know just what kind of a man provides its teenagers with entertainment."

I looked out of the window at the spears of buildings hiding the Sound. "Did you hear his new recording, boss? It'll probably get him another gold record."

Tenney sat up. "He's a rotten singer. He's got no voice at all." He wiped coffee drip from a corner of his mouth. "Only those depraved teenagers can stand him."

I rolled some smoke in my mouth and blew it out gently. "But you like Balboa, don't you, Stella?"

"Of course not," Miss Janicki snapped indignantly. "He has a voice like a crow."

Tenney got out of bed and took the letter from her. "I'm going to put this away," he said. "I may even send it to the postal authorities. There is no place for obscenity in our mails."

He walked bare-footed to the small wall safe and waited. Miss Janicki and I dutifully turned our heads away while he spun the dial.

While Tenney dressed, Miss Janicki, Cawber, and I had coffee in the kitchen.

"Of all the gall," Miss Janicki said. "That Jenny Williams has the nerve to use. That wanton slut!"

I put sugar in my coffee. "Tell me about it, Stella."

"Why, she had three lovers at the same time," Miss Janicki said.

I took a shocked breath. "Imagine!"

Miss Janicki was trying to. Her eyes were bright.

I leaned forward. "I missed the article."

She took an eager breath. "Well, this first one was a producer who . . ." She noticed something in my eyes and drew herself up. "I don't care to talk about such things."

I put my chin on my hands and stared at her. "I tried your door again last night, Stella. Why do you keep locking it? You're fighting fate."

She went scarlet and got to her feet. "Beast! That's all men like you think about." She stalked out of the room.

Cawber stirred his coffee. "The perpetual virgin. One of our greatest untapped natural resources. Her idea of love is a communion of minds. She'd get hysterics if anybody tried to touch her." He glanced at me. "Are you that desperate?"

I grinned. "I'd have to be drunk."

Tenney and I were in the entryway, ready to leave for his office, when the door buzzer sounded.

He jumped nervously, the way he usually does, and looked at me. "Don't take off the chain until you're sure who it is."

I opened the thick door as far as the chain would go.

Jenny Williams' smoke-gray eyes met mine. She looked me over. "I didn't come to see you." There was the faint odor of scotch on her breath.

"Who is it, Eddie?" Tenney demanded.

"Jenney Williams," I said. "She's primed to meet you."

Tenney's voice was peevish. "I don't want to see her. I don't want to see anybody. Get rid of her."

I unchained the door and stepped into the hall. Tenney snapped the lock behind me.

Jenny smiled faintly. "How cute. The little man's afraid of me."

I put my hand around the suede handbag dangling from her arm and fingered the outlines of a small gun. A twenty-five automatic, I figured. "Did you have the idea of using this?"

She shrugged. "I don't know. One more drink and I'd be sure."

"You're suing him," I said. "Be satisfied with that."

There was deep anger smoldering behind the haze in her eyes. "That's no damn good and I know it." Her words were slightly slurred. "That dirty bum," she whispered tensely. "Do you know what he did?"

"Sure," I said.

She shook her head and the ash-blonde hair swirled. "No, you don't." She swayed slightly and put her hand on my lapel to steady herself. "The best, the biggest part I ever had." She snapped her fingers. "Gone. Just like that."

She leaned closer and laughed lazily. "They don't want a woman who had three lovers in their damn movie."

She cocked her head and studied me. "How much do you get for bodyguarding that louse? A hundred a week? Two hundred?"

I smiled and said nothing.

She laughed. "Then you could stand the smell of ten thousand?" She stroked the side of my jaw. "That's what I'm offering you to get rid of that dirty rat."

"It's the liquor talking," I said.

She shook her head and the hair swirled again. "Ten thousand in cash."

Our eyes met and for a few seconds she was dead sober.

"I mean it," she said savagely. "I mean every word of it."

Then she smiled and kissed me lightly on the check. "Ten thousand. And anything else you want."

She made her way down the hall to the elevators. She pressed the button and looked back. "Phone me when it's over. I don't care how you do it, but make him dead."

Tenney's car has about a ton of extra steel in it and it's hell to handle in traffic.

He stared moodily through the heavy windows as I drove.

"What about that girl I had last night?" he asked. "What's her name? That model or something?"

"I kicked her out at nine this morning," I said. "You were still asleep."

He was silent for a while and then glanced at me suspiciously. "How much did you give her?"

"Five hundred," I said. It was really two-fifty. The other two-fifty was in my pocket. She raised a squawk, but a hand across her mouth made her satisfied with what she got.

He waited until I braked to a stop at a light. "I don't always have to pay them, you know."

"Sure, boss," I said.

"I'm an important man," he said. "They come to me."

The light changed and I stepped on the accelerator.

"Sometimes I don't even touch them," Tenney said.

Never is more likely, I thought. At least that's what I get from the stories the girls tell me. "Sure, boss," I said. "You just want companionship."

He was satisfied with the word. "A lot of them are diseased, you know. Especially the models."

I kept my face straight. "Why don't you see a doctor?"

He looked out of the window and shrugged. "Someday."

We were almost at the Randall Building when he spoke again. "What you thinking about, Eddie? You haven't said a word in ten minutes."

Ten thousand. I smiled. "I was thinking that the carburetor needs adjusting. I don't get the pick-up I want."

I turned the car over to the basement parking attendant and we took the executive elevator to the seventeenth floor.

When Tenney was settled in his soft insulated office, he used the inter-com to let his secretary know he was ready to grant audiences.

The picture editor brought in some layouts on Mavis Kennedy. She is a taut actress who is being mentioned for an Academy Award.

Tenney scowled as he examined the pictures. "Too tame. These are nothing but portraits. She was a model, wasn't she?"

The editor blinked cigarette smoke out of his eyes. "That was twenty years ago."

"So what," Tenney snapped.

"Get the photographs. Touch up the hair a little so they look like they were taken yesterday. Use your brush to make the poses look interesting. You know what I mean?"

The editor nodded.

"And get some pictures of junkies. Or better yet, get some of the spoons and needles and stuff like that. Let the public know what a dirty thing narcotics is."

The editor picked up the layouts. "It'll be a ticklish writing job. We can't say anything too definite about her. We don't know for sure."

Tenney glared. "Her first husband took dope. They lived together for three years. He probably got her started too. It always works that way."

The editor shrugged and left the room.

Sweeney came in to report. He was a heavy man with dull tired skin and he wasn't much interested in his job any more. He got out his notebook. "I found a couple open weeks on Howard. In 1952, he took a canoe trip up in the Minnesota lake country. He went alone and he was gone for two weeks."

Jeff Howard was now in television and he had a high rating.

Tenney's eyes brightened. "Two weeks? No witnesses? He can't prove he was there?"

Sweeney nodded.

Tenney smiled and pounded a small fist on his palm. "He used the trip as a cover-up. He was probably in St. Paul or Minneapolis all the time."

Sweeney sighed. "I'll work it that way."

"Pictures," Tenney said. "We want pictures of call girls."

Sweeney put the notebook back in his pocket. "I'll get a couple of girls to make statements. It'll probably cost a few thousand."

When Sweeney was gone, Tenney paced the thick rug. "Nobody can get as far as Howard has and still be a saint. Show business is dirty. What difference does it make if he was in a brothel in 1952 or 1955? The public has a right to know."

At four o'clock, Tenney's secretary buzzed. "There's a Mr. James Nitti to see you."

Tenney frowned, trying to place the name.

"Coppo Nitti," I said.

Tenney whitened. "I won't see him."

"He'll just want talk," I said. "It's too crowded in here for him to do anything."

Tenney bit his fingernails. "I can't see him. I refuse to be intimidated."

I lit a cigar. "I can see what he wants?"

Tenney thought it over. "You do that, Eddie. But remember, I don't back down."

I heard him snap the lock after me as I left the office.

Coppo Nitti was seated in the soft-lighted waiting room, waiting patiently. His long thin fingers absently stroked the brim of the Homburg on his lap.

He glanced up and raised a few lingers. "You look good, Eddie."

I sat down beside him. "Anything special, Coppo?"

"James," he said. "What about Tenney?"

"He refuses to be intimidated." I crossed my legs. "How did you hear that Tenney was going to run a story on you?"

Nitti showed even white teeth. "I still got devoted friends."

"You don't want it run?"

Nitti shrugged. "If it's just a re-hash of what I see every time I look at the Sunday papers, I don't care."

"But you don't want him to dig up anything new?"

"Or invent anything. I'm having trouble enough now with those investigating committees." He grinned. "They want to ship me back to Italy. What would I do in Italy? I can hardly speak the language any more."

He sighed. "I'm respectable, but nobody believes me. I get my income from General Motors and G.E."

"And you got a daughter at Vassar?"

He grinned. "She's not too bright. I got her in a Florida college majoring in tennis. She don't mind what kind of a reputation I got, just so long as I'm steady with her allowance. What worries me is Congress."

He stopped his smile and met my eyes. "What about the story, Eddie?"

"It's hot," I said. "Start brushing up on your Italian."

He was thoughtful and then raised an eyebrow. "Will money heal things?"

I shook my head. "He's as rich as you are. This place is a money maker."

He was silent as his eyes moved over the rich waiting room. "Is Tenney the keystone? Would this magazine fold if he weren't here?"

"I don't know," I said. "A lot of people with ten cents like to get their thoughts sweaty reading the sort of stuff printed here. This magazine is the kind of thing that doesn't die easy."

Nitti took a cigarette out of a gold case. He sighed. "It looks like I'll have to go back to the old ways then, Eddie." He lit the cigarette. "Would the story run if Tenney died?"

I took a while to examine my manicure. "It was Tenney's idea. His baby. Everybody else here is nervous about it. They know you still got teeth."

Nitti cocked his head. "What makes Tenney so brave?"

"Locked doors," I said. "And people like me. He's got great faith in these things."

Nitti waited.

"The story would be buried with him," I said finally. "That's my good guess."

Nitti got to his feet. "It's nice to know that, Eddie." He slipped into his gray gloves. "You look hungry. Would fifteen thousand look good to you?"

I said nothing. But I didn't throw him out.

He smiled and tapped me on the shoulder. "If you're nervous, farm it out. Hire somebody. That's the smart way."

When he was gone, I knocked on the door of Tenney's office.

"Who's there?" he asked.

"It's me. Eddie. I'm alone."

He opened the door cautiously. "Well?" he demanded.

"He was just curious," I said. "No threats."

Tenney looked relieved. "I print what I want. Nobody scares me."

I met his red-rimmed eyes for a moment. You're worth twenty-five thousand to me now, I thought. But you have to be dead. I wondered if I could arrange it; if it would be worth the risk.

I took Tenney back to his apartment for a nap at six, and at ten-thirty we were at the Club Majorca.

Tenney took his regular table in the safety of a corner and he picked at his food as he studied the other tables. His eyes brightened as he watched two couples make their way to a table.

He poked me with his elbow. "There's Ronnie Hendon."

Hendon was starring on Broadway. He was a pale young man who walked with a superfluous amount of hip motion. I didn't think it had to mean anything, but Tenney had other ideas.

He watched the table and after a while he ran his tongue over his lips. "Notice how he spends most of his time whispering in that other man's ear? He gives him all his attention."

Tenney scowled at the two hard-bright girls with Hendon and his companion. "Sometimes they go out with girls as a cover-up. So that the public won't know the real truth."

Tenney sipped his ice water. "I think he uses lipstick. I can see it from here."

"You got good eyes, boss," I said.

He nodded. "Nothing escapes me." He took out his notebook and wrote down Hendon's name. "I can't stand people like that. They're depraved."

I glanced across the big room and noticed the headwaiter talking to Rick Balboa and his manager. Rick was about Tenney's size, but what was there was hard. I set myself for trouble.

The headwaiter, followed by Balboa and his manager, began threading his way toward an empty table.

Tenney noticed Balboa and he clutched my arm. "You see him, don't you?"

Balboa almost passed us. Then his eyes flicked in our direction and he stopped in his tracks. Dark temper flooded his face.

He stalked over to our table and stood glaring down at Tenney. "You dirty liar!"

Tenney's face was white and his eyes big with panic.

Balboa's hand reached for a fistful of Tenney's shirt, but it never got there. I stood up and overturned the table. I spun Balboa, to get behind him, and pinned his arms to his sides. He cursed and tried to dig into my shins with his heels, but he was helpless.

Tenney's fright dissolved fast and a yellow glow came into his eyes. He lunged forward, his small fists flailing at Balboa's face.

I waited until he drew a little blood from Balboa's lip before I freed my left arm. I chopped Balboa under the chin with the edge of my hand. He collapsed and I lowered him to floor.

Tenney wasn't through with Balboa yet. He began kicking the unconscious singer.

I dragged Tenney away. "Take it easy, boss. No use in killing him."

After a while Tenney calmed down, but there was still a wild satisfaction in his eyes. He reached for his handkerchief and wiped the dribble from his chin.

The club manager forced his way through the half a hundred excited diners surrounding us.

Tenney stopped his loud talk by reaching for his wallet. He pulled out a couple of hundreds and his sharp little teeth showed in a smile. "This ought to help clear up the mess."

Tenney followed in my footsteps as I shouldered my way through the crowd and out into the street.

The attendant had just brought up our car, when the doors of the club opened and Balboa staggered out, his face still dark with rage. He was a bantam cock who never knows when he's had enough.

The whiteness came back into Tenney's face and he looked for me to hold Balboa's arms.

"I'll take care of this alone, boss," I said. "You shouldn't strain yourself."

I hustled Balboa back into the club, nearly carrying him. I put both my hands on his shoulders and pressed him down into a chair. "Give it up, Rick," I said. "You won't get anywhere. Not today and not while I'm in the way."

I guess that then he really saw me for the first time. Before that I was just a wall that kept him from doing what he wanted.

The fighting anger seeped slowly out of him. He ran his fingers through his hair and started at the floor. "My wife's going to divorce me. All because of that damn article."

His fingers touched the cut lip. "She'll get the kids too." He looked at me. "Is Tenney something extra special to you?"

I shrugged. "I don't give a damn one way or the other."

I think I knew what was coming next. I had the feeling and I waited.

Balboa looked me over before he spoke again. "I'd give ten thousand to *go* to Tenney's funeral. You know what I mean?"

His face flushed. "I'm serious. What the hell you grinning about?"

"Nothing much," I said. "I was just thinking that things come in threes." And that they add up to thirty-five thousand dollars, I added in my thoughts.

He grasped the sleeve of my coat. "You can get to him," he said urgently. "You'd know how to do it without taking a risk."

"Maybe," I said. "Just maybe."

Tenney was sitting in the car when I came out. I tapped on the window.

He came out of his happy dream and looked at me. "It's unlocked," he snapped.

When I pulled the big car into traffic, Tenney was back to smiling at his thoughts. "I think it was that last right that knocked him out."

"Sure," I said.

"They don't scare me," he said. "Nobody."

I nodded absently. "You're small, but wiry."

"Eddie," he said. "I almost killed him. You got to help me control my temper."

"That's right," I said. "You got a terrible temper."

He nodded. "That's part of your job, Eddie. To help me control my temper. That's my one danger. I'm liable to lose my temper and kill somebody."

"Sure," I said. "You got a mean punch."

He agreed. "I don't know my own strength."

I looked at him. He really believed it.

At the apartment, Tenney walked back and forth with his excitement and he told me what happened. As far as he was concerned, I hadn't been there.

Then he went to the buzzer and pressed it twice.

"Cawber's not here," I said. "This is his night off."

He shrugged. "Fix me a drink, Eddie."

I hesitated. Tenney isn't the kind that can take liquor and he usually knows it.

He frowned. "Do it now, Eddie. Not next week."

I went into the kitchen and got the only bottle of whiskey in the house. Tenney keeps it for his guests.

I made drinks for both of us.

Tenney took a couple of swallows. "Get me that girl in the accounting department. The brunette."

I knew which one he meant. She had been here before.

"Offer her five hundred," Tenney said. "No more."

I dialed her number. There was no answer. "She's probably out on a date," I said.

"Damn," Tenney said. "Damn it. I know that tonight . . ." He was through with his drink now and he felt two inches taller. It showed in the way he walked back and forth, almost on tiptoe. "Get me that one who paints," he ordered.

I dialed the number of the cat-eyed blonde who claims she earns a living painting portraits. There was no answer.

Tenney made himself a second drink. He walked back and forth and rubbed his head irritably. "It ought to be in all the papers."

I was thinking about thirty-five thousand. "What?"

"The fight," he snapped. "The fight."

I shrugged.

"Get me the newspapers," Tenney said.

"It's too early. It wouldn't be in yet."

Tenney was six feet tall now. "I said get me the newspapers."

For a second I considered throwing him out of the window. Then I put aside the idea and got my hat. I took the elevator down and walked two blocks to a newsstand and bought the latest papers. There wasn't anything about Tenney in any one of them.

I walked back slowly and I was still thinking about the thirty-five grand.

Upstairs in front of the apartment door, I pressed the buzzer and waited. After a while I used my keys.

Miss Janicki stood frozen in the middle of the living room, staring down at something on the floor. Her eyes were large with fright and her hands were in front of her mouth as though she were about to eat her fingers.

I tossed the papers aside and went to see what she was looking at.

Tenney lay sprawled on his back, the upper part of his body lying on the tile around the fireplace. The blood around his head had a dull shine.

"He's dead," Miss Janicki whispered. "He's dead." She began crying and the dry-sounding sobs grated on my nerves.

I pulled the hands away from her face and slapped her hard. "What happened?"

Tears trickled down her cheeks. "He rang for me," she said, her voice breaking around the words. She looked at me for desperate confirmation. "He often does that. Even late at night when he wants to dictate a letter."

"Go on," I said.

Her face was splotched with color. She tried speaking and then shook her head helplessly.

I thought I could figure it out. I knew what Tenney was like when he drank. "He started getting damn friendly?" I asked impatiently.

She nodded dumbly. "It was horrible. He was never like that before. Never." She stared at the body again. "I just pushed him . . . and he fell. He hit his head on the tile."

I looked down at Tenney. Dead, he could be worth thirty-five thousand to me. But not this way. Not if some hysterical female took the credit for it. I could feel the money slipping away.

And then the answer came to me. I would have to make an accident look like murder.

"I guess I'd better call the police," Miss Janicki said dully.

"Sure," I said. "Do that."

She saw what I wanted her to see in my eyes. She licked her lips uncertainly. "It was an accident. Nothing can happen to me."

I laughed softly. "You got witnesses?"

She spoke in frantic hurry. "He had some drinks. I could smell the liquor."

"Think of the publicity," I said. "Jealous secretary kills boss."

Her voice was high with denial. "But that's ridiculous. There was never anything between us. I respected him as a . . . a person, a mind."

I grinned. "You live in his apartment, don't you?"

It was true. Locked doors or no locked doors. Separate suites or no separate suites. Technically she lived in Tenney's apartment. He was the one who paid the rent.

Her face showed that she had never quite thought of it that way.

I lit a fresh cigar. After a while I spoke softly. "You don't have to go through that. It doesn't have to be that way."

She looked at me and after fifteen seconds I was the god who was going to save her.

I moved closer. "This is the way things went. Tenney and I came home at eleven. He seemed exhilarated and he began drinking. Both of us were in here with him. He wanted company."

She nodded.

"And then the buzzer sounded. I let in a man of about twenty-five. Everything about him was medium. He was about five foot six or seven. His hair was brown. His eyes were brown. Neither of us had ever seen him before, but Tenney seemed to know him."

I met her eyes. "We won't be able to identify him. Not if we look at a thousand pictures. You understand?"

She swallowed. "I understand."

"Tenney told you and me to leave the room. He wanted to talk to the stranger privately. We went into the kitchen and had coffee."

I began pacing he room. "After about a half an hour, I began to worry. I'm his bodyguard and that gives me the right. I came into this room and you came with me. You wanted to ask if they'd like some coffee."

I stopped in front of her. "Remember. We were never out of each other's sight. Neither one of us was in the room alone with Tenney after the stranger arrived. That protects us both in case the police get ideas."

She nodded.

"We found Tenney just as he is now and the poker was next to his body. The stranger was gone."

Her eyes went to the clean poker in its stand and then she looked at me. "Why are you doing this?"

"It's the only thing to do," I said. "There's no need for your life to be ruined because of this . . . this accident."

There was a warm glow in her eyes. "Is it for me?"

"Of course it's for you,'" I snapped. And then I got it. Good Lord, I thought, it's got to be personal with her. I killed the laugh I felt coming. So much the better. She'd really stick to our story then.

"Remember," I said. "We identify nobody. Tenney had a thousand enemies who could hire a thousand killers. We'll let the cops try to figure it out."

"I understand perfectly, Eddie," she said softly.

"We can't forget the little things that might trip us up," I said. "You'd better go into the kitchen and make some coffee."

She was calm now. "All right, Eddie." She went into the kitchen.

I sat down to think about it again. It was so simple and I was even on the side of the angels. I was actually helping someone. No murder. No risk.

I grinned and took out my handkerchief. I wrapped it around the poker and dipped the end of it into the blood.

And then Tenney groaned.

I froze in my crouch and looked at his face. His eyes were half-slitted with returning consciousness and he stirred faintly.

The tips of my fingers were ice cold.

Miss Janicki's voice came from the kitchen. "The coffee's ready now, Eddie. Would you care for a cup?"

"Just a second, Stella," I said. "I'll be right with you."

I took a firm grip on the poker and swung hard. I don't think the sound carried to the kitchen.

Stella made good coffee.

Fair Play

April 1959

After sixty seconds of television commercial, the large man came to the screen for his epilogue. He sighed regretfully. "Of course Miss Haskins, the tea cup murderess, was apprehended by the vigilant police eventually. We thought you might like to know that if you can't stand those happy endings for bad people." He closed his eyes for a moment of critical distaste. "And next week we'll be bringin' you the strange story . . ."

I adjusted my glasses and consulted our program guide.

My wife Edna's voice was rich with scorn. "That stupid woman. Arsenic is out. It's too easy to detect. An autopsy gets them every time."

I got up and switched to another channel. "What would you use, dear?"

I regulated the brightness and the sound and returned to my easy chair. I folded my hands. About a minute later, it came to me. Edna hadn't answered the question.

I turned my head to look at her.

Her fingers were busy with her knitting, but her eyes were in a world that brought a self-satisfied smile to her lips.

I felt a draft of uneasiness. "Are you all right?"

She remembered me and frowned. "Who said I'd use poison? I haven't mentioned a thing about it." The ice cubes in her glass of soda rattled as she took a sip.

My eyes went back to the television set. A detective was describing the wretched city he lived in. It was hot and humid and Tuesday and twelve minutes after eight when he checked in at headquarters.

I stole a glance at Edna. She was still Madame Defarge to me after fifteen years of marriage. Her lips moved, counting the stitches, but I had the feeling she was simply practicing for something bigger.

I tapped the tips of my fingers together and watched the set. A woman's body had been discovered. She had been brutally beaten. Her husband couldn't be found. Suspicion? Murder.

I leaned forward.

Edna's voice was sharp. "Can't you get something else?"

I was defensive. "Now be fair, Edna. Just because this time the victim is a woman I don't think . . ."

Her eyes were cold. "I said I wanted another channel. That means right now."

Edna is a big woman and I am a small man. I have been aware of this for some time. I turned to a quiz program. A taxi driver was making his twenty-seventh appearance.

"Henry," Edna asked after a while. "Have you paid the premium on your insurance this month?"

"Yes, dear. And I paid yours too."

She sniffed. "I still think it's a waste of money to insure me."

"No, it isn't dear," I said absently. "You never know when something might happen."

She stared at me with narrow eyes.

I got to my feet. "I'm out of cigars, dear. I think I'll go down to Miller's and get some. I'll be right back."

It was a thoughtful walk for me. I played with a suspicion.

Mr. Miller handed me the five nickel cigars. "Did you get rid of the rats, Henry?"

I lit a cigar. "What rats?"

"The ones your wife talked about when she got the poison."

I rolled the cigar in my mouth pensively.

Mr. Miller chuckled. "Don't you worry about her poisoning you, Henry. That stuff I sold her is harmless to dogs, cats, and humans." He kept grinning. "She seemed a little disappointed when I told her."

My cigar seemed to taste better.

He leaned on the counter. "Besides, if she wanted to poison you, Henry, she could just as well get something better from that brother of hers. He's a chemist too and he can lay his hands on all kinds of stuff."

I could see Gerald's sneaky face right now. I had to look at it eight hours a day at the laboratory.

On the walk back home, I ground my teeth several times.

Edna's eyes held a glitter when I entered the living room. "If you're hungry, you'll find two sandwiches in the refrigerator. They're wrapped in wax paper."

I was thoughtful as I walked into the kitchen. The sandwiches were on the second shelf.

I unwrapped one and lifted the top slice of rye.

Ah, ha! On the swiss cheese, and principally in the holes, I detected small grains of a white powder.

The second sandwich was exactly the same.

By George, she wanted to make sure.

I was quietly furious and almost stamped my foot.

Emma was rushing me into immediate action.

I hadn't planned to get rid of her until the end of the week.

I re-wrapped the sandwiches and hid them behind a canister on one of the top cabinet shelves.

I went to the refrigerator. Yes, I thought, lettuce and tomato sandwiches. Edna liked them because they were low in calories.

I prepared two and cut them diagonally.

I smiled to myself and rubbed my hands. Now for the seasoning. I got the small cardboard carton I'd hidden in the toe of my overshoes in the back hall and used the powder liberally on one of the sandwiches. I thought that was clever of me. I might have to eat the other one if Edna got suspicious.

I had just returned the poison to my hiding place when Edna walked into the kitchen.

Her eyes flicked to the sandwiches. "What are you doing?"

I laughed lightly. "Just making you a couple of sandwiches, dear."

Her eyes surveyed them suspiciously, "How come?"

"Now, dear," I said. "You act as though I'd never made sandwiches for you before."

"Let's just say you never volunteered until now." She looked me over carefully. "Did you eat your sandwiches?"

"Yes, dear."

"Hm," she said slowly. "I must say that you ate them extremely fast." She made her voice casual. "How did they taste?"

"Delicious, dear." I smiled and raised an inquiring eyebrow. "Well . . . perhaps just a trifle metallic?"

"Don't be ridiculous," she snapped. "I told you that only a fool would use . . ." She frowned and went to the step-on garbage can. "Well, I see that you ate the wax paper too."

She came back to the kitchen table and put her hands on her hips. She picked up a sandwich and lifted a triangle of bread.

The woman didn't trust me.

At the same time, however, I was pleased. My powder had melted and left no trace.

Edna eyed me thoughtfully. "Why don't you have one of these too, Henry?"

I picked a section of the safe sandwich, but I didn't get it to my mouth.

Her hand went over my wrist.

"I'll take that one."

She smiled like a cat as she elevated it to her mouth.

I smiled too. It was just a nervous smile, but evidently Edna didn't think so.

She put the sandwich down uneaten. "I don't believe I'm hungry. I'll just have a glass of milk."

Edna got the bottle out of the refrigerator and poured herself a glass. She paused and her eyes searched me.

She went to the cupboard and got a bowl. "On second thought, I believe I'll make eggnog." Her smile was firm. "For both of us. You watch what I put into it because you're going to drink half of it. I wouldn't want either one of us to get indigestion."

When the nog was done, I took a very small sip and waited.

Edna did the same and indicated that it was now my turn.

It took us ten minutes to finish our glasses.

We both felt quite confident as we went back into the living room to watch television.

The Inspector, a man with an eye patch, was explaining an interesting point. "Ah," he said. "The reason Mr. Lawrence did not succumb, even though he drank the same tea as Sir Anthony, is that he had, through the course of months, built up an immunity to the poison. Every day he took just a little bit, until . . ."

Edna beat me to the bathroom. I had to go out into the back yard.

I didn't sleep that night and I know that Edna didn't either. I lay in the moonlight, quite hungry, and evaluated the situation. It was absolutely clear. We were antagonists and only one of us could survive. The cleverer one.

That was what put the issue in doubt.

I considered other methods. A blunt instrument? Good heavens, no. Edna would probably wrest the weapon from me and bash my brains in.

Hire a killer? But where could I find one? Besides, he would probably be too expensive. Edna would never give me the money.

I wasn't worried about disposing of the body. That would be simple. I would drive out into the country late at night and find a secluded place to bury her. The police would be suspicious about her disappearance, of course, but what could they prove without a body?

The real problem was to get her to take the poison.

The answer came to me at five o'clock in the morning. I sat up in bed, pleased with myself.

Edna rose on one elbow. "Why the hell don't you go to sleep?"

I was elated by the tone of her voice. Evidently she hadn't come up with anything yet.

I got up at seven and went downstairs. Edna hadn't made my breakfast in fourteen years and I knew that she wouldn't start now. Not even to keep an eye on me.

She was probably lying in bed, smiling to herself, and thinking that I could adulterate anything I had a mind to, but she wouldn't be tricked into tasting a thing in the house. Perhaps she was even hoping that I'd manage to poison myself with some devilish thing she'd spiked.

I chuckled to myself as I made my solution and poured it into the tray.

At seven-thirty I left the house so that I could have a leisurely and secure breakfast at a cafeteria before going to the laboratory.

During the course of the day I beamed at Gerald twice. The first time he dropped an Erlenmeyer flask. The second, he burned the small finger of his left hand with a mild solution of hydrochloric acid.

At five, I was out of my lab coat and going to the elevators.

When I reached my house, I opened the front door with my key and listened.

There was silence. Big beautiful silence.

Out of respect for the dead, I walked into the living room on tiptoe.

Edna lay sprawled on the sofa, an empty glass on the rug next to her. She had taken the pause to refresh that I had anticipated, and she had paid for it. I notice that she had been careful. The large bottle of soda on the cocktail table was a different brand from those in the refrigerator. She must have gone out to get it.

I bent over her to make certain that she was dead. There was still a certain formidability about her, but it was not that of the living.

I went into the kitchen and emptied all the ice cube trays into the sink. It hadn't entered Edna's mind that there was enough poison in any one of the cubes to kill two or three people.

I felt a sense of freedom. of exhilaration, actually.

Perhaps that is what gave me the physical strength to drag Edna's body to the car later that night.

Really, that woman was grossly over-weight.

It was beautiful and star-lit in the country and when I cleaned the earth from my shovel, the moon still rode high in the early morning sky.

I drove home with the window of my car open and drank the bracing air.

I'd have to get rid of all the food in the house, of course. Everything that was eatable and drinkable. I smiled to myself. I couldn't very well allow Edna to kill me now that she was dead.

And I'd have to report Edna's disappearance to the police. There would be no elaborations. I would simply state that she had left last night, saying that she was going to a neighborhood movie, and that she hadn't returned.

I hadn't noticed her absence until this morning because I had gone to bed early.

At home, I went to bed and slept until the alarm rang. I sang in my shower and then went to the bathroom mirror to shave.

Poor Edna. That ice cube business had been pure genius. The old brain was really clicking that time.

I thought about poisons fondly as I shaved. About the varieties and classes, the metallics, the alkaloids.

Now take curare, for instance. It has to be injected directly into the blood stream itself to be effective. Perhaps I should have tried one of the derivatives we have at the laboratory.

I dabbed iodine on a small cut on my chin.

That stuff was so powerful that even if you diluted it with . . .

I stared at my reflection and my hand went to the cut.

"Now, Edna," I said out, loud. "That was a dirty trick."

I shook my head at the insidiousness of it.

"That was really . . . really . . . a dirty . . ."

Shatter Proof

October 1960

He was a soft-faced man wearing rimless glasses, but he handled the automatic with unmistakable competence.

I was rather surprised at my calmness when I learned the reason for his presence. "It's a pity to die in ignorance," I said. "Who hired you to kill me?"

His voice was mild. "I could be an enemy in my own right."

I had been making a drink in my study when I had heard him and turned. Now I finished pouring from the decanter. "I know the enemies I've made and you are a stranger. Was it my wife?"

He smiled. "Quite correct. Her motive must be obvious."

"Yes," I said. "I have money and apparently she wants it. All of it."

He regarded me objectively "Your age is?"

"Fifty-three."

"And your wife is?"

"Twenty-two."

He clicked his tongue. "You were foolish to expect anything permanent, Mr. Williams."

I sipped the whiskey. "I expected a divorce after a year or two and a painful settlement. But not death."

"Your wife is a beautiful woman, but greedy, Mr. Williams. I'm surprised that you never noticed."

My eyes went to the gun. "I assume you have killed before?"

"Yes."

"And obviously you enjoy it."

He nodded. "A morbid pleasure, I admit. But I do."

I watched him and waited. Finally I said, "You have been here more than two minutes and I am still alive."

"There is no hurry, Mr. Williams," he said softly.

"Ah, then the actual killing is not your greatest joy. You must savor the preceding moments."

"You have insight, Mr. Williams."

"And as long as I keep you entertained, in one manner or another, I remain alive?"

"Within a time limit, of course."

"Naturally. A drink, Mr. . . . ?"

"Smith requires no strain on the memory. Yes, thank you. But please allow me to see what you are doing when you prepare it."

"It's hardly likely that I would have poison conveniently at hand for just such an occasion."

"Hardly likely, but still possible."

He watched me while I made his drink and then took an easy chair.

I sat on the davenport. "Where would my wife be at this moment?"

"At a party, Mr. Williams. There will be a dozen people to swear that she never left their sight during the time of your murder."

"I will be shot by a burglar? An intruder?"

He put his drink on the cocktail table in front of him. "Yes. After I shoot you, I shall, of course, wash this glass and return it to your liquor cabinet. And when I leave I shall wipe all fingerprints from the doorknobs I've touched."

"You will take a few trifles with you? To make the burglar-intruder story more authentic?"

"That will not be necessary, Mr. Williams. The police will assume that the burglar panicked after he killed you and fled empty-handed."

"That picture on the east wall," I said. "It's worth thirty thousand."

His eyes went to it for a moment and then quickly returned to me. "It is tempting, Mr. Williams. But I desire to possess nothing that will even remotely link me to you. I appreciate art, and especially its monetary value, but not to the extent where I will risk the electric chair." Then he smiled. "Or were you perhaps offering me the painting? In exchange for your life?"

"It was a thought."

He shook his head. "I'm sorry, Mr. Williams. Once I accept a commission, I am not dissuaded. It is a matter of professional pride."

I put my drink on the table. "Are you waiting for me to show fear, Mr. Smith?"

"You will show it."

"And then you will kill me?"

His eyes flickered. "It is a strain, isn't it, Mr. Williams? To be afraid and not to dare show it."

"Do you expect your victims to beg?" I asked.

"They do. In one manner or another."

"They appeal to your humanity? And that is hopeless?"

"It is hopeless."

"They offer you money?"

"Very often."

"Is that hopeless too?"

"So far it has been, Mr. Williams."

"Behind the picture I pointed out to you, Mr. Smith, there is a wall safe."

He gave the painting another brief glance. "Yes."

"It contains five thousand dollars."

"That is a lot of money, Mr. Williams."

I picked up my glass and went to the painting. I opened the safe, selected a brown envelope, and then finished my drink. I put the empty glass in the safe and twirled the knob.

Smith's eyes were drawn to the envelope. "Bring that here, please."

I put the envelope on the cocktail table in front of him.

He looked at it for a few moments and then up at me. "Did you actually think you could buy your life?"

I lit a cigarette. "No. You are, shall we say, incorruptible."

He frowned slightly. "But still you brought me the five thousand?"

I picked up the envelope and tapped its contents out on the table. "Old receipts. All completely valueless to you."

He showed the color of irritation. "What do you think this has possibly gained you?"

"The opportunity to go to the safe and put your glass inside it."

His eyes flicked to the glass in front of him. "That was yours. Not mine."

I smiled. "It was your glass, Mr. Smith. And I imagine that the police will wonder what an empty glass is doing in my safe. I rather think, especially since this will be a case of murder, that they will have the intelligence to take fingerprints."

His eyes narrowed. "I haven't taken my eyes off you for a moment. You couldn't have switched our glasses."

"No? I seem to recall that at least twice you looked at the painting."

Automatically he looked in that direction again. "Only for a second or two."

"It was enough."

He was perspiring faintly. "I say it was impossible."

"Then I'm afraid you will be greatly surprised when the police come for you. And after a little time you will have the delightful opportunity of facing death in the electric chair. You will share your victims' anticipation of death with the addition of a great deal more time in which to let your imagination play with the topic. I'm sure you've read accounts of executions in the electric chair?"

His finger seemed to tighten on the trigger.

"I wonder how you'll go," I said. "You've probably pictured yourself meeting death with calmness and fortitude. But that is a common comforting delusion, Mr. Smith. You will more likely have to be dragged. . . ."

His voice was level. "Open that safe or I'll kill you."

I laughed. "Really now, Mr. Smith, we both know that obviously you will kill me if I *do* open the safe."

A half a minute went by before he spoke. "What do you intend to do with the glass?"

"If you don't murder me—and I rather think you won't now—I will take it to a private detective agency and have your fingerprints reproduced. I will put them, along with a note containing pertinent information, inside a sealed envelope. And I will leave instructions that in the event I die violently, even if the occurrence appears accidental, the envelope be forwarded to the police."

Smith stared at me and then he took a breath. "All that won't be necessary. I will leave now and you will never see me again."

I shook my head. "I prefer my plan. It provides protection for my future."

He was thoughtful. "Why don't you go direct to the police."

"I have my reasons."

His eyes went down to his gun and then slowly he put it in his pocket. An idea came to him. "Your wife could very easily hire someone else to kill you."

"Yes. She could do that."

"I would be accused of your death. I could go to the electric chair."

"I imagine so. Unless. . . ."

Smith waited.

"Unless, of course, she were unable to hire anyone."

"But there are probably a half a dozen others. . . ." He stopped.

I smiled. "Did my wife tell you where she is now?"

"Just that she'd be at a place called the Petersons. She will leave at eleven."

"Eleven? A good time. It will be very dark tonight. Do you know the Petersons' address?"

He stared at me. "No."

"In Bridgehampton," I said, and I gave him the house number.

Our eyes held for a half a minute.

"It's something you must do," I said softly. "For your own protection."

He buttoned his coat slowly. "And where will you be at eleven, Mr. Williams?"

"At my club, probably playing cards with five or six friends. They will no doubt commiserate with me when I receive word that my wife has been . . . shot?"

"It all depends on the circumstances and the opportunity." He smiled thinly. "Did you ever love her?"

I picked up a jade figurine and examined it. "I was extremely fond of this piece when I first bought it. Now it bores me. I will replace it with another."

When he was gone there was just enough time to take the glass to a detective agency before I went on to the club.

Not the glass in the safe, of course. It held nothing but my own fingerprints.

I took the one that Mr. Smith left on the cocktail table when he departed.

The prints of Mr. Smith's fingers developed quite clearly.

The Queer Deal

December 1961

I examined the twenty under the lamp. "It's counterfeit."

Big Ed swore and brought a handful of bills to the light. "They look all right to me."

I took a twenty from my wallet and handed it to him. "Try them side by side. There's a slight difference in the coloring and in the feel of the thing. The grain in the paper doesn't look right either."

Big Ed glared at me.

I shrugged. "How was I supposed to figure that something like this would happen? The hundreds are phony too."

Jimmy Becker left the open suitcase on the bed and joined us. "They don't look too bad—unless you got another bill handy to compare. I think we could pass them."

"It would be a long, long job," I said. "And it's not smart."

He didn't agree with me. "So we go into a drugstore, buy a pack of cigarettes, and get the change in the real stuff."

I smiled patiently. "Small time stuff and too risky. We'd leave somebody to identify one of us with every bill we passed. We couldn't stay in any town long enough to do us much good. We'd have to keep moving. And besides that, half the money is in hundred dollar bills. Do you expect to take a hundred into a drugstore and get change?"

Big Ed crumpled his handful of bills. "So we're stuck with two hundred thousand and it's just paper. We got nothing for our troubles."

"It's not that bad."

They looked at me.

"We'll have to sell the stuff," I said.

Two weeks before, I'd scouted Pete Fargo, and when I was satisfied I'd gone back to the West Coast to pick up help.

I'd settled on Big Ed and Jim Becker.

Big Ed was heavy, with a bearlike hunch to his shoulders, and Becker was a small, tense man. The thing they had in common was not being too particular about how they made money.

In my hotel room I'd seen that they had cigars and a couple of whiskies before I did my talking. "There's fifty grand in it for each of you."

They liked that part of it fine and smiled.

Big Ed only half joked. "Who do we kill?"

"Nobody. We kidnap him."

Big Ed gave that only two seconds' thought and then put down his glass. "Count me out. I don't monkey around with things that interest the Federal boys. Everybody and his cousin would be on my neck. Not a drop of sympathy anywhere."

Becker agreed with him. "Nothing doing."

"Think about the fifty grand while I'm talking," I said. "The man we take is Pete Fargo."

Big Ed snorted. "You're worse than crazy. Fargo's a big man in the Midwest. Nobody fools with him."

Yes, Fargo was an important man. And so was his brother, Frank. In the county they called home they ran at least a half a dozen clubs, and other things, that I knew about.

"We take Pete Fargo," I said again. "And for our work, we get two hundred thousand."

Big Ed raised an eyebrow. "Your cut would be a hundred thousand?"

"I'm providing the brains."

He let that go. "Just for the sake of conversation, suppose we do take Pete Fargo. You got any plans for him after we get the money?"

"We let him go."

Big Ed pitied me. "And so he goes straight to the cops."

"He won't. They'll never know a thing about it." I took a newspaper clipping out of my pocket and handed it to him. "The Fargo brothers have been in a little trouble with the income tax people. Nothing serious, but enough so that they got tagged to pay a little more than they did. The Government and the Fargos have more or less settled down to calling their incomes twelve thousand dollars a year each, for the last five years. The Fargos claim that they're businessmen and they've got a small ice cream plant to prove it."

Becker laughed. "Twelve thousand a year? Everybody knows they pull in at least ten or twenty times that much every year with the set-up they have."

I smiled. "Everybody *knows*, but nobody can prove it. Especially the Government. But if the Fargos go to the police, they'd have to mention the little thing that they paid two hundred thousand dollars to get Pete back. Before they knew it, the income tax people would pay them a fast return visit and this time, because they'd have the help of the police and the Federals, they'd really dig. They'd want to know *how* the Fargos managed to raise that much money on only twelve thousand a year. Even if the Fargos lived on water, they couldn't have raised that much legitimately. And saying that they borrowed from generous friends wouldn't be the answer. They'd have to name the friends. And the friends the Fargos have wouldn't like to be brought to the attention of the income tax people either. They wouldn't like that at all."

Big Ed worked on his cigar. "Suppose—and I'm just thinking—suppose we just dumped Fargo in the river after we got the money?"

"That would really bring the police in and we don't want that for ourselves. If we do things my way, they won't even know that anything happened. The Fargos won't tell them. They might get steaming mad, but there's nothing they can do but try to forget it."

Becker had an unpleasant thought. "What's to stop Fargo from putting his own organization on us?"

"What organization?"

He thought I was kidding. "He's got a couple of hundred people working for him."

"And you think that adds up to a couple of hundred hoods? A little army that will be searching for us?" I shook my head. "No. When you take off the waiters at his clubs, the bartenders, the croupiers, the girls, the clerks, the bookkeepers, the janitors and what have you, I doubt if you'd have more than half a dozen musclemen left—if that many. And that few can't look far. Figure it out for yourself. You think the Fargos are going to throw out money on an army of killers who just stand around ready to put somebody away once every three or four years?"

Becker was almost convinced. "But what about the Syndicate? The way I read, the Fargos are part of it. And that stretches all over the country."

I killed that. "The big boys might get together once every ten years to shake hands, drink whiskey, and maybe settle a little territory trouble, but as an organization, it's mostly a dream. If the Syndicate was half way as organized as the papers make out, it would need a building the size of the Pentagon filled with clerks just to take care of the paperwork."

I studied their faces and they seemed about ready to go along with me. "There won't be any nation-wide search for us by the Syndicate, but even if there were, the Syndicate wouldn't know who it was looking for. We're not going to leave our calling cards. Fargo doesn't know our names and our faces can melt into the two hundred million population without any trouble."

Becker thought of something else. "How do we get to Pete Fargo? According to what I read, his home is like a fort. All kinds of alarms gadgets, and electric eyes. We couldn't get near it. And he's supposed to have a couple of goons living with him."

Big Ed nodded. "When he travels somebody's always riding with him—somebody easy with a gun. And we couldn't take him at one of the clubs. Too many of his people around."

"I watched him for two weeks," I said. "And I know that he's alone—if you want to call it that—a couple of nights a week. I don't know the lady's name, but when he stops at her apartment, he doesn't feel that he has to have the help of a bodyguard."

We took the next morning's plane back to the Midwest and I bought myself a car.

We picked up Pete Fargo at 3 A.M. two days later as he left his car and was about to enter his girl friend's apartment building. The three of us took him to the small cabin I'd rented about twenty miles from the city.

Fargo was a slim man, but wide-shouldered, and he wasn't showing much scare. "Well?" he demanded. "What are you punks after?"

"Two hundred thousand," I said. "And then we'll give you back to your brother."

He tried a laugh. "You got the wrong man. We don't have that kind of money."

I smiled. "The two hundred thousand is for returning all of you. If we have to cut off an ear and send that to your brother, we'll lower our asking price to one-hundred and ninety thousand. Two ears, only one hundred and eighty thousand. We'll work our way down to ten thousand. There might still be some of you left."

Fargo's eyes went over us and he was memorizing our faces. "Do you know who you're tackling?"

"We know and we're not worried about it." I put the tape recorder on the table. "We'll use this—just in case your brother doesn't believe your handwriting. Tell him not to go to the police. If he should get that silly idea, we'll send you back right away. But he might have trouble recognizing your body. We want two hundred thousand. Nothing bigger than one hundred dollar bills."

His lip dragged at a sneer. "You think he'd mark big bills?"

"I'm not worried about your brother. But the bank would keep a record of the serial numbers of bigger bills—if that's where he's going to get the cash—and I won't feel comfortable if anybody at all has a list."

I unraveled the microphone cord. "Your brother has one week to raise the money. No more. And when he has it, I want him to put an ad in the Lost and Found column of both the daily newspapers. *Lost. Wallet, Initials J.G.L. Keep cash. Please return papers.* When we see that, we'll get in touch with him about the delivery."

Fargo's eyes flickered. "What's to stop you from putting a bullet through me once you get the money?"

"Nothing. Except that we're just as anxious to keep this thing a little private affair as you are. And I think you are. We don't want the police or anybody else in on this and they would have to be if we gave them a body. We'll kill you only if we don't get the money. We'd be mad enough for that."

I held the microphone in front of him. "Time to talk, Fargo, Give your brother a real horror story so that he'll feel sorry for you."

Fargo darkened with anger, but when I flipped the switch he began talking.

When he was done, I put the tape and a printed note in a small box and addressed it to Frank Fargo.

When Fargo's answer appeared in the Lost and Found column four days later, I phoned him from a bus depot and made the arrangements for the delivery.

He was to put the money in a suitcase and drop it in the ditch beside county trunk J a hundred feet past its junction with OC at nine the next night. Both J and OC were gravel roads in a lonely section of the country.

When I got back to the cabin, Big Ed and Becker were anxiously waiting.

"Everything's arranged," I said.

Big Ed rubbed his neck nervously. "Suppose Frank Fargo's got the place covered by a few of his boys?"

"I told him not to plan any surprises. The man we'd send to make the pick-up wouldn't know where to find us or where we kept his brother. We'd get in touch with him after he picked up the money. But if we didn't meet him on time and alone, we'd finish off Pete and send him the pieces."

Becker frowned. "We're letting somebody else in on this?"

"No. I just used those words. I'll make the pick-up myself."

Big Ed smiled. "You *and* I will make the pick-up."

My smile was mild. "You're afraid that I won't be able to lift the suitcase by myself?"

"I just think that you might not be able to resist the temptation to keep right on traveling."

"Ed," I said. "Suppose I did cross you? What would you do about it?"

His eyes narrowed. "I'd kill you."

"What if you couldn't find me?"

He glowered. "Maybe I'd get mad enough to send the police a few hints about how you got the money. Even if it hurt me too."

"That's right," I said. "And since I know that, you can bet your teeth that I'd rather have just my hundred thousand clear and nobody looking for me than two hundred thousand and no safe place to hide."

"Could be," Ed conceded. "But I'd just as soon go with you so that you don't get tempted even for a second."

The next evening at eight, Big Ed and I parked the car on a hill about a half a mile from the intersection of J and OC, turned off our lights, and waited.

At a quarter to nine, a car pulled off the main highway and turned onto J. We watched the beams of the headlights move slowly down the road and stop just past OC.

A big man carrying a suitcase crossed the headlights and disappeared on the side of the road. When he returned, his hands were empty.

We waited until the car turned back toward the highway and melted into the traffic before Big Ed started the engine.

He slowed down at the intersection.

"Right about here," I said.

I got out of the car with my flashlight and walked along the ditch. When I came back to the car, Ed took the suitcase impatiently. "Let's see if it's there."

He whistled softly when he snapped open the lid. "Now isn't that pretty."

We drove around for a while to make certain we weren't being followed and then headed back to the cabin.

Becker had untied one of Fargo's arms and was letting him have a smoke.

Big Ed put the suitcase on the kitchen table and let Becker have a look.

Becker's eyes glittered. "Are you sure it's all there?"

Big Ed chuckled. "If it isn't, it's close enough. We didn't stop to count every bill."

Pete Fargo took a couple of nervous puffs on his cigarette and I thought I knew what he was thinking. Now that we had the money, were we really going to let him go, or did we have other plans?

I grinned. "Take it easy, Fargo. You'll be talking to your brother before midnight."

He shrugged as though he hadn't been worried at all.

"What do we do now?" Becker asked. "Drop Fargo off on the road somewhere?"

"We just leave him here and go ourselves," I said. "He'll work his way out of those ropes in an hour or so. We'd better not stick around here any longer than we can help it."

We left Fargo where he was and got into the car. We drove about ten miles to a medium-sized town and checked in at a hotel.

Big Ed put the suitcase on the bed and opened it. "Time to divide the stuff." Then he smiled. "Becker and I been thinking and we come to the agreement that the only fair thing to do is split this three ways. All even."

I looked them over. "I did all the planning."

"Maybe," Big Ed said. "But we figure the pay-off should be on the chances we took. We think they were about even all around."

Their eyes told me that they were ready to make something out of it if I got stubborn. I took a deep breath and then shrugged. "Let's start counting."

I picked up one of the packs of hundreds and riffled through it. I hesitated a moment and then slipped one of the bills from the paper band and examined it. I frowned and went to the lamp for a better look.

Big Ed and Becker stopped their counting and watched me.

"What's the matter?" Big Ed asked finally.

I didn't answer him. I got a pack of twenties from the suitcase and slipped a bill from that. I swore softly.

Big Ed and Becker stared at me.

I held the bill against the light. "It's counterfeit."

"We'll have to sell the stuff," I said. "We got rooked, but we still ought to bring something out of this. To pass those bills you need an organization—a lot of little men who cash the stuff, take their percentage, and bring back the change in good money. But we don't have an organization. If we tried shoving the queer ourselves we'd be operating as amateurs and we'd be asking to get caught. But there are organizations that can do the work for us."

Big Ed regarded the suitcase without joy. "How much could we get for this pile?"

"I don't know. Maybe thirty, forty percent. I never did that kind of business before."

Becker figured that and looked a little happy. "Sixty grand? Or more? Where do we find an organization like that? How do we get in touch with one?"

"I wouldn't know any of the boss men myself," I said. "But I do know a passer in St. Louis. He ought to be able to get us a connection. We can give it a try."

"Start phoning," Big Ed said.

I didn't have Harry Owens' number or his address, but I did know several places where he might be at this time of the night. On my third call to St. Louis I got him at a bowling alley.

"Harry," I said. "This is Mike Randall."

"So?"

"I've got something in your line. Some merchandize I'd like to get rid of."

"Why tell me? I'm just a private in the big army. I don't freelance."

"I don't know the general. But you ought to be able to get through to him. I've got two hundred thousand units. If you can arrange the sale, you get ten percent of what I get."

There was a little silence and then, "I'll see what I can do. Where can I reach you?"

I gave him the town and the name of the hotel. "Something more, Harry. I want the meet here and tonight."

"That's asking for fast work."

"I haven't got the time to waste."

There was a little more silence. "I'll see what I can do. But I don't give orders. I just ask."

Harry called back forty minutes later. "They're going to send a buyer up there."

"When?"

"They told me right away."

"He'll have the money?"

"Sure."

"How much?"

"I don't know. It all depends on what quality stuff you got. And remember, my cut is ten percent. But don't mention that to the man you see."

It was about eleven-thirty when the knock came at the door.

He was a small man, wearing glasses, and he carried a brief case. "Mike Randall?"

"That's right." I looked him over. "What's Harry's last name?"

He smiled thinly. "Owens." His eyes went past me to Big Ed and Becker. "Your friends?"

"Partners."

He came into the room and took off his hat and topcoat. "Where's the merchandise?"

Big Ed pulled the suitcase from under the bed where we had shoved it.

The small man picked up several of the bundles and studied them casually. Then he slipped a few hundreds and a few twenties from their packs and sat down. He took a folding magnifying glass from one of his pockets.

After two or three minutes he smiled slightly. "Jim Bryant's plates made these. I recognize his work. He usually sells his stuff on the Pacific coast." He looked up. "By the way, he's back in prison now. Tried to pass his own work again. Some people never learn. Where did you get these?"

"We found them," I said.

The little man shrugged. He went through the rest of the stacks, taking a random bill here and there and examining it cursorily. He folded his magnifying glass. "You've got two hundred thousand there?"

"Yes."

He pursed his lips. "I can offer you twenty thousand."

Big Ed's mouth dropped. "Twenty thousand? That's only ten percent."

He nodded. "Ten percent. That's a good price. And I'm willing to offer that only because this is Bryant's work. Rather good engraver." He regarded us. "Evidently this is your first venture in this field and you may have heard that the offers go up to thirty or forty percent. You heard wrong. The average is closer to eight percent. And we pay the standard prices."

Big Ed sighed. "All right. Twenty thousand is twenty thousand."

Becker nodded glumly. "What's the sense in spending time shopping around and maybe even getting a lower price?"

The little man opened his brief case and took out a thick manila envelope. He counted out the hundreds and when he was through the envelope was empty.

"You're sure that's *real* money?" Big Ed demanded.

The little man was mildly offended. "I assure you that those bills are the best the Government can print."

When he was gone with the suitcase, I put two thousand in an envelope and addressed it to Harry Owens. We divided the remaining eighteen thousand three ways.

Big Ed scowled as he shoved his six thousand into his pocket. "Hardly worth the chances we took."

Becker was more philosophical. "It's better than nothing."

I took off my necktie. "Let's get some sleep."

"Not me," Big Ed said. "I'm putting a little more country between me and the Fargos first."

Becker agreed with him. "I'll sleep better then, too."

"You're worrying about nothing," I said. "I'm beat and I'm staying here. And I got the car keys."

"Keep them," Big Ed snapped. "There's a bus depot across the street and I'm taking the first thing moving west."

After they left, I went to the window and watched the depot. They got a midnight bus. I didn't know where they were headed and I didn't care.

I put my necktie back on and went down to the car.

It was close to one o'clock when I found county trunk J and followed it until it hit OC.

I stopped the car and walked along the road playing the beam of the flashlight into the ditch until I found the suitcase.

There had been two suitcases.

One I had planted the night before and it had contained the two hundred thousand dollars in counterfeit money I had bought on the West Coast. That was the suitcase I had picked up earlier.

The one I now carried back to the car had been dropped by Frank Fargo and the money had to be real.

There was no sense in dividing two hundred thousand dollars three ways—if you could help it.

And best of all, nobody knew what I had done.

Nobody would be looking for me.

Going down?

July 1965

Several floors below me, firemen were stringing up a safety net.

Sergeant Morgan had eased himself out on the ledge too and now he stood up. "It's a long way down, mister. When you land you'll be nothing but a wide mess."

"The configuration of my remains does not concern me at the moment," I said coldly.

It was evidently part of the sergeant's job to keep me talking. "What's so bad that you think you can solve it by jumping?"

"Nothing specific," I said. "It is simply that the sum total of existence is impossible to bear. I am Everyman and Everyman is a failure."

He took a well-worn cigar stub out of his mouth. "Look, I don't go for this Everyman jazz. You got trouble with your wife? What would she think about you doing this?"

"I rather suspect that she would encourage me to take one or two steps forward."

Morgan listened for a few seconds to someone leaning out of the window behind him and then spoke to me again. "You're registered as Amos Dawson?"

"Yes. However don't bother asking me for my actual name."

He worried the cigar. "You got children, ain't you? What would they think if they seen you up here?"

"I have one son and he is a disappointment. He became a pharmacist."

"You got to learn to take the good with the bad," Morgan said. "Like I wanted my boy to be on the force, but it didn't work out."

"I suppose your father was a policeman?" I asked acidly. "And his father before him?"

"Well, no," Sergeant Morgan said "But you got to start a tradition somewhere. Lance is a carburetor man at Len's Auto Service."

"Lance?"

Morgan shrugged. "I didn't have nothing to do with that. The name was my wife's idea." He began searching through his pockets. "You don't happen to have any Tums on you?"

"No."

He sighed. "I'll bet it's mostly wife troubles bothering you? That right? You don't get along now? But remember, she was the girl that you was in love with when you got married."

"She was?"

"Sure," Morgan said. "Why else did you marry her?"

"Fatal propinquity."

"Now take my case," Morgan said. "She was the girl next door. Weighed in at one-twenty." He thought about that. "You could double that now easy."

I had chosen the side of the building sheltered from the wind and normal conversation was possible. "Everyman is born and doomed to failure," I said. "The sooner he realizes that and defies fate and the universe by a positive-negative action, the better. . . ."

"So things didn't work out," Morgan said. "But life's still worth living."

"Why?"

"Well. . . ." He rubbed his jaw. "If it weren't, then why do people keep on living?"

"Because they are either idiots or cowards afraid of death."

He looked me over. "You wouldn't put yourself in the idiot class, would you?"

"Of course not," I said coolly.

He nodded. "So then if you lived all these years only because you're a coward, I'd think that by now you'd be used to it?"

I thought the sergeant's face seemed rather gray. "Do heights bother you?" I asked a trifle maliciously.

He shook his head. "Not especially. It's my insides. What the fumes done."

"What fumes?"

"Auto fumes. I directed traffic on Third and Wisconsin for seventeen years and then the department medics decided I ought to transfer. So now I'm in bunco."

"Really? And the police sent *you* up here to talk to me?"

"Nobody sent me," Morgan said. "I just happened to be walking to the subway minding my own business when I looked up and seen you. So I rushed up here and started talking. And now nobody inside wants to relieve me. They say they don't want to change horses in mid-stream. But personally I think they're just afraid you'll jump on their time and it might look bad in the newspapers."

He glanced down at the stalled traffic. "See that big truck over there? Looks like you're on television." He exhaled wearily. "That's where I should be now. At home watching this on TV." His face became pensive. "In the old days I could sit in front of TV with a case of beer and watch the ball games all afternoon. But now one bottle makes me sick as a dog. The fumes, you know."

I sincerely wished someone else had arrived here first. "Very well, so you can't drink beer. I'm sure you've managed to fill in your time with something else."

Morgan shook his head. "It was the only hobby I had. Television just ain't the same."

I gazed out into space. "If Everyman is to be more than simply a compliant mote in this universe, then he must. . . ."

"There's one thing I got no trouble with, though," Morgan said. "My ears."

"I wasn't aware that *I* was shouting."

Going Down? 167

"Not you. My wife. I could use a little deafness around the house, but in the ears I got twenty-twenty."

"Women feel unfulfilled unless they are making noise," I said. "Basically it is their desire to be noticed, to be want . . ."

A suspicion descended upon me. Was Morgan engaged in the stratagem of pretending that his miserable cares were important in order to belittle my own? I smiled firmly. "Now concerning my son. My family has been Liberal Arts for generations. We did not even *speak* to anyone with a B.S. And when my son blithely announces that he has registered in . . ."

"My boy didn't even make it through high school," Morgan said. "And the parole board got him the job with Len's Auto Service."

I still smiled. "My wife absolutely hates me."

He brushed that aside. "Hate? My wife saves it up all day and hits me with it at supper. Ever since I told her the boy was no good and that was ten years ago."

I invented a progeny. "My granddaughter got a D in spelling."

He trumped. "*My* granddaughter failed the first grade. She's got to take the whole thing over and she's eight already."

I folded my arms. "The roof of my house leaks."

He was still with me. "We're living in a three-room apartment and my mother-in-law's the landlord."

That did it. "See here," I said. "It is quite evident that you have completely rejected my Everyman motive for departing this world and prefer to think in terms of family trouble. So be it. However I must warn you that I am quite aware of your attempts to minimize my difficulties by creating imaginary ones of your own."

Morgan had large blue eyes. "Huh?"

"My dear man," I said. "If all you say is true—if you are plagued with the fumes and eternally deprived of the creature comfort of beer—if you have a corpulent, nagging, shrill, hating wife—if you have a delinquent son, a moronic granddaughter, and a mother-in-law for a landlord, then I submit to you that you are one of the most miserable creatures in existence. And that being the case, why are you standing here gabbling like an old woman? I see absolutely no reason why *you* shouldn't step off this ledge. Why don't *you* jump!"

Morgan stared at me.

"And furthermore," I said. "If we should delve into your intellect, I'm sure that . . ." I stopped and watched him uneasily.

Morgan's face was white and he stared down at the street. He teetered.

My eyes widened. "Now, just one minute . . . !"

But Sergeant Morgan had stepped off the ledge into space.

The psychiatrist and I had an enjoyable two hours of conversation before a police lieutenant entered the room to interrupt us.

He put the facts on the line. "We've been checking up on you. You pulled this same stunt in Chicago, in St. Louis, and now here. What's the matter, you an exhibitionist, or something?"

"I am *not* an exhibitionist. I approached every ledge with the utmost sincerity. I merely lost my nerve at the last moment."

The psychiatrist was understanding. "However you have definitely decided that never, never again Will you consider taking your life?"

"Absolutely never," I said firmly. "When I saw Sergeant Morgan step . . . slip off that ledge, I suddenly realized that perhaps inhaling and exhaling still had their virtues." I sighed to prove it. "By the way, how is Sergeant Morgan?"

"He got a few rope burns from the safety net," the lieutenant said. "But otherwise he's okay. Except maybe for a little shock. Keeps babbling about how good it is to be alive."

I agreed. "No matter how bitter life is, it is still worth living." And that reminded me of something. I removed thirty cents from my wallet and handed it to the lieutenant. "The next time you see the sergeant, would you please present him with a pack of Tums. My compliments."

**THE STORIES FROM
MANTRAP, MURDER! AND
SMASHING DETECTIVE STORIES**

Anniversary of Death

Smashing Detective Stories
May 1956

They're all positive that Willie won't get me.

The Sheriff has his two deputies here, and there's the lieutenant with six State Troopers. They're all primed and ready sitting here in my living room. About twenty more men are waiting outside to shoot Willie if he shows up.

Clem Purdy and Freddie Houston didn't have this kind of protection. When Freddie died he was alone. Clem was alone, too, when his throat was cut, but that was his own fault. He could have had a bodyguard, but then he had his big idea and he decided he didn't need one.

The red-headed reporter just brought the cat over and took another picture of me with the cat at my feet. That's how it all started, with those cats. Not directly the killings, but how Willie Taver was and what happened later.

People began finding cats hanging dead from trees and bushes; and sometimes at night there'd be a blaze—and somebody would come on a dead cat that had had gasoline poured on it and lit. We all thought at first that it was done by some of the kids and so didn't get much excited. We don't place especial high store on cats, except for maybe a widow woman here and there who keeps one for a house pet.

But when it happened to dogs, that made it different, everybody got powerful indignant and hollered for the sheriff to do something. He was willing enough and did some running around, but he was getting nowhere at all.

Four good hound dogs were lost before the break came—and it was pure luck. That was the Sunday when Clem, Freddie, and me, Walt Harris, took our rods down to the river for some fishing; We three most grew up together and none of us were married. Me and Clem ran the meat market in town and Freddie and his mother were doing the same for the grocery store.

Sitting there on the river bank having a few nips prior to tossing out our lines, we seen Willie Taver sneaking mysterious through the woods. Willie always was a queer one, even when he was a boy; and now when we saw that he hid a brown and white tabby under his arm, we stopped our talking and watched quietly.

Willie stopped next to a willow tree fifty feet short of us and set down the cat. Then he reached in his pocket and pulled out some strong cord.

"I'll be damned," whispered Clem. "Looks like Willie's the one who's been doing the killing."

After making a hangman's knot, Willie looped it around the cat's neck and threw the other end of the cord over a branch and began pulling.

The three of us jumped to our feet yelling and started after Willie. His face got white and he turned and took off like a rabbit. He ran fast, dodging through the bushes real tricky, but at the end of a half mile we caught him and brought him down.

Willie was squealing and cursing when we dragged him to face the sheriff. We got handshakes from everybody and some of the citizens passed the hat for us; it came to about forty-five dollars and that was fifteen for each of us.

Willie wouldn't say a thing to the Sheriff, being either smart or stubborn enough to want a lawyer. The ones in town all claimed they was mighty busy and not able to take on another client at this time. I didn't blame them; you can get pretty unpopular defending a man who kills dogs. Finally Willie's uncle had to go clean to Perryville before he could get one.

The lawyer, Willie, and Willie's uncle did some conferring and then Willie admitted to taking care of those cats. The sheriff tried hard to get him to admit killing the dogs, because that was a more serious charge, but Willie just clamped his mouth shut and wouldn't say another word. We was all hoping for a trial in town, but Willie's lawyer was plumb canny. He got the case transferred to the county seat.

Freddie, Clem, and I went on the witness stand, telling what we saw. Then they put Willie on the stand despite his lawyer doing a flock of objecting.

Willie answered a few questions real normal, but then he got to raving about evil cats and how voices had told him to kill as many of them as he could. The prosecutor asked Willie what the voices said about dogs, but Willie's lawyer was up and hollering and the judge said Willie could let that question ride.

The judge listened to Willie's rambling some more and then he stopped the proceedings. He turned Willie over to some doctors to be worked over, and the upshot of it was that Willie was packed off to the county asylum.

Willie was gone for three years and then one day he was back. The doctors must have figured he was cured, though looking at him, we couldn't understand how they come up with that answer.

Willie was more or less paroled to his uncle, working at the lumber mill hauling boards around and anything that was simple. When he wasn't working, he'd wander around talking to himself.

At first some of the kids heaved stones at him, but that stopped when Willie chased the Simpkins boy clear across town before the boy had sense enough to run into the sheriff's office.

The sheriff locked Willie up again until Willie's uncle got that Perryville lawyer again. There was a lot of argument, with the doctors and the judge who'd sent Willie away getting in on it.

It set most everybody on their heels when they let Willie go and things was made worse when the judge gave the Simpkins boy a tongue-lashing with regard to throwing stones.

The town was buzzing about outside justice for a long while, and Willie's uncle kept him close to home most of the time, but eventually things simmered down. And then about three weeks later Buzz Norbie's setter was found split down the middle with an ax. That dog was worth at least fifty dollars to Buzz, and his wife had to hide his shotgun to keep him from using it on Willie Taver.

The sheriff was burning and he pulled Willie in. But with no witnesses, and that pesky Perryville lawyer pounding on the jail door, he had to let Willie go.

The black looks and the talk didn't bother Willie at all. He'd walk down main street jabbering away to himself and paying no mind to anyone.

Willie built himself a small shack on public land down by the river. He didn't live there, having a room at his uncle's house, but he'd put in a table and a few chairs and he'd stay in there for hours brooding with his thoughts.

A week after Buzz's dog got cleaved, Freddie, Clem, and me took us down to the river for celebrating. Freddie had just give a ring to Margie Carter and he brought along a couple of bottles of white mule.

We lay along the bank passing the bottle now and then and generally getting happy. There was some joshing about how I'd always been the one who carried Margie's books home from school.

"You did all the work, Walt," Freddie said, grinning. "And I got the credit."

"I admire everything about Margie except her judgment," I said. "If you'll quit hogging the bottle, I'll see if I can drink enough to forget a broke heart."

"Here comes Willie," Clem said, pointing up the river. "Hey, Willie!" Clem called. "Come on over and have a drink."

But Willie just gave us black looks and gave us a lot of space as he kept walking down to his shack.

Clem took the bottle after I had a drink. "You fixing to live with your Ma, Freddie?"

Freddie frowned. "I guess I'll have to; I don't think she could take care of herself."

Freddie's Ma was something like Willie, only not so bad. At least right then she wasn't so bad.

She'd come from a big town when she'd married Freddie's Pa and some said as how she'd even been to college. She hadn't been much to look at then, I heard tell, but she was chock full of book learning. She didn't take much to neighbors, claiming that they never talked about anything real important.

After Freddie's Pa died, she took up chess in real earnest. Sometimes she'd go all the way to Perryville for a game with the doctor who lived there. But mostly she'd be studying a board by herself and solving problems. I don't believe anybody in town but her played the game, at least as far as I knew.

She claimed this chess improved her mind, but from what I could see it wasn't doing her much good. There wasn't much housework got done when she was poring over that chess board.

We were near to finishing the bottles as the sun was beginning to set when we got to talking about Willie Taver.

Freddie was grinning kind of foolish. "I think we folks in the community ought to do something about Willie. He's dangerous to have around."

Clem Purdy hiccupped. "How about lynching him?" he said. "Or is that a mite too severe?"

Freddie took a drink and wiped his mouth with his sleeve. "We just seen Willie go to his shack. Suppose when he was coming back he'd see a cat hanging in the path. Right then we jump out of the bushes and collar him. We could all swear we actual seen him string it up."

"It's a dirty trick," I said, but the white mule was working on me and I got to thinking about the forty-five dollars we collected last time we caught Willie. There might be more in it this time.

Clem was pondering on it too. "Considering that we know Willie killed Buzz's dog, but can't prove it, maybe it would be our civic duty to get Willie put away permanent."

"Where you going to find a cat?" I asked.

Freddie giggled somewhat. "It was seeing that one lying on the log over there give me the idea."

Sure enough, sitting there and watching us was a gray striped cat. We caught that cat and strung it up with fishing line to a bush along the way Willie would come back, and then we hid in the bushes with what was left in the bottles.

We had them finished and it was getting almost too dark to see when we heard Willie coming. When he saw it, he stood there looking at it with his mouth open and full of surprise. And then we stumbled out of the bushes and rushed him.

Willie let out a high-pitched curse and started running like a deer. We took after him, but the whiskey hadn't done us any good and after a couple minutes of running and stumbling over roots, we gave up.

We were panting and wondering what to do, when Freddie said, "We don't have to catch him. All we need to do is tell the sheriff we saw him hang the cat."

We all agreed on that and made our way back to town where we told our story to the sheriff. He rubbed his hands and the first thing he did was to make us deputies. He had to help Freddie pin on his badge because Freddie was a mite unsteady.

The sheriff took his two deputies down to comb the tracks and sidings, reckoning that crazy or not, Willie would have enough sense to hop the first freight out of town. He sent Clem and Freddie to search Willie's uncle's house and he told me to get my shotgun and try Willie's shack, in case Willie backtracked.

In the morning I reported back to the sheriff's office and told him that Willie hadn't come back to the shack. The sheriff was tired and sweaty from the night search and he said that no one had seen hide nor hair of Willie.

I was just about to go home and make me some breakfast, when Mister Halley, who runs the Farm Equipment store, came staggering into the sheriff's office. Mister Halley's face was red mad and he had a big bump alongside of his head. When he could calm down enough to talk, he told his story.

Along ten o'clock the night before when the store was closed and he was working on some accounts alone in the back office, he heard a rap on the back door. Through the glass, he seen that it was Willie. Mr. Halley hadn't heard that we were looking for him.

"I was glad to see him," Mr. Halley said. "Sometimes I have Willie get me a cup of coffee and a sandwich from the Diner and right then I was feeling hungry. Willie picks up a few bits that way and I thought that was what he was after now."

But as soon as Willie got in, he pulled out a knife and stuck it against Mr. Halley's stomach. Then he made Mr. Halley sit in a chair and used some wire to tie him up.

"He asked me for the combination to the safe," Mr. Halley said. "It had this month's receipts in it, and I was going to tell Willie to go to hell. But then I got a look at his eyes and remembered those animals he had killed. I gave him the numbers without argument."

Willie filled a paper bag with the money—about eight thousand dollars—and then he gave Mr. Halley a bounce on the head with a paperweight. It wasn't until morning that the first clerk showed up to free Mr. Halley.

That took some of the tiredness out of the sheriff and he set about appointing deputies wholesale and organizing them into searching parties. In the afternoon, when the sheriff came in fuming because Willie still wasn't found, he got the letter. It had been mailed from one of the boxes in town and it was a storm of words from Willie.

Cats were his downfall, Willie wrote. They followed him and they spit at him and they were his enemies. He killed them when he could; and he hated dogs, too, because they always snapped at him.

For that matter, the whole world was against him, with people hating and conspiring against him. They thought he was crazy, when all the time he was the sanest man in the world. Mainly they hated him because they were jealous of his power to talk with the voices.

He was going away for a while and he took the money from Mr. Halley so that he would have a stake and not have to work for any of the mean people who hated him.

The last paragraph was written in what looked like brown ink. It was a fancy curse saying that Willie was going to return one day, and when he did, he was going to kill Freddie, and Clem, and me.

The sheriff sent the letter with what he knew to be Willie's handwriting to the police laboratory in the city. When they were through with their tests, they wrote back that the handwriting was Willie's all right and his fingerprints were all over the letter.

The brown part was written in blood, and by checking with the asylum, they found that it was Willie's blood type.

The next few weeks there was a heap of searching and there were people who claimed to have seen Willie, but all the leads turned sour. The sheriff finally had to admit that Willie had got clean away.

So time went by and people began forgetting Willie and thinking of other things. One of the things that got them to talking was Freddie's accident.

Two weeks before Freddie and Margie's wedding they were out riding and it happened. I've always told Freddie that drinking and driving don't mix, but the only impression that made on him was to remind him that he needed another drink. Drunk or sober, he always drove like a maniac, not allowing any consideration for curves, and this time he didn't make one.

Margie Carter was killed outright and Freddie got about as near to being killed as was possible. He was broke in a dozen places, but he was alive and was rushed to the hospital.

They kept him there for more than six months before they let him go and even then he was still beat up and had to get around with crutches.

The accident, and Freddie's almost dying, made his mother queerer than ever. While he was in the hospital she ran the store, but it made only a bare living for her and I don't know what she did about the hospital bills. The way she muttered and her far-away stares scared away a lot of customers.

She seemed to get somewhat better when Freddie was let out of the hospital, but that lasted only while Freddie was alive.

One night when she came back from playing chess in Perryville she found him dead in the living room. He was sitting in an easy chair with his throat cut from ear. to ear; and beside him was a dead cat.

The sheriff might have made it a routine hunt for motives, and such, but the cat pulled him up short. And then somebody pointed out to him what he was already thinking of. It was exactly one year the day that Willie had disappeared!

The word that Willie was back went around like wildfire and there were more volunteer deputies than the sheriff could handle. They combed that countryside, looking everywhere a man could hide, but they just couldn't locate Willie.

"I don't know where that boy could be hiding," the sheriff said after two days of searching. "But wherever it is, it's a beaut."

He assigned each of his deputies to following us, and Clem and me bought ourselves pistols. They were with us most of the day for about a month and then the citizens started complaining. They didn't like how those deputies concentrating on us cut down on protection for the rest of the town. The tramps down at the switch yards were getting mighty bold, and the deputies ought to look to controlling them instead of wasting their time on us. The elections was coming on, so the sheriff listened to them and took away the deputies.

The months went by with nothing happening, until at last we decided to put the pistols away. We reasoned that if Willie had any more killing in mind he was going to save it for the Anniversary Day. That's what we started calling it—the Anniversary Day.

And so when a year passed and the anniversary came around, we were ready. We closed the butcher shop and spent the entire twenty-four hours in the house that Clem rents. The sheriff came down in the evening with his deputies, having one patrol the outside while the other stayed in the house with us.

Toward the last few hours the tension began building up. The last one was the worst, and Clem was putting away liquor fast. But the minutes went by and the clock finally struck midnight without anything happening. We all let out a breath at once and poured another round of drinks.

"It's my guess that Willie has decided to forget about the whole thing," the sheriff said, tossing off his drink. "Either that or he's come to the conclusion that it's too dangerous to try."

The sheriff wasn't taking any chances though. He had us guarded the rest of the night and the next day before pulling his men away.

Life went back to normal and it would have stayed that way, but then Clem began getting his idea.

When you grow up with a man, going to school with him, fishing and hunting and working with him, you get to know him pretty well. And that was why I could tell when the idea began working on him. He nursed it a long time, working it over, and then one day about eleven months later he came down to the store wearing his gun.

"You can never tell about Willie," he told all the folks who asked him about the gun. "He might strike at me any time."

A week later he took me aside and began talking. "I'm selling out my half of the shop," he said. "There isn't really enough business for two of us in this town."

"We been doing all right, Clem," I said; "we ain't exactly starving."

"Maybe not, but I'm heading for Perryville. It's a bigger place and I aim to make more money there," Clem said. "I'm giving you first chance to buy me out."

We talked it back and forth until I seen it was no use. I went down to the bank for a loan and didn't have much trouble getting it. I paid Clem off and had the partnership papers changed.

"When you thinking of leaving town?" I asked him.

I could see his Big Idea shine in his eyes. "I'm staying until the Anniversary Day," he said; "just to show I ain't scared of Willie, and I'm giving him one more try."

When the day came close, the sheriff talked to us about providing guards.

"Sheriff," Clem said. "I don't think. Willie is going to try anything. Besides, I can sure enough take care of myself." He patted the pistol he had holstered to his belt.

Seeing that was Clem's attitude, I turned down the sheriff's offer myself. "I guess I can take care of myself too," I said.

On the morning of the Anniversary Day when the woman next door to Clem looked out of her kitchen window, she saw him lying on the pavement outside his back door. Clem's throat was cut and he was dead in a pool of blood.

When the sheriff rushed over he found some things to puzzle about. A case of dynamite was under the kitchen table and a dead cat was on the floor. One of the deputies got a shock when, he opened a closet door in the house. Another body, with its face bashed in, was huddled in a corner.

No one could identify the extra body—especially because of the way his face was worked on; but nobody in town was missing so the sheriff figured that he must have been one of the hobos from the switch yards.

People were scratching their heads, but the sheriff came up with about the best answer. He reckoned that Willie broke in with the intention of setting up that dynamite to blow Clem to kingdom come!

"While he was fixing things up, this tramp must have broke in too, looking for some food or money and Willie had to kill him," the sheriff said. "Then maybe Willie changed his mind, or Clem came home unexpected. Whichever way, Willie met him at the back door and sliced him real good."

It was as good an explanation as any, but it didn't cover why the hobo's fingertips had been gone over with sandpaper.

But that was only the beginning of the day, and the sheriff was plagued with more trouble. Mr. Halley had got himself robbed again. One of his clerks made an estimate that it was of about six thousand dollars. Mr. Halley couldn't tell us exactly how much because Mr. Halley was dead. He was tied up in a chair and gagged and before he had been stuck twice with a knife, his feet had been burned with matches.

The story was really big news now and all the state papers took it up. The Governor sent down State Troopers to take charge of the case. They blocked all roads for thirty miles in every direction and then closed in.

Three State Troopers were assigned to me personally, each one taking an eight hour shift and I got into the spirit of things by unpacking my revolver once more.

The searching and the guarding went on for two weeks before I took things into my own hands and told the Sheriff I was selling out and leaving.

"The strain of waiting to get my throat cut is too much," I said. "I'm getting out of this state and find myself a place that Willie never heard of."

The sheriff was all for the idea, being peeved at having so many troopers under foot, but when the lieutenant in charge of them heard about it, he and some other police officials came swarming down on me.

"This guy Willie had us completely baffled," the lieutenant said. "We haven't the faintest notion where he is. But considering that he's nuts, he's bound to make a try for you one of these days."

"Look," I said, "I don't like being bait in a trap. I don't care if you get Willie or not; I'm leaving while my throat is still in one piece."

But they jawed at me for hours until I finally gave in somewhat. I said I'd stay for just one year, up to the Anniversary Day. If they hadn't caught Willie by then, I was moving out.

They kept hammering at me, but I stuck to my guns and in the end they had to settle for it my way. They would keep a guard on me all year long, and then the day after Anniversary Day if Willie still hadn't got me, I could clear out.

And that's the way it is right now. I'm in my living room and it's full with more than a dozen people; it's been exactly a year since Clem was killed and by midnight tonight it'll all be over.

The sheriff is here looking lost and unhappy among all the blue uniforms and two reporters have been let in to cover the waiting. One of them's brought Freddie's mother along, saying that it would pep up the story.

"Grieving mother waiting for the killer of her son," the red-haired reporter said, sounding pleased with his words. "Get a couple of pictures, Al."

The other reporter has the camera and he's taking a lot of pictures. Some are of the sheriff and the State Police, but more are of me looking determined not to get killed.

He's taken a couple of Freddie's mother too, with a shotgun across her lap and the black cat at her feet. The papers are calling Willie the Cat Killer, and the reporters brought along the cat to pose with us.

All these people have got it figured out that Willie must be reading the papers and that he must know that tonight is his last chance at me. So they're sitting here on the edges of their chairs or pacing around.

Freddie's Ma is staring bleak-eyed at the rug, her lips moving in soft whispers. She's still got that shotgun across her knees and the cat is sitting a few feet away, his tail waving slow and his eyes green and watching.

I have to work hard to keep from busting out laughing right in their faces.

They're all going to have to wait a long, long time if they want to see Willie. He isn't going to show up tonight or any other night, for that matter. Willie's been dead and buried these four years!

I know this for a fact because I'm the one who killed him, and I'm the one who buried him!

It was on the night when Willie got away from Clem, Freddie, and me and the sheriff made us deputies. I was on my own and sent down to Willie's shack by the Sheriff.

When I found that it was empty, I waited around outside for a couple of hours, thinking that he might decide to come back. And around eleven o'clock he did and he was carrying a paper sack.

He was acting so peculiar and secretive that I kept hidden and let him get into the shack. Then, peaking through a crack in the wall, I saw Willie light a lamp and take out writing paper.

He sat down and commenced to scribbling furious. He had about a page and a half down and I was ready to walk in on him when he stopped and took out his jackknife. I held off a while longer to find out what he was up to. Willie made a cut in his arm and dipped his pen in the blood and went on with his writing.

I let him finish the letter and address an envelope before I put a shoulder to the door and barged in.

His eyes got wild when he saw me and he grabbed that jackknife and came for me. He was roaring crazy, and there wasn't much else I could do but slap him hard on the side of the head with the barrel of my shotgun. Willie dropped in his tracks with a moan and I stepped over him to the rickety table to see what he had written. Then I looked in the paper sack and whistled at seeing so much money.

I didn't have any particular notions about it then, but when I glanced down at Willie I saw that he wasn't breathing. I knelt down beside him and shook and talked to him, but it wasn't no use. There was hardly any bleeding, but Willie was dead.

I was wondering what to do next, the thought of all that money interfering with my thinking, and then I saw the shovel in the corner. That was what did it.

I carried Willie outside in the moonlight and buried him under a bush fifty feet away, replacing everything careful so that nobody could tell the ground had been messed with. When I was through, I cleaned the shovel, stuck Willie's letter in my pocket, and took the money home with me.

At my house I hid the money in the attic and then went out and mailed Willie's letter.

It was different with Freddie. When I killed him it was because I was burning with hate for him and what he did to Margie.

I don't guess that anybody really knew how I felt about Margie Carter. I knew she didn't love me the way I loved her, but she liked me and I thought that in time things would work out right for me.

It seemed like a pretty good bet because she didn't seem serious about no one else. Freddie was around once in a while, but I never even thought about him that way.

It hit me pretty hard when she said yes to Freddie. Not enough for killing, but real hard. But I kept it to myself and decided that if that was what she wanted, I wasn't going to interfere. The main thing to me was that she should be happy.

And then Freddie went and killed her with his drinking and driving! It was murder to me, just plain murder!

I was boiling enough to kill him right away, but it looked as if he was going to die anyway, so I waited. Only he didn't die.

And so I waited until the Anniversary Day. Willie wasn't going to care if a killing was charged against him. I went to Freddie's house and cut his throat. I felt worse killing the cat.

The second Anniversary Day was funny to me, but I had to go along with everybody else. It passed without Willie making his appearance, of course, but it gave me an idea.

But then Clem got the idea, too, and I waited.

I knew Clem was thinking about something big because I knew him so well. And I was able to figure out what it was because, as I said, I've been thinking about it too.

That money was still in my attic and it was disturbing me how to spend it. If I'd let any of it go in town, people would begin wondering where I got it. And the sheriff might wonder too and come up with a different answer about Willie.

I was certain that Clem would pull off his plan on the Anniversary Day because that was the logical time to do it in order to put the blame on Willie. So a few days before the day, I kept my eye on Clem and began following him when he went out nights. I wasn't far away when he bought the case of dynamite or when he killed the cat and brought it to his house.

I was only thirty yards away when he killed that tramp two nights before the Anniversary and lugged the body home. And I was close enough to hear Mr. Halley gurgle under his gag when Clem stabbed him with the knife.

Clem's plan was simple and direct and just about the way I had been thinking of doing it. He'd take the money he stole from Mr. Halley and what he got for his half of the meat market and headed for new territory.

To give himself time to get away and to put the blame on Willie, Clem would use the hobo, the dynamite, and the cat.

He'd set a long fuse to the dynamite and when he was twenty or more miles away the house would be blown to smithereens. There wouldn't be much to identify but pieces of a man and a cat. Even if some parts of the body didn't get destroyed, there'd be no fingerprints and Clem made sure that the hobo had no face either.

Once again everybody would get excited and once again Willie would be held responsible for another killing.

When I followed Clem to where he killed Mr. Halley, I was just admiring how smooth, things were working out. But when I saw him raking that money out of the safe, I got other ideas.

They say that killing gets easy after a while and I guess they're right. When Clem got back to his house I was waiting for him in the bushes, and when he put the key to his back door, I came on him and cut his throat from behind.

Maybe I should have felt sorry, but I didn't. I remember that I even got a little sore because some of Clem's blood got on the money—but I took it, anyway.

And now this is another anniversary and they're here waiting for Willie to crawl out of his grave and cut my throat. It sets me to wondering whether Willie really would have gone for us if he'd had the chance. You never can tell with someone like Willie.

I lit a cigaret just now and I let my hand tremble. It's a good touch, and the reporter seen it like he was meant to. "Getting a little nervous?" he asked.

"I ain't scared," I said, but I swallowed and made it loud enough to hear.

The reporter smiled to show that he wasn't being fooled by my brave talk.

In the corner, Freddie's mother is mumbling to herself louder now. I wonder if she's really thinking about Willie at all or whether she's working out one of her chess problems.

All these people are beginning to get on my nerves.

It's pretty close to midnight now. I just lit up another cigaret and got careless with the match. It was still lit when I flipped it toward an ashtray and missed. It landed on the cat and he let out a yowl of pain.

The sound seemed to get to everybody and they all jerked up and some of them licked their lips like they was dry. They must have thought that Willie had come at last.

But Freddie's mother didn't jump. She just took her eyes off the floor and she's looking at me.

Her eyes are burning black and they make me squirm. A woman like her ought to be locked up. She's crazy enough to be dangerous.

"Only about five minutes to twelve," the sheriff said, "Willie hasn't got much time."

The red-haired reporter checked his wrist watch. "I hope this doesn't turn out to be a fizzle."

I wish Freddie's mother would take her eyes off me and I wish somebody would have sense enough take that shotgun away from her.

She's smiling in a funny way now, as if she just solved one of her chess problems.

It's dead quiet except for the ticking of the clock and far away a dog is howling. Somehow, everyone seems to be watching Freddie's mother; she's moved that shotgun and it's pointed straight at me.

The State Police Lieutenant is speaking softly and urgently. "Get that gun away from her, Clancy, but be careful about it. It's loaded and the safety is off."

There's a fleck of saliva on the corners of her secret smile and her finger is squeezing that trigger. She's got it all in that crazy head of hers! She's got it all figured out, or maybe just enough of it!

The clock is striking and I can't move or take my eyes away from hers. They're shining yellowish and they know!

The cat is beginning to arch his back and he's yowling again; the trooper is moving fast now for the shotgun, but he's too late.

He's just too late, and the world is exploding in my face!

A Torch For Tess

**Mantrap
July 1956**

Steve Kaiser smiled at us now the way he always smiled when we came to question him. "You're bothering me again," he said.

He slouched in the easy chair with the first drink of the day in his hand. He was a big man in shirt sleeves and he had eyes that laughed at all the little people in the world and especially at me.

"Why the hell do you boys come to me every time," he complained with a grin. "I could be innocent."

Kaiser was too important a man now to get his own hands dirty. But he pushed the button and the job was done. The little punk Vasco had his last look at life in a dirty alley and then he left it stitched from chin to belt buckle with .45 slugs.

"Vasco was pushing snow where he had no business to be," I said. "He set up a stand of his own. We know you don't like free enterprise."

Kaiser clicked his tongue sadly. "Imagine," he said. "Snow. That's a dirty racket."

Berg tested the tip of his ballpoint and was ready. "How about it?" he asked. "What lovely alibi have you got made for last night?"

"Just the usual," Kaiser said. He took his time sipping at his bourbon. "I hosted a poker game here last night. Played until two in the morning with Benson, my lawyer, Hilliard, my doc, Durbin, my Banker, and Judge Moore."

"Your judge?" Berg asked.

"Let's refer to him as the Eminent Jurist. That has a nice ring."

"And after that?" I asked. And then I wished the hell I'd kept my mouth shut.

Tess Paterson was on the arm of Kaiser's chair watching me with those strange gray eyes. A lock of her taffy colored hair dangled over her forehead.

Kaiser ran a hand slowly along the length of her thigh and smiled at me. "You tell, Ryan, baby," he said. "He'll get a thrill out of it."

She patted him absently on the head. "I'll testify in court if I have to." There was no expression in her voice.

"Thanks," Kaiser said. He scratched an eyebrow and grinned. "I'm getting ahead of the script. What time did poor Vasco leave us?"

"Around ten," Berg said. "Did it go according to schedule?"

"Ten is a nice time," Kaiser said. "Not too early. Not too late." He turned his grin on me. "So what do you care what happened after ten?"

Tess rose and stretched her long slim body. "Can I fix anybody a drink?"

"Never mind," I said. "We're not here because we like the company."

"Baby's only trying to help," Kaiser said. "You'd be surprised how useful she is."

I tapped a cigarette on the cocktail table. "You can get some good dames for twenty bucks a night. How much is she costing you?"

Tess's eyes glittered, but she said nothing.

"She's expensive, but worth every penny of it," Kaiser agreed amiably. "Not every man could afford her."

Tess turned her back on us and walked over to the small corner bar.

Kaiser's dark eyes sparkled. "I get a kick out of you, Ryan. I've been spreading the word around and all the boys do too. They all know this torch you're carrying for Tess."

I flicked on the lighter and held it to my cigarette. "I can forget I'm a cop," I said. "I can forget it easy."

Kaiser rattled the ice cubes in his glass. "Don't do it on account of me. I got a headache and I'm out of condition. Besides, I don't think Berg would just sit there and watch."

"If you two are through talking your fight," Berg said, "let's get back to the thing we're here for." He flipped a page of his notebook. "The gun that killed Vasco did the same for Bannion three months ago. It also took care of Waldek last year. That's according to Ballistics."

"Amazing," Kaiser said. "Just like a signature."

We asked fifteen minutes more worth of questions, but they were routine and got us nothing. They never did with Kaiser, but it was our job to ask them. We left at a quarter to eleven.

In the car, Berg said, "Do you always have to make some crack about the dame?"

"Think I hurt her feelings?"

"So she's not a good little girl. We know it and she knows it. Why get hot and bothered?"

He lighted a cigar and puffed at it. "I guess we better see Willie now. He said to make it around eleven."

I nosed the car into the traffic lane. "What good does this do us, besides the exercise? Kaiser's so worried he's laughing."

"When I was young I was impatient too," Berg said. "But I've seen them come and go. Some taller than Kaiser."

Berg regarded me seriously. "I guess it's easier for me to wait," he said. "I got only one reason for hating him."

He drummed his fingers idly on his knee and told me, "You know that dame could put her shoes under my bed any time. I'm not as young as I used to be, but I'd try."

I skidded to a stop as the traffic light ahead of me changed. "Why the hell don't you shut up, Berg?"

Willie Shank is a small blond man who earns his bread and butter by visiting people's homes while they're at the movies.

Once in a while Willie gets caught. But he considers it one of the risks of his trade and he has a forgiving nature. He doesn't hate cops.

Willie also has a part-time job. He collects information and sells it.

We found him in his usual bar hunched contentedly over a short beer. He waved us to chairs. "Make me an offer."

Berg took a seat. "Where else can you peddle it? Five bucks if I think it's worth it."

"Let's toss it back and forth."

Berg shook his head. "Wouldn't do any good."

Willie sighed. He saluted us with the glass and emptied it. "Yesterday afternoon I accidently run across Pinky Newton carrying a suitcase down the main drag. I wonder why he's in town, knowing his reputation and such, so I keep him in sight. He registers at the Holton."

"This is a big crime?" Berg said.

"I'm getting to it," Willie said. "He just registers, see? And has his suitcase sent up to his room. Next he leaves the joint. I got nothing else to do, so I tag along about a block behind."

"You like the way he walks?" I asked.

Willie's eyes were reproachful. "He went up to Steve Kaiser's place and stayed there for about an hour.'"

"And when he came out?" Berg asked.

Willie opened his mouth, and then hesitated. "Nothing. I lost him."

Berg turned to me and lifted his shoulders. "So Pink's in town. He wants to get away from his mother-in-law."

"Now don't be that way, Berg," Willie said. "We all know how Pinky earns money for his Dacron suits. And I heard Vasco got his last night."

"Do you think that's worth five bucks, Willie?" I asked.

He closed his eyes. "I'm glad this is only a sideline. I could starve." His lids raised. "I'd like to point out that Pinky was in town too when Bannion tried to eat those .45 slugs."

He folded his hands. "I thought it was worth ten."

"Pinky's probably back home by now," I said.

Willie put the five dollar bill Berg handed him into his wallet. "This is for free. He was still checked in at his hotel half an hour ago. Looks like he hit the bottle and forgot to leave."

At the desk of the Holton we found there was no Pinky Newton registered. But a bellboy recognized his description and that helped the clerk to remember that a Mr. Morgan in 1214 must be the man we were looking for.

Berg and I rode the elevator to the twelfth floor and rapped on the panel of door number 1214.

"Who the hell is it?" Pinky's irritated voice wanted to know.

"The police," Berg said. "We'd like a few words with you."

We heard the creaking of bed springs and then Pinky opened the door. He was short and slightly overweight. Carrot hair retreated untidily from his forehead.

His blood-shot eyes looked us over. "Thought I recognized your voice, Berg. I see you're still working, Ryan."

"Mind if we come in?" Berg asked.

"Sit down anywhere," Pinky said.

We followed Pinky in. He made his way to the unmade bed and sat down on it. He rubbed his head gingerly.

"Like to tell us what you were doing last night?" Berg asked.

"If I look like I feel, you ought to be able to guess," Pinky said. "I sat here in this room just drinking quiet. I started at eight and the last I remember it was twelve."

"Got anybody to agree with you?" Berg asked.

"I'll shop around," Pinky said. "Do I need anybody?"

"You know Vasco?" I asked.

"Never heard of him," Pink said. A smirk came to his lips. "I been hearing about you, Ryan. Kaiser got to talking about you."

I came up close to him and the smirk disappeared.

Berg put a hand on my shoulder and pushed me away. "You saw Kaiser?" he asked.

Pinky thought about it. "All right," he said. "I saw Kaiser yesterday afternoon. We talked over old times. So?"

"Mind if we look your room over?" Berg asked.

"Have I got a choice?" Pinky asked. "Be my guest."

Berg and I combed the room while Pinky dragged on a cigarette. We found nothing interesting.

I went through Pinky's coat lying on the bed and then ran my hands over Pinky.

He was patient about it. "See," he said. "Clean."

"That's what smells, Pinky," I said. "I hear you feel naked without a gun."

"I left it home," Pinky said. "Didn't think I'd need it in this town."

I put Pinky's hat on his head and handed him his coat. "You got objections to answering a few questions down at headquarters?"

"I got objections," he said. "Does it make any difference?" He slipped into his coat. "What's the book? Suspicion of what?"

"We'll let it be a surprise," Berg said.

Downstairs in the car I got into the back seat with Pinky. I snapped cuffs on his wrist and mine.

"Afraid of me?" Pinky asked curiously.

"How about it, Berg?" I asked. "Could you use some country air?"

"I like the idea," Berg said. "But let's just keep it only an idea. With my pension coming into focus I like to do things by the numbers."

"It wouldn't do you any good," Pinky said complacently. "I been massaged by professionals." He considered it. "Sometimes I even think I like it."

He watched the scenery. "I don't think it's the pension stopping you, Berg. You're not the type." He glanced at me. "With Ryan it's different."

We covered a dozen blocks and then I tapped Berg on the shoulder. "Pull up at the next corner. I'm out of smokes."

Berg eased the car to the curb and idled the motor.

"Hell," I said. "Be an obliging policeman and get me a couple of packs. Otherwise I got to unlock these cuffs."

Berg switched off the ignition and groaned his way from behind the wheel. "Okay. But you got to scratch my next itch. And you know where that's going to be."

I waited until Berg was inside the supermarket and then I unlocked the cuffs. "Get in the front seat, Pinky. And don't argue about it."

"Who's arguing?" Pinky said. He did as he was told.

Berg was deep inside the store with his back toward me. As I started the motor Pinky opened his mouth to yell for Berg. I clipped Pinky's Adam's apple with the side of my hand and he gasped for air.

Even if Berg saw me, I figured he wouldn't have time to get out of the store and do anything about it. I spun the car around the corner.

I would have preferred someplace out in the country, but I knew I couldn't make it. Berg would have a general alarm out in a few minutes and every cruiser in the city would be looking for me.

The warehouse district was near and it was quiet. I parked behind a shed near the river.

Pinky fingered his throat nervously. "Now what's on your mind?"

I said nothing while I looked him over. He was scared the way a hard guy is scared. I could work on him until my knuckles were raw, but in between sobs he'd spit in my face.

"Pinky," I said finally, "you take your beatings with a smile because you know they're going to be nothing more than just beatings. You know even a tough cop will go so far and no further."

"You're not gonna be a cop long," Pinky said. "How you figure on squaring this?"

"Pinky," I said. "I'm not a cop now."

He blinked, thinking about what I'd said.

"I won't know when to stop," I said.

"What if I do talk," Pinky said. "What good will it do you? You can't use anything I say in court."

"Don't worry about court," I told him. "Just worry about me."

I slashed at him twice. Short, sharp jabs that broke the skin.

When Pinky shook himself out of it, he pulled out a handkerchief and wiped at the blood coming from his nose. His voice was muffled. "Hell," he said. "Why should I take a beating when it don't mean anything? You know damn well I gunned Vasco."

"And how does Kaiser come in?"

"Just the way you think."

"About the gun?" I asked.

"I threw it in a sewer. I don't remember where."

"Don't hand me that," I said. "You kept it after the Bannion job and after you took care of Waldek. Where is it, Pinky?"

He shook his head. "This is where I stop talking."

I snapped a short left to the bridge of his swelling nose. "I told you once I'm not a cop now. I'll keep this up until I kill you if I have to."

He waited until the pain lessened and then looked into my eyes. "It's that dame, ain't it? She's driving you crazy."

The rage came swelling into me and I saw Pinky only as something I wanted to kill. I jerked out my .38.

His eyes met the barrel of the gun and then they shifted to me.

He knew it then. He knew he was going to talk fast or die.

My voice was tight. "You might beat the chair, Pinky. But you can't beat this." I began a slow squeeze on the trigger.

His eyes went away from me and the gun and stared at the dashboard. He was hard and tough, but he didn't want to die. Sweat misted his forehead.

"Think about it fast," I said.

His face became gray and weary. "It's in a locker at the bus station."

"Where's the key?"

"I haven't got it. I left it with the clerk down there. Told him I was afraid of losing it."

"You can lie to me this once, Pinky," I said. "But it'll be the last time you lie to anyone."

"I'm not lying," he said angrily. "Let's get out of here."

I holstered the gun and handcuffed Pinky's wrists together. During the ride to headquarters he leaned back against the seat with his eyes closed. He shivered every once in a while.

I made it to headquarters without being stopped and there I handed him over to Lieutenant Shaw. I told him what to look for.

Shaw's gray-blue eyes were alive with question, but he put them off. He sent a couple of men to the bus station and gave me orders to wait in the squad room.

I borrowed cigarettes from one of the detectives and began walking the room. By five my mouth was parched and the cigarettes were gone.

At six, Berg came in. "All I told the Lieutenant was that the car was gone when I got out."

"Thanks," I said.

"But he knows what Pinky looks like and can put the pieces together. Pinky himself is too busy fretting about his rap to care about what you did to him."

"How about the gun?" I asked.

"They found it," Berg said. He was uneasy. "The Lieutenant says for me to bring you to him."

Lieutenant Shaw looked at me with brooding eyes. "We did a rush job on the gun. It's the one that did the job. Fingerprints crawling all over it."

"How about Pinky? Has he got anything to say?"

"He thought about it for a couple of hours. Then I showed him what we had. I got his statement right here."

"Is it enough to bring in Kaiser?"

"It's enough," Shaw said.

"I'll get him," I said.

Shaw put the tips of his fingers together. "Don't bother, Ryan. You're suspended. There'll have to be an investigation."

"I'll get Kaiser first. Then investigate."

Shaw's voice was hard. "Don't tell me how to run my department."

I took out my wallet and unhooked the badge. I tossed it on his desk. "Keep it. I'm through."

He stared at the badge moodily. "Sometimes I wonder if I know all that's going on around here." He looked at me. "What's got into you, Ryan? Not a blot on your record and suddenly you go berserk."

Behind me Berg cleared his throat. "Could I see you alone a minute, Lieutenant?"

"Shut up, Berg!" I said. "You got nothing to say."

Shaw glanced at Berg and then back at his desk. He flipped the badge with a forefinger. "I don't want your badge, Ryan. The suspension takes effect tomorrow. Bring in Kaiser, if that's what you're living for."

Berg and I went down to the car and made the trip to Kaiser's hotel in a fast ten minutes.

Tess Paterson in a mink coat was in the lobby talking to a bellboy. Three fine leather suitcases were at her feet.

Her face paled as she watched us approach.

"Looks like Kaiser got the word," I said. "You wouldn't care to tell us where he is now?"

She bit her lip. "Why not? He's upstairs in the apartment doing last minute packing."

Berg started for the elevators.

"Don't take it too hard," I said. "With your talent you ought to be able to turn up another sucker with money."

"Come on, Ryan!" Berg called impatiently.

"Maybe he'll get you two mink coats," I said.

Color came back into her cheeks.

"He might," she said. "Maybe three. Or a dozen."

I gripped her wrists hard. "That's what you want, isn't it?"

She twisted away. "And you haven't got a damn cent. So let me alone, can't you?"

I heard the car horn, but I wasn't paying attention. It was Berg who noticed. "It's Kaiser," he yelled, coming on the run. "He's in that car outside."

Evidently Kaiser didn't know that we were in the lobby. He leaned on the horn. He wanted to get away fast and he wanted Tess to come with him.

He saw me before I got to the swinging doors. For a fraction of a second he stared at me, and then he stepped on the gas. The car lurched away from the curb.

The traffic lights on the corner were against him, but Kaiser tried to shoot through. His big black car plowed into the side of a delivery truck.

I got to within fifty feet of the smash-up when Kaiser shouldered open the jammed door on the driver's side of his car. He leaped out holding an automatic and dashed across the intersection.

At the edge of a parking lot he stopped long enough to fire. Flakes of red brick chipped from the building on my right.

I ducked behind the corner mailbox and returned the shot. A windshield behind Kaiser snapped into a spiderweb of cracked glass. Kaiser sprinted in among the parked cars.

Berg came up panting and crouched beside me. "Don't go after him in there," he said, breathing hard. "Wait until we get help."

I pulled away from him and dashed across the street and into the lot. A bullet skittered off the bumper of a Buick.

"Don't be stupid, Kaiser," I yelled. "You know I'll kill you if I get half a chance. Come out of there with your hands high."

He was four or five cars away and I could hear his feet crunch the gravel as he ran. He came into sight as he crossed an open spot and headed for the alley.

"I'm not talking again, Kaiser!" I shouted. "Stop or I'll kill you!"

Kaiser stopped and turned. He stood there a man alone. Then he raised his gun and leveled it swiftly. The automatic barked and the bullet sang as it passed my ear.

I fired before Kaiser could pull off another shot.

He reeled and staggered with the heavy load of the .38 slug in his chest. He fought to keep standing, but it took more strength than he had. He dropped to his knees and then sprawled forward. The automatic jumped from his hand and pin-wheeled to a stop ten feet away.

I came to him slowly and looked down. His black eyes burned with hate and he began a painful crawl for the automatic.

Berg trotted up and scooped up the gun. "Don't try any exercise, Kaiser," he said. "We'll get you to a doctor."

Kaiser's face twisted with pain and he buried his head in the crook of his arm. The fingers of his left hand made claw marks in the dirt. His body shuddered several times and then he gave up.

Berg got down on one knee. He lifted Kaiser's head and looked at it carefully. He lowered it back to its resting place.

"He won't give anybody trouble," Berg said, flatly. "He's dead."

They came now from doorways, from automobiles, and from the streets. It was a crowd that murmured and became bolder as it grew in numbers. It became a ragged circle around Kaiser, gripped with the terror, the curiosity, and the delight of another man's death.

Behind it, in the tired darkening day, sirens moaned their searching way closer to the target.

The prowl car men came first, and on their heels the ambulance, and then the technicians to measure, to take pictures, and to classify.

I smoked as I used methodical words to tell the Lieutenant what happened. I used words that were facts; long and wide, but with no depth, no meaning.

I told him about a man I had killed. I did not tell him how it feels to kill a man, even if you hated him, and even when there was nothing else you could do.

They turned to Berg at last, and I backed away. I backed away into the eager-eyed crowd, and then I turned and walked back to Kaiser's hotel.

The lobby was deserted except for the desk man and a bellboy who was picking up Tess's suitcases.

"Never mind taking those outside," I said. "She isn't going anyplace."

The little man looked at me curiously. "I wasn't taking them outside, Mister," he said. "Before the excitement started I was about to take them back upstairs."

I stared at him and he got nervous. "Put those down," I said, finally.

I fished half a dollar out of my pocket and tossed it to him. I walked to the elevators carrying the suitcases.

The door to Kaiser's apartment was half open. I closed it behind me and put down the bags.

Tess was at the window, a slim silhouette against the crawling darkness. Her mink coat lay on the floor in the gloom beside an easy chair.

"He's dead, isn't he?" she asked without turning.

"That's right," I said. "He's dead."

The clock on the fireplace mantle ticked off seconds.

"I'm the one who killed him," I said. "It was me, Ryan."

Her voice was tired and low. "It was me, Ryan," she repeated.

"I didn't mean it that way," I said.

I came close to her. The edges of her hair were delicate featherings against the last remnants of light.

"You weren't going with him?" I asked.

"I should have," she said. "He was good to me."

"But you changed your mind. Why?"

She turned to face me. Her face was shadowed, but there was the glitter of tears. She passed around me and walked away.

I turned on one of the floor lamps and the mink on the floor was bright.

I knew what I wanted to do. I wanted to grind my heel into the soft blue white fur until it was in shreds.

Tess watched me and waited.

I picked up the coat carefully and put it on the chair. "I won't be bothering you any more."

Tess put her hand on my arm. "Don't you every ask for anything? Are you always too proud?"

Those strange gray eyes were near and the scent of clean perfume was in the air.

Dead Cops Are Murder

Murder!
September 1956

"Killing a cop is never a bright idea," I said, "It makes everybody mad."

"I don't give a damn what you think," Reagan said. "You're getting paid good to do it."

I shrugged my shoulders. "All right. I won't worry about it. I'll be back in St. Paul on the first plane out, but you'll still be here and you're liable to get squeezed rough. They'll have an idea who called for the job."

"They won't squeeze hard if they're smart," Reagan said. "If they decide to pull me in for talk, some of the boys will give me advance warning. I got a doc who'll examine me before. And when my lawyers get me back home, he'll do it again. If I got so much as a busted fingernail, there'll be hell raised."

I sat there with my drink and considered Reagan. He was a big florid man with black hair that straggled wetly over his forehead. He ran everything in this town that operated best at night. Reagan used to take care of killings himself, but now that he could wear evening clothes without feeling uncomfortable, he let others do them for him.

"How come one man can bother you so?" I asked. "I thought you owned the force."

"I control pieces of it," Reagan said. "You can't buy a whole police force. It's a simple matter of human stubbornness on the part of some people and also basic economics. You just buy the key pieces, the ones that can be bought, and hope for the best."

He got up to refill his glass. "I don't mind an honest cop here and there, as long as he's stupid. But Randell's got quite a brain."

He tonged ice cubes into his glass. "Nobody can control a town all the time. Every ten years or so the citizens put down their comic books and decide to pick up the cleaning broom. They even go out and vote."

He measured his whiskey by ear. "I don't mind taking a vacation for a while. I need the rest anyway. But I want to do my resting in a nice sunny place where I don't have to march to the dining hall in formation.

"An honest cop—a real honest, smart cop—stands out in this town like a monk in a convent." He blew cigar ash off his vest. "I'll tell you what's going to happen, Trapp. These amateur boys will win the election, no matter what we do about it. And as soon as they do, they'll look into the clear blue eyes of Randell and hand him the gold badge.

"Randell's been around a long time and he knows what's going on. And what makes it worse is that he'll know exactly what to do about it.

"I could pack up right now and go to Mexico or Cuba and let them have their fun trying to get me to come back. But I don't want to stay out of the good old forty-eight forever. Some day when things are back to normal, I want to come back without the Feds meeting me at the border."

His eyes met mine. "How you gonna do it?"

"The simple way," I said. "Things don't go wrong that way."

"And what time? I got to arrange a party."

I thought it over. "This Randell married?"

"No. No complications. He lives alone in a small apartment on the corner of 12th and Franklin."

"Then you pick it," I said.

He scratched his jaw. "Around eight should be right. Everybody'll still be sober enough at my party to remember I was there."

"You can give me the money now," I said.

I went back to my hotel room and napped until about seven. Then I checked the .38 and fitted on the silencer. I shoved it into the briefcase, which I put under my arm, and went downstairs for a bite to eat. I finished at twenty to eight and walked slowly toward 12th and Franklin.

It was a three story building with a foyer just big enough to let two people pass each other. I studied the directory and found that Randell had apartment 25.

I walked up the carpeted stairs until I found the door I was looking for and pressed the buzzer.

He was a medium-sized man in shirt sleeves and he held the evening newspaper open in one hand. His sharp blue eyes flicked over my face.

"Lieutenant Matt Randell?" I asked.

He nodded his head.

"I'd like to talk to you about something important," I said. "Reagan figures in it."

"Can't it keep a couple more years." he said. "I'm full of Reagan right now."

"It might keep," I said. "But you should be interested right now."

His eyes went over me once again and then he stepped back. I walked into the apartment and sat down. It was a single room with adjoining bath and kitchenette. I put the briefcase on my knees.

Randell stood watching me a few more seconds and then he decided to take a chair opposite me. "I never saw you before," he said.

"And never will again," I said, smiling. "That's why right now is so important to both of us."

His eyes went to the briefcase. "If it's information, I'm listening. If it's money, you're wasting your time."

I unzipped the case and put my hand inside. "No, you're guessing bad." I brought out the .38 and pointed it at his chest.

He sat without the slightest movement, his eyes traveling from the silencer to my face.

"Do you think you could be bought now?" I asked, interested.

He almost smiled. "I'm considering it."

I shifted my weight to make myself more comfortable. "Can you guess why I'm here?"

He did smile thinly then. "If it's to scare me, you won't go away disappointed."

"No," I said. "It's more serious than that."

His eyes shifted slightly and I knew what he was looking for. His short-barreled .32 was hanging in its holster from the door knob of the closet about six feet away.

I could see that he was going to try for it, but he needed a little talking time to think over the best way to do it.

I wouldn't have minded some talking. I'm always interested in how a man meets death, but I couldn't take a chance. The trouble with these silencers is that they have the habit of jamming the gun after one shot.

I might get him as he made his dive, but the chances were that I'd need more than one shot to put him away. I didn't like the idea of me with a gun that didn't work and him pulling up one that did.

Regretfully, I squeezed the trigger.

Randell grunted slightly as the slug bored into his flesh and he flopped out of his chair with the uncoordination of instant death.

I put the gun back in the briefcase, went to the door knob with a handkerchief and let myself into the hall. I was dabbing at the surface of the buzzer with the handkerchief, when I noticed the brown-haired girl at the door of the apartment next to Randell's.

She had two large bags of groceries in her arms and she was having difficulty using her keys to get into the apartment.

She smiled at me. "I hope you don't mind," she said. "But would you hold one of these while I get the door open?"

"Not at all," I said. I took one of them while she unlocked the door.

"Thank you very much," she said as I returned the bag.

She had a nice smile and so I smiled too. I touched the brim of my hat. "No trouble at all," I said.

Outside on the sidewalk, I took a look at the palm of my hand under the first streetlight. Not even moist, I thought, in a pleased way.

Sure, she could identify me if she ever saw me again. But she never would. Randell's body most likely wouldn't be found until somebody came to find out why he wasn't reporting for work, and by that time I'd be in St. Paul. She could look through all the mug prints at headquarters until she needed glasses. My picture wasn't in anybody's files.

In my hotel room I packed the briefcase away with the five grand in the suitcase. I glanced at my wrist watch and saw that I had about an hour to kill before I could catch a plane.

I picked up the suitcase and checked out of the hotel. About a block down the street I found a hamburger joint. I got a pack of cigarettes out of the machine and sat down on a stool.

"Two burgers with," I said. "And coffee."

The counterman, a wiry little man of sixty or so, splayed out two balls of meat on the hot sheet. He drew my coffee and slid the sugar to me.

"Kind of chilly tonight," he said.

"Yeah," I said. "A little nippy." I looked idly around and saw that the only other customer in the place was a sandy-haired man working on a piece of pie in one of the booths.

The counterman put the burgers on a plate and he was just setting them in front of me when the door opened and the two punks walked in. I picked up one burger as I took a look and a prickling came to the back of my neck. Both of them were high on the brown cigarette stuff and the tiny pupils of their eyes glowed. They were in their late teens, pale-faced boys with the thin-shelled bravado of the perpetual delinquent.

I chewed slowly and wondered if they were going to go through with it. They hesitated for a moment as they looked around and then the taller of the two moved to the juke box and turned his back to it. He brought out a rusty looking revolver and swept the room with it.

"This thing works," he said, his voice high. "Everybody behave and you'll live to tell your grandchildren about it."

The other kid had a better looking gun. "Move away from that cash register, Pop. I'm coming in to take a look."

I noticed the man in the booth lay down his fork. His head went slowly back and forth as he alternately watched one and then the other.

The short, chunky kid went behind the counter and rang up a No Sale. His face twisted in disgust. "A lousy twenty-two bucks."

"What did you expect," Pop said dryly. "This ain't no bank."

The short kid stuffed the money in his pocket and moved out from behind the counter. "Throw your wallets out on the floor," he ordered.

I took mine out carefully and tossed it down. I watched the sandy-haired man get to his feet. He licked his lips for a few seconds and then seemed to take a deep breath. His hand went to the button of his suitcoat.

He didn't quite get the snub-nosed .38 out of the belt holster. The tall punk's gun spit angrily twice. The man in the booth crumpled and he slid between the table and the bench.

The punk's eyes turned toward me glowing with killer madness.

I dove over the counter as the shots came and landed hard against the shelf of coffee mugs. I lay there hugging the floor, my heart pounding wildly.

After a couple more shots, I heard the sound of a hard slap. "Snap out of it, you damn fool," I heard the chunky kid say. "Let's get the hell out of here."

I heard their footsteps moving fast toward the door, and then I heard the door slam. I lay there unable to get up right away and marveling in a detached way at my trembling and weakness.

Finally, Pop straightened up. He looked over the counter and his mouth got tight. He walked over to the phone.

I came to my senses. It was time to get out. I couldn't get mixed up in anything like this. I got shakily to my feet.

Then I saw the faces pressed against the windows and far away I heard the cat wail of a siren. Pop didn't have to phone, I realized suddenly. Somebody had heard the shots and done it for him.

I picked up the suitcase and looked at the glass door. My stomach tightened around fear. It was too late to get out.

There were about twenty people out there and more coming. Their fascinated eyes traveled a thrill circuit from the body of the sandy-haired man, to Pop, and then to me.

I put down the suitcase and wiped the palms of my hands on my trouser legs. I looked at Pop with a weary indignation. "Why did he do it?" I asked hoarsely. "Why did the damn fool go for his gun?"

Pop sat down on one of the Stools and reached automatically for the pipe in his shirt pocket. "He had to, mister," Pop said. "He had to because he was a cop."

Pop glanced once more at the body and then looked away. "Joe Farley," he said. "Just a rookie cop. Off duty and all he wanted was quiet and something to eat."

Pop's eyes hardened. "The force ain't all perfume and flowers," he said, "but there's one thing that gets every cop mad. You just don't kill a cop, mister."

His hand brought out a tobacco pouch. "Those two punks are going to fall down a lot of stairs before they ever get to court. A lot of stairs."

Two cops elbowed their way through the outside crowd and into the diner. They looked down at the sandy-haired man silently and then one of them went back out to the squad car.

I picked up my cup of coffee, but I was spilling so much of it that I set it down again. I lit a cigarette instead.

The homicide detectives were there in less than ten minutes and a pair of them took me to one of the booths.

"I'm Sergeant Wilson," one of them said. He was as tall as I am, but thinner and his hair was graying. He cocked a thumb at the other man. "And this is my partner, Sergeant Cooper. Your name, please."

I didn't see how it could hurt to give my right name. I figured they'd want to see my identification papers anyway.

"Trapp," I said. "Charles Trapp."

"Address?"

"2489 North Wendell." As he wrote it down, I added, "St. Paul, Minnesota. I'm just here visiting friends. I have a plane to catch at ten."

"Mister," Sergeant Wilson said, looking up. "A cop's been killed. Your plane can wait."

"Tell us about it," Cooper said. "From the beginning."

I gave them the story and described the two punks.

"You'd recognize them if you saw them again?" Wilson asked.

I hesitated. "Well, I don't know. I was pretty scared."

"You gave a pretty good description," Wilson said. "I think you will." He got up. "You and Pop better come down to headquarters with us. We'd like to have you look at some pictures."

"Look," I said. "Making this plane is important to me."

"I don't hear you, mister," Wilson said.

At headquarters they took Pop and me into a small room and began bringing in folders of mug shots.

"Put the suitcase in the corner if it bothers you," Wilson said.

"It doesn't bother me a bit," I said irritably.

After two hours my cigarettes were gone and Wilson brought me a fresh pack. I was pulling off the red strip, when I glanced down at the next page and there was the tall kid who did the killing.

I lit a cigarette and puffed slowly as I thought it over. Finally, I looked up. "This is one of them," I said.

Wilson got to his feet and came over. He studied the picture and the record. "All right." he said. He picked up the book and took it over to Pop.

Pop blinked his red-rimmed eyes a couple of times before he looked. "It sure is," he said. "It damn well sure is."

I shifted in my chair. "I got a pretty important appointment in St. Paul. Pop ought to be able to spot the other one."

"Keep looking," Wilson said. He left the room with the book and returned about twenty minutes later.

Sergeant Cooper came into the room chewing furiously on a kitchen match. "You mad?" he asked Wilson.

Wilson raised an eyebrow.

"Get a lot madder," Cooper said. "Matt Randell got it too."

"No kidding!" Wilson exclaimed. Cooper walked to the water cooler. "His brother dropped by to borrow Matt's golf clubs. He buzzed, but there was no answer, He tried the door and found Randell on the rug with a slug in his chest." Cooper took a drink of water, crumpled the paper cup and left the room.

I turned a few more pages in the book. I found a photograph that I thought would pass.

"Here's the other one," I said.

Wilson carried the book over to Pop. I glanced at my watch.

Pop shook his head. "Nope."

"Pop can't see," I said.

"Maybe," Wilson said. "We'll put it aside. Sit down, Mister, and look some more."

Cooper came back. "Found a witness," he said. "A girl who lives next door to Randell saw a man coming out of Randell's apartment this evening. She got a pretty good look and they're bringing her here to look at the pictures. She says he has the first joint of the little finger on his right hand missing. She noticed it when he touched the brim of his hat."

I closed my right hand and looked at the mug prints until I found one that looked like the chunky kid. "Here he is," I said.

Pop studied the photograph for a minute and I watched him closely.

He sighed. "Nope. A lot like him, but nope."

"You're crazy, Pop," I said. "That's him. I was right there."

"So was I," Pop said. "And I still got twenty-twenty."

I stared at Sergeant Wilson and then went back to the books. The door opened and I jerked involuntarily.

It was a deep voice that spoke from the doorway. "We got them, Sergeant."

I put my hand on the suitcase and got to my feet. Pop took his time getting up, and he stretched.

"Come on, Pop," I said. "Let's get this over with."

Wilson and Cooper took us into a large room and we saw the two punks sitting on a bench. They were interested only in their pain. The tall thin kid was crying into a handkerchief wet with the blood from his mashed nose. His face was ragged with cuts made by the ring on somebody's fist. The chunky one was nearly blind from the beating he'd gotten, only a thin slit of iris showing on one eye. He sat with his head low and he crooned in soft misery.

The big beefy bluecoat standing next to them grinned as he reached out for the hair of the chunky kid and jerked his head back so that we could get a better look. "They're a mite messy," he said. "Fell down a couple of times."

I looked down at his big hands and saw the blood crusted on his knuckles. I wiped my forehead with the back of my hand.

"We damn near have to guess—the condition they're in," Pop said. "Not that it makes me cry."

Wilson looked them over and turned to the big cop. "You're getting kind-hearted, Harris," he said. "They still got faces."

Harris' grin broadened. "They was just brought in, Sergeant. I ain't had much time."

"It's them," I said, and the timbre of my voice startled me.

"Take your time," Wilson said. "Be sure."

"Damn it," I said. "I'm sure. I'm positive."

"How about you, Pop?" Wilson asked.

Pop tilted his head and considered. I looked up at the wall clock and followed the red second hand as it moved from four to six.

"Come on, Pop," I snapped. "Don't take all day."

"Take it easy," Pop said. He looked them over carefully. "Yep," he said.

"Hold it, Mister," Wilson said. "A few more things we got to do."

They took me and Pop into another room with desks in it and Wilson handed me a sheaf of papers. "Read this carefully, check for any errors, and sign it. It's your statement."

I paged through rapidly and scrawled my signature.

"You read fast, Mister," Wilson said. He looked at my right hand and frowned as though he were trying to remember something.

I went to the door and Wilson came with me. "You're in an awful hurry," he said. "You might as well spend the night in town. No planes leave after eleven."

"I'll take a train," I snapped.

"We'll keep in touch with you," Wilson said. "You'll have to testify at the trial."

"Sure," I said. "Sure."

Wilson kept pace with me as I hurried down the corridor. We clattered down the stairway and as we turned at the first landing, I saw her.

She was between two plain-clothesmen and she raised her eyes. They widened in recognition.

The fear tore at my mind and I knew there was only one thing for me to do now. There was just one way out. I dropped the suitcase on the landing and my fingers tore at the clasps.

"What the hell . . ." I heard Wilson say in surprise.

"That's him!" the girl screamed.

I had both the side clasps open in a second and was snapping the lock. My fingertips just touched the butt of the gun when Wilson's foot lashed out.

It caught me on the side of the face and I clutched at the air as I began falling.

I rolled down the stairs, unable to stop, and the sharp marble edges of the steps slammed into my face and body.

It hurt. It hurt a lot.

But I knew that this was only the beginning.

Death Rail

Mantrap
October 1956

What does a man think about when he's falling? Is he still possessed with hate that has fingers of steel? Does he shriek against the death that waits for him after all of the lighted windows have flashed by? Is he a human being who will smash against the pavement or has he already become a terror-stricken animal screaming against the night air? . . .

The long car patiently threaded its way through the narrow dirty street and halted in the middle of the block in front of the Club Luna.

Simon Laskar uncrossed his legs and waited for the chauffeur to come around and open the door. His yellow-brown eyes went contemptuously over the shuffling, ragged men; the winos, stubble-whiskered and with begging eyes, who waited for him in the warm afternoon.

He stepped onto the windblown sidewalk and irritably blinked a mote of dust from his eyes. He was a man in his late thirties, trim and of medium height with dark brown hair and tense shoulders.

Laskar watched Harley close the door firmly and return to the driver's seat. His eyes speculated at Harley's back and he made a mental note to add him to the list. It could be anybody, he thought; anybody.

The derelicts made room for him and he passed through them and went up the three stairs to the door. He turned and put his hand in his pocket. He rattled the half a dozen halves in his right hand like a pair of dice and tossed them to the sidewalk.

They scrambled for the bouncing, rolling half-dollars, grating worn cloth on the coarse concrete. Laskar's eyes followed the short struggle and then he moved inside the club.

He walked past the tables with the chairs stacked on them. He took the small elevator past the gaming rooms to the fourth floor.

When he opened the door to the paneled office, Otto Lund and Chris Taber got to their feet. Otto took his hat and Chris began fixing him a drink.

"How's the wife?" Otto asked.

Laskar sat down at the desk and accepted the drink Chris handed him. He looked at Otto. No, he thought, it couldn't be you. You're damn near sixty and that paunch is no beauty mark. You got no hair worth mentioning and your jowls flap when you talk.

"She's fine," Laskar said.

Chris Taber reached for the brief case on a chair and zippered it open. He glanced at the sheaf of accounts and laid them on Laskar's desk. Then he moved in easy strides to a chair and sat down.

Laskar followed his movements. But you're different, he thought. You're smooth as a seal and that mustache is just too damn tailored.

"You ever take ballet lessons?" Laskar asked.

Chris lifted an eyebrow and wondered how to take that.

Go ahead, get sore, Laskar's eyes said. He turned his attention to the papers. He spent fifteen minutes going over them and when he finished he looked up at Chris.

"It's going slow at the Highway Club," he said.

Chris shrugged his shoulders. "I told you it was an elephant when you bought it. It's too far out for one thing and the overhead is high. We got to take care of both the State Troopers and the county boys. My advice is to get rid of it and take the loss."

Laskar folded his hands. "No."

Otto's thick lips moved. "He's right, boss. I been out there a couple of times and it's pitiful."

"I don't take a loss on anything," Laskar said. "Make it pay."

"Those farmers go to bed at nine," Chris complained.

"You're getting paid to see that they don't," Laskar snapped. "Put off a few of your manicure appointments and use the time to think of something."

He stacked the papers and rapped them on the desk to even the edges. Chris came and took them out of his hand.

He riffled the papers and reached for the drink on the desk. He put it down quickly when he saw the yellow in Laskar's eyes glowing. "Sorry, boss," he said. "I guess my drink is over there."

Laskar sat quietly for a few minutes after they left and then went to the window. He adjusted the Venetian blinds so that he could see down into the parking lot in the rear of the building.

Chris Taber slipped into his car, backed out of the space, and pulled into the street. A moment later a gray sedan eased from the curb and followed him.

Laskar went to the phone and dialed.

"I've got one more for you, McMaster," he said when he made his connection. "Ed Harley. He's my chauffeur."

McMaster repeated the name slowly as he wrote it down. "Got it. He live at your place?"

"No," Laskar said. He checked his pocket notebook and gave McMaster the address.

"Got anything for me?"

"Nothing," McMaster said, and paused. "Look," he said finally. "I'm enjoying the business and it's your money, but I think you're wasting it."

"You're right," Laskar said. "It's my money," He cradled the receiver.

Laskar caught a taxi outside the club and took it to the Finley Hotel. He rode the elevator to the top floor. At the door of the penthouse he slipped the key into the lock and turned it carefully and quietly.

He moved into the apartment leaving tip-toe prints in the heavy rug. Celestine was in the living room idly playing solitaire.

Her black eyes met his. "Yes," she said. "I'm alone. You can walk on your heels now."

Laskar flushed. Celestine stood as he came to her. He ran his hands along the curve of her breasts and down to her waist. She tilted her head and allowed him to kiss her.

Laskar gripped the shining raven hair in his hands and looked at her. You're my wife, he thought. You belong to me completely and alone. He saw the secret independence in her eyes and he knew that he didn't own her. He'd bought her, over a year ago; but he didn't own her.

But someone did. Who?

He twisted her around hard, into him; his mouth found hers. His hands played over the firm, young, rounded body. The body that belonged to him.

She didn't fight him. She didn't respond. Lasker's left hand found the V of the $200 dress, ripped it off her, the filmy underthings giving way with it. Her flesh was hot to his touch, but her eyes mocked up into his. Take me, they said, if you want to, but don't expect anything. He swore and let her go.

Celestine was as cool, as poised as if nothing had happened. She glanced at her wrist watch. "You said you'd be back at seven."

"There wasn't as much to do as I thought."

She smiled faintly as she stepped away from him, pulling the dress together covering the front of her.

Laskar reached for his cigarette case as he watched her. His fingertips left wet marks on the engraved silver.

She accepted a cigarette. Her eyes half-lidded as she drew in the smoke. "By the way, there's a man who's been following me," she said.

"It's your imagination."

"Of course. My imagination. But in that case I may be losing my mind. Don't you think I ought to see a psychiatrist?" The smile edged toward laughter.

"Don't talk nonsense," Laskar said.

"But it isn't nonsense, dear. You will get me an expensive one, won't you?"

Laskar went to the French windows and stared out at the terrace.

"What agency is it, dear?" she asked. "The best, I should suppose."

Laskar faced her. "All right," he said. "The best I could get."

"That's nice. You love me, but you don't trust me." She considered the contradiction and seemed amused by it.

"You're my wife," Laskar said tightly. "I've got a right to know if there's anything going on."

Celestine sat down at the cocktail table and picked up the deck of cards. "Why don't you invite your friends up more often, dear. Some of them are so interesting."

Laskar ground out his cigarette. "Get some things on and we'll go downstairs for dinner."

Celestine's hands moved over the layout. "No. I'm not hungry and besides this card game is just too damn interesting."

Laskar's eyes brooded down at her. He reached down and tipped the table so that the cards slithered to the floor.

Celestine leaned back indolently. "Unless you decide to pick them up, they're going to stay there a long time."

Laskar turned on his heel and walked toward the door.

In his office at the Luna Club he pulled a bottle of scotch from the liquor cabinet and opened it. When Otto brought in a check to be okayed at nine-thirty, a strand of Laskar's hair stuck damply to his forehead.

Laskar regarded the check dully before he reached for the desk pen. He put his initials on a corner of the check and handed it back.

Otto lingered a moment. "Something wrong, boss?"

Laskar poured himself another drink. "Why the hell should anything be wrong? Mind your own damn business."

Dullness crept into Laskar's arms and legs as he drank, but the tautness in his neck was still there. When the phone buzzed he listened to it for half a minute before he reached for the receiver.

"Laskar," he mumbled.

"McMaster. I think we got something."

The slouch in Laskar's back slowly dissolved.

"He's up in your apartment now," McMaster said. "Might not be anything to it, but if this is what you were waiting for, it's as good as the real thing as far as evidence is concerned."

Laskar's numb lips moved. "Who?"

"This Chris Taber guy. We tailed him here and he took the elevator to the twenty-first floor. Since you lease the whole thing, it was no strain to figure where he was going."

Anger began driving the haze from Laskar's brain. His hand went to the back of his neck and began rubbing.

"You coming over or do you want us to handle it alone? We can wait until he comes out and have the house dick there for another witness. Or we could break in. But we'll need you there for that or it could mean our licenses."

"I'll be over," Laskar said.

Outside the club Laskar flagged at the passing taxis. A wino whose dirty-white sleeve lining showed at the shoulder-seams regarded him with a smile of liquor contentment.

Laskar reached automatically for a quarter and tossed it on the sidewalk. The derelict's moist blue eyes went down to the coin. He spit at it expertly. "Not tonight, Mr. Laskar. Tonight I don't bend down."

Laskar sat in the taxi, his stomach tight with irritation at every stop light. He leaned forward in urgency the last half mile and had a dollar bill ready when the taxi braked to a stop.

He hesitated in front of the hotel and his eyes traveled up the waffle indentations of the windows to the top of the hotel. He cursed softly and moved for the glass doors.

McMaster fell into step with him as Laskar strode for the elevators. He was a big man whose beef had acquired an overlay of suet.

He puffed keeping up with Laskar. "I think we ought to wait a little longer. At least until after midnight. That way we got it sewed up. It always looks bad if they stay after midnight, even if nothing happens."

Laskar stepped into the elevator and McMaster followed him. A thin man weighed with a swinging camera joined them before the doors closed.

"This is Harry," McMaster said. "But with giving them only a half hour up there, I don't think we'll get much in the way of pictures. Unless he's a fast worker."

McMaster rocked on his heels as the elevator rose. "All right, then, if you don't want to wait, this is the way we'll do it. You unlock the door yourself quiet-like and we rush in fast before they got time to think about it. If there's anything worth taking, Harry will be ready."

The elevator came to a silent stop and Laskar got out. He turned and faced the two. "Go back down," he said. "I'll handle this myself."

McMaster and Harry glanced at each other with sudden uncomfortable understanding.

"I'll take care of this in my own way," Laskar said.

"Now look," McMaster said hurriedly. "You're not thinking of doing anything you'll be sorry for?"

"I'm not going to be sorry."

McMaster's voice was a surprised complaint. "I thought this was just routine divorce stuff."

A nerve in Laskar's cheek twitched uncontrollably. "I don't give a damn what you thought. Just take your boy and get out of here."

They felt obligated to linger and reason with Laskar, but looking at him they knew it was no use. They came to a wordless agreement to wash their hands of this case and left with the hope that the agency wouldn't get involved if something nasty happened.

Laskar waited for their elevator to begin its descent and then turned to the door and inserted the key. He swung open the door to an empty room. He went swiftly and silently through the apartment, but the other rooms were empty too. He finally saw them outside in the gloom of the terrace.

Chris Taber leaned on the chest-high guard rail and smoked a cigarette as he watched the city lights. Celestine's laughter came to Laskar's ears as he stood at the open French windows and watched.

Chris flipped his cigarette over the rail and watched its firefly arc. Celestine, her eyes glittering in the moonlight and her lips faintly parted came close to Chris. She put her arms around him and, her white shoulders trembling as she pressed closer, met his lips. Chris put her gently away, surprised. Surprised, Laskar's mind raged, now that they knew a tail was on them.

Laskar's fingers tensed for action as he shoved aside the French door and stepped out.

Chris and Celestine parted abruptly as they heard him. Their faces were pale in the moonrays as they faced him. Celestine stepped to one side as Laskar came forward, his lips tight over sharp teeth.

The back of Chris' hand went to the dark stain on his lips but he saw it was useless to try to rub away the lipstick. His eyes darted to Celestine and back to Laskar.

"Wait a minute, boss," he said. "This isn't what you think."

Laskar moved with cat speed as his fingers darted for Chris' throat. They crashed together, writhing as Laskar strained to kill with a madman's hate and Chris raked defensive fingernails on his wrists.

They twisted and staggered, their bodies a tight jerking shadow. Chris gasped rawly for air as he was pressed against the guard rail. Laskar's hands forced his head backwards until his feet were off the terrace and he kicked frantically.

As Chris slipped over backwards, his fingers clung to Laskar in a vise grip that took Laskar along with him . . .

What do men think about when they are falling?

Does this new thing, this new way of dying, this inexorable plunge make them forget everything except that they do not want to die? Do their eyes widen in horror as they fall? Do their hands stretch desperately to keep away the sidewalk that rushes toward them like a monster?

And what does a woman think of as she stands with her hands firm on the guard rail?

What does she think about as she looks down twenty-one stories to the street?

And smiles to herself, knowing she has it all now. Everything that was her husband's. Including his chauffeur.

Rainy Afternoon

Murder!
December 1956

There wasn't anything I could do about it, so I shuffled the cards again for another hand of solitaire.

The tall one called Hank leaned on the cabin window still watching the rain, and the man who gave orders had his eyes on Annette.

She met his stare for awhile and then she looked away.

"You can call me Pete, baby," he said grinning.

Hank left the window and picked up the satchel. He emptied it on the table. And his lips mumbled as he started counting the money.

I bent down to pick up some cards that had fallen from the table. "Twenty-four thousand and two hundred," I said. "It didn't melt."

"I didn't ask for you to talk," Hank said.

Pete tilted his chair and looked at me. "What do you find in a place way out here that makes it worthwhile, besides her?"

"I don't like to be crowded," I said.

Pete's interest went back to Annette. "How about you? What keeps you here, baby? Is he that good looking to you?"

Annette moved out of his line of sight. "Don't let it worry you," she said to him.

Pete turned his chair. "Think about all this money," he said. "And think about all the things it could buy."

Hank riffled a stack of hundreds. "I'd like to know, Bud," he said. "How do you scratch a living in a place like this?"

I transferred a black seven to a red eight and studied the layout.

"The man asked you a question," Pete said. "Answer it."

Annette told him. "He does trapping."

Pete's fist spun me off the chair. "I'd like to hear you tell it."

I got up and stood there tasting the split lip with my tongue. The automatic in Pete's hand was waiting for me to argue.

I sat down in the chair. "I do trapping," I said.

They had come out of the driving rain two hours ago, with their satchel and their guns. They settled down to wait for a break in the weather, and my 30/06 lay in its rack unloaded and ornamental.

Hank finished his counting and stared at the pile of money. "How about some light?"

Annette lit the lantern and slipped the handle over the ceiling hook.

"I like the way you move, baby," Pete said.

Annette's face was white. "Stop calling me baby."

Pete showed uneven teeth as he laughed. "Sure, baby, sure."

Hank paused as he put the money back in the bag. "You have any dough in that bank?" he asked me.

"A few hundred," I said. "It's covered by insurance."

Hank thought about it and nodded. "Not bad. Nobody lose but the insurance company."

Pete rubbed his stomach. "I'm hungry. Fix up some sandwiches."

Annette went to the cupboard and brought out the bread, butter, and ham.

"Too bad you ain't got a car," Hank said. "We could be out of here."

"It bothers me too," I said.

Pete's eyes left Annette for a moment and went to Hank. "I'll remember you nearly killed us."

Hank shrugged. "The road was lousy. And you're the one who wanted speed," he said.

Annette put a plate of sandwiches on the table and then brought the cups and coffee.

Hank picked up a sandwich. "I saw a bottle on one of them shelves," he said.

Annette paused for a thoughtful moment, but she brought the whiskey and glasses.

They ate slowly and when they finished there was one sandwich left on the plate. "Eat it," Pete said to me.

I pushed the cards together for another hand.

Annette touched my shoulder. "Eat it, Sam," she said.

I picked up the sandwich and ate.

Pete poured himself a shot. "I'm serious, baby," he said. "How about it? I got money now and it won't make me mad to spend it."

Annette reached for the empty plate and the cups.

"I can make lots of excitement," Pete said. He put his hand on her, and she stiffened. I shifted in my chair.

Pete laughed as she walked away.

The beat of the rain on the roof speeded up. Pete was smiling, thinking, to himself. Hank finally yawned, and Pete had his mind made up.

"Keep awake for awhile, Hank," he said. "I'll be in the bedroom."

Hank yawned again. "Don't dream all night. I need sleep too."

"I won't be sleeping," Pete said.

The sodden oaks outside creaked with the wind. I put down the cards I was holding.

Pete looked over his shoulder at Annette. "You ready, baby?"

Annette's face was pale, and I got to my feet to face their automatics.

"A man with a bullet in his chest coughs real hard," Pete said, smiling.

I looked at their waiting and I knew I was going to try.

Annette stepped quickly in front of me and put her arms around my neck. "No," she whispered. "It won't help. You know that."

"Be a hero," Pete said softly.

"Please," Annette's voice was soft. Her lips met mine lightly, and she held me tight. "It won't matter that much."

She let go of me and went into the bedroom.

Pete followed her in, shut the door, and I sat down to watch the .45 in Hank's hand.

"I might take my turn too," Hank said after a time.

The sound of the rain was slackening, and I watched Hank as we listened. My hands absently shuffled the deck of cards.

And in a little while we could hear them.

Hank's eyes moved slightly to the bedroom door, and he began to smile, think ahead.

He was dreaming about it, and I waited for the clouding in his eyes and was ready.

I threw the cards at his face. As he ducked, instinctively, my hands shot across the three feet of table top and clamped on his gun hand. I twisted until he was staring, with horror, into the muzzle of the gun. My hands pressed his finger until the trigger moved back and the gun exploded.

He kicked over the table as he fell and died.

I snatched up the gun, aware of the strong stink of cordite. I stood ready.

Pete pulled open the bedroom door, angrily, and then he saw it wasn't Hank standing there.

I looked past his naked shoulders to where Annette lay on the bed. Her eyes met mine, and then she turned her face away.

I motioned Pete slowly into the kitchen. His mouth was working desperately for words, but failing to make a sound.

The fear in him watched as I picked up the whiskey bottle by the neck and smashed its bottom on the table.

Whiskey gushed to the floor, and I put the automatic in my pocket.

Pete backed up until there was no place to go. His body shrank as he saw the jagged edges of the bottle come closer. There was the fascination of terror as his eyes clung to the gleaming sharp claws of glass that would rip and tear.

And then I began killing him.

Jack Ritchie (1922-1983) Bibliography

"Always the Season" News Syndicate, Dec 1953
"Three-Quarter Moon" News Syndicate, Mar 1954
"License for Cupid" *Today, The Philadelphia Inquirer*, Mar 1954
"My Game, My Rules" *Manhunt*, Jul 1954
"Take Him in Six" *Men*, Aug 1954
"Replacement" *Manhunt*, Nov 1954
"Record Breaker" News Syndicate, Nov 1954
"The One to Do It" *Western Short Stories*, Dec 1954
"Wait for Me" News Syndicate, Jan 1955
"Mr. Can't Fix It" News Syndicate, Feb 1955
"Snowball" News Syndicate, Mar 1955
"Poet Cornered" News Syndicate, Mar 1955
"Let Me Help You" News Syndicate, Apr 1955
"Hold Out" *Manhunt*, May 1955
"Wife Beater" News Syndicate, May 1955
"Ape Man" *Male*, Jun 1955
"Interrogation" *Manhunt*, Jun 1955
"Champs Don't Dive" *For Men Only*, Jul 1955
"Solitary" *Manhunt*, Jul 1955
"The, Saints Go Stumbling On" *Ten Story Sports*, Jul 1955
"Open House" News Syndicate, Jul 1955
"The Hero Husbands," News Syndicate, Jul 1955
"Vancouver Killer" *Liberty*, Aug 1955
"Try It My Way" *Manhunt*, Aug 1955
"Let Me Handle This" News Syndicate, Aug 1955
"Mock Chicken" News Syndicate, Sep 1955
"The Best of Friends" News Syndicate, Sep 1955
"Family Affair" News Syndicate, Oct 1955
"Handy Man" *Family Weekly*, Oct 1955
"The Tie That Binds" News Syndicate, Nov 1955
"Fair Game" News Syndicate, Dec 1955
"Silver Buckle" *Western Action*, Jan 1956
"Square Snowball" *Today, The Philadelphia Inquirer*, Jan 1956
"The Required Tingle" News Syndicate, Feb 1956
"Devil Eyes" *Manhunt*, May 1956
"Anniversary of Death" *Smashing Detective*, May 1956
"The $300 Question" News Syndicate, May 1956
"The Canary" *Manhunt*, Jun 1956
"A Torch for Tess" *Mantrap*, Jul 1956
"Honor at Steak" News Syndicate, Jul 1956
"Saline Solution" *Today, The Philadelphia Inquirer*, Jul 1956

"Good-by, World" *Manhunt*, Aug 1956
"The Wire Loop" (as Steve Harbor) *Manhunt*, Aug 1956
"Sim" *Sir!*, Aug 1956
"Flight Plan" *Stag*, Aug 1956
"The Partners" *Manhunt*, Sep 1956
"Dead Cops Are Murder" *Murder!*, Sep 1956
"Death Rail" *Mantrap*, Oct 1956
"Popular Guy" *Ten Story Sports*, Oct 1956
"Degree of Guilt" *Manhunt*, Dec 1956
"Rainy Afternoon" *Murder!*, Dec 1956
"Past Performance" News Syndicate, Dec 1956
"Picket Ticket" News Syndicate, Dec 1956
"Color Scheme" *Today, The Philadelphia Inquirer*, Dec 1956
"Bullet Proof" *AHMM*, Jan 1957
"Taste Test Tells" News Syndicate, Jan 1957
"Divide And Conquer" *Manhunt*, Feb 1957
"Ditto Man" *Today, The Philadelphia Inquirer*, Mar 1957
"You Should Live So Long" *Manhunt*, Apr 1957
"Double Exposure" *Today, The Philadelphia Inquirer*, Jun 1957
"Minor Engagement" *Today, The Philadelphia Inquirer*, Jul 1957
"Bomb #14" *AHMM*, Aug 1957
"Sound Alibi" (as Steven O'Donnell) *AHMM*, Aug 1957
"Space Bounder" News Syndicate, Aug 1957
"Lady Luck's Own Alfred" *Brotherhood of Locomotive Firemen and Enginemen's Magazine*, Sep 1957
"Welcome to My Prison" *AHMM*, Oct 1957
"The French Bachelor" *Men's Digest #3*, Oct 1957
"Inside Pitch" News Syndicate, Oct 1957
"Single-Minded" *Today, The Philadelphia Inquirer*, Oct 1957
"Sauce for the Gander" (Unpublished) News Syndicate, Oct 1957
"Kill Joy" *Manhunt*, Nov 1957
"Community Affair" *Nugget*, Nov 1957
"Unadulterated Product" *Sir!*, Nov 1957
"Double Feature" News Syndicate, Dec 1957
"Hospitality Most Serene" *AHMM*, Jan 1958
"No Shroud" *Mr. Magazine*, Jan 1958
"A Sheriff for Murder Town" *Adventure*, Feb 1958
"Talent Scout" *Rogue*, Feb 1958
"The Uncounted Way" News Syndicate, Mar 1958
"Out of Order" News Syndicate, Mar 1958
"Don't Twist My Arm" *Manhunt*, Apr 1958
"What Frightened You, Fred?" *AHMM*, May 1958
"Ambition Takes a Detour" (with Irma Ritchie) News Syndicate, May 1958

"#8" (a.k.a., "The Killer with Red Hair") *AHMM*, Jun 1958
"A Gentleman From Argentina" *Today, The Philadelphia Inquirer*, Jun 1958
"Triangle With Four Sides" (with Irma Ritchie) News Syndicate, Jun 1958
"Saucer for the Gander" News Syndicate, Jun 1958
"Brains Against Lead" *Mr. Magazine*, Jul 1958
"Blue Feather" *Man About Town*, Sep 1958
"No Speck of Dust" (with Irma Ritchie) News Syndicate, Sep 1958
"Where the Wheel Stops" *AHMM*, Oct 1958
"Deadline Murder" *Manhunt*, Oct 1958
"Man on a Leash" *AHMM*, Dec 1958
"Antitogetherness" News Syndicate, Dec 1958
"22 Stories Up— 22 Down" *AHMM*, Jan 1959
"Training Camp Champ" *Argosy*, Jan 1959
"A Square Foot of Texas" *Good Housekeeping*, Mar 1959
"Frame-Up" *AHMM*, Apr 1959
"The Woman Behind the Gun" (as Steven O'Donnell) *AHMM*, Apr 1959
"Fair Play" *Manhunt*, Apr 1959
"The $5,000 Getaway" *AHMM*, May 1959
"Such Things Happen At Night" *AHMM*, Jul 1959
"Between 4 and 12" *AHMM*, Oct 1959
"Painless Extraction" *AHMM*, Dec 1959
"The Reluctant Baton Twirler" *Today, The Philadelphia Inquirer*, Dec 1959
"Falcons Fly Far" *AHMM*, Jan 1960
"Death, Taxes, And . . ." (as Steve O'Connell) *AHMM*, Feb 1960
"The Enormous $10" *AHMM*, Feb 1960
"Fragrant Puzzle" *AHMM*, Mar 1960
"Fly By Night" *Escapade*, Apr 1960
"Lily-White Town" *AHMM*, May 1960
"The Return Engagement" *Today, The Philadelphia Inquirer*, May 1960
"When Buying a Fine Murder" *AHMM*, Jun 1960
"The Fabulous Tunnel" *AHMM*, Sep 1960
"Shatter Proof" *Manhunt*, Oct 1960
"9 From 12 Leaves 3" (as Steve O'Connell) *AHMM*, Nov 1960
"Politics is Simply Murder" *AHMM*, Nov 1960
"Pigment of the Imagination" News Syndicate, Nov 1960
"The Reckoning" *Spree #25*, Jul 1961
"The Long Wait" *Topper #1*, Jul 1961
"The Crime Machine" *AHMM*, Jan 1961
"You Can Trust Me" *AHMM*, Feb 1961
"The Third Call" *AHMM*, Mar 1961
"That Year's Victim" *AHMM*, Apr 1961
"Play a Game of Cyanide" *AHMM*, May 1961
"Put Together a Man" (as Steve O'Connell) *AHMM*, May 1961

"For All the Rude People" *AHMM*, Jun 1961
"Remains to Be Seen" (as Steve O'Connell) *AHMM*, Jun 1961
"Under Dim Street Lights" *AHMM*, Jul 1961
"Goodbye Memory" *AHMM*, Aug 1961
"The Quiet Eye" (as Steve O'Connell) *AHMM*, Aug 1961
"Ring Around Dulcie" News Syndicate, Sep 1961
"How Near to My Heart" News Syndicate, Sep 1961
"The Traveling Arm" *AHMM*, Nov 1961
"Punch Any Number" *AHMM*, Dec 1961
"The Queer Deal" *Manhunt*, Dec 1961
"A Christmas Tree Caper" *New York Mirror*, Dec 1961
"There Has to Be More" News Syndicate, Jan 1962
"The Deveraux Monster" *Manhunt*, Feb 1962
"Holdout" *AHMM*, Mar 1962
"Upside Down World" *AHMM*, May 1962
"Meeting At the Bridge" (as Steve Harbor) Newspaper Enterprise Association, Jun 1962
"Where the Finger Points" *AHMM*, Oct 1962
"The Eyes Have It" *AHMM*, Nov 1962
"Travelers Check" *AHMM*, Dec 1962
"A Taste for Murder" *AHMM*, Jan 1963
"Just Between Us, Dad" *AHMM*, Feb 1963
"Ripper Moon!" *Manhunt*, Feb 1963
"The Green Heart" *AHMM*, Mar 1963
"The Operator" *AHMM*, Jun 1963
"Grounds for Marriage" *New York Mirror*, Jul 1963
"The Egghead and I" *New York Mirror*, Jul 1963
"Oh, Give Me a Home" *New York Mirror*, Aug 1963
"Ten Minutes From Now" *AHMM*, Oct 1963
"The Fullback From Liechtenstein" *Boy's Life*, Nov 1963
"Anyone for Murder?" *AHMM*, Jan 1964
"Cricket in the Heart" (with Irma Ritchie) News Syndicate, Mar 1964
"Silence is Gold" *AHMM*, Apr 1964
"Everybody Except Wilbur" *AHMM*, Jun 1964
"Kill the Taste" (as Steve O'Connell) *AHMM*, Jun 1964
"Captive Audience" (as Steve O'Connell) *AHMM*, Aug 1964
"Who's Got the Lady?" *MSMM*, Sep 1964
"Fourteen Beds" *Showcase*, Oct 1964
"Upon My Soul" *Signature* (Diner's Club), Jan 1965
"Preservation" *Mil lionaire*, Feb 1965
"Blisters in May" *Signature* (Diner's Club), Mar 1965
"Sing a Song for Tony" *AHMM*, Apr 1965
"Mr. Policeman" *MSMM*, Apr 1965

"Swing High" *AHMM*, May 1965
"Approximately Yours" *Mil lionaire*, May 1965
"A Piece of the World" *AHMM*, Jun 1965
"Businessman" (as Steve O'Connell) *Signature* (Diner's Club), Jun 1965
"Chicken Charley" *Cavalcade*, Jul 1965
"They Won't Touch Me" *Signature* (Diner's Club), Jul 1965
"Going Down?" *Manhunt*, Jul 1965
"Memory Test" *AHMM*, Aug 1965
"Package Deal" *AHMM*, Sep 1965
"Queasy Does It Not" *AHMM*, Oct 1965
"Look Ma, No Hands!" *Boy's Life*, Oct 1965
"We Will Come Back" *Signature* (Diner's Club), Oct 1965
"A Dame on Ice" *Adam*, Dec 1965
"The Holdout" *Signature* (Diner's Club), Dec 1965
"Copy Cat" *AHMM*, Jan 1966
"The Little Green Book" *Intrigue*, Jan 1966
"The Pickup Man" *MSMM*, Jan 1966
"Gemini 74" *Signature* (Diner's Club), Feb 1966
"The Trouble With Double" *Practical English* (Scholastic), Mar 1966
"Plan 19" *AHMM*, Apr 1966
"The Id of Irving" *Adam*, May 1966
"The Liechtenstein Swing" *Boy's Life*, Jun 1966
"Twenty-Two Cents a Day" *AHMM*, Jul 1966
"Speaking of Murder" *MSMM*, Sep 1966
"Big Tony" *Adam Reader #25*, Oct 1966
"Killing Zone" *Mil lionaire*, Oct 1966
"The Almost Magic Toe" *Young Catholic Messenger*, Sep 1966
"The Silver Backside" *Adam*, Nov 1966
"The Tree is the Same" *Boy's Life*, Dec 1966
"Exit Point" *Adam Reader #27*, Feb 1967
"Hungary for Love" *Adam*, Apr 1967
"McCoy's Private Feud" *Adam Reader #28*, Apr 1967
"Goodbye, Sweet Money" *AHMM*, Apr 1967
"The Negotiators" *Adam*, May 1967
"The Fifty Cent Victims" *AHMM*, May 1967
"Six-Second Hero" *Signature* (Diner's Club), May 1967
"Give Me Your Criminals" *Elks Magazine*, May 1967
"The Trouble With George" *Sensation*, Jun 1967
"The Push Button" *AHMM*, Jun 1967
"Hot Air Pilot" *Signature* (Diner's Club), Jun 1967
"With One Stone" *AHMM*, Jul 1967
"Run With the Tide" *Adam Reader #30*, Aug 1967
"The $15,000 Shack" *AHMM*, Aug 1967

"Put Your Head Upon My Knee" *Signature* (Diner's Club), Aug 1967
"The Best Driver in the County" *AHMM*, Sep 1967
"When I Look Back, I See Everybody" *Boy's Life*, Sep 1967
"By Child Undone" *AHMM*, Oct 1967
"Piggy Bank Killer" *AHMM*, Nov 1967
"The Moonlighter" the *Girl From U.N.C.L.E.*, Dec 1967
"Basketball, Ach Nein!" *Practical English* (Scholastic), Mar 1968
"That Russian!" (a.k.a., "The Commissar") *AHMM*, May 1968
"The Killing Philosopher" *AHMM*, Jun 1968
"Pearls Before Wine" *MSMM*, Aug 1968
"You Got to Watch Ben" *MSMM*, Sep 1968
"Wearing of the Green" *MSMM*, Nov 1968
"Dropout" *AHMM*, Jan *1969,*
"Under a Cold Sun" *MSMM*, Jan 1969
"At Face Value" *AHMM*, Apr 1969
"Welcome to the Club" *MSMM*, Apr 1969
"Where Am I?" *MSMM*, Jul 1969
"Pardon My Death Ray" *AHMM*, Oct 1969
"A Finger Here . . . a Finger There . . ." *AHMM*, Dec 1969
"Bon Appetit, Captain" *Adam*, Mar 1970
"The English Draw" *Zane Grey Western Magazine*, Apr 1970
"The Havana Express" *AHMM*, Jul 1970
"Living By Degrees" *A New Leaf and Other Stories*, Apr 1971
"Take Another Look" *AHMM*, Aug 1971
"The Violet Business" *AHMM*, Sep 1971
"The Griggsby Papers" *MSMM*, Oct 1971
"Listen, Pigs, Listen" *AHMM*, Nov 1971
"The Liechtenstein Toe" *Boy's Life*, Nov 1971
"Home-Town Boy" *AHMM*, Dec 1971
"The Beholder" *Man's Pleasure*, Feb 1972
"In Open Hiding" *AHMM*, Mar 1972
"Let Your Fingers Do the Walking" *AHMM*, Apr 1972
"Tight Little Town" *AHMM*, May 1972
"Rights and Wrongs" *AHMM*, Jun 1972
"Setup" *AHMM*, Jun 1972
"Finger Man" *AHMM*, Jul 1972
"The Value of Privacy" *AHMM*, Aug 1972
"The Killer From Earth" *Swank Magazine*, Sep 1972
"The Gesundheit Caper" *Boy's Life*, Oct 1972
"Center of Attention" *Boy's Life*, Jan 1973
"Four on an Alibi" *AHMM*, Apr 1973
"The Magnum" *Debonair*, May 1973
"But Don't Tell Your Mother" *AHMM*, Aug 1973

"End of the Line" *AHMM*, Oct 1973
"Flasher Fever" *Boy's Life*, Oct 1973
"The Wastebasket" *AHMM*, Dec 1973
"Freddie" *Elks Magazine,* Sep 1974
"When the Sheriff Walked" *AHMM*, Dec 1974
"Major Effort" *More Teen-Age Football Stories*, Jun 1975
"Too Solid Mildred" *AHMM*, Mar 1975
"To the Barricades!" *AHMM*, Apr 1975
"Bedlam At the Budgie" *AHMM*, May 1975
"Little Orphan Annie" *Story World*, Aug 1975
"The Angler" *AHMM*, Oct 1975
"The Many-Flavored Crime" *MD*, Dec 1975
"The Weather Man" *Elks Magazine*, Jan 1976
"Finger Exercise" *AHMM*, Mar 1976
"Next in Line" *AHMM*, Apr 1976
"Kid Cardula" *AHMM*, Jun 1976
"To Kill a Man" *Mystery Monthly*, Jun 1976
"Nobody Tells Me Anything" *EQMM*, Oct 1976
"My Compliments to the Cook" *AHMM*, Jan 1977
"The Cardula Detective Agency" *AHMM*, Mar 1977
"Good-Bye Mayor Barkin" *Young World*, Apr 1977
"Odd Pair of Socks, An" *AHMM*, May 1977
"Beauty is As Beauty Does" *EQMM*, Jun 1977
"The Canvas Caper" *AHMM*, Aug 1977
"The Seed Caper" *EQMM*, Aug 1977
"Variations on a Scheme" *AHMM*, Sep 1977
"Box in a Box" *AHMM*, Oct 1977
"The Willinger Predicament" *EQMM*, Oct 1977
"Cardula to the Rescue" *AHMM*, Dec 1977
"Hung Jury" *EQMM*, Dec 1977
"The Scent of Camellias" *AHMM*, Mar 1978
"The Invaders" *Boy's Life*, Mar 1978
"The School Bus Caper" *EQMM*, Mar 1978
"Cardula and the Kleptomaniac" *AHMM*, Apr 1978
"No Wider Than a Nickel" *EQMM*, Oct 1978
"Cardula's Revenge" *AHMM*, Nov 1978
"The Return of Bridget" *AHMM*, Dec 1978
"Delayed Mail" *Elks Magazine*, Dec 1978
"The Hanging Tree" *AHMM*, Jan 1979
"The Midnight Strangler" *EQMM*, Jan 1979
"The Little Room" *MSMM*, Jan 1979
"Stakeout" *AHMM*, Apr 1979
"The Brown Paper Bags" *EQMM*, May 1979

"You Could Get Killed" *AHMM*, Jun 1979
"Some Days Are Like That" *EQMM*, Jul 1979
"The Victory" *Milwaukee Magazine*, Jul 1979
"Friend of the Family" *MSMM*, Aug 1979
"The Gourmet Kidnaper" *EQMM*, Sep 1979
"The Sliver of Evidence" *EQMM*, Nov 1979
"Focal Point" *MD*, Dec 1979
"The Davenport" *A Chilling Collection*, Feb 1980
"Appointment on the Barge" *Microcosmic Tales*, Nov 1980
"The Way to Do It" *EQMM*, Jan 1980
"The Alphabet Murders" *MSMM*, Feb 1980
"The Third-Floor Closet" *EQMM*, Jun 1980
"More Than Meets the Eye" *EQMM*, Sep 1980
"For the Good of Society" *MSMM*, Dec 1980
"That Last Journey" *AHMM*, Dec 1980
"The Absence of Emily" *EQMM*, Jan 1981
"In the Public Eye" *Woman's World*, Mar 1981
"This Gun for Hire" *Woman's World*, Mar 1981
"Win Some, Lose Some" *EQMM*, Mar 1981
"The Rules of the Game" *Twilight Zone*, Jul 1981
"Body Check" *EQMM*, Jul 1981
"The Connecting Link" *EQMM*, Oct 1981
"The Message in the Message" *EQMM*, Dec 1981
"A Case of Identity" *EQMM*, Jan 1982
"The Return of Cardula" *AHMM*, Feb 1982
"The Orange Murders" *EQMM*, Mar 1982
"Cardula and the Locked Rooms" *AHMM*, Mar 1982
"Murder Off Limits" *EQMM*, Jun 1982
"The Golden Goose" *EQMM*, Jul 1982
"The Fifth Grave" *EQMM*, Oct 1982
"The Method" *MSMM*, Nov 1982
"The Final Truth" *EQMM*, Feb 1983
"The Customer" *MSMM*, Mar 1983
"The O'Leary Conspiracy" *EQMM*, May 1983
"Cardula and the Briefcase" *MSMM*, Jun 1983
"Dial an Alibi" *Woman's World*, Jun 1983
"The Liechtenstein Flash" *Boy's Life*, Aug 1983
"The Liechtenstein Imagination" *Boy's Life*, Sep 1983
"The Journey" *EQMM*, Dec 1983
"The Second Letter" *EQMM*, Feb 1984
"The Investigator" *MSMM*, Apr 1984
"The Ghost of Claudia McKenny" *EQMM*, May 1984
"The Two Percent Solution" *EQMM*, Jun 1984

"The House of Yorick" *TSMM*, Jul 1984
"The Big Day" *Toys "R" Us Magazine #2*, Jun 1986
"A Helping Hand" *Woman's World*, Jan 1986
"The Fabricator" *AHMM*, May 2009

Key:
AHMM = *Alfred Hitchcock's Mystery Magazine*
EQMM = *Ellery Queen Mystery Magazine*
MSMM = *Mike Shayne Mystery Magazine*
TSMM = *The Saint Mystery Magazine*

Also available from Stark House Press:

The Best of *Manhunt*
A Collection of the Best Stories
From *Manhunt* Magazine
Foreword by Lawrence Block
Afterword by Barry N. Malzberg
Edited and Introduction by Jeff Vorzimmer
ISBN: 978-1-944520-68-7 $21.95

The Best of *Manhunt* 2
More of the Best from *Manhunt* Magazine
Foreword by Peter Enfantino
Introduction by Jon Breen
Edited and Introduction by Jeff Vorzimmer
ISBN: 978-1-951473-05-1 $21.95

The Best of *Manhunt* 3
More of the Best from *Manhunt* Magazine
Introduction by Jeff Vorzimmer and David Rachels
Edited by Jeff Vorzimmer
ISBN: 979-8-8860-1003-9 $21.95

The *Manhunt* Companion
The complete issue-by-issue compendium
to *Manhunt* Magazine, January 1953
to April/May 1967, with story and
author indexes.
Edited by Peter Enfantino and Jeff Vorzimmer
ISBN: 978-1-951473-44-0 $19.95

www.ingramcontent.com/pod-product-compliance
Lightning Source LLC
LaVergne TN
LVHW021811060526
838201LV00058B/3335